CHASING SHADOWS

Kevin W. Luby

Cojamiba Publishing Company
Portland, OR

CHASING SHADOWS

ISBN–13: 978-1727894882
ISBN-10: 172789488X

Cover Photograph by Chad Hastings

Published by
Cojamiba Publishing Co.
Portland, OR
www.cojamiba.com

Dedicated to the lovely and talented Jane K. Luby, without whom I would be nothing; also to my intelligent, beautiful, and always feisty daughter, Moira E. Luby; and always to Conner Patrick Luby - never forget; never forgotten.

ALSO BY KEVIN W. LUBY

A Life Short & Loud: And the Long Road Back

Murder in Bridge Citys

ACKNOWLEDGMENTS

I would never have completed this—my first novel—without the encouragement and assistance of numerous people including Jane Luby, Mike Kelley, Brian Bice, Susan Giles, LaRae Burke, Mike Moody, Jeff Brown, Ken Cruickshank, and Mike Nelson. They all read early drafts of the book and gave well-reasoned critiques (some of which were accepted with grace and aplomb) and corrected multiple grammatical and punctuation errors.

I'd also like to thank Mike Weston for his guidance in educating me about some of the military ordinance described in the book.

Thanks to my business partner, Hafez Daraee, for tolerating this frolic and detour when I should have been working on billable time.

The real Roger Boulden has been a great sport about this. I was warned to not name the megalomaniacal antagonist after my future son-in-law but, like most advice I receive, I disregarded it.

To all of the others who have offered encouragement and/or recommendations for this endeavor, please accept my sincerest gratitude.

Contents

When someone shows you who they are,
believe them the first time.
—Maya Angelou

Nothing is perfect. Life is messy. Relationships are complex.
Outcomes are uncertain. People are irrational.
—Hugh Mackay

PROLOGUE

Jack Withers was tired. He was now officially six months into his one-year commitment with the Peace Corps in Ecuador. The position was as a business advisor, living and working in a small village outside of Nueva Loja, near the border with Columbia.

The experience, so far, had been wonderful and came after he finally gave up managing fast food restaurants. A long-term career in restaurant management was not something he wanted and the opportunity with the Peace Corps came at a perfect time. He had no career, no girlfriend, and nothing tying him down. He left his dog with his folks and headed to Ecuador.

The most difficult part of the mission was not the language or being away from his family but rather, having to live with a host family. Ever since graduation from high school, Jack had lived on his own and cherished his privacy. Now he was living in a small four-room house with a host family and his bedroom was nothing more than a closet. It was comfortable enough for sleeping, although with only one little window, the heat and humidity could get oppressive. The host family was comprised of a mother, father and three young children. It was always noisy and busy.

When he wasn't working with local business owners, Jack spent much of his time just walking from village to village, with occasional forays into the jungle to find some peace and quiet. He would sit and listen to the wildlife and try to identify as many animals as he could.

As access to the Internet would be sporadic, Jack kept a daily journal. These were his final three entries.

February 15

It was a good day today. Nico got permission from the local governor's office to open a second garage in N.L. Now he has to finalize the lease and buy the equipt., really happy for him. He's a good man. His eldest will manage the local garage while Nico spends M-F in town and comes home on weekends.

Louisa wasn't having as much luck. The samples she sent into Quito have disappeared. I suggested next time she should take them down there herself. Buyers want to put a face to a name and a voice and she should be using that smile of hers.

Strange thing happened down at the river this afternoon. The capuchin monkeys were unusually active and I loved watching them. I heard a couple of howlers but couldn't see them. One capuchin was stumbling around and came walking up toward me. Generally, I never offer food to them because it creates mayhem. This one, however, looked weak and hungry.

I threw him a small piece of my sandwich and he picked it up but with no enthusiasm. He sniffed it, all while staring at me. His eyes looked glassy. He put the sandwich into his mouth and started slowly chewing it as he continued walking toward me. He stumbled once and I thought he was going to fall.

I told him I'd give him one more piece but that was it. I tossed him one more piece and then put the rest of the sandwich in my mouth. At that point, he bared his fangs and screamed at me.

He swung his hand at me, almost like a roundhouse punch but without the fist. I felt his hand graze my sleeve and stood up and yelled back at him. He scampered away but I noticed that after about thirty feet, he stumbled again and, this time, fell to the ground. He slowly picked himself up and disappeared back into the jungle.

When I got back to the house, I noticed that I had a small scratch from where the monkey swung at me. It was only about two inches long and I put some Neosporin on it.

Tomorrow, I need to go into town and get some supplies. I need razor blades and toothpaste. Kelley is supposed to be there. I'm really looking forward to having a couple of beers with him and speaking English again.

February 16
I decided to cancel the trip to town. I just don't feel very well. Maybe I've been pushing myself too much or maybe it's the heat but I'm dog-tired.

The scratch on my arm is starting to look red and I've been applying more Neosporin every couple of hours. It's a little sore, almost like when I got the vaccinations. Whatever it is, I'm hoping that sleep will do the trick and I can meet up with Kells tomorrow

February 17
This is not good. I've definitely got something. If it was just the head-ache, I could deal with it even though it's a bad one. The problem is that my arm is getting worse. The swelling runs from shoulder to elbow. I also have a fever. I hope it's not malaria.

Senora Morena agreed to drive me into N.L. so I can see a doctor. She wasn't happy about it, but she can see that I need more attention than she can give me.

I'm curious about what this might be.

CHAPTER ONE

Smoke from a Distant Fire

His favorite thing about this house was the view. The glow of the rising sun would first light the sky with a yellow and orange radiance and then, ever so gradually, the sun would peek over the horizon, just to the right of Mt. Hood. It was a view which always left him with a sense of hope that the day was going to be something special. This day was going to prove, at least to himself, that he was born for something, if not great, at least memorable. As it turned out, he was right in part, although not in a way he could ever have imagined.

John Thomas Callahan, like just about everyone, had a morning routine. This involved awakening well before everyone else. This was his quiet time; his time to luxuriate in solitude and slowly come to grips with the new day. Long ago, he would have picked up the morning paper and read it from front to back. Now, he got all of his news either on television or online. Whenever possible, he would stop, stand by the large front window and just watch the sunrise, letting the sun shine on his face. During certain times of the year, like now, the timing was perfect.

Once he greeted the sun, and while the coffee brewed, John checked his emails to see if there was anything of import or urgency. Next, he checked his calendar for the day. He'd looked at it the night before as he was leaving the office but always checked again in the morning. It would be a pretty light day. There was a partners' meeting at 10:00 a.m. and a client meeting in Gresham at 2:00 p.m. Other than that, he could just work on projects with varying deadlines in his office.

By now the coffee was ready, and he poured himself a cup. Sitting down in his chair in the living room, he checked his watch. It was a Fitbit and he noted that, in addition to the present time, he'd slept for slightly over six hours the prior night. This was good.

With 30 minutes of quiet time left, John opened his iPad and first checked social media. It was mostly just the same posts by family and friends with a variety of social and political chatter— nothing of much interest.

Out of habit more than actual curiosity, he checked to see what was new with the Celtics and Bruins—his father was from Boston and had instilled a love for all Boston sports teams into him. He then perused the *OregonLive* website for local news before moving onto the various national new services.

A small headline caught his attention, but he didn't bother pulling up the article. When he saw another similar headline at the *Washington Post* website, he clicked on the link. There was an outbreak of a new virus. Other than there were two stories about it, John didn't know why he found it of interest. There were always viruses out there, whether Zika, the avian flu, or something else. Perusing the article, he noted this new virus, described as being similar to Ebola, was different in how it arose in the Zamora-Chinchipe region of Ecuador. Maybe this was what prompted him to read the whole article. As best he could remember, most viruses arose in Africa or, like the avian flu virus, in China.

He couldn't remember when, or even if, there had been a new virus arising in the Americas before. John was scheduled to travel to Argentina in the fall for an international tax conference. Even though it was six months away, he reminded himself to keep an eye on this.

Looking at his watch again, John stood up and refilled his cup, grabbed a second one, and padded upstairs to wake up Liz. She was curled up in a relaxed fetal position. Generally, she stayed on her side of the bed but whenever he got up in the morning, she seemed to migrate over to his side. He put the coffee cups on the nightstand and curled up behind her.

"Good morning, love."

"Mmmmm, mmmmm," was her sleepy response.

In a singsong voice, he whispered, "It's time to rise and shine and greet the brand-new day; to wake up with a cup of coffee and be off on your way."

She gave him a sleepy smile. "Just five more minutes?"

"Sorry, love, we've got things to do."

She grunted but rolled over to accept his morning kiss. Her breath was rank, as morning breath is, but her lips were perfect and soft. Starting to rise, he said, "I'll wake the kids."

John walked down the hall and tapped first on Brian's door. "Hey Boyo, it's time to get up." He opened the door to the room, which was dark and smelled like teenage boy. "Brian, time to get up," he said again, only this time a little louder.

"Dad, I told you I set my own alarm. I've got another ten minutes." The exasperation in his voice was such that could only be expressed by a teenage boy.

"Okay, just remember, Mom's leaving at 7:35 and you need to be ready. You know how she'll be if you make her late."

"I will," the whine rising in his voice. "Just leave me alone and let me sleep."

John slipped out the door, keeping it cracked open, just slightly, behind him. He smiled remembering what he had been like at fifteen and how much he hated it when his father used to wake him up.

Moving onto Cassie's room, he tapped lightly and called out quietly, "Hon, it's time to wake up." There was no response. He knew better than to just walk into a twelve-year-old girl's room, so he again tapped and called out, "Can I come in?"

"I'm sleeping," came the drowsy reply.

Slowly opening the door, John quietly said, "Cat? It's time to get up. Do you want a waffle?"

The room was dark, but he could hear her sleepy voice. "No thanks, Daddy. I'll do it. How much time do I have?"

"You have to get up now if you want to beat your brother into the shower."

"Okay."

John couldn't see her, but he heard the bed sheets rustling and turned, closing the door behind him. Both girls and boys need their privacy but, at least in this house, Cassie always got just a bit more privacy than Brian.

He walked back to the master bedroom. Liz was sitting up in the dark, the only light coming from the bathroom. She was sipping her coffee.

"You know I hate you," she said.

"Of course, you do," he chuckled. "I'm going to jump in the shower."

"Don't jump," she said. "You might fall."

It was an old joke, but one made almost every day.

As the shower heated up, John brushed his teeth and looked at himself in the mirror. "Not bad," he thought, patting his stomach with one hand while brushing with the other. The belly was definitely too large and, if he was to be honest with himself, he was starting to develop moobs—man boobs.

Leaning over the counter and into the mirror, John looked closely at his face. The bags under his eyes were noticeable but not too large; the crows' feet, however, were becoming conspicuous. Using his hands, he pulled on the sides of his face but that only took away the sagginess of his cheeks and made the wrinkles on his forehead more prominent. John thought to himself that middle-age was not being kind to him. At least he still had his hair.

Spitting the toothpaste out and stepping onto the scale, John shook his head when he saw that his weight had crept up to 232 pounds.

"Dammit," he muttered. "OK, time to seriously start dropping some of this weight. No more donuts and no more ice cream, at least during the week."

He wondered what else he might do but then Liz walked in. Fortunately, she didn't notice him staring at himself in the mirror or how he was obviously sucking in his gut.

"Yeah," he thought to himself, "I really need to lose weight. It's not fair to Liz. She still looks as good as she did 20 years ago."

With that, he turned and walked into the shower and then, afterwards, put on his work uniform. It was always the same—a dark two-piece suit with a white or light blue shirt. Over the past five or six months, he had begun to show his rebellious streak by wearing colorful socks and not wearing a tie. Of course, he kept a few ties in his office but only wore them if he was seeing a client or attending a partner meeting.

John Callahan was a tax attorney working for a small boutique firm in Portland, Oregon. He was good at what he did, mostly national and international taxation, but he knew he wasn't anything special. He was just another cog in the machine of everyday life, one with an ever-expanding stomach and sagging features. He and Liz used to joke that he wasn't overweight, merely well-upholstered.

In hindsight, he remembered that particular morning only because it was the first time he learned of the virus outbreak. True to his promise to himself, he followed reports over the following weeks and months. Viruses had never been of any great concern to him before. He remembered hearing about the Zika virus but in his little segment of the world, it was of minimal consequence. He and Liz weren't going to have any more children and Brian and Cassie were still years away from worrying about pregnancies. Anyway, they lived in America and the only viruses that were of any real concern were the annual flu bugs.

There weren't news articles every day, at least not at the beginning. For the first month or so, he would see an article about every other week. They weren't overly alarming but gradually, news reports about this new virus became more common. One article referenced the ever-increasing threat of a pandemic and John did a little online research on what a pandemic really was. The last serious pandemic was back in 1918. That pandemic, often called the Spanish Flu, was thought to have infected five hundred million people with an estimate of twenty million to fifty million or more fatalities.

The news always mentioned that the biggest difference between 1918 and now was the progress in medical science over the last century. Scientists now understood how viruses worked. Modern science knew how to develop treatment protocols for various illnesses and diseases. Scientists had mostly mastered the development of vaccines, even if the manufacturing process, at least on a large scale, was still a work in progress.

Despite these assurances, reports became more frequent and provided more details. This new virus was apparently different than others and was even more deadly than Ebola. The news articles described it as air-borne and the initial symptoms were excessive mucus resulting in difficulty breathing and harsh coughs. The virus would enter into the body's cells and rapidly reproduce, bursting through the cell walls and causing internal bleeding, eventually overwhelming the body's ability to survive.

CHASING SHADOWS

The news suggested that this new Ecuadorian virus had nearly a 100 percent mortality rate, at least to date. What was even more disturbing were the articles suggesting that health workers, despite their training and safety gear, were also being infected and dying.

Even with all of these reports, there were few outside of Ecuador and the surrounding countries who, like John, paid attention or showed much concern. People were accustomed to reports of new and deadly viruses and the threats of pandemics. The danger from any particular virus was just too remote to truly register with the common man, at least not yet.

It was in early May when the evening news finally began reporting on the virus outbreak. Teams from both the World Health Organization and the Center for Disease Control were already in the region to investigate.

Within a week, the media began reporting daily stories of the virus. The WHO and the CDC, together with the United Nations, announced an unprecedented quarantine of all three countries—Ecuador, Columbia, and Peru. All traffic in and out of those countries, whether by land, sea, or air, was halted. The US Navy and Coast Guard placed a blockade along the coast.

While this was alarming, the media was continuing to report on advances in developing a vaccine for the virus. Vaccines were a wonderful discovery first developed for smallpox and then for diseases such as diphtheria, measles, mumps, and polio. By their nature vaccines stimulate and bolster the body's immune system in order to allow a person to become immune to the particular disease. Reports suggested a vaccine might be available as soon as the first of August.

Being a cautious man John wondered what, if anything, he could and should prepare for. At this point with the summer rapidly approaching, there wasn't much to do. He did cancel his trip to Argentina but other than that, and as long as the virus was restricted to Central and South America, he believed his family to be safe.

By the Fourth of July there was a growing and palpable sense of concern everywhere around the globe, at least by leaders of most nations. This virus was something completely different from its known predecessors. The outbreak was serious and stories ran daily in the news. The scientists named the new virus the EC-1 Virus, but people initially called it the New Plague and, ultimately, just the Curse.

Evangelicals used the term to support their theory that God was punishing people for turning their backs on Him and otherwise engaging in sinful behavior. For environmentalists the term was used to suggest that Mother Nature was striking back for centuries of mankind's rape and pillaging of the Earth and its resources. For conspiracy theorists the Curse was an attack by foreign nations, the Deep State, and/or otherworldly entities.

For everyone else the name just seemed to fit. It was a curse; a curse capable of being an extinction level event, and no one was quite sure how or when it might eventually be lifted.

The WHO and the CDC continued to issue press releases regarding the imminent development of a vaccine. Both agencies issued at least weekly reports assuring the public that it would only be a matter of time before the vaccine would be deemed effective and then, shortly thereafter, be distributed for large-scale manufacture. All of the major pharmaceutical companies were working independently and around the clock to create their own vaccines, knowing that the first successful vaccine developed would be hugely profitable.

It was mid-August when it was revealed through multiple news sources how the quarantines and blockades weren't working. Realistically, there was no way to stop highly motivated people from going or leaving the areas. There is little motivation stronger than the motivation to protect one's self and family from certain death. The survival instinct drove people to flee the affected countries and seek refuge wherever they could. While the airports and roads were closed down as part of the international quarantine, people fled through the jungles and mountains. Some used cars and trucks, others used mules and others left on foot or on bicycles. Some used boats, while the wealthy snuck out in private planes, flying low to avoid detection. All travelled under cover of night and it proved to be impossible to stop them.

Outbreaks were gradually reported in Brazil, Venezuela, and Panama. The national armies and local militias were enlisted to protect the borders, but their efforts were often as brutal and inhumane as they were ineffective. People were being slaughtered yet some still made their way through.

Almost overnight, all media reports from the first three nations affected—Ecuador, Columbia, and Peru, as well as the border regions on the neighboring countries—stopped. There was a total media blackout—a complete void. Even shortwave radio from the area was quiet. It was impossible to tell whether this was a self-enforced media blackout, a military effort or something far worse. In any event, the blackout from the affected countries was unprecedented. Some speculated that there was no one remaining to report on conditions there.

What was particularly concerning to most people was how there were no communications through the Internet—nothing on Facebook or any other form of social media. There were no emails emanating from these countries.

The White House announced that it was merely a malfunction of the local electrical grid and communication networks in those countries. A press release advised that the Navy was actively preparing to locate and assist American and other western journalists to return home. Strangely enough, no journalists, western or otherwise, from those countries were ever heard from again. At this point, only the most trusting of American citizens actually believed the White House on this issue.

It was about this time when the virus went from being just *a* news story to be *the* news story. There were articles in every form of print and internet media, as well as it being the lead story on all television and radio broadcasts.

With all of the media frenzy, John and Liz began discussing options should the Curse reach the United States. School was just starting for the kids and there were only mild disruptions at their jobs. Deciding that it might be a good idea to locate and rent a house away from the metropolitan area, someplace more remote and safe, they began their research

As they both still had to work, and the children were still in school, it had to be somewhere relatively close but still at least isolated should the Curse reach Oregon.

John and Liz focused on the coast as it was now the off-season, which meant vacation rentals would be available and reasonable, especially for longer terms. Liz began their search online and quickly found a house just east of Manzanita. It was a small three-bedroom cabin with a fireplace, small garage and a carport. It wasn't something that would ordinarily interest them as, even in off-season traffic, it would take at least thirty minutes to get to the beach. It was, however, reasonably priced for a six-month rental and relatively remote. The cabin was on a small dead-end road toward the top of a steep cliff with an ocean view only on very clear days. There were streets both above and below them, but they were separated enough so they weren't visible to one another. The cabin was set back from the road and was heavily forested. They would be able to see their immediate neighbors' houses but not much else.

While Liz was negotiating a lease, John decided it would be prudent to purchase some guns. He had never owned a gun and, in fact, had never even fired a real gun before. When he was younger, a friend had an air pellet gun, but they only fired it a couple of times before the friend's parents took it away after finding a dead squirrel in the yard.

John's concern was that if the Curse did make it to Oregon, panic might ensue. It didn't take much to imagine how panic could transition into riots and he didn't want to be the guy carrying a butter knife to a gunfight. Being practical, he decided on a shotgun, a handgun and a deer rifle. On his way home from work on a Friday, John stopped by Cabela's, a specialty retailer of all things outdoors, in Tualatin. Never having been there before, John was amazed at how big it was and how many different outdoor activities it catered to. There were huge sections of the store for fishing and camping, and others for archery. He didn't care about any of that though. He was there for guns.

It was disconcerting how many guns there were and how many different types. He saw what looked like assault rifles as well as handguns that looked like they could take down an elephant. It was crowded and clear to John that he wasn't the only one concerned about possible riots.

With the help of a very attentive salesman, John purchased a Taurus Judge revolver, capable of firing both .45 caliber bullets and .410-gauge shotgun shells together with a Winchester 12-gauge shotgun, and a Montana Rifle ALR. Despite never handling a gun before, John was amazed how good they felt in his hand and how strangely beautiful they were. The rifle, in particular, had a wood stock and black barrel and just seemed to speak to him.

In addition to the guns John purchased a couple of boxes of cartridges and a carry bag for all of them. As he would assure Liz that evening, once life returned to normal, as it surely would someday, he would either return the guns to Cabela's or just sell them. He also promised to take a gun safety course as soon as he had the time to do so.

In his heart, John knew that while he could sell the handgun and the shotgun, he would want to keep the rifle. It was just so damn beautiful, like a work of art. It felt good in his hands and seemed to give him the confidence to handle whatever might present itself in the future. At one point that weekend, as John was demonstrating his prowess in holding the various firearms, Liz laughed.

"I swear," she said, "you are standing straighter than I've seen you do in a long time. Are you puffing out your chest?"

In the glare of her laughter, John turned red-faced and muttered, "no", sheepishly returning the guns to the carry bag. Despite his embarrassment, he knew Liz's vision of him didn't match his own. He was a 51-year-old tax attorney. What he *wasn't* was a hunter or a military guy. He hadn't even been in a fight since sixth grade so while the guns might make him feel like John Wayne, he wasn't. He was more schlub than gunfighter and, at least for the immediate future, that was all right. He had no desire to actually use any of the guns; he just wanted them to allow him to believe that, if necessary, he could and would protect his family.

ॐ

CHAPTER TWO

QUESTION 67 AND 68

I t was early October when they spent their initial weekend at the coast. This was to be a work weekend for all of them, involving first cleaning the cabin and then stocking shelves and closets. They loaded up the SUV with food and had each child pack a suitcase full of clothes. They left early on Saturday morning, and it took them a little over two hours to get there. Any questions posed to the children by either John or Liz were met with monosyllabic responses and sullen glares. When they arrived, the children walked quickly into the cabin to claim their bedrooms.

Chores were doled out and Brian and Cassie silently performed their assigned tasks with ear buds firmly planted in their ears. They did nothing more than what they were asked. John overheard an occasional telephone conversation one of the children would have with friends and the anger and frustration was obvious.

Both children were, of course, aware of the Curse as they practically lived on the Internet. Nonetheless and at least publicly, they shared the belief, like most kids their age, in their own invulnerability and immortality. They never said anything to either of

13

their parents and neither John nor Liz knew how, or when, they should discuss it with them. Both children were upset when they were told the family was going to spend weekends down at the coast beginning immediately. Brian was on the varsity football team, albeit only second string, and fumed when informed that he would have to quit the team.

Cassie was on a travelling soccer team and cried when she was told.

Both children's anger and disappointment gradually diminished when, over the next couple of weeks, other teammates quit the teams and they were officially disbanded by the third week of October.

It was just prior to that first weekend when John considered allowing the children to invite friends to go with them, at least on the initial weekend excursions. Liz overruled him. Her rationale was that if they were going to start establishing a safe house to avoid infection, the fewer people who knew the precise location of the cabin, the better. John agreed but wondered whether they weren't becoming paranoid. He could see the children looking at them warily from time to time.

Even before that first weekend at the coast, John and Liz made a few attempts to have serious family discussions about the virus but were quickly shut down with cries of "I know" and sighs of exasperation. Both parents watched the children to see if there were any signs of fear or if, alternatively, it was just teenage angst about the inconvenience and separation from their friends. John and Liz could only hope that if things got worse, the kids would eventually open up, so they could really talk about this virus and what impact a global pandemic could have on their lives.

While Internet service had been set up before they got there, the children were both given explicit instructions as to what they could, and could not, tell friends about the cabin. They could say that their parents were crazy and/or paranoid. They could tell them that they would be back on the following Monday, and this was just a temporary panic by their parents. They were not, however, to ever tell anyone exactly where the cabin was located, nor were they to post any pictures of the cabin.

John and Liz discussed this at length. They decided that in a worst-case scenario, they needed to know they were safe from anyone who might want to take advantage of their preparations. They understood how heartless this might sound, especially to Brian and Cassie, but their responsibility was first and foremost to keep their children safe.

They could deal with rolled eyes and sighs of exasperation but hoped that when things got back to normal, they would all be able to laugh at their paranoia.

It was during that first Saturday evening at the coast that John tried again to have a serious discussion about the virus. He started up the grill and cooked cheeseburgers for everyone. Liz cooked broccoli and opened a bag of potato chips.

With everyone sitting around the dinner table there was still little communication coming from Brian or Cassie.

"So, kids, what do you think?" John asked.

Brian stared at his plate, fumbled with his potato chips, and muttered, "Of what?"

Before John could respond, Cassie looked at John and said, "Dad, you're really scared about this thing, aren't you?"

She really was the more intuitive of the children. John looked at his wife and their eyes locked. In times like these, parents naturally want to protect their children. They are willing to lie to their children in order to keep the sometimes-horrific aspects of the real world from them. Both John and Liz wanted to lie to their children. They wanted to, but they couldn't.

"I am," John said simply and quietly.

"Is it going to reach Oregon?"

"I wish I could tell you for certain one way or another."

John fumbled with the neck of his beer bottle and took a sip.

"Dad, if the Curse reaches Oregon, are we going to die?" This was Brian and John could hear the nervousness in his voice.

This time Liz spoke up. "Honey, we don't know what's going to happen. This virus is bad, which is why your dad and I have rented this cabin. We should be safe here. If there is ever a case of the virus anywhere in Oregon or Washington, we'll immediately come down here until it blows over.

"We don't know how long it might take, which is why we want to stock the cabin with enough food and supplies to last a couple of weeks...just in case."

Brian drank down his can of Diet Coke and, while still looking at the cheeseburger sitting on his plate, slowly passed the empty can back and forth from hand to hand.

"Mom, I've heard some really bad stuff about the Curse," he said.

"Brian, first of all, we would prefer you not use that term—the Curse. It is just something people started saying to scare everyone even more. This isn't some otherworldly force or malevolent being that is trying to kill people. It's a virus, just like the flu. I just read this morning about a breakthrough and how they might be able to start manufacturing a vaccine in a couple of weeks.

"There are people a lot smarter than your father and I who are working day and night on this. They *will* find a way to stop this thing and well before it comes anywhere near us."

Liz had to force herself to sound convinced because she was anything but. Ever since the virus started being described as a possible global pandemic, she'd read everything she could about it. She knew how deadly it was. She knew the media reports of an impending vaccine might be nothing, but a ruse intended to install false hope and avoid panic.

Nonetheless, she, like John, tried to maintain an air of confidence and calm, at least in front of Brian and Cassie.

John stood up and looked out the window. In the distance he could sense, even if he couldn't see, the ocean. "Look, we wish we could tell you that everything is going to be all right but, honestly, we can't. We believe it will be and we will do everything we can to protect you, but we can't be absolutely sure.

"What we can be sure about is that we are a family, and we will stay a family. Mom and I are doing our best to protect you and I realize how us coming out here, even if just for the weekends, may look like we are panicking. We're not. We're just trying to prepare for the worst. You know me; I'm the guy with unopened packs of socks and underwear in the garage, just in case. I've always said I'd rather have something and not need it than to need it and not have it. That's what this cabin is.

"For tonight, just try to get some rest. Open your window and you might be able to hear the ocean in the distance. I want to do a little more work around here tomorrow and we should probably run into town just so we know where the stores are."

Everyone stood up and Brian, followed by Cassie, walked over to Liz and gave her a kiss. Brian said, "I love you, Mom."

They then walked over to John and Brian gave his dad a hug first. This was the first time in years that Brian had hugged him.

"We'll get through this, Boyo," John said quietly.

"I know we will, Dad," Brian responded. Whether or not it was false bravado, Brian seemed to have regained his age-appropriate sense of invulnerability.

Cassie walked up to John and wrapped her arms around his waist. He could feel her give a little sob and knew how frightened she really was.

He leaned over and whispered in his ear, "It's okay, Cat. I'll protect you. I promise."

She looked up at him for almost longer than was comfortable and then reached up and gave him a kiss on the cheek.

"Okay, Daddy, goodnight."

17

꿍

CHAPTER THREE

Darkness on the Edge of Town

I t would be close to Halloween before it became common knowledge about what made this particular virus so virulent. It was unusually small and had a unique ability to adapt to different hosts—primarily people. As even the non-medically inclined people came to learn, most viruses range in size between 20 and 300 nanometers. This virus, throughout all of its mutations, could be as small as 5 nanometers. Most common respiratory masks were useless against a virus of such a small size.

The first reported case in the United States was in Tucson, followed quickly by cases in Miami and Houston. All reported cases were fatal, and none were contained. Simultaneously, reports were confirmed on every continent. Australia declared a complete quarantine, banning all air and sea traffic in or out, but it was too little and too late.

The news became erratic and unreliable. It was difficult to differentiate between true fact and fear mongering. The media was trying to keep up with developments as quickly as possible, but they didn't have the opportunity to fully fact-check the reports. There were reports that the virus was a biological warfare agent, which had been accidentally released. Other reports claimed terrorists were behind it. There were even reports of zombies.

What wasn't reported would have been of even greater interest to the general public. The federal government was in the process by mid-summer of establishing plans should the virus continue its inexorable spread. These plans involved how and when to shut down Congress and the Courts. The federal government already had multiple contingency plans to deal with a wide range of catastrophes. Now, those contingency plans had to be tailored to fit this impending crisis.

The president met with the director of the Federal Emergency Management Agency with instructions to prepare for the worst. FEMA, in turn, placed an emergency order for Level A hazmat suits, waiving the standard federal regulations for public contracts. The suits, when they were received, were first distributed to the military and federal law enforcement, as well as those considered to be essential personnel within the government.

The Federal Communications Commission was instructed to prepare for implementation of the Emergency Broadcasting System. This involved greater testing on both radio and television.

The Joint Chiefs of Staff received the most attention and instruction. The president and Congress realized that in the event of a full pandemic, the United States would be vulnerable to attack. Of course, if the virus was truly a global pandemic, there was always the question of who would actually be able to sustain a legitimate attack. Nonetheless, preparations were required. Rather than officially declaring an increase in military readiness, it was decided to keep the United States at a DEFCON 3 level. Behind the scenes, however, the military was busy.

The Navy ordered all of its ships out to sea and increased the security at all naval stations. With the ships at sea, it was thought they would be less vulnerable to infection. Troops from all branches of the military were called back to the United States, leaving minimal forces at foreign bases and posts. Active military engagements in countries throughout the world were suspended with the troops being instructed to remain on base and in a solely defensive posture.

Military reserves were called to active duty. This included a 37-year-old sheriff's deputy from Pendleton, Oregon by the name of Roger Boulden. While on active duty, Boulden served two tours in Iraq with the Army achieving the rank of Specialist. There had been issues during his second tour whereby he was sent back to the States after an internal investigation of excessive force was dismissed for lack of evidence. His second marriage was in the process of dissolving and Boulden welcomed the chance to once again answer his nation's call and defend it against any enemies, foreign or domestic, human or biological.

The timing was fortuitous for Boulden as his soon-to-be second ex-wife filed a complaint of spousal abuse. Due to his status as a sheriff's deputy in Umatilla County, the complaint was forwarded to the nearby Morrow County Sheriff. The small staff there, however, was depleted by the call to active duty of many of its deputies and so the investigation was shelved temporarily.

Training for military personnel focused more on law enforcement on the chance that martial law might be declared. With his background in law enforcement, Boulden was quickly promoted to the rank of Corporal and put in the position of training less skilled warriors on the duties and procedures for that form of service.

The U.S. had a sporadic and limited history of declaring martial law. All prior declarations of martial law were limited in both geographic area and time. General Andrew Jackson declared martial law prior to the Battle of New Orleans. Abraham Lincoln and Congress had declared a limited form of martial law during the Civil War in an attempt to legitimize Lincoln's unilateral suspension of the doctrine of *habeas corpus*. At other times, local leaders declared martial law in the wake of disasters in order to avoid looting and maintain law and order.

In the present case, however, the president was contemplating a declaration of a national state of emergency and ordering martial law throughout the nation. This had to be a last resort, as it would undoubtedly cause serious opposition by many and panic by even more. Nonetheless, planning commenced and governors in each state were consulted and included.

Perhaps most nefariously, the federal government began implementing procedures to allow it to control all forms of communication, if necessary. In the process of doing this, the National Security Agency, in conjunction with the Central Intelligence Agency, the National Reconnaissance Office and various military intelligence agencies, confirmed they could control or disable all communication satellites, as well as ground-based communication networks and providers. Some of the private communication providers, such as Comcast, CenturyLink and AT&T were briefed on how they would be expected to respond should martial law be declared. They were also advised that such briefing was highly confidential and if any reports were leaked to the general public, the government would pursue treason charges.

In fact, and this was communicated without any pretense or apology, any such leaks might well result in extrajudicial remedies. Anyone suspected of leaking any confidential information would be immediately arrested without the right to counsel or prompt hearing. This was not the time for whistleblowers or to countenance leakers. Of course, nothing of this scale could be accomplished without leaks but these threats minimized them.

The more radical and extremist media outlets, whether professional or amateur, were disabled either voluntarily or involuntarily. Suddenly people found many popular websites and podcasts went dark and weren't updated. Well-known conspiracy theorists such as Alex Jones and Mark Levin just seemed to disappear overnight.

21

They were said to have gone on vacation and few in the mainstream media seemed to notice. Only the most paranoid of their followers suspected the truth.

While all these steps were being implemented on a national level, local governments were also developing plans to deal with what was not yet officially designated a pandemic. These plans involved everything from shutting down schools and public meetings to increasing staffing of hospitals and medical clinics.

There is an old saying that the best laid plans of mice and men often go awry. In this case, that was exactly what happened. While the federal government was able to implement much of its planning without publication by the media, local governments were not as adept. As word got out about the possibility of closing schools and government offices, panic began setting in.

There were runs on banks as well as supermarkets and hardware stores. Gun stores had brisk business, even with substantial markups on weapons of all kinds.

Unbeknownst to the general public was that the virus was far more dangerous than they were told. There were two aspects to the virus causing the greatest difficulty in developing a vaccine. First of all, it appeared to mutate constantly. It seemed to mutate upon contact with the DNA of a host, creating a new, individualized virus. The experts could examine two victims side by side and the viruses in both, while obviously related, were sufficiently different that one could not be used to develop a vaccine against the other.

The second factor was that the virus' gestation period was constantly shortening. In effect, the virus in its multiple permutations was becoming more efficient. It appeared to be increasing its potency, resulting in the shortening of the period between infection and death.

The original victims in Ecuador lingered for weeks, allowing medical teams to observe and document how the virus impacted and destroyed human cells. Victims of newer versions of the virus were dying within days of infection. It was becoming a morbid race to see which was moving quicker—the decrease in the Curse's gestation period or its spread around the globe.

By Thanksgiving, panic was in full bloom globally. Hospitals were overflowing with patients and the morgues even more so. The Curse maintained a nearly 100% mortality rate and there was still no substantive progress on the long-promised vaccine. Many of the research scientists reluctantly, and only in private, suspected the only hope for survival was if the virus, like a hurricane turning back out to sea, just died out on its own. This had happened with other pandemics throughout human history but there were no signs that this particular virus would follow suit.

The outbreak was rapidly becoming a cataclysmic event, akin to the asteroid that wiped out the dinosaurs. Religious loonies declared it the End of Times and even non-religious people began to accept that as a possibility.

ↀ

CHAPTER FOUR

Takin' It to the Streets

In the weeks just before Thanksgiving, John stopped going
into the office on a regular basis. There was little point as
most of the firm's clients were shut down and there was no
one working at the Internal Revenue Service. What little work
needed to be taken care of could be done from home.

His last trip into the office was the Friday before Thanksgiving
week. He and the family had been in town since Tuesday making
final arrangements for a longer, more permanent stay at the cabin.
School for both children was cancelled through the remainder
of the year. The family spent the week packing their remaining
personal items. They also worked on buying whatever dry goods
they could find in the grocery stores and Costco. They loaded
up on flour and sugar as well as spices and any fresh fruits and
vegetables they could find. They bought as many bottles of water,
in all sizes, that they could find as well as boxes of macaroni and
cheese and other instant meals. They were not alone in hoarding
food and supplies, but they persevered.

On Friday, Liz drove down to the cabin with the children in

the SUV packed with supplies. They left at the crack of dawn, so they could make it there, unload the SUV, and get back to Tigard for a second and final trip with John.

After they left, John spent the rest of the morning closing up the house. He shut off the water at the meter and tried to cancel the utilities, but no one answered the phones at either Portland General Electric or Northwest Natural Gas. He unplugged all the appliances and then jumped into the BMW and drove downtown.

The streets were mostly empty and a quick survey of the various neighborhoods on the way showed most houses with curtains drawn tight. Occasionally he would see someone loading up a car but noted the people invariably avoided making any eye contact. Other than those few loading cars, no one was on the street. Nobody was raking leaves, nobody was waiting on the corner for the bus and there were no children playing in the park. John thought to himself how eerie it was.

Entering the downtown grid, there were a few more cars on the road but more noticeable was the unusually large number of homeless people wandering about. Portland always had a large homeless population who, due to the mild climate, slept in doorways and under overpasses and congregated on sidewalks, public parks, and plazas during the day. On this day, the number of homeless was larger than anything he had seen before. Also, they didn't appear to be sedentary. There were small groups of four or five people, mostly younger people, walking around and yelling at the few passing cars. John had his window rolled up and while he couldn't understand what they were saying, he recognized the hostility in their faces and movements.

Driving into the parking lot in the basement of the PacWest Center, John felt a measure of relief to be out of the open. Locking the car behind him, he strode over to the elevator, noting how few cars were parked down there, and quickly rose to the 24th floor. DiCioccio & Braun, P.L.L.C. had twenty-one lawyers and at least another forty people on staff. The firm resided on the entire floor with a few offices located on the 23rd.

Usually on a Friday the office would be a beehive of activity. Today John found it nearly empty. Only the most ambitious of associates were still there in an attempt to impress whichever partners might show up. John said hello to a few of them and then spotted his principal associate, Hafez Daraee. Hafez had an admirable intellect surpassed only by his work ethic and ambition. He knew he was up for partner in the spring and didn't want to risk missing the opportunity merely out of fear of the Curse.

"Good morning, Boss, I didn't think I'd see you here today."

"Hafez, I didn't expect to be in either, but I wanted to pick up a few more things for home. Why aren't you working from your house?"

"You know me, John. Someone needs to be manning the fort in case a client comes in with an emergency."

John chuckled and softly shook his head.

"Hafez, you really should go home. Until this virus blows over, it's not safe here. Hell, it's not even safe out in the streets."

"That's why I'm still here. I'm probably as safe here as I can be anywhere. We're twenty-four flights up and it's not likely a law office will attract a lot of looters," he said.

It was difficult to argue with that type of logic, so John said, "Well, I'm going to grab a few things and then get out of here. You take care of yourself, all right? You know I'm always just a telephone call away, right?"

"Of course, Boss. You take care of yourself and your family too."

"Will do. I'll see you after the Holiday."

Both of them suspected this might not be true but they kept up the pretense and waved to one another as John walked away. Striding to his office, John sat down at his desk. He really didn't need anything involving work. What he did need was his backup drive. This contained a copy of all of his personal records, including a library of family photographs. Whether or not there would be any work to come back to, John wouldn't risk losing access to all of his digital memories.

With the backup drive in his briefcase, John walked to the kitchen, grabbed a bottle of water and headed for the elevator. While he waited for it to arrive, he turned and surveyed the office. He had never seen it so empty, not even on Saturdays. He wondered whether he would ever be back and, if so, what he might come back to.

The bell announced the arrival of the elevator and it seemed unusually loud as it echoed around the vacant lobby. With a heavy heart John entered and headed down to the garage level.

The building's garage was just as empty as it had been when he arrived. Out of curiosity he first drove down to the bottom level before heading back up toward the exit. He counted a total of nine cars for a building with thirty-three floors.

As he drove up the ramp to the exit, a loud buzzer sounded warning pedestrians that a car was exiting the parking lot. This was exactly what John did not want. As he pulled out into the street, everyone milling around turned to look at him.

Turning onto S.W. Fourth Avenue John drove slowly. There seemed to be an almost palpable sense of danger. He felt a light sweat break on his brow as the hairs on the back of his neck stood straight out. Everyone on the street was disheveled and many seemed intoxicated. There were no young professionals heading out to lunch. These people were the homeless and those ignored or scorned by society. Their hostility was obvious. John did his best to avoid eye contact or make any sudden movements that might set someone off.

Suddenly, he heard a can bounce off the passenger side door. Through the closed window, he could hear some people laughing. In the rear-view mirror, he saw a group of ragged men and women walking in his direction. He picked up the speed of the car just a little and, simultaneously, they started running. They were throwing things at him. At the same time, he saw a group of young people on his right who were also running toward him from the driver's side of the car. Ahead of him, people began throwing garbage cans into the street to block his way.

John increased his speed again as he weaved around the garbage cans, as well as the people who were now hitting his car with their hands. He looked again in the rear-view mirror and saw one of the men crouch down and point something in his direction.

Instinctively he ducked down and, just as he did, he heard a bang and the rear window of his car shattered, spraying him with glass. At that point, John no longer worried about drawing attention to himself or avoiding garbage cans and people. He hammered his foot down on the accelerator and sped away. He struck a garbage can sending it flying into the air, and nearly hit a cyclist crossing the road ahead of him but, at this point, he didn't care.

It wasn't until he pulled into the driveway and closed the garage door behind him that John allowed himself to relax and breathe again. He started shaking and suddenly felt nauseous. Opening the door quickly, John bent over and vomited onto the floor of the garage. Wiping his mouth with his handkerchief, he took a few deep breaths in an effort to calm himself down. Looking around, he was relieved to see the SUV parked there. After a few minutes, he was collected enough to be able to go into the house.

"LIZ? Kids? We need to go," he said, making no attempt to mask the urgency in his voice.

From upstairs, he heard Liz say, "John? Are you all right? Did something happen?"

"Pack up, we need to go now!"

He could hear her footsteps coming around the corner.

"John? Oh god! John, what happened? You're shaking."

"Someone shot at me. I was leaving downtown, and someone shot at me."

"Are you hurt? Did you call the police?"

"Hon, I'm fine but you don't know what it is like out there. We need to get out of here. I'm not sure there are any police left. Is the car packed?"

"Just about. Cassie is upstairs getting dressed and Brian is just down the street at JB's."

Without saying a word, John reached for his phone and texted Brian, "*Get home NOW!*"

John looked up and Liz was staring at him.

"Is this really it?" she asked.

"I don't know but if it isn't, I don't want to be here when the shit really starts to hit the fan. Where the hell is Brian?"

Just then, John's cellphone buzzed and there was a message from Brian. "*On my way.*"

"Liz, we need to go right away. Please get Cassie now. I need to collect myself. I don't want the kids to see me so shaken."

"Okay, we'll be right down."

John went into the downstairs bathroom and had to rush to avoid soiling himself. The excrement flew out like diarrhea and John worked to slow down his breathing.

"Dad, I'm home. What's going on?" It was Brian.

"Grab your stuff and get in the car. We're leaving now." John realized that his voice was loud, with a noticeable, at least to him, quiver. He stood up to wash his hands and kept taking deep breaths to calm himself.

Walking out of the bathroom, John looked at Brian who was still standing there and noted the fear in his eyes.

"Brian, grab your gear. We need to go now. I'll explain later. Don't leave anything behind that you might need."

They were in the SUV within fifteen minutes. John focused on the road ahead while Liz and the children were all looking backward at their home. It was unsaid but he could sense each of them wondering when they would be back. While he couldn't tell them, he silently mouthed the answer to himself—never.

∾

CHAPTER FIVE

SLIPPIN' INTO DARKNESS

In the Oval Office, the president sat his desk looking at the leather binder in front of him. His chief of staff, ten members of his cabinet, the speaker of the House and the Senate majority leader were fanned out behind him. The Joint Chiefs of Staff were standing in front of the desk as were the heads of the Federal Bureau of Investigation, the Central Intelligence Agency and every other federal intelligence and law enforcement agency. Everyone stared at the president.

The president's chief of staff walked up to him and whispered in his ear, "It's time, Sir."

The president continued to look at the binder. He rubbed his hand over the smooth warm leather and felt the embossed seal of the United States on the front cover. He picked it up, the weight of the binder hiding the slight, but noticeable, tremble in his hands. Taking a deep breath, he laid the binder back down, opened it and picked up his pen. Fearing any hesitation might lead him to a change of mind, the president quickly put the pen to paper and signed his name.

"Gentlemen, I have now signed Executive Order 14132. Martial law is hereby declared throughout the United States. General Moody, as chairman of the Joint Chiefs of Staff, you are now instructed to implement Project Bravo. Do your best and remember that you are being entrusted with the safety and welfare of our fellow citizens. Do us proud."

As everyone turned and filed out of the room, the president turned to his chief of staff and said, "Ed...God help us all."

He then stood and strode out the side doors to the Residence. The president and First Lady were to be flown to Camp David and the Federal Government, or what remained of it, would operate remotely from there. First, however, he needed to address the nation.

CHAPTER SIX

It's the End of the World as We Know It (And I Feel Fine)

The roads were crowded with people fleeing town. The ordinary rules of the road were irrelevant. People would strike other's cars without stopping to exchange information. John was able to get on Highway 26 toward the Oregon coast and the further away from town they got, the lighter the traffic was. He suspected most people would head east toward the mountains and the plains. There was a lot more empty space east than there was on the coast.

Turning on the radio, he heard the distinctive buzzing sound, which he had grown up with but only for tests. John stared at the radio and then turned to Liz. The buzzing stopped.

"This message is being brought to you by the president of the United States." There was a brief pause before he heard the voice of the president.

"My fellow Americans. As you are all aware we are amidst a

global pandemic of catastrophic proportions. In order to maintain order and for the protection of our fellow citizens, I have declared martial law.

"What this means is that our judicial system has been temporarily closed and the police and military will be running all federal, state, and local offices. This is a temporary situation and, in itself, is no cause for alarm.

"We have instituted a national curfew from seven in the evening until seven in the morning. All citizens, other than emergency responders and the military, must stay at home and off the streets during those hours. Anyone who violates that order will be arrested and jailed for the remainder of the emergency.

"It is critical that we all remain calm and maintain a sense of order. Any lawbreakers will be immediately arrested and detained indefinitely. In order to discourage looting, the police and military have been authorized to use whatever force is necessary to maintain order.

"My friends, I understand how frightening this situation is. This virus is a dogged and determined foe, but we will not give up. I have pledged all available resources to both private and public medical and educational institutions, including the CDC and countless hospitals, research facilities and medical schools. They are dedicated to finding a vaccine. The brave men and women of these various institutions are working around the clock, and I have been assured that we are making progress each and every minute of each and every hour of each and every day.

"All is not lost. We, as a people, have weathered difficult storms in the past and will do so again this time.

"Please keep calm and reach out to your friends and neighbors. There will be some sporadic interruptions in utilities, and we need to band together, as friends, as family and as a nation, to help one another. Keep in contact with your neighbors and please help them in any way you can.

"I vow to give you updates each and every day. This is an unprecedented challenge but one that we are up for. I give you my word as the president of the United States that we *will* prevail, and we *will* survive.

"Until we speak again, be brave and abide by the curfew. Law enforcement and the military are here to help every one of us so please treat them with the respect they deserve. Like you, they would prefer to be with their families but have agreed to serve their country by maintaining law and order during this time of crisis.

"Good night and God bless the United States of America."

The grating buzzing came on again, followed by a gentle, disembodied voice of a woman, "That was the president of the United States. My name is Susan Giles and I will be with you for the next four hours or so. The president has ordered all media to consolidate for the duration of this crisis and broadcast news as one.

"The purpose of this is to ensure that every American has the opportunity to hear the news—the real news, and to understand exactly what is going on and what they need to do. We'll be reporting on the weather every twenty minutes, with news, both local and national, the rest of the time.

"The first story this afternoon, and as many of you just heard, is that the president of the United States has declared martial law and..."

John shut the radio off. He turned to look at Liz and he saw tears welling up in her eyes. He gave her a half-hearted smile and then reached across and grasped her hand tightly.

While he hoped the children were listening to their music on their headphones, he looked back and saw that they weren't. Turning back around, he could feel their eyes on the back of his head and looked at them through the rearview mirror.

"Dad, what is martial law?" Cassie asked.

"Well, as far as you should be concerned, it isn't that much different than regular law. By declaring martial law, the president

34

authorized the police to arrest people without having to go through the normal channels of getting warrants. Also, once arrested, people won't have a quick court hearing to find out if they should be released on bail or not. In effect, once someone is arrested, they can keep him or her in jail for as long they need to."

"But that isn't fair," Brian chirped in.

"Of course, it's not fair but as long as we don't break any laws, we don't need to worry about it. The only law we'll have to be careful of is the curfew. So long as we stay in the cabin between seven and seven, we should be fine."

"Dad," Brian asked, "what's going to happen to us?"

"OK, Boyo, I'm going to be as straight with you as I can. Absolutely no one, and I mean *no one*, knows what is going to happen." John noticed how his voice seemed to be getting higher in tone, but he couldn't stop it. "This fucking virus is like nothing anyone has ever seen or heard of before. We are in uncharted waters. I don't know when, or even if, a vaccine will be ready or whether the virus will just magically disappear, but whatever happens, I hope it happens soon."

John felt Liz's hand on his forearm and stopped, taking a deep breath. Liz started, "Kids, your dad and I will always do our best for you. We will be safe at the coast. We have enough food for at least four weeks, six if we are a little careful. Let's all just hope the scientists come through and figure this thing out."

"This isn't the end of the world, regardless of what it looks like. It's going to be rough for a little while, but we've got a safe place to live, we've got supplies, and most importantly, we've got each other."

Continuing to look at them in the mirror, John saw both children look at one another then, simultaneously, reach down for their headphones and put them back on. They turned away from one another to look out the windows.

"Thanks, Dad."

"You're welcome, Boyo."

They drove the rest of the way without anyone talking. John couldn't bring himself to even look at Liz because he was afraid of what they might actually say to each other. Perhaps it was better not to voice their deepest fears. Maybe it was better just knowing that they were there for one another. John would occasionally look at the children in the back seat and see them either listening to music or texting. He knew they would have a lot of questions and only hoped he could find answers to provide some comfort.

∽

It was just starting to get dark when they pulled into the driveway of the cabin. That first night the children said little as John and Liz did their best, with forced cheerfulness, to try to project an air of normalcy. Liz recruited Cassie to help make the pizza and salad while John and Brian finished unloading the car and lighting a fire in the fireplace.

As they sat down for dinner, they could hear the raindrops splatter against the windows on the west side of the cabin.

"Brian, what is JB doing?" Liz asked.

"He's at home with his folks, I guess."

"I always liked JB and his family," Liz said but she knew it sounded forced. It was clear Brian wasn't going to expound on his answer and give her any additional information. He wouldn't even look up at either of his parents. He ate his pizza but just picked at the salad.

John tried next. "Cassie, do we have any movies you'd like to watch tonight?"

"Thanks, Dad, but I think I'd prefer just to go online and talk with my friends."

John and Liz looked at one another and both of them knew there was little they could do that evening.

"If you want, you two are excused. Your mom and I will clean up. Please remember when talking to your friends, don't tell them where we are."

"I know, Dad." The annoyance in Cassie's voice was clear.

"Cassie, this is important. It can be very dangerous if people start looking for us out here."

This time Cassie didn't even respond. John couldn't tell if the look on her face was contempt or fear. Whatever it was, he hadn't seen it before and didn't like seeing it now.

"Thanks, dinner was good," Brian muttered, still looking at the floor as he too headed upstairs.

John looked at Liz and she just shrugged. "I really hope this isn't how it's going to be."

"John, give the kids a break. It's been a pretty traumatic day for them too. They just need a little time. They're good kids but worried about their friends. I don't blame them."

"I know, it's just that I'm frustrated. I don't know what to say or do to fix this. I've always felt in control before, but this thing is too big. I hate having to be reactive rather than active. I'm starting to feel so fucking helpless and that's not me."

Liz walked over to John and put her arms around him. Resting her head on his shoulder, she said, "Honey, we can only do what we can do. I know you'll do your best for the kids and me and I know that your best will be more than enough.

"It's going to be rough for a while, but I think we're safe here. We've got food and shelter and, most importantly, we have one another. I'll always be there for you just like you've always been there for me."

John could feel tears welling up in his eyes but wasn't quite ready to show how scared he really was. Taking a deep breath, he gave her a squeeze and whispered to her, "You really are too good for me."

"Yes. Yes, I am"

John looked up and held her out at arm's length. She had a sly smile on her face.

"You're mocking me, aren't you?"

"Yes. Yes, I am," Liz responded.

He spun her around and with a gentle pat on her butt, he pushed her toward the kitchen. "To the kitchen, woman! You have work to do." He gave her his best smile and began picking up the empty plates.

CHAPTER SEVEN

WE JUST DISAGREE

Corporal Boulden wasn't surprised when he was advised of the president's declaration of martial law. It was becoming increasingly obvious the virus was attacking not only people but civilization as a whole.

The order for all senior staff to appear at the briefing came in the morning with the briefing to start at noon. The presiding officer, Colonel Jeremy Bice, wasted no time.

"Gentlemen and ladies, this morning the president has signed an executive order declaring martial law. What this means for us, is that the operation of all civilian governments has been temporarily suspended and we have been put in charge. The region we are responsible for starts at the California border and then north all the way across the Columbia River to the Vancouver, Washington area. We are also responsible from the Coast to the Cascade Range.

"There may be some overlap with other commands and an extension as time goes by. There are no strict borders, and we will need to coordinate with our fellow forces in neighboring regions. This is an unprecedented situation, and we need to be flexible.

"As matters of priorities, the first thing we will be doing is establishing a formal base for all military and law enforcement personnel in our region. We have identified the Portland Community College campus at Sylvania for that purpose. I have already ordered fencing to be constructed to surround the entire campus. By the way, we are using the terms "campus" and "camp" rather than "base" in order to alleviate some of the fears people may have about martial law.

"Temporary housing is being erected and we anticipate we will have three to four thousand personnel at the campus by the end of the month. If you have any questions regarding logistics related to the campus, you are to direct such questions to Major Nelson.

"We will be incorporating all remaining law enforcement personnel and they shall continue their efforts to maintain a police presence throughout the community, just under our supervision. Corporal Boulden, you are in charge of coordinating with all law enforcement agencies, municipal, county and state and supervising them. Also, the remaining federal law enforcement agencies, including the DEA and the FBI, are now under our jurisdiction."

Boulden could feel all eyes on him. He fought the urge to smile. This was his time. Never again would he have to handle the crap shifts or be stuck partnering with morons. He was "The Man" and it was now his time to shine. Wouldn't Sergeant Major Bush, the fuckhead who had him sent back from Afghanistan, be surprised?

Colonel Bice continued, all the while looking directly at Boulden, "Remember that you are charged with maintaining law and order. I am not worried about investigating crimes. If you see someone breaking the law, you are to take them into custody immediately.

"Please note martial law also suspends the doctrine of *habeas corpus*. The courts won't be in session, and we won't be having arraignments or trials for the immediate future. We will implement a process for establishing what to do with citizens who have been arrested. First Lieutenant Garrahan has been working on this for some time and he will brief the staff and implement the plan. We're already setting up a holding area for these people but hopefully won't need too much space.

"Gentlemen and ladies, this is not only a historic occasion as martial law has never previously been declared on a national basis, but it is also critical. People are afraid and when people are afraid, some of them will panic. Some people will overreact to what they perceive as a threat to the welfare of their families and themselves. Some will use this as an opportunity to riot and loot.

"Corporal Boulden, this will require you, in particular, to both calm people's fears and enforce law and order. You are taking the lead on the law enforcement. Please remember that many of the people you will be supervising have years, if not decades, of experience and you should rely upon them. Let's not recreate the wheel. It's a matter of organizing the various law enforcement agencies so as to create a single efficient force.

"I want regular patrols and any riots must be immediately quelled. If you see any looting going on, you can use such force as may be necessary to stop it. Remember, however, our primary goal is to keep the peace and project an aura of safety for our citizens. You are authorized to use force on an as-needed basis but remember, force *must* be a last, and not a first, option.

"Are there any questions?"

"NO SIR!" was the unanimous response.

"Very well, you are dismissed."

As the others straggled out of the briefing, Boulden stayed behind. "Colonel Bice, may I have a word please?"

Bice looked up from his papers and said, "What can I do for you, Corporal?"

"Sir, I recognize you are busy, and we are in crisis. With that being said, however, I have a concern about my ability to work

41

with Major Nelson and First Lieutenant Garrahan. I have nothing against either of them personally, but you have given me significant responsibility and I'm concerned how my current rank might impact my ability to work with those two officers."

A sigh escaped Bice's lips and he clenched his fists in order to control his anger. "Are you telling me that with all of the shit we are going through right now, you are concerned that you might have to sit at the children's table? Is that really what you are fucking telling me, Corporal?"

"With all due respect, Colonel, this is not an ego thing. When I was in Afghanistan, there was a significant rift between commissioned and non-commissioned officers. We are in a situation now where we have a relatively small core of mid-level and senior-level officers and I'd hate to see the situation arise where my requests might be treated with less import, or even disregarded, because of my rank."

"Corporal, do you know how fucking stupid your request sounds? We are involved in an unprecedented event, and you expect me to care about your rank?"

Boulden stood his ground and continued to stare his superior officer in the eyes. "Colonel, battlefield promotions are not unheard of."

"And what battle do you think we are engaged in, Corporal? You are in charge of law enforcement. Do you see yourself as being in battle with your fellow American citizens?"

Now it was Boulden's time to try to maintain his composure.

"Colonel, I'm not sure what the fuck…excuse me, I'm not sure what you think is going on right now. We, not just as a nation but also as a species, are in the battle of our lives. The president, our Commander in Chief, declared martial law for the first time in American history and you somehow think this is just an ego thing for me?

"Again, with all due respect, Colonel, you need to get your

head out of your ass and recognize that the only way we survive is for those of us with the organizational skills to be able to maintain some semblance of structure. In order for us to succeed, we need to work with one another and not allow potential delays to arise because of a perceived gap in rank.

"In other words, if there is even the slimmest of possibilities that the gap in rank between me and the senior officers is going to cause a problem, you have an obligation to address and correct that situation."

Boulden saw Colonel Bice's face turn bright red as he was saying all of this and a vein in the colonel's neck was bulging. Through clenched teeth, the colonel said, "Corporal," the word practically dripping with contempt, "I will take your recommendation under advisement. More importantly, I want to make myself completely clear. If you ever talk to me that way again, if you ever use that tone with me again, one of two things is going to happen. Either I'm going to throw you in the stockade and you won't see the light of day for a long, long time or, alternatively, I will kick your ass from here to D.C. and back again.

"Have I made my position clear enough for you, Corporal?"

"Yes, sir."

Boulden turned and strode out the door, fighting to keep the smile from fully forming. Once outside, he called for a meeting of his senior law enforcement staff. He instructed them to immediately contact every law enforcement agency in the region. This included state police, county sheriffs and local police as well as the Feds. After advising them as to whom they were to report to, they would be instructed to give a complete report as to personnel and equipment.

There were only three military armories in the Portland area. Camp Withycombe in Clackamas served maintenance, logistics and warehousing functions for the Oregon Air National Guard and the Oregon Army National Guard. It did, however, house the principal armory for the state of Oregon. There was also a smaller armory in Hillsboro and another small one in northeast Portland.

Boulden ordered squads to each of the armories with directions to seize all personnel, vehicles, weapons, and materials and bring them back to the campus. Without information as to what weaponry might be available from local law enforcement, he needed to make sure his troops were sufficiently equipped to accomplish their mission.

He also wanted to make sure none of the military grade weapons made it into the hands of ordinary citizens in panic mode.

❧

It became quickly apparent to everyone that consolidating all military personnel in the Oregon region in one campus was a two-edged sword. On the one hand, it allowed for clear communication of orders and directives, as well as being able to monitor personnel. On the other hand, the military personnel at the campus were not immune to the Curse and the close quarters were dangerous.

Within days, almost a quarter of the campus was infected and within only a few more days, they were dead. Included were Colonel Bice and Major Nelson, as well as several of Boulden's staff.

Bice's second-in-command, Lieutenant Colonel Kenneth Cruickshank, assumed command of the camp. His first order involved isolating the ill and the dead. His second order was that everyone remaining should first be tested for the virus and, assuming they were healthy, issued hazmat suits as soon as possible. He also established shower facilities before anyone was allowed to remove their hazmat suits and come into contact with other personnel.

As to the dead, they had to be disposed of. The number was too large for any sort of burial, so it was decided to create a funeral pyre. Just south of the campus and most importantly, downwind, was a large field. The corpses were respectfully piled up, drenched in gasoline and incinerated. The smoke from the pyre was dark and could be seen for miles around. Ash from the fire slowly settled on the adjacent landscape, rendering it a gray and somber reminder of what had been and what was to come.

ↀ

Boulden listened to an aide explain that there was a riot in downtown Portland. He didn't have many details but apparently the local police were being attacked by a mob. Many of the policemen were forced to retreat to the police station where they were under siege. Boulden wasted no time ordering a squad of thirty soldiers to immediately head downtown. They were dressed in full combat gear under their hazmat suits. It was bulky and uncomfortable, but Boulden understood the need to protect his soldiers from the Curse. Combat deaths were always an unfortunate but acceptable, risk. Losing his soldiers to this virus was both unacceptable and avoidable.

The soldiers loaded into four Stryker Infantry Carrier Vehicles as well as two Humvees. The ICVs were large vehicles, almost twenty-three feet long and nine feet wide. Each of the ICVs carried a .50 caliber M2 Browning machine gun atop of them. The ICVs were built for a crew of two, with nine passengers.

Unlike the ICVs, the Humvees were basic light military vehicles with six soldiers crammed into each.

As this was the first real action in the area since martial law was declared, Boulden jumped into the lead Humvee as they raced up the highway. The road was mostly empty, so they completed the nine-mile drive quickly. Entering the downtown core, the caravan slowed as it drove down S.W. Fourth Avenue. The riot at the police station could be seen and heard from blocks away. The police were firing tear gas and rubber bullets from the protection of the Justice Center's columns, doors and windows. The mob, which Boulden now estimated at more than five hundred, was mostly in front of the Justice Center. While some had firearms and were shooting at the building, others were hurling rocks and Molotov cocktails from behind the cover of flipped cars and trucks.

The police had better armaments, but the mob was larger and very aggressive. Someone noticed the military vehicles advancing north on the avenue and the fighting slowly came to a stop. The mob, almost as one, turned and stared at them.

Using the radio to communicate between the vehicles, Boulden positioned three of the ICVs in front of the Humvees and side-by-side. The fourth ICV was placed in the rear to protect their flank. Together, the front three ICVs spanned the entire width of the street. Just one hundred feet south of the melee, the vehicles stopped and using a speaker system in his Humvee, Boulden said: "This is Major Roger Boulden of the United States Army. Martial law has been declared and you are all ordered to drop your weapons and immediately disperse."

Boulden smiled. This was the first time he had used his new, self-declared rank and he liked the way it sounded. With Bice and Nelson dead, and the fact he was in charge of most of the military and police weaponry, Boulden was pretty sure neither Cruickshank, Garrahan, nor anyone else, would call him out on it. If he had to give himself the much-deserved promotion and rank, so be it.

As he spoke, the crowd stared at the vehicles. Just as he was about to start giving more orders, someone in the mob yelled "FUCK YOU!" This was all that was necessary to return the mob into a state of frenzy. They began, almost as one, to run toward the ICVs, screaming and hurling rocks. The rocks began to hit the ICVs and then bullets. Boulden couldn't believe these idiots were actually stupid enough to be attacking them. Didn't they have any concept of what they were facing?

Boulden thought about trying to continue communication but knew any further delay would result in the mob overwhelming them. Screaming into his radio, he yelled "Drive! Full speed!"

Either the mob would be dispersed or they would be destroyed.

Glancing through the small gaps between the ICVs, Boulden saw the looks on the rioters' faces change from contempt to fear as they began to recognize exactly what was happening. The ICVs were coming toward them and picking up speed.

Many leaped up onto the sidewalk, but others weren't quick enough and the ICVs rolled right into, and over, them. Some people were thrown into the air and flung into those standing on the sidewalks. The ICVs were clearing a swath through the crowd. The only sound that could be heard over the screams and noise of the ICVs' engines was the sound of breaking bones. The ICVs bucked as they ran over fallen bodies but didn't slow.

The two Humvees lowered their windows and, with Major Boulden leading, the soldiers strafed the rioters huddling on the sidewalks. No quarter would be given. It was time to send a very strong message that rioting would not be tolerated.

While it seemed to happen slowly and for what seemed like an hour, the slaughter actually took less than a minute. The military vehicles completed their pass through the rioters and then went an extra block before turning around. Boulden again got on his speaker, "This is the United States Army. We are going to come back down the street and anyone not a policeman will be shot!"

The vehicles began driving back down the street. This time the soldiers fired indiscriminately on anyone they could see who was still standing or looked to be holding a weapon. These remaining rioters were the enemy and no mercy would be shown.

Stopping directly in front of the Justice Center, Boulden stood up in his Humvee and using the speaker, stated, "Ladies and gentlemen of the Portland Police Department, we will lead you to the campus we have set up in Southwest Portland. Who is in charge?"

From behind a column, a short and stout woman in riot gear walked out. "I am Captain Cate Morris of the Portland Police Department. Who are you?"

"I am Major Roger Boulden and have been charged with coordinating with local law enforcement to implement the president's declaration of martial law and to keep the peace. How many people do you have?"

"I'm not sure of the exact count but we should have about thirty or more officers here, together with a few staff."

Boulden stood there for a minute and considered his options. "I'd like you and your people to load up your vehicles with all the contents of your armory and to follow us back to camp."

"If it is all the same to you, Major, I think we would rather stay here. Some of my people live nearby and they are worried about their families. Also, we can do a better job of protecting people down here by staying here."

Staring at her, Boulden called out, "Captain, if you interpreted my statement about you loading your people up and following us as a request, you were mistaken. This is an order. You will load your people up immediately…all your people.

"Under the executive order signed by the president establishing martial law, the military is in charge of all law enforcement. I have been directed and empowered to organize and coordinate all military and law enforcement and am doing so. At this point, it is imperative we consolidate all police and military units so we can do the most good.

"Do you have any questions about my orders?"

Captain Morris looked at Boulden and then at the broken and battered bodies littering the street. She also looked at the four ICVs and their .50 caliber M2 Browning machine guns. It didn't take her long to realize she had no choice. Nonetheless, she spoke up, "What about the remaining people living downtown? What about the people who are hurt right here?"

"As to the remaining residents in the downtown area, we will send a squad back out to locate and bring them back to our campus. As to the people injured, they were rioting and in violation of martial law. They will have to take care of themselves."

"But how do you expect them to do that? I doubt any of them have medical training. We can't just leave them here. They'll die."

Major Boulden and Captain Morris stared at one another as each of their respective subordinates looked back and forth between them. The cries of the injured and dying filled the empty spaces between and around them.

"These people were rioting. They refused my order to disperse. They attacked my people. Hell, Captain, they were attacking *your* people. They will get neither my sympathy nor my pity.

"Now, do you have any further questions before you follow my orders?" The contempt in his voice was obvious to all.

Captain Morris averted her eyes as she reached for her radio. Instructing her people to gather weapons, equipment, and vehicles, she turned back to the street. She was sickened by the sight of so many dead and mangled bodies and struggled to maintain her composure and not tear up. It took all of her strength to avoid begging Boulden to help the injured. "Major, I will supervise the loading of the vehicles. It will take about thirty minutes. Our vehicles will be leaving from the east side of the building and will then follow you out."

"You have fifteen minutes. After that, I am sending my men in to seize whatever weapons and personnel remain. This is not an idle threat, Captain.

"I will not allow my men to be exposed to the obvious dangers of rioters any longer than absolutely necessary. They have been shot at once and it will not happen again. I recommend you get your ass in gear and get it done. The clock is ticking and I won't have any more patience with your people than I did with the scum laying here. Am I clear enough?"

"Yes sir." Captain Morris turned and walked into the building using her radio to order her people to move quickly.

In exactly seventeen minutes, a fleet of vehicles started pulling onto S.W. Fourth Avenue, just south of the military vehicles. They were primarily a mixture of Ford Crown Victoria cruisers and Ford Explorers. There were a couple of white vans, as well as two SWAT armored trucks and a large Mobile Command Center that looked like a converted motor home.

Captain Morris climbed out of the lead SUV and approached Boulden's Humvee. "Sir, my people will follow you now. Where exactly are we going?"

"Just follow our lead. When we get to the campus, your people will be quarantined until we can confirm they aren't infected. Assuming they are healthy, they will be issued hazmat suits and given instructions on how to proceed."

Boulden nodded to his driver, and they pulled out, followed by a caravan of ICVs and police vehicles. Downtown Portland was now officially abandoned, even if they believed it was only on a temporary basis. A better man might have tried to get word out to any remaining residents who might want the military to escort them to safety. Major Roger Boulden wasn't that man.

ॐ

CHAPTER EIGHT

THAT'S THE WAY OF THE WORLD

Life at the coast quickly fell into a mostly comfortable routine. John and Liz would wake up early and begin the often-rainy day. John would get the fire going in the fireplace, while Liz would either do a load of laundry or start breakfast. They would then sit down and have a cup of coffee together. Sometimes they talked but more often they didn't. The important thing was how, for just that moment in time and in the early morning light, there was peace. Words weren't as important as the fact they each knew they were there for the other. John had learned that, as important as his quiet time had been in their former life, now it was just as important, and perhaps even more important, to be sharing it with his wife.

When Brian and Cassie awoke, they were given chores to keep them busy. These might involve stacking firewood or cleaning the cabin or baking. Many of the chores weren't really necessary but John and Liz thought it important to keep the children busy. Their afternoons involved three hours each day of online schooling and they were required to read books for at least another two hours. John and Liz monitored their chores and schoolwork and would try to spend at least an hour each day discussing various topics. In particular, John liked to talk about dynasties and civilizations that had come and gone to illustrate that mankind had previously weathered calamitous collapses. They discussed the Greek and Roman empires as well as the Mongols and Persians. They discussed at length the British Empire of the late 16th century through the early 18th century as being the largest in history, characterized as the empire on which the sun never set. John and Liz felt this to be particularly important so the children were able to learn how an empire could crumble, but a nation and a people could survive and, over time, still thrive.

The hope was that by having some sort of schedule and attempting to put the current crisis in historical perspective, the children would feel a sense of normalcy and security. John and Liz couldn't be certain their hoped-for results would ever be achieved; all they could do was their best.

From time to time, the family would drive into town, but such trips became less frequent as fewer and fewer stores were open. Rarely would they even see anyone in the street. If they did, the person's eyes were averted in order to avoid making contact. No one dared communicate with a stranger. The sense of isolation was both unsettling and frightening.

If the weather was nice, which occurred rarely at that time of year, they would drive down to the beach and have a picnic. The beach was almost always deserted other than the seagulls calling to them and begging for food. Nonetheless, there was joy in skipping stones, playing touch football, or even just basking in the sun.

The isolation was also present in the neighborhood. While they could see a few of their neighbors' houses, they rarely saw their neighbors. John found out that the neighbor just to the south of them was named Ray Marshall. They would see him from time to time but never got more than a nod of the head. Even that seemed to be an effort for him and was, at best, reluctant.

John walked toward his house one afternoon in an attempt to open a line of communication and to see if he might be a source of assistance should a need arise some time in the future.

As he walked up to the house, Ray Marshall opened the front door and stood there with a shotgun dangling from his arms. The gun was pointed down, but Ray was staring at John and just shaking his head from side to side.

Ray didn't need to say a word for John to understand exactly what he was saying. He was not going to be *that* kind of a neighbor. He wanted nothing to do with John and John should expect nothing from him.

Thereafter, they began to refer to him, facetiously, as "Good Neighbor Ray" and the children were told never to go anywhere near his house.

The neighbors directly to the north were named Dave and Laura Baloun. The Callahans never saw them other than peeking out their windows. They were an older couple and made absolutely no attempt at friendliness or even common courtesy. John preferred to think it was fear rather than rudeness, but he didn't really know.

John didn't bother checking on any of the other neighbors because it was clear by the time they moved into their cabin that no one was ever going to interact with them. Everyone was too scared of the virus to take a chance by having physical contact with anyone else, especially newly-arrived strangers. Anyone, and everyone, could be a threat. Anyone, and everyone, could destroy them and everything they knew.

ॐ

While television and radio were limited by the bland and monotonous news on the Emergency Broadcast System, John still listened from time to time, if for no reason other than for the weather. The actual news was almost always the same. A vaccine is imminent, and the worst of the virus was in the past. There were always assurances that the virus was a worldwide epidemic and no continent or country was unaffected. Presumably this information was given to provide some sort of assurance that this was not just an American scourge.

The problem with this information was, at least for John, it just meant that people were dying around the globe. Whether these people were Pakistani or Dutch, whether they were Chilean or Congolese, they were dying and John found no comfort in that.

He became accustomed to the voices of the rotating roster of faceless announcers. The genders of the announcers alternated and their dialects varied. There were multiple television and radio stations, but they all broadcast the same thing, only in different languages—English, Spanish, Vietnamese, Chinese, French, Italian and countless others.

For the first week or so, the president did make daily addresses to the nation. After that, it was announced that he was unavailable, as he had to address various unnamed emergencies. No one was fooled. It was assumed that the virus had reached the White House, or wherever the president had been hiding, and he hadn't survived. John found it disconcerting how there were no current photographs or videos of the president or whomever might have succeeded him. The announcers just kept referencing "the president," without giving his last name.

The reports of medical breakthroughs were given on a daily basis but were largely ignored by John and Liz. They had come to believe the Curse would disappear, not when modern science came up with a cure but rather, when it finally just burned itself out. This is what happened with the Plague, the Spanish Flu, and other older pandemics. Science wasn't the savior. It was nature that ultimately resulted in these deadly viruses mutating into a nonlethal form. The question was when that would happen and whether they could survive until then. John was determined to do whatever he could to improve the odds of his family's survival.

The Internet was available but unreliable. The government was now regulating and monitoring the major social media sites and negative posts were always deleted within minutes with the posters then permanently blocked. Accordingly, the social media sites were mostly helpful for just confirming the status of some friends and family. Unfortunately, there was never an announcement of someone's death. All that would happen was a friend or family member just stopped posting. The unspoken presumption would be that they had died.

Independent online communities would, however, still pop up from time to time and were a great source of information before they were shut down. The difficulty with these pop-up sites was that the news was often anecdotal and unverifiable. People would post about what they saw or heard and, oftentimes, the information would be second or third hand. Despite the obvious unreliability of the information, John and Liz, as well as the children, were able to glean certain information they considered accurate.

Within weeks, it was clear there was no real government any longer, whether at the federal, state or local level. Martial law was in place everywhere and little, if any, tolerance was granted to anyone who violated curfew or engaged in any sort of protest. It was unclear, however, who was actually in charge.

There was little to no military presence at the coast. From time to time, John could see military vehicles in the distance and even on one occasion, three military Humvees drove down their street. All of the military personnel were garbed in hazmat suits with windows rolled up in their vehicles. John, Liz, and the children watched them from the windows, doing their best to remain unseen. If asked, they wouldn't have been able to say why they hid from the military. In fact, that night at dinner, this was the principal topic of conversation.

"Dad, what do you think those army trucks were doing up here?" Brian asked.

"I don't really know," John responded. "They may have been looking to see if anyone was around or they might have just been making a statement that they were here. Sometimes law enforcement does that, both to send a message to the bad guys and to reassure the good guys.

"It didn't seem as if they were looking for anything or anybody in particular, so I think it was much more likely they were just showing the flag. They were sending a message to us that there is still someone in charge, even out here."

"So, why did we hide?" This was Cassie. All three of them, Liz, Brian, and Cassie all looked at John.

"Okay, the way I figure it is, I don't know them and I have an innate fear of martial law. I've heard of it being declared in various second and third world countries and it never turns out well for anyone but the military.

"As far as I'm concerned, the only people I completely trust in this world are the three of you. I'm sure there are many other good people out there and those army guys are probably good people too. The problem is…I just don't know. What I do know is that it is best if we just stay to ourselves and hunker down until the virus burns itself out and we can start getting back to normal."

"Will we ever get back to normal?" Liz asked.

John looked at her and tried to send a mental message that those types of questions were best posed outside the hearing of the children. Of course, he didn't know when, or even whether, life would ever regain a sense of normalcy, but this wasn't something he could admit to their children.

"Sure, we will. I don't know when, but I suspect it will be no later than the spring. It will be a new normal, but we can at least get back to school and work. We can go home and start working with friends and neighbors to rebuild our lives and our community."

John looked back at Liz and hoped she understood the purpose of his answer. He didn't really believe what he said but now was not the time to explore their deepest fears; now was not the time to acknowledge the complete uncertainty as to the future.

Liz stared back at John before looking away, nodding her head softly. "Okay kids, let's clean up and we can play some games tonight. I think it is finally time I learned how to play Settlers of Catan so I can kick your father's butt. Who's in?"

Everyone smiled, agreed, and proceeded with the clean-up. As John was washing a pot in the kitchen, Liz walked up behind him and whispered, "I'm sorry. I knew as soon as I said it that I shouldn't have. I'll do better."

John turned around and wrapped his arms around her. With an exhausted smile, he leaned in and gave her a kiss. "I really do love you, you know."

Liz quietly responded, "I know."

CHAPTER NINE

THE NIGHT THE LIGHTS WENT OUT IN GEORGIA

The children were too old to believe in Santa Claus but, as a family, they had numerous traditions and were determined to keep as many of them as possible. John cut down a small fir tree from the back of the property and Liz and Cassie strung popcorn and cranberries to decorate it. Brian decided to try his hand at making their Christmas Eve dinner and, with the help of the Internet, made a passable pot roast.

When they sat down for dinner, each of them attempted to avoid talking about anything of substance. They focused on what the spring would be like and how the children would make up for lost school. Unfortunately, every thread of conversation led to the same place. If they talked about school it led to questions as to when, and even whether, school would reconvene. If they talked about friends or cousins, it led back to whether their friends and cousins were even still alive. The Curse, even without being named, haunted every topic.

Eventually they gave into the inevitable and began discussing what was happening. Perhaps it was the forced, but empty, frivolity of Christmas but for the first time John and Liz didn't make attempts at artifice. They decided to be truthful with Brian and Cassie figuring there was no real point in shielding them anymore from what was really going on.

"Dad, what happens if the Curse doesn't burn itself out? What happens if it kills everyone?"

"Brian, I don't have an answer. I still have faith that the two most likely things to happen are that the virus will either burn itself out or a vaccine will be discovered. Remember, there have been pandemics before. There was the Spanish Flu back in the early 20th century and there was the Black Plague back in the Middle Ages. Both of those viruses eventually ran their course and the world recovered. While this virus is much deadlier than either of those, I have to believe that the same thing will happen."

"But what if it doesn't?" Cassie said this with a look of real concern on her face.

"If it doesn't..." John paused, looking for the right words. "If it doesn't, then everyone is going to die, including us."

There was silence all around. Liz started up, "I know we're not a religious family and have really never discussed spirituality but maybe it is time. Do either of you have any thoughts about what happens when someone dies?"

Both of the children shook their heads. John, speaking softly, reached out and took their hands. "Look, kids, let me tell you what I think.

"I think that one of two things happen when we die. One is that somehow, we continue on in some form. I don't care if you call it a person's soul or spirit or even just the person's essence, but a certain part of you continues on after our bodies fail. That part of you will reunite with loved ones. You'll see your grandparents again. You'll see your friends who may have already passed on. Most importantly, if the virus gets all of us, we will all be there together.

"If that happens…if we die, I don't think we should be afraid. If there is some sort of judgment, kind of like what various religions preach, I'm satisfied that we are all good people and will all pass on together."

John looked back and forth between Brian and Cassie, trying to sense what they were feeling and what he could say to help.

"Dad," Brian asked, "what's the other possibility?"

"Well, the other possibility is that nothing happens. The lights just go out and there is nothing next. The nice thing about that possibility is that there is nothing to fear because there will be no regrets. The lights will just go out and that will be all there is.

"I really don't believe in that, though, and I want you guys to understand why. We've all heard about ghosts and psychics. I think much of that stuff is crazy but there has also been enough that hasn't been, and can't be, explained to lead me to believe we do continue to exist in some form or another. I really believe there is a hereafter. I can't prove it and I don't know what it will be like, but I believe in it. I'm not ready to say goodbye to the two of you and your mom. I love all three of you so much, I can't help but believe this really is just a temporary thing. I just can't."

John felt the tears start to well up in his eyes, as well as the fear start in his chest, and so he closed his eyes and tightened his grip on the children.

"Does that help at all?" he whispered, his voice starting to break.

"Dad, it does. I've been thinking about this for a while." This was Brian talking. "I came up with the same idea. There's got to be something else out there. If there is a God, I can't imagine he would be so cruel as to separate all of us. If there isn't a God, then I still believe there is *something* out there. I don't know what it is but there has to be something, doesn't there?"

This time it was Liz who said, "Brian, there absolutely has to be something out there. What we are afraid of is the unknown. I choose to believe there is a God who will protect us and that takes away some of my fear."

They sat there in silence. The wind was active and they could hear it blowing through the trees. The fireplace crackled and just as John got up to throw another log on the fire, the lights went out.

John quietly cursed, grabbed a flashlight from the front closet, and trooped out to the circuit breaker box. He flipped each of the circuit breakers, but nothing happened. "Fuck!" John banged his hand on the side of the cabin.

As he walked back to the kitchen, John looked out at the neighbors' houses. The Balouns' house on the one side was dark but Good Neighbor Ray's house on the other side had its lights on.

"I'm not sure what the problem is. I can't believe the power just went out for some houses and not for others," John said. "Let's enjoy the rest of our evening and, if the lights aren't back on tomorrow, I'll go next door and find out why Good Neighbor Ray has power but we don't."

Liz took candles out from under the sink and gave one to each child. "Be careful with these. I'd really prefer we not burn down the cabin."

The children smiled and, holding their candles, walked upstairs to wash up.

John was clearing the table and Liz was starting to pile the dishes alongside the sink when she said, "John, there's no water."

"What the fuck?" John said quietly.

"Dad! The water isn't running!" Brian called from upstairs.

Watching as the flickering lights from the candles descended the stairs, John looked at his family. He was too tired to put up a false front so he just said, "When the power went out, it must have also affected the pumps bringing water up to us. For tonight, we've got water bottles you can use to brush your teeth and wash your faces."

"Will the toilets still work?" Cassie asked.

Shaking his head, John looked at them and said, "No, they won't. Well, they will work for the first flush, but we'll need to fill them up by hand. So, at least for tonight, don't flush if you just peed. If you pooped, you can go ahead and flush."

The three of them just stared at him.

"I'm sorry, guys. There's nothing else I can do right now. We'll have plenty of time tomorrow to figure out what to do."

"Okay, Dad." John watched as Brian put a protective arm around Cassie and walked with her upstairs. That was something he had never seen before. His son was becoming a man right in front of his eyes.

⌘

Christmas morning started, as with every other day, with John and Liz being the first awake. Unlike every prior morning, the only light inside the cabin was coming from the windows. It was cloudy and drizzly outside; just the type of day John didn't want.

Once the fire really started burning, John and Liz sat down in front of it.

"Is this what it is going to be like now?" Liz asked.

"What do you mean?"

"Is this what it's going to be like now? No electricity, no running water, and heat only from the fireplace? John, I don't know if I can do this."

"Hon, we'll figure something out. At least we're not outside or sleeping in a tent. We've got a solid roof over our heads, and we should have enough food to last us a while. We are safe but we might just have to really rough it for a while."

"But what about the food? The food in the refrigerator and the chest freezer isn't going to keep very long without electricity. We can't cook what we have without electricity, and we can't keep the food fresh."

"Well, first of all, we'll use the gas grill out on the deck to cook. It won't be great, but it will work. As to the food, maybe the guy next door, if he still has electricity, will allow us to store some stuff over there. Hell, maybe we can move the chest freezer over to his house?"

"You mean Good Neighbor Ray? Isn't he the guy who pointed a gun at you the last time you tried to talk to him?"

"Hon, he didn't point the gun..." John gave up trying to explain. "I'm not sure what choice we have. After the kids get up, I'll walk down the street and see if any other houses lost their power. Maybe it was just our cabin and the house to the north."

Before they could say anything else, they turned with a start and heard the children singing from the bottom of the stairs. "We wish you a Merry Christmas, we wish you a Merry Christmas, we wish you a Merry Christmas and a Happy New Year."

John and Liz couldn't help but start laughing. The children walked over to them, both wrapped in their blankets.

"Dad, it's cold."

"Yeah, Brian, it is. I'll put a few more logs in the fireplace but we're going to have to dress warm until we can figure out what to do."

The children sat down right in front of the fire and Brian wrapped his blanket around Cassie's shoulders. John and Liz watched them for a bit before sitting down next to them. Without saying anything, they all just watched the flames.

There were no presents in the stockings and, in fact, there were no stockings hung on the mantle. There were no presents under the tree. John and Liz rummaged through the pantry and returned with pop tarts and potato chips. They also had a gallon container of milk and poured glasses for everyone. The family quietly ate in front of the fire.

John started, "Well, think of this as how the early settlers would have awakened on Christmas morning."

"You mean with pop tarts and potato chips for breakfast?" Liz inquired.

This made all of them laugh and he didn't even bother trying to further explain his statement. Eventually, John stood up and said, "I need to find out what is going on out there and figure out if we're going to get our electricity back."

He stood and walked upstairs to get dressed. Returning downstairs, John was clad warmly and he put his raincoat on, as well as his duck boots.

"Dad, can I come with you?"

"Not this time, Boyo. I'm going to need to talk to our neighbor Ray and I don't want my strapping young lad of a son to scare him."

John opened the door and walked out into the morning drizzle.

❧

CHAPTER TEN

THE FOOL ON THE HILL

T he city of Portland is a mid-sized city in Oregon. It shares its northern border with the state of Washington, with the Columbia River serving as the line of demarcation between much of the two states. The Willamette River cut Portland in half along a mostly north-south axis. The west side contained the downtown core of the city. To the west and south of the downtown area were the Tualatin Foothills, commonly referred to as the West Hills. The West Hills contained some beautiful neighborhoods with commanding views, mixed with mostly middle-class neighborhoods, as well as a medical complex. To the west and past the West Hills, the land flattened out and turned into fertile farmland until reaching the Pacific Coast Range. This consisted of a string of smaller mountains extending from Alaska to Central Mexico. Just beyond the Pacific Coast Range was the spectacular Oregon coastline and the Pacific Ocean.

To the south, and beyond the various, mostly middle-class suburbs, was the Willamette Valley with its fertile farmland.

To the east, the land was mostly flat and highly populated until you started into the foothills of the Cascade Mountains with Mt. Hood positioned to dominate the eastern skyline. Close in on the east side were warehouses and older residential neighborhoods, some being very exclusive and expensive. Once you got a few miles east of the Willamette River, the neighborhoods became less exclusive and less expensive and melded into Gresham. Beyond the Cascade Mountains, there was high desert throughout most of Eastern Oregon and leading into Idaho.

Portland has various nicknames. It was once referred to as Stumptown after large swaths of forest were cleared from what became the downtown area. It was also known as the City of Roses for the miles of roses that were planted leading up to the 1905 Lewis and Clark Centennial Exposition. It was also commonly called Bridge City or Bridgetown because of the twelve bridges spanning the Willamette River.

Just south of downtown Portland is a particularly large part of the West Hills with a commanding view to the east. A medical complex consisting of the Oregon Health Sciences University, with its hospital, medical, dental, and nursing schools, as well as supporting buildings and structures, dominates this area. Also, on the same campus are the Veteran's Administration Hospital, Doernbecher Children's Hospital, and the Shriner's Hospital for Children.

Portlanders commonly refer to this medical complex as "Pill Hill" or just "OHSU." Despite the number of hospitals and schools on the campus, there are limited roads. The principal road is Sam Jackson Park Road, a steep and winding two-lane road leading up to and through the campus. This is the road usually taken by anyone approaching from downtown Portland.

To the south and east of the campus, there is another winding road, S.W. Terwilliger Boulevard that runs below the campus and has a couple of small offshoot roads leading up to it. To the west is a single road, S.W. Gibbs Street that left the campus and winds through woods and a number of upscale neighborhoods.

Due to overcrowding, OHSU established a second campus just below Pill Hill and on the waterfront. An aerial tram and buses allow hospital workers, students, and visitors to park down by the waterfront and travel up the hill to the main campus.

Just south of the downtown core where the Willamette River widened, is a series of small islands. The two largest islands, Ross Island and Hardtack Island, are connected by an artificial levee built in 1926 by the U.S. Corps of Engineers in order to form a lagoon between them. The combined islands are referred to as just Ross Island and, throughout much of the prior one hundred years, had been used for mining gravel.

The east side of the combined islands is as close as three hundred feet from the shore and the west side could be as close as five hundred feet.

⌘

Boulden was frustrated. He expected the difficulties experienced in coordinating the various and varied law enforcement agencies. The real problem, however, was how many of the men and women from these law enforcement agencies were disappearing. Some of them succumbed to the Curse, but others slipped away to be with their families. For those whose families were already dead, some left to mourn while others just gave up and let the virus do what it would with them.

Boulden didn't have these issues. If his ex-wives were dead, it just meant less alimony for him to pay once things got back to normal. He had neither understanding nor sympathy for the deserters. This was an emergency and, as far as he was concerned, they were cowards and traitors.

It became incumbent upon him to assemble a loyal staff on which he could rely. It was mid-December and he was now the *de facto* leader of the Oregon Territory. He was not given this command but, rather, it was thrust upon him. The Curse had decimated senior leadership and now, he was the senior military officer.

Out of necessity, he gathered teams to organize sanitation and food handling. He had other teams responsible for coordinating the disinfecting of everyone coming onto the campus, as well as keeping track of the current residents. As the campus was clearly not immune to the Curse, it was critical that these teams identified those infected, whether alive or dead, and have them removed. In order to do this daily roll calls for all residents were required.

Boulden had to be creative in order to provide benefits to his staff and give them an incentive to stay. While their best chance of survival was to remain at the campus, Boulden knew this wasn't enough for everyone. He needed to provide better living quarters and food for *his* people. He found out what special needs they might have—whether alcohol, drugs, or women, and would ensure that they had enough, but not too much, to remain incentivized to stay and work for him.

Among the many services required, the most distasteful was assigned to a small squad of soldiers responsible for disposing of the infected and dead. This team stacked the dead and incinerated their bodies. The first funeral pyre was not the last and fields were cleared in order to ensure the fires were always downwind. After the fires burned out, large bulldozers were brought in to crush the bones and spread lime on the remains. Once a pyre had been crushed, leveled, and limed, it was then ready for the next. There never seemed to be an end to the bodies needing cremation.

Boulden established communications with a medical community at OHSU. While the hospitals had been shuttered due to the lack of medical personnel to treat victims, there were still researchers working on finding both a vaccine and a treatment for those currently infected.

Boulden quickly realized that it didn't make sense to maintain two camps—one for the military and one for the medical community. He decided to combine them. The OHSU campus was chosen for various reasons. First of all, being situated on a large hill, it gave him a tactical advantage from a military standpoint. The roads leading up to the campus were limited and winding with sharp drop offs. This would limit an enemy's ability to focus a direct attack. Secondly, it was not practical to move the equipment being used for research. The equipment was far too delicate, and he did not have the personnel to accomplish such a move without damaging it.

The lead administrator at OHSU was Dr. Moira Kessel. While they had spoken by radio on numerous occasions, their first face-to-face meeting was tense. It took place while Boulden was still working on developing his teams to run the combined camp.

With a small coterie of his top aides, Boulden suited up in his hazmat suit and drove up to the OHSU campus. The meeting was scheduled at Dr. Kessel's office on the third floor of the Hatfield Research Center. Kessel was waiting when Boulden strode into her office.

"Good afternoon. I'm Major Roger Boulden. I assume you are Dr. Kessel."

"I am but please call me Dr. Mo, everyone does and with the limited staff we have now, I try to maintain a level of informality in order to keep up morale."

Kessel stared at her as she was talking. She was a petite woman in her late forties or early fifties. She wore a pair of pale slacks and a white lab coat. Her hair was short and blond and she was only a little over five feet tall. She looked tired and it was apparent that whatever sleep she was getting wasn't enough.

The office was sparse with only a desk lamp on. The rest of the room was illuminated by sunlight streaming in through a bank of windows overlooking the Willamette River.

"How many people do you have here?"

"Well, Major, or may I call you Roger?"

"I prefer to be called Major."

"Very well, Major, I'm not exactly sure how many people we have here. The numbers fluctuate based upon the virus and people leaving to be with their families. There are 12 research scientists, together with another 20 to 30 medical personnel—doctors, nurses, interns, etc. We also have another 30 or 40 support staff who try to keep the generators going and take care of maintenance issues."

"Good. What type of disinfecting program do you have to avoid having your people infected?"

Dr. Mo looked at him. He was clearly attempting to establish his dominance, but she could tell this was as much based upon some innate insecurity as it was any level of competence. He was clearly not comfortable dealing with a woman with authority.

Taking her time, she sat down at her desk and took a sip of coffee from her cup. "Major, won't you sit down? Can we get you a cup of coffee?"

Boulden hated her immediately. She was just the type of smug academic who always assumed they were smarter than everyone else. While he might not have a college degree, he was smart enough to be in control of the entire Oregon territory. He remained standing in front of her.

"I asked about your disinfecting system. Do you have one?"

"Of course we do." Dr. Mo took another sip of her coffee, all the while knowing her patience in answering his questions was driving him crazy.

"We disinfect everyone who comes here before allowing them into the general population. We also require everyone to shower every morning and evening." She took another sip of her coffee.

"We also quarantine anyone who shows any symptoms of the virus, even if it is just a cough." She gave him a smile that she would describe as pleasant and he would describe as smug.

"We came here, and you didn't attempt to disinfect us," Boulden said with a trace of contempt in his voice.

"Well, Major, first of all I assumed because of your position and rank that you would be smart enough to take your own protections so as to not *be* infected. Secondly, as you were all wearing hazmat suits when you drove in, it suggested to me that you had taken adequate precautions to ensure you wouldn't infect the only people in the area who might be able to discover a vaccine and develop a course of treatment.

"Was I right?"

"Doctor, as *you* well know, this virus has the potential to end all human life. And yes, I am smart enough to know all of that, but I also know that making assumptions when dealing with something like this virus is both dangerous and stupid."

The smile completely left Dr. Mo's face. It wasn't the fact that he was talking to her with a complete lack of respect but, rather, that he was right. With such a small margin of error, she couldn't afford to assume that everyone would know how to protect themselves.

"You're right, Major, and I apologize. Now, I assume you are here with a proposal."

Boulden smiled, this time with an uneasy attempt to mimic Dr. Mo's earlier smug smile. It came across as awkward and Dr. Mo noticed but failed to react.

"It is not a proposal but, rather, a plan. I am going to be moving my people up here."

This surprised Dr. Mo and Boulden noted her reaction.

"How many people do you have, Major?"

"Our number also fluctuates but we have approximately 3,500 people right now, mostly soldiers and police officers. We'll be adding as many of their families as are still alive and unaffected.

I also intend to round up as many other survivors as I can and bring them here."

"But why? Why would you bring them to a medical campus?"

"Because this is a campus we can isolate and protect. This will become the principal home to every survivor in the area and when the virus is done, we will then begin to methodically repopulate the state, using this campus as our base."

"Major, I'm not sure we can handle that many new people."

"With all due respect, Doctor, they will be handled. I'm going to start sending crews up here tomorrow. We'll need to convert various hospital buildings into living spaces. We will also need to demolish unnecessary buildings in order to clear the lines of sight. Finally, we will also construct a fence to surround the entire campus.

"No one will be allowed to enter or leave the campus without due authorization. Any questions?"

"I am somewhat dumbfounded right now, but I expect I will have a lot of questions when I start to think about this further."

"Well, Doctor, I don't have time to wait so let me tell you what you need to do. Right now, there are a couple of hospitals up here, correct?"

Dr. Mo looked at him, her coffee forgotten, and her hands clenched in her lap. Taking a deep breath in order to control her voice, she said, "We actually have four hospitals here—the OHSU hospital, the VA hospital, the Shriners Hospital, and the Doernbecher Children's Hospital. They are, however, all closed."

"Well, I want you to decide which buildings you need to continue your research. I won't disturb you and you will have the complete ability to continue your work. You will need, however, to move any necessary medical equipment and supplies and consolidate them into one hospital.

"The other hospitals and buildings you don't need will either be converted for use by the general population or will be demolished."

"Why would you demolish any of the buildings?" Dr. Mo's

eyes were large and she was clearly alarmed. Boulden wasn't just a bully, but he might be verging on going mad.

"In order to ensure the safety and security of this campus, I can't and won't allow unused buildings to remain. By destroying them, it will make it easier to maintain order and control. It will also allow us to better monitor the campus and surrounding areas."

Boulden turned and as he strode to the door, said, "Doctor, you better get your people going. We'll be up here tomorrow morning to start outlining our plans and I anticipate that construction, and demolition, will be starting within the week."

As he walked out the door, Dr. Mo heard him say "Goodbye and thank you for your time." She was actually a little surprised by what she perceived as a measure of courtesy and respect. She didn't know him well enough yet to recognize the sarcastic tone in his voice.

☙

As promised, ten soldiers, all garbed in their hazmat suits, appeared at Dr. Mo's office the following morning at 9:00 a.m. after being processed through the disinfection protocol. She offered to take them for a tour, but it was clear they had already studied maps of the campus and planned what they wanted to do.

The leader identified herself as Captain Morris and the only way Dr. Mo could identify her from the others was that she had a clipboard. Taking off the helmet of her suit, she addressed Dr. Mo.

"Have you selected which buildings you need for your research, Doctor?" she asked.

"Well, most of our research is being done here and in the Biomedical Research Building."

"Okay, you can have those two buildings. We need one of the hospitals for ordinary medical care. Given the location of the two research buildings, we'll use the OHSU hospital building."

Dr. Mo let out a silent sigh, as that was what she was hoping for. While all of the hospitals located on the campus were good, she was most familiar with the OHSU hospital.

Captain Morris began again, "The VA Hospital will be demolished as will all of the buildings south of SW Veterans Hospital Road. Also, both the Casey Eye Institute and the Dental School will be demolished.

"We'll convert the Children's Hospital into the principal residential building.

"The debris from the demolition will be used to block off all the roads in and out of the campus other than Sam Jackson Park Road and S.W. Gibbs Street. This will allow us to limit the number of vehicles coming in and out.

"Doctor, do you have any comments or concerns about this plan?"

For the second time in less than twenty-four hours, Dr. Mo was stunned and silent. Gathering her thoughts quickly, she said, "With all due respect, these buildings cost millions of dollars, if not more, to construct. It seems to me to be foolish to destroy them just because we don't need them right now."

"Duly noted, Doctor. Unfortunately, our orders are to downsize this facility in order to make it a safe and functional base. We don't know how long we will have to use this as our main base, but we can't take a chance of keeping buildings that won't be useful in the foreseeable future.

"Further, your power and water supplies are limited and we can't waste them on buildings we don't need.

"Doctor, I recommend you get your people going immediately. If you need more hands to help you, please let me know and I can send some people up to provide you with whatever additional labor you may need.

"We'll be working simultaneously on demolishing the VA hospital and converting the Children's Hospital so you should focus on stripping those buildings immediately of any medical equipment and supplies you might need."

Captain Morris recognized that Dr. Mo was feeling overwhelmed and actually took some pity on her. Softening her look, she said, "I know Major Boulden can be intimidating and difficult to work with, but he really is trying to do what he believes is necessary to protect as many survivors as he can. He may lack tact, but he doesn't lack motivation. It would be in your best interest to find a way to work with the major. We all know that we need you and your team, and we will do whatever we can to accommodate you, but you are merely a part, albeit an important part, of this operation.

"What you may not know is that while we have been having an influx of people at our camp, the total number of people—survivors—really hasn't changed. We seem to lose as many people to the Curse and desertion as we get new people. Doc, can I ask you a question?"

"Absolutely."

Captain Morris turned to the other soldiers with her and said, "Will you excuse us for a moment?"

They all turned and walked out the door, closing it behind them. Captain Morris walked closer and bent over the desk and quietly asked, "What is going to happen? Are you going to be able to find a cure?"

Dr. Mo stared across her desk at Captain Morris. Whatever air of confidence Captain Morris displayed when she first arrived was gone and she looked like just another scared human being.

"I don't really have an answer for you, Captain. This virus is like nothing we've ever experienced before. We are working on a vaccine but, quite honestly, I just don't know if we'll develop it in time."

"In time?" Morris interrupted.

"In time to save our species. This is a cataclysmic event, one that may well end up with the extinction of the human race. There have been numerous mass extinctions over the life of our planet. Some have been caused by extraterrestrial objects, such as the asteroid or comet most believe wiped out the dinosaurs. Others have involved climate changes like the Ice Age.

"We don't know if there has ever been anything before like a virus that wiped out an entire species. It is possible but we just don't know.

"In any event, and assuming we can't create a vaccine, our only hope will be for the virus to continue to evolve to the point that it is no longer so deadly. That isn't an unrealistic hope. With viruses that evolve so quickly, it is always possible it will eventually turn into a largely harmless one.

"The difficult thing about this particular virus is how quickly it evolves. All viruses mutate and evolve but I've never known one that moves this quickly. This creates the greatest obstacle to developing a vaccine. By the time we develop one, the virus has evolved through so many iterations that the vaccine no longer has any practical application.

"Again, the fact it evolves so quickly does offer some hope. If it is going to burn itself out, it may do so sooner rather than later. Of course, we have no way of really knowing that with any certainty, but it might just be our best hope."

Standing up, Captain Morris walked around the desk to Dr. Mo and offered her hand. She silently took it.

"Doctor, I look forward to working with you on getting the camp set up. Even more importantly, I'm looking forward to the day we can all go home. Until then, please feel free to talk to me if you have any problems with the major."

She then turned and walked out the door, putting her helmet back on. As the door closed behind her, Dr. Mo softly whispered, "Merry Christmas." She then put on her coat and walked to a gathering of her staff as they celebrated Christmas Eve with a small dinner and the remainder of the good wines they had been saving for the hoped-for celebration of the discovery of a vaccine.

In her mind, Dr. Mo gave thanks to have connected with someone in the military with whom she might be able to work. She hoped Captain Morris could act as an intermediary between her and Boulden. What Dr. Mo didn't know as she was sipping her wine was that Captain Morris would be infected with the virus by the end of the day. Morris would start coughing that very evening and be dead within forty-eight hours. What was left of her would go up in a pile of smoke and then be crushed for the next funeral pyre.

CHAPTER ELEVEN

The Time of the Turning

Walking down the front steps, John noticed how quiet everything was. He could hear the light rain falling as well as the wind in the trees. Other than that, there was nothing. There were no sounds of cars. There were no voices. There weren't even dogs barking. There was nothing at all and he found it disconcerting.

He first headed to the street and proceeded to walk up and down, past at least six of the neighbors' houses. He was looking, if not for lights, at least smoke curling out of chimneys. Again, there was nothing.

He walked slowly up to Good Neighbor Ray's house. It was dark now. He stopped thirty feet from the front door and called out, "Ray?" There was no response.

Walking another ten feet forward, he again called out and, again, there was no response other than the trees rustling in the wind.

The curtains in the living room were slightly apart but he could see no light or movement. He walked up to the front door and knocked loudly—no response. He knocked again. He yelled out, "Ray? Ray, are you there?" He could hear the rain dripping down the downspouts but that was the only sound coming from the house.

He walked up to the bay window by the side of the front door. Through the slightly parted curtains, he peered in. This was the living room. It was tidy and the furniture looked old but barely used. He noted a television and small stereo on a bookshelf but neither had any lights on. Everything seemed to be orderly.

Going around the side of the house, John reached up on his tiptoes to look through the kitchen window. There appeared to be a few dirty dishes in the sink but nothing else of interest. Continuing, he turned the corner and wandered into the backyard. There was a picnic table and a brick fireplace toward the back of the property, closer to the cliff. As he approached the fireplace, he could see, through a gap in the trees, the grayness of the ocean in the distance. Holding his breath to create even more silence, he could hear the faint sounds of the waves crashing.

Turning around to look at the back of Ray's house, he noticed that there was a generator next to the house. He walked over to it and wondered why it wasn't working. It must have been working last night if all of the electricity in the area was out. Otherwise, Ray's house would have been as dark as the cabin. Had Ray left overnight and shut off the generator while he was gone? Had it run out of fuel? No, that was unlikely. While he didn't know much about generators, he figured they had to be built to be able to operate for more than just a day or so.

Completing his encirclement of the house, John headed back to the cabin. It was time to update Liz and the children so they could, as a family, discuss how to proceed. Entering through the front door, he shrugged off his raincoat and hat and saw the three of them sitting in front of the fire.

Liz looked up and said, "Did you find anything?"

John shook his head. Looking at the three of them huddled in blankets he had to fight the despair welling up in his stomach. "No, it looks like Ray may have gone somewhere and the good news, other than Ray being gone, is that his house has a generator. If he's not back in a couple of days, we might try to move into his house."

Cassie looked up at him and said, "What if he comes back?" John saw that she was shivering slightly, hopefully just from the cold.

"We'll deal with that if and when it happens. Sometimes in desperate times, you have to take desperate measures."

"John, I don't like that idea." Liz said. "It is still his house, and I don't feel right about just moving into a stranger's home, particularly one who has been so openly unfriendly. I'd prefer to stay here as long as we can. We've got the fireplace and plenty of wood. It might not be warm but at least we won't freeze…or be shot. We'll have to figure something out to collect rainwater, so we can flush the toilets but, other than that, we should be all right for a while. We'll cook the food in the freezer as long as it stays good and then we can switch to dry goods. We've got those camping meals out in the garage. We can also go into town to get more when we need it."

John looked at her and nodded his head. He was almost over-whelmed with love for his wife of twenty-three years. A slight smile came to his face and John felt much of the weight of responsibility slide off his shoulders. He didn't need to do everything. Liz was a remarkable woman and together they could handle whatever came their way. Silently however, he wondered whether she truly grasped the enormity of the situation they were facing. This wasn't just having to deal with a lack of electricity or water. This was a global catastrophe and who knew what life might be like when it was over. Maybe she and the children just weren't ready to address the "big picture" yet and that was fine with him. If it were up to him, he would also just focus on the here and now, but his mind and his imagination kept leading him to places and concepts that terrified him.

The fear gnawing at him was for the safety of his family, balanced with the knowledge of how compromised it already was. The biggest fear, and the one he constantly fought to prevent from completely overwhelming him, was what would happen if *he* should die. As he explained to the children, it wasn't a fear of what might happen after death. He had no fear of judgment or retribution from some greater being or deity. What he feared was dying and leaving his family to fend for themselves. While he might be ill prepared for this holocaust, he still felt he could handle it better than they could.

Every parent fears for his or her family. Responsible parents make sure there is life insurance to address at least some of the financial needs for their spouses and children. With estate planning, parents can also address who they want to raise their children in the event of an unexpected death. The current situation was completely different. Money meant nothing right now. The investments and insurance John and Liz had built up over the years were useless and worthless at this point. There were no family or friends nearby who could provide assistance to Liz and the children should something happen to him. There were, apparently, no neighbors to help either.

He knew Liz was smart and resourceful, but she had even fewer survival skills than he. If something happened to him, what would they do? He again tamped down those thoughts and tried to just appreciate how Liz was stepping up and trying to help. He focused on his gratitude for that, although he didn't agree with her, at least not about Ray's house. In all likelihood Ray was dead and no one was coming back to his house. People don't leave a refuge in the middle of a crisis. Ray, like them, would have stayed as long as possible. They would know in a matter of days whether he'd died or, in fact, just left for some reason. If, at some time in the future, Ray reappeared they'd deal with it. John couldn't focus on the distant future, he needed to provide for and protect his family now and not concern himself with the possibility of offending someone who had been so completely unfriendly, and even hostile, to them.

Looking back at Liz, he said, "That's fine. Maybe we'll go exploring tomorrow and see if we can't find someone else around here. People are out there, maybe we just need to find them."

"Are you hungry?" Liz asked.

"I would love something. Whatcha' got?"

Liz turned and walked into the kitchen and began making breakfast for all of them. It was Christmas morning and she decided to use as much of the food as possible before it spoiled. She instructed John to start the grill out on the deck.

Using all of the eggs, they made scrambled eggs and bacon, with pancakes and orange juice. As they sat down at the table to eat, Liz said, "I know we're not religious and we don't say grace, but I'd like to try something. I'd like all of us to hold hands and, just for moment, close our eyes and give thanks for each other."

The children looked at John for a response and he just smiled and reached out his hands. With them looking from one to the other, John started saying "thank you, thank you" to each of them, using a silly French accent. Each of them quickly picked up on this and began repeating "thank you, thank you" to one another before the laughter overwhelmed them. They then got to work with their knives and forks and seemed to eat their respective weights.

Over the next several days, the family ate well. They set up tarps to collect rainwater into buckets and used it to flush toilets. They even rigged up a device to allow them to boil water over the fire in the fireplace.

Before losing electricity and running water, they were all accustomed to showering every day. Within days, they began to feel rank. By boiling rainwater, they could take baths. This, however, was a labor-intensive operation as they could only boil limited amounts of water at any one time. It wasn't a perfect solution, but John and Liz knew how important it was to maintain a semblance of cleanliness both for their physical and mental health. They ended up alternating, with the girls bathing one day and the boys the next.

In the afternoon, all four of them would bundle up and walk through the neighboring areas. They never found anyone or even any evidence that anyone was still in the area, but they kept looking. For John, he knew it was important for each of them to get their bearings and know which houses had generators...just in case. He was mildly surprised to find that Ray's was the only house around with a generator.

John also got out the guns and began teaching Liz and the children how to use them. While his knowledge was limited, he was able to teach them how to load the guns, as well as how to aim them. They practiced shooting at cans along the top of the cliff behind the cabin. At first, John wondered if the noise of the gunshots would cause the military to come looking for them, but they never did.

Perhaps most importantly, John taught them the basics of gun safety. He stressed the number one rule, which was to never point a gun at anyone. He explained how their inexperience with firearms increased the possibility of a gun going off accidentally. The lesson he hoped not to have to teach them, but which he eventually did, was that if you ignored rule number one and pointed a gun at a person, you should damn well be ready to pull the trigger and kill them.

❧

John and Liz woke up early on the morning of December 31st and began their standard preparations. Stepping over the children as they were all now sleeping in front of the fireplace, John quietly placed a couple of logs on and watched as they quickly caught fire. He and Liz then walked into the kitchen and sat down.

"John, I'm concerned about the rest of the food in the freezer. I've tried to keep the door closed as much as possible, but the food is defrosting. I've got an idea."

"I'm listening."

"What if we just cook all of the food we have left? We have roasts and steaks and chicken in the freezer. We've also got some partially frozen vegetables. This is New Years' Eve. How about if we just have a feast to end this miserable fucking year?"

John smiled but was a little startled by Liz's language. She rarely cussed and then, only if she was really angry. She wasn't angry now and John wanted to tease her about starting to talk like a sailor. For just a moment, however, he wondered if the stress wasn't starting to get to her. Tamping down that thought, John said, "I think that's a great idea. I'll start the grill and we'll cook all day if we have to."

As the food became ready, they placed it on the table and watched the children as they slowly woke up. It was the scents, rather than the noise, waking them.

"Wow," Brian said. "Something smells really good."

They both shuffled over to the kitchen table and stopped with mouths agape.

"What is all of this?" Brian asked.

"Well, we all know the frozen food won't last forever so we decided to end the year with a feast. We will be cooking everything we can today and end the year with full stomachs."

"But, Mom, I'm not sure how much I can eat," Cassie said.

"Don't worry about it. This may be the one and only time I won't yell at you for wasting food. Come and sit down. Let's eat as if there is no tomorrow."

જી

The feast continued all day. They didn't worry about chores. They didn't worry about cleaning up. They ate and then fell into food comas and napped. When they awoke, they would eat some more and play board games and cards. In between eating, John and Liz would tell stories from their childhoods, at least a couple of which neither child had heard before.

When night fell and they had all eaten as much as they could, they gathered up the rest of the perishable food, both cooked and un-cooked, and walked to the edge of the cliff at the back of the property. At John's urging, they all screamed into the night as they tossed the food over the cliff.

Making a pact to stay up to midnight and greet the new year, they played games as midnight slowly approached. The clock in the living room was battery operated and they counted out the last ten seconds of what had been a terrifying year.

"Ten…Nine…Eight…Seven"

The gathered up their pots and pans and their wooden spoons.

"Six…Five…Four…"

Standing up, they raised the pots and pans to the sky.

"Three…Two…One…HAPPY NEW YEAR!"

They screamed and bashed on pots and pans, creating a cacophony that even the neighbors must have heard, assuming there still might be living neighbors anywhere nearby. They danced and hugged.

Finally, finished and exhausted, they settled onto the mattresses in front of the fireplace. Their spirits were lifted and while no one knew what the next day or the next year might bring, they were momentarily content. John threw one last log on the fire. With everyone saying goodnight to one another, John and Liz told both of the children that they loved them.

They all closed their eyes, sated and happy for what seemed like the first time in months. John and Liz held hands as they started to drift off to sleep.

And then Brian coughed.

CHAPTER TWELVE

KING OF PAIN

The move to the OHSU campus progressed and Major Boulden renamed the area "Camp Oregon." He and his staff were successful in establishing the basic, but necessary, logistical aspects of running the facility. Construction of living facilities at the former Children's Hospital were under way and the hospital's kitchens were being used to process meals for the approximately thirty-five hundred residents. There was sufficient power and water, at least for the immediate future.

A crew was dispatched to set up a transmission station using the radio towers on the other side of the hill. Communication was critical for numerous reasons. After declaration of martial law, but before its total collapse, the federal government disabled all but military satellites. This allowed Boulden to be able to communicate with the forty-four remaining bases identified around North America. The closest was at Fort Stevens, just south of Seattle, with others nearby in Boise and Sacramento.

The other bases were in similar straits as Camp Oregon. Most had some sort of medical facilities and a few were established at nuclear power plants. The consensus amongst the various bases was that they would operate independently but share whatever information they could. There was not much discussion about what would happen when the Curse either died out or a vaccine was created. These were all military leaders, mostly mid-level, with limited training on how to create or recreate a nation.

It was decided to use only rudimentary encryption software for communications between the bases, as there was little fear of invasion. What contact there was with foreign bases across the globe established that North America was no worse off than any other continent. The African nations, lacking the technical skills and equipment to fend of the Curse, had been decimated and the only communications from that continent were isolated and by small groups of survivors. Most of the nations of Europe were lost due to their proximity to one another and porous borders. Countries like Germany and France, despite the sophistication of their governments and militaries, were unable to stop refugees seeking safety and were overrun by those infected by the virus.

China appeared to be the only other country in a condition comparable to North America. While its government also collapsed, the military established outposts throughout the country, although the number couldn't be ascertained.

The medical staffs of the various bases also used the satellite communications. They were able to compare strategies being used to develop vaccines, as well as for treating those infected. All breakthroughs were short-lived as the virus continued its constant mutations, rendering all treatment of limited value.

For non-military and base-related communications, the survivors used single sideband broadcasts. A few ham radio operators were able to communicate globally and the camp maintained a single ham radio to monitor these communications. Walkie-Talkies were used for communications among the residents of the camp.

Boulden's initial plan was to maintain a number of satellite camps for farming and ranching. That, however, was deemed impractical as he realized he could not adequately control and safeguard assets beyond the camp's fences.

He ordered his staff to start mapping out how the camp could be set up to provide for livestock. For grains, Boulden realized he would likely be able to obtain a sufficient supply by ransacking supermarkets and food warehouses. When the spring came, he might be able to set up some basic farming processes but that was something that could wait. As of now, the camp would survive on whatever livestock, warehoused grains, and processed food they could find.

For security, Boulden ordered the construction of a six-foot chain-link fence around the camp. Boulden knew this wouldn't be enough, but it was a start. As soon as it was completed, he then had a second fence erected, ten feet in height and located about eight feet behind the first fence. Both fences were topped by razor wire and guard dogs patrolled the area between. The double fences were necessary to slow anyone or anything that might try to break through. It was also a deterrent for any resident considering leaving the camp.

Gates were installed along the north and south ends of the camp on Sam Jackson Park Road and S.W. Gates Street. The other streets were blocked by the debris from the initial demolition of various buildings. Guardhouses were constructed at both gates and manned by armed guards around the clock. Eventually, decontamination facilities were constructed beside the guardhouse to ensure that no one entering the camp was carrying the virus.

The biggest potential issue was not how to provide for, or even to protect, the camp's residents but how to keep them busy. Boulden remembered his mother telling him, "Idle hands are the devil's workshop." He would have to keep the residents busy and hopeful about the future if he had any chance of controlling and maintaining the camp. Everyone was experiencing grief for family members and friends who had already succumbed to the Curse. The residents were grieving over the loss of their past lives and were scared of what the future might bring.

For Boulden to have any chance of maintaining the camp, he would need to find a way to inject hope into the population. He marveled at how society had been turned upside down by this cataclysm. In the past, the wealthy had most of the power. Corporate kingpins, financial advisors, high-tech entrepreneurs, professional athletes, entertainers, and trust fund babies held an inordinate amount of influence on politicians who, in turn, wielded an inordinate amount of influence over the rest of the country and the world.

Now those titans of industry and politics were of little value. Money was irrelevant. Property ownership was irrelevant. At the top of the new societal food chain were those in the military because they understood a chain of command and, even more importantly, had weapons and knew how to use them. After that, those with practical skills were mostly highly valued. Carpenters, plumbers, electricians, and like-skilled tradesmen brought abilities critical in a world where things like the Internet and the financial sector were extinct. Likewise, medical skills were highly valued.

Boulden recognized the need to both identify those in the camp population with useful skills, as well as to train people to develop these useful skills. A problem with this was, despite his best efforts, the population of the camp continued to slowly shrink.

The Curse was responsible, in part, for this attrition but there was also natural diminution due to illness, disease and desertion, as well as suicide. While his efforts to fence in the camp slowed people from abandoning it, he couldn't completely stem that tide.

Boulden suspected there were significant numbers of survivors outside the camp simply staying in their homes. They might still be there to mourn their deceased family members or just to protect their property. Outside of the camp, they were of no value.

If he could somehow bring them in, at least some of them might have useful skills.

He gave orders to organize search parties. They would be comprised of no less than four soldiers and up to four additional civilians. They would use a minimum of three vehicles. Two would be either a jeep or some type of SUV. The third would be a truck capable of transporting survivors back to the camp. The search parties were to go from neighborhood to neighborhood throughout the territory.

Boulden understood that many people died in their homes. As such, his instructions were to have the front door of every house broken down by the soldiers. They would then be able to tell, merely by the smell, whether a house contained one or more corpses or, alternatively, might have a survivor.

If the soldiers detected the scent of decaying flesh, they were ordered to burn the house down. This would not only resolve the possibility of spreading diseases created by decomposing corpses but would also allow them to prevent survivors from sneaking back into a neighborhood already searched.

Boulden believed it was likely most survivors would be staying in single family residences rather than large apartment complexes where the smell of the rotting corpses of neighbors would make it too uncomfortable to remain. For those larger apartment complexes and high rises, Boulden instructed them to be destroyed. He was fortunate to have a former Navy Seal on his staff, Warrant Officer Fernand Dutile. Dutile had served on multiple missions in Afghanistan, the Middle East and Africa. For reasons never really clear, as he had no discernable sense of humor, his peers called him "Tex" despite the fact that he was born and raised in Maine and New Hampshire.

While all Seals are trained in the use of some explosives, Tex Dutile developed a particular expertise with all types of explosives and, in between missions, served as an instructor to new recruits.

Dutile was tasked with the destruction of larger buildings where corpses might create a health risk. It was determined that the buildings themselves would be of little use given the decimation of the human population. When the camp's small cache of explosives was exhausted, Dutile and his squads resorted to using tanks and artillery. The hope was that the weight and volume of debris from the destroyed buildings would entomb the corpses and limit the health risks to the survivors.

Other squads were sent in all directions with the intent to focus on primarily residential areas. They would first go to West Portland and then fan out to Beaverton, Hillsboro and beyond, eventually reaching the coast. To the north, they would go to Northwest and North Portland and work their way up to Vancouver, Washington and its surrounding suburbs. To the east, they would first cover the inner-city neighborhoods and then work their way out past Gresham. To the south, they would investigate all of the South Portland neighborhoods and work their way down to Tigard, Wilsonville and, eventually, all the way down to Eugene and beyond.

The immediate results of the program were positive, and a substantial number of new survivors were brought to the camp, almost all of them unwillingly. Before these new survivors could be assimilated into the general population, they would have to be examined and disinfected under protocols established by Dr. Mo.

After the disinfection, Dr. Mo or her staff would conduct a full medical examination while Boulden had his staff conduct background interviews. After that, the residents would be classified. The standards for classification were based upon a survivor's utility in the camp.

Class I residents were those deemed most important to the camp. These included anyone with a medical, dental, or emergency services background or whom Dr. Mo considered important for purposes of medical research. Anyone with a military or law enforcement background would also be deemed part of this category, as was anyone with skills in any of the construction trades or with engines and mechanical devices.

Class II residents were able-bodied and experienced with food service, livestock or like trades. Truck drivers were of significant value given the importance of bringing supplies into the camp. This group was generally comprised of people who could either currently provide useful service to the camp or develop sufficient new skills so as to eventually become a Class I resident.

The final category, Class III, was for those with no discernible skills that would be of benefit in the current times. Manual laborers, as well as writers, lawyers and accountants were superfluous. Salespeople, stockbrokers and musicians were of little consequence. They were all considered expendable.

Those with physical and mental disabilities, to the extent they were permitted to remain in the camp, were also categorized as Class IIIs based upon Boulden's belief that it was not efficient to allow their limited resources to be used for anyone not deemed "able bodied and able minded."

Class IIIs were given the most difficult and dangerous duties. They were responsible for cleaning bathrooms and operating disinfecting stations, as well as the demolition of nearby buildings. The demolition work was difficult and dangerous. There were many injuries even under the guidance of Warrant Officer Dutile. For those Class III individuals who did suffer injuries, minimal medical treatment was provided. They were just not considered useful enough to waste resources on.

The search parties sent out to look for survivors were comprised of soldiers and Class IIIs. Unbeknownst to them, these Class IIIs were always used first if a dangerous situation arose. They were provided with the least effective hazmat suits. If a large group of survivors were discovered, the Class IIIs would be left behind with the promise of being picked up the next day. Many times, they weren't.

Everyone was expected to contribute in some fashion to the maintenance and well-being of the camp. This included children, unless a child's parent was already either a Class I or Class II resident. Anyone who was unable to provide some genuine benefit to the camp was escorted out and left to fend for themselves. This was effectively a death sentence and Boulden accepted the responsibility for that. While many of the camp residents quietly grumbled about turning away the needy, they did nothing for fear of being turned out themselves. Some of the soldiers looked to Warrant Officer Dutile for guidance on this issue but he remained silent and inscrutable.

⁊

In the week between Christmas and New Year's Day, everyone was working very hard to set up the camp. Boulden realized, however, that he couldn't just constantly work the survivors. He had to provide some form of entertainment and release. In the days leading up to the end of the year, Boulden implemented his plan.

After ensuring that the Veteran's Hospital and the other buildings south and east of the OHSU hospital had been stripped of all useful supplies, he set up a row of tanks and artillery. As darkness fell on New Year's Eve, he ordered a feast to be served to all of the camp residents. There was turkey with all of the fixings, roasts, and fresh vegetables, as well as whatever desserts the kitchen crews could come up with.

The few religious leaders who remained among them stood up and led the residents in prayers. At that point, recorded music was played and there was laughter and dancing. Boulden released enough liquor to satisfy almost everyone. At 11:30 pm he started to lead the residents out of the cafeterias and to the eastern end of the camp.

The night was cool with a light mist no one seemed to notice. The residents all enjoyed being able to let off a little steam and, for the first time in months, smile and laugh. As they approached the fence, Boulden ordered the lights to be turned on. Spotlights and mobile light fixtures sprang to life and bathed the old Veteran's Administration Hospital and surrounding buildings in a bright, white light.

Just below the fence and lined up on the road, were six tanks and four Howitzers. They were all aimed at the old hospital.

Over a loudspeaker, Boulden began the countdown to midnight. Ten…Nine…Eight…Seven…Six…

The crowd joined in the count and their voices got louder and higher with each count. The artillerymen and tank crewmen placed their hands over the controls to discharge their weapons.

Five…Four…Three…Two…One…Fire!

The buttons were pushed and immediately the quiet of the evening was destroyed by the sound of artillery guns and tanks firing at the old hospital. For effect, Boulden had installed large containers of natural gas and butane throughout the building. As the artillery discharged and crashed into the buildings, these gas containers offered a secondary explosion and the building collapsed with a roar.

A loud cheer went out from the viewers. If nothing else, it served as an aggressive, albeit futile, strike against an unseen foe that had already destroyed life as they knew it. This might only be a symbolic counteroffensive, and while everyone knew it would not stop or even slow down the virus, it was something and it was glorious. For just a fleeting moment, these residents—these survivors of the destroyer of humankind, could say goodbye to a year of devastation and death and hope that this new year would allow them to regroup and recover.

CHAPTER THIRTEEN

I Am a Rock

John and Liz opened their eyes simultaneously and stared at one another. Both of them heard the cough but neither wanted to say anything to alarm the other. In the flicker of the firelight, they just stared and tried to communicate that it was just a cough. They held their breaths and tried to hear Brian's breathing.

Then they heard it again. While the first cough had been dry, this cough sounded wet. They both slowly sat up and saw both children were still asleep. Brian, however, appeared to be restless. Liz placed her hand on his forehead, and she could feel unnatural warmth. He didn't appear to be sweating.

Quietly standing up, they worked their way to the kitchen.

"John, he's hot! He's got a fever." Liz's voice was quiet but urgent.

"Okay, let's not panic. This doesn't mean it's the Curse. This could be anything. He's a kid and this wouldn't be the first time he's had a fever. Let's just watch him. I'll stay up for a bit and keep an eye on him and you can go back to sleep."

Liz looked at him with incredulity. "Really? You really think I could fall back asleep right now?"

"Okay, okay, we'll just sit and both keep an eye on him."

They silently walked back into the living room. Liz sat down on the couch and wrapped her blanket around her. John put another log on the fire and settled down beside her. Putting his arm around Liz's shoulder, she leaned into him, and he kissed the top of her head.

"It's going to be all right, honey. I promise."

Liz didn't respond and they just sat there, both fearing the worst but refusing to admit it to the other.

Brian would lie quietly for a while and then begin tossing and turning. In the firelight, John could see a glisten of sweat begin to form on his face. A soft moan escaped Brian's lips and Liz got up to feel his forehead.

"John, he's really hot now. We need to do something. We need to do something now!" This time her voice was slightly louder and with a greater sense of urgency.

"All right wake him up and put him into his coat. I'll start the car and take him down to the hospital. There has to be someone there."

"I'm coming with you. I'll wake up Cassie and get her dressed."

"No, let her sleep and I want you to stay here with her. We shouldn't alarm her, especially as we don't know whether or not it's the…" His voice dropped off. He didn't need to say anything further. They both knew what was left unsaid.

Liz tried to wake Brian up, but he was unresponsive. John picked him up and put his jacket on. Carrying him to the car, John gently laid him down on the back seat and buckled a seatbelt loosely around him. With a cursory wave of his hand back to Liz standing at the door, John started the car and gunned it down the street.

Despite not previously using a hospital at the coast, John had done his research and knew there was an Urgent Care Center in downtown Manzanita, as well as a larger Medical Center in

Cannon Beach. There was also a full-sized hospital just north of there in Seaside.

Driving quickly but carefully, he spotted the Urgent Care Center. It was a drab two-story building with a parking lot in back. Turning off from the street, John weaved through cars parked at all angles and apparently abandoned. There were no lights on in the building, not even emergency lighting.

With a look at Brian in the back seat, John noticed that his breathing was becoming erratic. John jumped out of the car and ran to the front door. It had been broken in and the building was trashed. Most of the emergency lights were either damaged or burned out.

"Hello? Hello? Is there anybody here?"

There was no response and John decided he didn't have time to explore and hope he might find a doctor. Running back to the car, John jumped in and started weaving his way out of the parking lot.

Brian coughed again. It was wet and just by hearing it, John could tell how painful it must be. Fortunately, Brian appeared to be incoherent. He would occasionally mutter or moan but didn't open his eyes.

With a growing sense of urgency, John turned onto Highway 101 and drove north fast. There were no streetlights and no cars. Coming around a curve, John caught sight of an elk crossing the road ahead of him. A few seconds earlier and they would have run right into it.

It took them only a little over ten minutes to reach Cannon Beach. John knew the risk of running into something or someone increased the faster he drove, but he didn't care. His son was sick and had no time to spare.

The Providence Medical Center in Cannon Beach was a u-shaped building with cedar shingling. The medical offices were on the first floor and John parked on the street in front. The entire complex was dark, and John didn't even bother getting out of the car. Again, he decided against wasting time looking for help in what was obviously an abandoned facility.

Just north of there, in Seaside, was the full-fledged hospital. There had to be someone there who could help Brian. It was only another ten miles or so further and John immediately headed there. With no concern about the risks involved, he put his high beams on and sped up the highway. When coming up to curve, he would honk the car's horn in order to alert any animals that might be on the road ahead, but he didn't slow down.

Providence Seaside Hospital was just west of downtown and only minutes off Highway 101. Turning off the main road into the entryway, John saw the large two-story building on his left. While it was mostly dark, there were still some lights on inside. Following the signs for the Emergency Room and with some hope restored by the belief that if there were lights, there should be people, John drove around to the back. He focused mostly on avoiding the cars littering the parking lot, while aiming for the front door of the Emergency Room. Even from this distance, he could see light inside the lobby.

Coming around a BMW lying on its side, John ran over some debris in the road, causing the car to jump. He slammed on his brakes right by the front door. The sliding doors were broken and there were various pieces of furniture stacked up behind them. John could see that the lights shining were the backup emergency lights. Down the hall, some of them were flickering, giving the impression of someone moving down there.

Jumping out of the car, John stepped over piles of debris and walked through the smashed doors. Looking into the entry area, John saw everything in disarray. Chairs were knocked over and computer monitors and papers were strewn all around.

His mind raced. There had to be someone still in there. He looked down the corridor to where the lights were flickering and yelled out, "HELLO! MY SON! I NEED HELP!"

There was no response.

Taking a look back at the car, he turned and raced down the hallway yelling. He passed overturned chairs and gurneys. The rooms he passed were all dark and he stopped to listen but heard nothing.

"HELLO?" It felt unnatural and even improper to be shouting at this point. The building was so deserted that his voice echoed and reminded him of being in an empty cathedral. John placed his hand on a gurney beside him, immediately noticing something laying on it, covered only by a sheet. He didn't need to pull back the cloth to know what it was.

He looked carefully and saw other gurneys also covered in sheets. On the floor were bodies laid along either side of the corridor, one after another. The number of bodies took John aback. They were so still and for just a moment, John thought about what they must look like underneath the sheets. He headed back to the car.

Standing outside of the broken sliding glass doors, John leaned against the SUV and let his mind race. Where was the next closest hospital? Did he have time to make it? Was it really possible everyone here was dead?

"Dad?" The voice sounded raspy and weak.

John turned and opened the SUV's back door. Brian's face was red and puffy. His eyes were wet and it appeared that tiny rivulets of blood were leaking from their corners, as well as from his nostrils. John's first thought was that he was crying bloody tears.

Unbuckling the seatbelt, John picked up Brian's head and sat down on the seat. He gently lowered Brian's head onto his lap. Taking his handkerchief out of his back pocket, John wiped away the sweat and blood from his son's face. He bent over and kissed Brian's forehead. He could feel the heat emanating from it.

"I'm here Boyo. I'm here." He spoke softly and tried to keep his tears at bay. His job now was to comfort his son and not cause him any concern.

In the dim glow from the dome light, John saw Brian try to open his eyes while moaning. The sweat instantly returned to his face and John could see him trying to move his lips.

John bent close and said, "Brian, I'm here. Just hold on, a doctor is coming."

Brian started shivering and John held him close.

"I don't feel very good," Brian whispered. "I'm scared."

Summoning every inch of courage he could, John whispered, "Don't worry, Boyo. I'm here for you. I'll always be here for you. There's nothing to be scared of. Everything will work out just fine."

John would forever swear he saw the sides of Brian's mouth turn up as if in a wry smile. He knew, logically, it was more likely a grimace, but John wanted to believe he provided some comfort to his son in his last conscious moments.

They sat there, in the back seat, father and son, bound by love.

Looking out the car windows, John silently prayed, "God, help me. Somehow, help my boy. Please, please help me!"

He looked back down, and Brian was again moaning and writhing in obvious pain. John closed his eyes and thought, "Goddammit! Goddammit! How the fuck could this happen? He was fine only a few hours ago! How the fuck could he get this sick so quickly?"

He yelled out to the window, "PLEASE, SOMEONE! SOMEONE HELP US!"

The only response was the rustling of the wind in the trees and the chirping of the crickets. Brian didn't even flinch at his father's cries.

John sat there and held his son. Was there anything worse than a parent's impotence to save a child? Closing his eyes, John slowly shut down his emotions. He would stay with his son until the end. He would hold and comfort his son as long as he could, but he would not cry and he would not mourn. Remembering days from his youth when older kids would pick on him, John refused to show any pain. He was a rock...and nothing can hurt a rock.

It was just as the morning sky started to lighten when Brian's breath became particularly labored. John began singing songs he remembered singing to him when he was just a baby. John had been fortunate to be able to take three weeks off after Brian was born and spent as much time as he could just holding him and singing to him. They were nonsense songs, but the words came back to him without effort.

Brian was no longer thrashing. In between songs, he would whisper in Brian's ear, "I love you, Boyo. Everything is going to be okay. There is nothing to fear. If you have to go, you can. I'll catch up with you soon enough."

John was gently running his hand over Brian's head and felt his skin begin to grow cool. Brian's eyelids fluttered open and John saw that his pupils were bloodshot. Nonetheless, Brian was looking at him. John felt himself hold his breath at the thought the fever might be breaking and Brian might survive. He looked down and smiled at his son. "How ya feeling, Boyo?"

Brian just stared, then exhaled, and John could see a glaze come over his son's eyes. Brian was still.

John clenched his eyes shut as a guttural wail erupted from his lips. He bent over and held Brian as closely as he could. He had no idea how long he stayed like that but gradually the wailing stopped, and John fought to calm his breathing. With his eyes still shut, he listened for the sound of Brian's breathing but there was nothing.

He sat up and looked down at his son. His beautiful, beautiful boy looked peaceful. His hair was damp, but the pain was gone. John freed up one hand and reached down and gently closed Brian's eyelids.

"You are a rock," he whispered to himself. "You will not break."

The sound of crickets now became noticeable and seemed to

shake John out of his stupor. "You are a rock…and now you have to go back and tell your wife and daughter that Brian is dead."

John again closed his eyes but efforts to hold back the tears were useless. He wept and his tears fell on Brian's lifeless face. As he sobbed, his body wracked with convulsions of grief, heightened by the weight of the lifeless body in his arms. He would be a rock later when his remaining family needed him to, but right now, he needed to mourn.

After some time, John looked up to see the sky turning a brilliant blue. He gingerly lifted Brian's head off his lap and eased his way out of the car. Just before he stood up, he kissed Brian on the forehead.

His back ached but he barely noticed as he looked around. In the light of the coming day, he saw the debris piles around the hospital were, in fact, bodies. There were dozens of them just laying all around the area in front of the entrance. These bodies weren't carefully placed like those in the hospital. These bodies weren't covered by sheets. These bodies looked like they lay where they had been dropped and had clearly been there for some time. Some bore evidence of local scavengers, whether rats, wild dogs, or other, starting their handiwork.

John hadn't noticed the swarms of flies last night, but he did now. The air was thick and dark with them. The buzzing was what John had mistaken for crickets.

He closed the back door of the SUV and slowly walked around the car, mindlessly swatting at the flies. Climbing into the driver's seat, John turned the car around and drove away from the hospital, attempting to avoid running over any of the bodies now clearly visible throughout the parking lot. There was no rush now. Once on Highway 101 again, he rolled down the windows to let the cool morning air envelop him. He could not look back at Brian. He would not cry again. He would not break. Now he could, and would, be a rock. That is what Liz and Cassie needed him to be and he would not fail them.

CHAPTER FOURTEEN

WEAPON OF CHOICE

"I will not do it," she said adamantly.

"Doctor Kessel, you *will* do it and not just because I am ordering you to. Let me remind you what our situation is. We are basically treading water right now. The number of new residents we're finding is barely offsetting our attrition rate due to this fucking virus.

"That being said, I don't expect us to be able to continue finding new recruits indefinitely. We are continuing to expand our search radius but there is only so much ground to cover and eventually we will reach a point where there are no other survivors out there...at least not within our region.

"At that point, and unless you have discovered the magic bullet to kill this fucking thing, we, both you and I, as well as every other human being on earth, will die. I find that potential result to be unacceptable.

"Now you've told me you have discovered five individuals who have somehow developed an immunity to this virus. You have also told me you don't understand how they developed this immunity and why their immunity seems to be able to handle the mutations. You've told me all of the testing you conducted so far has been of no value so..."

"I didn't say it was of no value," she interrupted.

Major Boulden stared at her. She could see his face getting red and a vein in his neck was starting to bulge. He stood stiffly and was clenching his fists.

"Doctor Kessel," he said slowly, measuring out each syllable. It was clear that he was restraining himself although neither of them knew how long he would be able to do that. "You will not now, or ever again, interrupt me. I am your superior officer, and you will only talk to me when I ask you to or otherwise allow you to. Do I make myself clear?"

"Yes," she responded.

"Yes....what?"

She hesitated for a moment. She wasn't, and had never been, a part of the military and was unused to be treating with such obvious disrespect and contempt. Nonetheless, she knew when to pick her battles. "Yes, Sir."

"We have five individuals who may be the only people from our camp who might survive. Is that correct?"

"Well, assuming we are unable..."

"DOCTOR!" he said loudly and sternly and then slammed his fist on the desk. "I asked a question that *only* requires a simple yes or no answer. I'm not looking for a discussion or a debate. What I'm looking for is an answer. The question is whether we currently have five individuals who may well, at the end of the day, be the only survivors from this camp. Is that correct—yes or no?"

She looked at him and then diverted her eyes to the floor. "Yes."

She could feel his eyes upon her and finally looked up. He was staring at her and seemed to be waiting. She then remembered and, again looking down at the floor, said "Yes, Sir."

"Thank you. Now you've conducted a full battery of tests and have still been unable to determine how and why these individuals have survived while almost the rest of the entire human race has been destroyed. Am I also correct as to this?"

"Yes, Sir."

"And no one else in the camp has been determined to be similarly immune to this virus. Is that correct?"

"Yes, Sir, but..."

He didn't wait for her to complete her sentence. "So, unless you figure out why these five individuals have survived, you and I and everyone else in this camp are going to die a miserable and painful death. Am I still on track here?"

"Yes, Sir, but..."

"And given the dire consequences we are facing, do I understand you are suggesting that your holy ethics should take precedence over the survival of the thirty-three hundred people living here, not to mention the rest of the human race?"

Dr. Mo tried to gather her remaining strength and reason with the major.

"What you are asking me to do is to engage in quasi-medical testing that may well kill these five people. You're asking me to sink down to the level of a Dr. Mengele and to expose these people to dangerous testing that will, more likely than not, kill them. You want me to do this without any scientific basis to support that such testing will provide any useful data. That is what you are asking me to do, and I can't do it!"

"Doctor, we have neither the time nor the luxury of you holding onto some medical oath you took way back at the beginning of your career. Either you will immediately start this testing, or I will find someone else who will.

"If these survivors die, you will conduct an autopsy. Is there even the slightest possibility that an autopsy might provide some useful information?"

"Major, it is unlikely to provide any useful information and will cause extreme distress and likely death to these individuals. This just doesn't make sense."

"Unlikely or it absolutely *won't* provide any useful information?" The major was smiling now.

Dr. Mo realized her mistake. She had suggested there might be *some* useful information that could be gleaned from such testing even though it was highly unlikely. Nonetheless, Boulden heard what he wanted to hear and wasn't going to let it go.

"With all due respect, Major Boulden, there is no one else on my staff who could, or would, be willing to do this type of testing. I'm the only one left with the necessary training to conduct *any* of this. My staff is comprised at this point of a couple of dentists, some young physicians and medical assistants, a few lab technicians and three emergency medical technicians.

"There is no one capable of conducting and evaluating the testing you are suggesting. I'm the only one, Major, and I refuse to perform this type of testing."

Major Boulden stared at Dr. Mo from across the table. The smile faded and his face again turned red with the vein in his neck visibly bulging and throbbing. Then, suddenly, he let out a deep breath and normal coloring returned to his face. He seemed to relax and it almost looked like a little smile came to his lips.

"Doctor Kessel, I certainly respect your morals. At this point, and given that I am apparently unable to convince you, I now have to go to my Plan B."

"And what would that be?" Dr. Mo was nervous now, if for no reason other than his preternatural calm. This was a side of him she hadn't seen before.

"Well, first of all, as you have declined to engage in this testing, you really are of little, if any, value to our community anymore. Accordingly, you will be escorted out to the gates of the camp this evening and you can fend for yourself. Secondly, I'm not quite as confident as you are that your staff is unable and unwilling to conduct the necessary testing. I guess we'll find out soon enough. I will explain to them, however, that if they fail or refuse to attempt such testing, they will also be deemed of insufficient value and will be removed from the camp.

"My suspicion is that eventually I will find someone on your staff who is more...*flexible* with their morals and will do as I have requested. Now the problem, of course, is that whoever does the testing will be much less skilled than you. This means these five individuals, whom you obviously care so much about, may be subjected to a greater degree of pain and risk. It has been my experience that when the untrained attempt to do something only the trained should do, they often do it improperly. If this happens, I suspect that our lucky five survivors will suffer a great deal more throughout the course of this testing and the risk of death to them will greatly increase.

"So, as I see it, the testing will be done either with or without you. The only question is whether the testing will be done in the most humane way possible by you or in a possibly barbaric and inhumane fashion by someone without your training, compassion and morals.

"With all of that said, Doctor, I've got to get back to work. I'll be back at 5:00 this afternoon. When I return, you will either tell me you have reconsidered and will do as I've ordered or you will be escorted to the gates. Remember that your decision affects not just the five but, in all likelihood, each and every resident of this camp.

"Good luck with your decision-making, Doctor."

Major Boulden stood up, turned and walked out the door, leaving it open behind him. Dr. Mo sat for a moment and then stood and walked over to the door. She closed it quietly and then sank down onto the floor with her back against it. Cradling her head in her hands, Dr. Mo allowed herself to cry. Her tears weren't for the five survivors or even the other residents of the camp. No, this time the tears were for herself.

∽

At 3:00 that afternoon, Dr. Mo gathered her staff.

"I know each of you have been incredibly brave through this catastrophe and we would not be where we are without the aid each and every one of you has provided. You have performed admirably and done everything asked of you and much more than you have been trained to do. In fact, all of you have gone above and beyond and you should all be proud of yourselves. You've learned new skills and saved lives. I will forever be grateful to each and every one of you.

"I have been ordered to begin testing on the five patients who have shown themselves to somehow be immune to the Curse. This testing will go far beyond anything we have done so far and will be very dangerous to them. I have always taken my Hippocratic Oath very seriously and want you to know this testing will be contrary to that oath.

"I don't do this easily or even willingly. Major Boulden has made it abundantly clear this testing will be done one way or another. I have decided that I, and I alone, will conduct the testing. In doing so, I will do my best to minimize any pain to these patients. I can't make any promises other than that.

"Now in doing this, I'm not asking for either your permission or your forgiveness. Some of you may consider this testing to be inhumane and even evil and I won't disagree with you. I'm doing this with great reluctance and with the understanding that if there is any sort of judgment after we die, I will undoubtedly be punished for my actions. Please know that I accept the possibility of such judgment and, quite frankly, will even welcome whatever punishment is meted out.

109

"While I can't ask for your permission or forgiveness, I can ask for your understanding and maybe even some compassion. Please understand that this may be our only hope. Judge me if you must but understand that none of you will, or could, judge me more harshly than I am judging myself.

"While I am conducting this testing, I request you continue to do what you can to care for the health and welfare of our fellow residents. Finally, if any of you are religious, please take a moment to say a prayer for me. If there is a God, I'm going to need His forgiveness."

❧

CHAPTER FIFTEEN

MILES FROM NOWHERE

As he turned into the driveway, he saw the cabin up ahead of him. Before he could even shut off the car, the door opened and Liz stepped out.

"John." Her voice faltered but she stuck her arm straight out as if to tell him to stay away. "John, he's gone, isn't he?" Her eyes were red and even from a distance, he could see she had been crying for hours.

Standing beside the car, John looked at her and nodded. He was emotionally torn. He was a rock but if he tried to comfort Liz and Cassie, he knew he would break. He really wanted to be strong for them, but it was obvious from the pressure in his chest that he just wasn't strong enough. Nonetheless, he took a step forward, but Liz again motioned for him to stop and then doubled over with a thick and wrenching coughing fit.

Without any further hesitation, John ran toward the cabin and sprinted up the steps. Pulling her into himself, he wrapped his arms around her. She was burning up and drenched in sweat.

Laying her head against his chest, her legs gave out and John had to hold her up. Using his right arm to hold her, he opened the door with his left hand. "It's going to be all right. Where's Cassie?"

He didn't need to hear her answer. As he walked into the living room, he saw Cassie lying in a fetal position in front of the fireplace. The fire was barely burning but it didn't matter. The room was hot and smelled of urine and vomit. He laid Liz on the couch and knelt down over Cassie. Even before placing his hand on her forehead, he could see that she was burning up. The sweat glistened on her face and he stroked her damp hair.

Cassie stirred and struggled to open her eyes.

"Daddy?"

"I'm here for you, Cat." He could feel tears rolling down his cheeks but ignored them. He reached down and kissed her moist forehead and then stood and opened the door. While it was cold outside, too cold for ordinary comfort, this was the only way he could think to provide even a measure of relief to his girls from their raging fevers.

He tried to give them water, but they were both unable to swallow. Their coughing fits would come intermittently and John would rush from one to the other to hold them and try to calm it.

From his experience with Brian, John knew there was nothing he could do to save them. They were in pain, and he could only offer comforting words to them and keep cool washcloths on their foreheads. He reminded himself to be that rock. His wife and daughter were going to die, and he had to be strong. His mind was focused on everything around him and nothing at all. There was no cry for help because there was no help to be had. There was no prayer for divine intervention because John knew any such prayer would be pointless and would go unanswered. He would be a rock; a rock watching his family die. He would be a rock; a rock who could only hope that his death would quickly follow those of his family. He would be a rock.

CHASING SHADOWS

&

It was dark before it was all over. John didn't really remember exactly when he heard the last gasp of breath. He wasn't even sure who passed first. All he could remember was moving Liz down onto the floor next to Cassie, and going back and forth between them, giving them fresh washcloths drenched in cool water. When he finally closed his eyes, he was lying between their still bodies. His arm was around Liz and her head was resting on his shoulder. In his left hand, he could feel Cassie's cold and lifeless one.

It was silent and frigid, and the night air brought a chill, but John didn't care. It was now his time. He drifted off and dreamed of walking with all three of them—Liz, Brian and Cassie. They were walking down a street that looked familiar, but he couldn't place it. He was holding Liz's hand and the children were chattering alongside them although he couldn't understand what any of them were saying. Suddenly, he stopped but they didn't. He could see the connection between him and Liz, their joined hands, start to widen and then the grasp broke.

John couldn't move. He called out to them to wait. They all looked over their shoulders. They seemed so happy and were calling out to him, but he couldn't hear them and he couldn't move. He could see their mouths moving but couldn't hear anything.

He could only hear his voice asking, even begging them to stop and wait for him. His words floated in the air, but they didn't seem to react or respond. They just kept walking. Then they were gone and the darkness settled on John. He was still; he was quiet; he was alone.

&

It was the shivering that likely wakened him. John was cold and it took him a moment to realize where he was or why he was so

113

cold. Sitting up, he saw his wife and daughter lying beside him. They looked calm and peaceful. The sweat had evaporated and their faces were pale with just a tinge of blue.

He stood up. His legs and back were stiff and aching. Walking to the front door, he unzipped his pants and peed off the steps. Looking around, it was another cloudy day with a slight drizzle. There was almost no wind, and it was unnaturally quiet. He looked up at the gray sky and just muttered, "Fuck you!" His voice was dry and raspy.

His curse wasn't directed at God or anything or anyone in particular. Rather, it was directed at everybody and everything. Zipping his pants back up, he sat down on the stairs. He was cold and shivering but didn't care. He could feel his stomach gurgle from hunger but didn't care about that either. There was nothing left for him and all he could do was wait for the Curse to come for him. No, that wasn't true. He could make sure his family could rest in peace. He would give them the type of burial they deserved. He wouldn't allow them to be ravaged by whatever scavengers might live in the woods. They wouldn't be abandoned like those bodies back at the hospital in Seaside. The fact that there would be no one to provide him with a similar burial was irrelevant.

Without bothering with a coat or gloves, John took a shovel out of the garage and began digging in the back yard. He would dig a hole six feet deep and six feet wide. The work was slow and monotonous, but it allowed him to shut down his emotions and distract him from thoughts of his family. The only breaks he took were to drink water from time to time.

By the time he was finished, he was drenched in sweat and filthy. He welcomed the pain in his legs, back and shoulders. Looking down at his hands, he saw they were raw and bleeding. He climbed out of the hole with the ladder he had taken from the garage a few hours before. He stripped off his clothes and tossed them in the ditch. He then walked into the cabin to the kitchen and grabbed a couple of gallon bottles of water.

Walking out to the deck overlooking the hole, the cold air chilled him and he recognized the reason he welcomed the chill, as well as the pain in his legs, back and hands. It was because he deserved it. He went to the railing of the deck and looked down on his handiwork. He then lifted the first jug up and emptied it on his head. The water was cold and he began shivering uncontrollably but didn't stop. One small part of his mind wondered if this was an attempt to wash the dirt and sweat off or to wash away the guilt of knowing he had not been able to protect his family. He had failed them. The shock of the next gallon of water washed away all thought other than the cold now gripping him and causing his muscles to spasm.

John used his hands to wipe off the dirt and the sweat and after the third gallon of cold water, he turned and walked back into the cabin. He crossed the living room floor and couldn't help but look at Liz and Cassie. He went up the stairs and got dressed. John allowed himself to put on warm clothes, as he needed enough strength to complete his task.

Grabbing three white sheets from the linen closet, John walked downstairs. He slowly undressed Liz and washed her gently and lovingly. He even used shampoo to wash the dried sweat from her hair. He combed it and dressed her in the only dress she'd brought to the coast. He wrapped her up in one of the sheets and carried her to the grave. It was awkward getting her down and he ended up placing the ladder at an angle so he could use it more as steps. He placed Liz on the cold, wet ground and climbed back up for Cassie.

He repeated the same steps with her and then with Brian. With all three of them lying on the ground, he climbed back up and pulled the ladder up behind him. John picked up the shovel. Looking down, he noticed his hands were bleeding again. In other circumstances, he would have known to use gloves before trying to dig but this wasn't other circumstances. This was the burial of his family, of the life he had known and loved.

John then got an idea and dropped the shovel. Running back up to the cabin he grabbed a bottle of Knappogue Castle Irish Whiskey. This had long been a favorite of his and Liz's. Carrying it back to the hole, John stood on the edge and lifted the bottle high.

"I wish I could think of something lovely and comforting to say. You know I love you all and I'm so sorry I failed you. I hope you will find it in your hearts, wherever you are now, to forgive me and let me join you soon.

"I'm not meant to stay here without you. We are a family and will always be.

"Here's to the loves of my life!" John placed the bottle to his lips and took a deep draw. The whiskey burned on the way down and he coughed from the shock. He then looked down at the three bundled bodies at the bottom of the hole and poured out a shot for each of them.

"It's time."

He began shoveling. The only noise was of the dirt hitting the white sheets. As it slowly piled up and covered the bodies, the sound became less and less.

It was dark by the time he finished. Looking up, he could see the moon peeking out as the clouds began to dissipate. It was too dark to put the finishing touches on the grave. He would pile rocks on top to deter any animals from disturbing his family's final resting place. That, however, would have to wait until the next day. John sat down beside the grave and picked up the bottle of whisky.

Looking out over the dirt, he whispered, "I love you" and took a full drink from the bottle. After the burning in his throat went away, John lifted the bottle up toward the full moon and, this time using a much louder voice, said, "Fuck you Curse!" and took another large drink and then another.

He struggled to stand up straight as his muscles were showing the strain from all of the digging. He staggered back into the cabin. This time he didn't bother stripping off his clothes and didn't even try to start a fire. He just collapsed on the couch and instantly fell asleep.

There were no dreams that night. There was no joyful vision of his family again. There was nothing and when he awoke, he was cold and achy and totally alone. He reminded himself again that he was a rock, which allowed him to continue or, more appropriately, to wait—to wait for *his* time.

❦

CHAPTER SIXTEEN

WELCOME TO THE JUNGLE

Ann knew the time had come. Despite the fact that the Oregon Zoo had been closed for months, she and a small band of her fellow keepers kept showing up to care for the animals. Their small band, however, was now down to just her. Food for the animals was becoming scarce and likely wouldn't last to the end of the month.

She knew it was only a matter of time before the Curse would get her and it would likely be soon. It was time to implement the plan she and her fellow keepers agreed upon. The plan was to start freeing the animals in the hope of giving them at least some chance at survival. She could not, and would not, just allow the zoo's animals to starve to death in their enclosures.

The plan called for releasing the animals in stages. The first stage required her to open all of the gates in and out of the zoo. This included the front gates where visitors entered but also the gates around the exterior, which were generally used for the transport of animals to and from the facility and for maintenance.

Next, she began opening various animal enclosures. She actually had to lead the elephants out of theirs. For the gazelles, giraffes and bonteboks, she left a trail of food leading out to open areas of the zoo. For the birds, she cut the netting, leaving large holes for them. She knew some animals would leave and some wouldn't, but she didn't have time to spend working with every species to free them. She could only hope that some would recognize their emancipation and take advantage of the opportunity.

There was nothing she could do for most of the aquatic animals. She didn't have the ability to move seals but figured she could at least transport the beavers and otters down to the river. Putting a large cage on the back of one of the pickup trucks, she lured them in. Once secured, she quickly drove down to the Willamette River and opened the cages. She sat and watched for an hour as they waddled down to the river. The beavers disappeared into the bushes, but the otters began to play. Ann felt like she could watch them play all day but, of course, she knew she couldn't. There was still too much work to be accomplished on Day One of the plan.

Returning to the zoo, she checked on the progress of the released animals and found most of them just loitering around. She was disappointed but not surprised. Most of these animals only knew the world from the confines of their enclosures. Maybe during the evening hours, they might get adventurous and disperse into the surrounding forest.

It was now late afternoon, and the sky was starting to get dark. Taking a sledgehammer, Ann smashed the enclosures for the snakes, insects, and naked mole rats. She didn't expect they would get far but, again, it was better than letting them starve to death in cages.

She then headed home to rest. Ann was not only the sole zookeeper remaining, but she was the only person in her family who had survived the Curse. She slept fitfully.

She awoke the next day, January 15th, to a cold, driving rain. After quickly heating some coffee on her gas grill, she drove back up to the zoo. Ann noted that far too many of the animals were still just walking around or standing and eating leaves off the trees and bushes. Some, like the penguins, even returned to their pens. If they didn't have any great motivation to leave the zoo grounds yet, they soon would.

The bears were pretty lethargic as this was generally their season to hibernate. In the wild they would have never been roused. In captivity, however, they were slow but still mobile. She opened the enclosures for the brown, black and Malayan sun bears. Even in their lethargic condition, Ann knew they could be dangerous and she quickly retreated to her truck.

As the first black bear sauntered into the open, it drew the immediate attention of the gazelles and giraffes. They panicked and started running away. Some found the open gates, but some just ran until they were out of the sight and scent of the bear.

Ann sat in the truck and just watched all of the commotion. For each herbivore that ran out a gate, she smiled. She knew most would never survive but at least they now had a chance.

The next species released were the monkeys and apes. The zoo had a large and varied collection of primates and they needed to be freed before any of the more dangerous animals could be released. While the primates were accustomed to humans and their keepers, Ann had never worked with them before. She could not assume she would be welcomed. Running from gate to gate, Ann opened them and kept running until she could get back to her truck.

She watched as the primates slowly ambled out of their enclosures. They were wary but quickly began heading toward the woods on the other side of the fence. Some used the gates, but others just climbed over the fences. If any animals from these groups would survive, it would be the primates.

The next, and that day's final release would be the most difficult and dangerous so far. The zoo had a small collection of wolves, African wild dogs, hyenas and jackals. They were fast and smart and Ann had to be very careful. Gathering their daily feed, Ann dropped a double serving off at the far end of their enclosures and then quickly drove back and opened their gates. She had enough time to get to safety before they realized she had just granted them their freedom. It was still late morning but Ann figured she had done enough for the day. Tooting the horn of her truck, she tried to alert the canines to the open gates. She then drove toward the gate and stopped to watch.

As the first African wild dog wandered out into the open, the remaining animals panicked and began letting out howls and cries. A wolf was the next to come out and Ann saw it spot a gazelle and start tracking it. The gazelle was slow to notice but quick to start running when it did. Ann saw the gazelle run behind a building with the wolf in hot pursuit.

Sitting there in her truck, Ann ate her peanut butter and jelly sandwich and sipped coffee from a thermos. She was relieved that the plan had gone so well but she knew she still had one more day's worth of work. The plan allowed most of the herbivores at least a day or two head start before releasing the most dangerous animals. The wolves were predators, but they were still less dangerous than the big cats.

As she started to drive through the gate, Ann stopped and decided to go back. The polar bears were unlikely to be prey for the cats, but they were still somewhat lethargic and their best chance at survival would require them to have at least a single day's start. She drove to the rear of the polar bear enclosure and opened it as wide as she could without waiting around to see if they would come out. She hoped they would but did not want to be there if they did.

Ann called it a day but not before noticing soreness in her throat and an uncomfortable warmness. There was no fear at this point. With everyone she knew and loved already dead, the Curse was not anything she feared. She only hoped it would go quickly but not so quickly that she couldn't finish the plan.

The next morning confirmed the infection. She hurt all over and had a wet and painful cough. She didn't bother washing up or heating the coffee. Instead, she headed straight to the truck.

Driving up to the zoo was difficult as she started to drift into a fog a couple of times. Fortunately, there were no other cars on the road. Pulling into the zoo, she noticed it was a massacre site. There was a giraffe carcass lying on the side of the road and bits and pieces of penguins strewn about. She suspected it was the hyenas and jackals but at that point, she just didn't care. She had done what she could to at least give the animals a chance. If it wasn't enough, she could live with that. That thought brought out a small smile, which quickly dissolved into a wet and painful coughing fit. She covered her mouth with her handkerchief and saw blood as she pulled it away.

Driving to the back of the big cats' exhibits, she opened the gates to the lions, tigers, leopards, cheetahs and cougars. At any other time, she would have run back to the safety of her truck. This time, however, she had neither the strength nor the will. If one of the cats caught her, so be it. It might be more painful than the Curse but likely much quicker. Either way, she no longer cared.

Ann did make it back to the truck but barely. Opening the door was painful and climbing up into the cab took every bit of her remaining strength. Sitting there, trying to catch her breath, Ann spotted the cougars and the leopards slowly exit their enclosures and quickly disappear into the shadows. The lions and tigers were more cautious but still wasted no time leaving their enclosures. She had always wondered what would happen if a lion and tiger came face to face. Now she had her answer. They stopped and looked at one another, gave a low growl, and then just walked in different directions.

Off to her right, she noticed a flash of something white moving into the woods.

"With the power invested in me as the sole surviving keeper of the Oregon Zoo," she mumbled as she started to slump over, "I, Ann Dmohowski Forrestall, hereby declare you free and…" She didn't finish the sentence.

CHAPTER SEVENTEEN

Us and Them

Boulden tried to focus on the things going well so far. This mostly entailed the basic logistics of running Camp Oregon. Since the start of the new year, debris from the destroyed buildings was used to build large parking lots full of military vehicles, cargo trucks and fuel trucks. In order to operate the generators, they needed large diesel deliveries every day. Accordingly, every single day, crews went out to locate and bring back diesel and other fuels. This was pretty easy as there were oil terminals at the ports of both Portland and Vancouver, Washington. If they ever drained all of the gasoline and fuel oils from those ports, there were others within the Oregon region. If they eventually drained those, they could still access underground tanks at the thousands of gas stations throughout the region.

As for food, his scouts located all of the nearby food warehouses and trucks were loaded up and brought back to the camp. There were no fresh vegetables or fruit although they were all looking forward to late summer when crews could be sent out to orchards.

For meat, Boulden had pens set up and stocked with cows, pigs, and sheep. As it was still February, he wasn't prepared to actually start cultivating herds. For now, they would just transport any livestock they found back to the camp and butcher them as needed.

A group from Class IIIs was put in charge of maintaining the chicken operation and there were more than five hundred. As younger chicks matured, the older chickens were slaughtered for food. Boulden knew they could have a complete turnover in a six-month process, which was how long it took chicks to mature enough to be eaten.

Canned and dehydrated foods were used to supplement the meat and the bakery was operating twenty-four hours a day to produce breads of all sorts.

Boulden was proud of that part of the operation. While it was a lot of work to maintain the camp and feed its residents, it could be done for the indefinite future. Neither the supply nor the demand was an issue. The problem was, as with just about everything else in his dominion, the personnel.

There were only a limited number of residents who were experienced in operating big trucks. It seemed that about one-third of those were completely worthless. If he could get them to actually take a truck out, there was a substantial risk of them not returning. These were the serious drunks and addicts and, whether they drank themselves to death or overdosed, every day fewer came back than went out. Eventually a soldier or police officer was assigned to accompany the drivers, with strict instructions not to let a driver detour from his job. While this decreased the number of defections, when they did lose a driver, they also lost the soldier or police officer. Boulden didn't understand how much the soldiers, and especially the police officers, feared his wrath if a truck driver disappeared. Many times, the accompanying soldier or officer decided to just desert. This only enraged Boulden more which, in turn, increased the disappearance of his military and law enforcement personnel.

Another third of the truckers were scared. They were scared of leaving the camp and possibly being exposed to the Curse. They were scared of the wild animals they sometimes caught a glimpse of outside of the fences.

In order to get them to go on a fuel or food run, he sometimes established convoys, which only served to place further strain on his core group of soldiers and police.

The final group of truckers was both competent and willing to undertake its missions but had its own problems. The members of this group were mostly sullen and uncommunicative. Boulden suspected they were unafraid of the Curse because they were unafraid of death. Either they welcomed the thought of dying to join their loved ones or believed death to be inevitable. It was these truckers who, in their off-times and only in their off-times, would drink themselves blind and fight anyone who might be deemed to have offended them. He could arrest them and dry them out, but they were too valuable to impose any further punishment.

Another problem, and perhaps the most significant problem other than attrition, was camp morale. Everyone had lost loved ones and most, if not all, assumed it was only a matter of time before the Curse would complete its apparent mission to destroy the entire human race. Keeping people busy and holding out hope for a medical breakthrough was helpful but not enough. Boulden and his team tried to balance the carrot and stick. They engaged in various strategies to give some hope while, at the same time, showed little patience for those who were deemed detrimental to the good of the camp.

For the first month or so, the people seemed to be excited by the destruction of high-rises and office buildings. The explosions were like fireworks. Gradually, however, people figured out the destruction was really just a sign that those buildings were never going to be needed again. Life was never going to get back to normal. All of the luxuries people had come to take for granted, such as national and international travel, the Internet and readily available consumer goods, would not return in their lifetimes.

People began to understand that even if the Curse died out, they would have to rebuild the world without the technological advantages they had always known. They would need to learn to farm and ranch. They would need to learn how to build and operate utilities for power and water.

Given the assumed number of deaths already, even the most optimistic believed that recreating any semblance of what life had been like just a year before would take more than just years or decades. It would be centuries, if ever, before mankind would be anywhere near to being "back."

Adding to the natural attrition due to exposure to the virus, some people died of natural causes. Heart disease, cancer, diabetes, and other diseases did not just disappear and, in fact, with limited treatment options, the mortality rate from those diseases increased.

It was too emotionally taxing to establish funeral pyres anywhere near the camp. The smell of burning flesh and gray ash falling from the sky reminded people of Nazi death camps. In order to avoid this, Boulden ordered corpses to be trucked up to the Columbia River to the north. They would then be loaded onto barges and set adrift to have the current take them down toward the Pacific Ocean. Fortunately, it was winter and the abundant rains created a strong flow in the river. If the barges capsized or the bodies were otherwise washed off the barges, they would still be swept downstream and away from the camp. Even if the barges got stuck on the shore or otherwise grounded, they were far enough away to not present a health risk, either physical or mental, to the residents.

Alcohol and drugs were tightly controlled. Boulden set up a commissary charged with doling out liquor and certain recreational drugs to the community. Class I residents, of course, had the first choice and greatest freedom to consume intoxicants. The other residents had differing freedoms. The problem with this program, however, was that a robust black market arose throughout the camp.

Being in the middle of another dreary Portland winter, suicide was also an issue. Boulden convinced Dr. Mo to issue anti-depressants liberally but that proved insufficient. Every day, one or more bodies would be found. For those who couldn't commit suicide directly, they would sneak out of the camp with full knowledge they were walking into the grasp of the Curse. While Major Boulden used his best efforts to prevent people from leaving without permission and protection, even he was impressed with how creative some could be.

Boulden's greatest stress was the need for more people. Attrition, from the varied causes, continued to drain the camp. While pro-creation was encouraged and birth control prohibited, there were few pregnancies. People did not want to risk bringing a child into such an uncertain and dangerous world. People had already lost entire families and feared a newborn might be immediately infected and die. More frightening, however, was the fear that the parents would die, and a newborn would be left with no one to care for it.

What the camp needed, and what Boulden needed, was to show the residents how the community was actually growing despite all appearances to the contrary. As a result, he sent out more squads farther and farther away to track down more survivors. The entire metropolitan area had been swept and Boulden ordered the squads to focus on the towns and cities along the I-5 corridor, as well as coastal cities. Central and Eastern Oregon and Washington were just too remote to warrant the risks involved, at least at this point.

Through communications with other camps, he learned his problems were not unique. By the end of January, four bases just disappeared. They went out with a whimper more than a bang. The closest base, just to the north in Washington, started to falter.

Boulden saw this as an opportunity to both increase the population of the camp and to resupply his arsenal. He sent a caravan up to Fort Stevens to collect whatever assets they could find, led by First Lieutenant Michael Kelley.

The remaining residents of Fort Stevens were categorized and there were almost a thousand who would be deemed either Class I or Class II residents. On Boulden's orders, First Lieutenant Kelley declined to transport any of Seattle's Class IIIs and they were left to fend for themselves.

Upon their return, First Lieutenant Kelley reported to Major Boulden.

"Sir, we had a successful trip."

"Lieutenant, first tell me about the personnel."

"Sir, we brought back 953 people. Of these, 315 have a background with either active or prior military experience, while another 27 individuals have a law enforcement background.

"There were 613 women and 340 men. Of the non-military and non-law enforcement residents, we have 227 with construction experience, 112 with agriculture experience, and 54 with truck driving experience. The remaining 218 individuals appear to be of sound mind and body and were deemed to have potential."

Boulden smiled at this and asked, "Tell me about the material you brought back."

"Most of the people were brought back in busses, but we also collected ten M939 trucks, ten M35 trucks, five-gun trucks, three M109A6 Paladin howitzers, 20 Humvees of various types, a M1 Assault Breacher, a Bison armored personnel carrier and three M1128 Mobile Gun Systems. There were various other vehicles and material safeguarded in warehouses. I'll have a complete list of the warehoused equipment to you this afternoon.

"We also brought back ten cases of M16s with 10,000 rounds of cartridges."

Boulden stood up and strode over to Kelley with his arm outstretched. Shaking hands, Boulden said, "You've done good, Lieutenant. I assume all of our personnel returned."

"With one exception, yes."

A look of concern crossed over Boulden's face. "What is the *one* exception?"

"On the recommendation of Warrant Officer Tex Dutile, we sent a small contingent up to the Naval Yard at Bellingham. Dutile suggested we retrieve a large cache of C-4 explosives stored there. They were able to fill an entire cargo truck with the C-4, as well as some limpet mines, haversacks, and shaped charges. Unfortunately, Dutile's truck broke down on the way back to Fort Stevens. The rest of the contingent returned to Fort Stevens, and we sent a recovery crew back the next day to collect Dutile and the explosives.

"When they got back up there, both Dutile and the truck were gone. We have not heard from Dutile since then."

"Fuck! So, you're telling me we have a potential deserter with enough explosives to blow us all up and we have no fucking idea where he might be?"

"Sir, with all due respect, Warrant Officer Dutile gave us no indication he might be inclined to desert. I believe it is more likely he somehow was able to fix the truck but succumbed to the Curse before he could make it back. The truck is likely located somewhere off one of the many exits along I-5. We can, of course, send out search parties but that would take a lot of personnel and a lot of time."

Boulden turned and walked back to his chair. He closed his eyes while Kelley tried to read his mind. Finally, Boulden opened his eyes and said, "Overall, a good job Lieutenant. Get the new residents processed as quickly as possible.

"I want you to know, however, that if Dutile is still alive and causes us any problems, I will hold you personally responsible. Am I clear on that, Lieutenant?"

"Yes, Sir, completely."

First Lieutenant Kelley saluted, turned, and walked out the door.

Boulden was pleased with this influx of survivors but recognized they also brought with them a weariness likely surpassing that of the existing residents. These Seattle survivors had seen a camp falter. As much as Boulden would try, it was difficult to differentiate Camp Oregon from Camp Seattle and many might suspect they were just delaying the inevitable.

∽

At some level, Boulden understood he was starting to show physical manifestations of stress, although he remained ignorant of the psychological impact. He was having problems with insomnia and his fingernails were chewed down to the point where they were bleeding. It was understandable. He had never before been in the position of being responsible for the lives of so many people. He was confident, some might say excessively so, in his ability to do it all. Nonetheless, even Boulden recognized how much of what he was doing required him to learn on the fly.

His background was in law enforcement but now he found himself basically running a small community and having to make decisions about essential services. It was ultimately his responsibility to ensure the lights and the heating worked, that the water would run, and that there was enough food available on a daily basis. This was the first time he didn't have any superiors to direct him or to take on some of the burdens of responsibility. This was *his* operation and *he* was the person ultimately responsible for everything.

While he pushed his subordinates hard, he was pleased with how efficient most of them had become. These subordinates learned not to bother him unless absolutely necessary. Whether this was from concern for his health, as he believed, or because of fear of his unpredictable wrath, which was the actual reason, Boulden was generally able to focus on the larger issues.

These issues involved how to maintain and safeguard the camp until such time as the threat from the Curse disappeared. From what Dr. Mo advised him, the virus could only be transmitted through direct human-to-human contact. As long as they were able to maintain disinfectant procedures for all those entering the camp, they could minimize the risk to the resident population. It was not fail-safe, however. In the past six weeks, the camp experienced two significant outbreaks. While quickly contained, these outbreaks still resulted in the deaths of more than 50 people.

To deal with his daily rigors, Boulden initiated a strict personal regimen. He would rise at 5:00 am sharp. In addition to drinking coffee throughout the day, he began taking 30 mg. of Adderall three times each day. He found the Adderall assisted him with his focus and provided him with the requisite energy. He didn't eat breakfast but would have a lunch of grilled chicken and vegetables, whether he was hungry or not, and then a small dinner in the evening. When he finally went to bed, generally at 11:00 pm, he would ingest a 15 mg. dose of Ambien to assist him in falling asleep.

He rationalized the need for these prescription medicines. It was for the good of the camp. Boulden actually looked forward to the day when he wouldn't need either the Adderall or Ambien, but that would only occur after the Curse disappeared and he could start the rebuilding of America and the world. Until then, he would continue to self-medicate, as necessary, but only enough to allow him to do his work and maintain control.

ॐ

CHAPTER EIGHTEEN

The Forecast
(Calls for Pain)

John woke slowly and, for just a brief moment and with his eyes still closed, he felt good, wondering how long he had left before the alarm went off. Then reality came flooding back in—there was no alarm; there was no work to go to; there was no family. With the sense of reality, came the physical pain. He tried to roll over on the couch but found any movement was too painful. John's back, shoulders and legs screamed at him. Raising his hands to his face, he tried to wipe his eyes but the pain in them was too severe. They were bloody and swollen.

Opening his eyes, everything was gray. Turning toward the window, he heard the rain battering the glass. This wasn't the usual drizzle at the coast. This was real rain. Closing his eyes, John tried to will himself back to sleep but couldn't. The need to urinate was too great; it even surpassed the aching of his muscles.

He opened his mouth to say, "Fuck" but found he couldn't. His mouth was dry and his lips were cracked. With a grunt, John forced himself to stand and turn toward the bathroom. Starting to lumber in that direction, he saw a bottle of water on a side table and picked it up. This was when he first took a real look at his hands. They were a mess. The blood had dried but he could tell he had worn through the skin when shoveling. Even through the pain, he wondered how he could have done that. He'd never had a particularly high pain threshold but couldn't remember even feeling his hands yesterday.

His hands were so stiff John couldn't even use them to open the cap of the water bottle. Instead, he put it up to his mouth and grasped the cap in his teeth and turned the bottle. Spitting out the cap when it finally came off, John gingerly took a small sip of the water. He couldn't tell if it was cold or not, all he knew is that it felt as if he were swallowing razor blades. His throat was so parched the water hurt and he had to stop just to prevent himself from coughing.

Once the urge to cough subsided, the need to urinate returned and John resumed his laborious journey to the bathroom. There was no chance he'd be able to undo the button of his jeans and unzip himself, so he just pulled his pants down. Looking down, his urine was a dark shade of yellow. John understood this meant he was dehydrated. That might explain his headache, which of course, he hadn't even noticed until just then. With a grim chuckle, John considered whether the headache might also be the result of the Irish whisky and quickly decided it was probably a combination of both.

Finished, John clumsily pulled his pants back up and stumbled back to the living room. Sitting down on the couch, he looked around. The fireplace was black and cold. The mattresses were still laid out on the floor and the sheets were all soiled. The couch he was sitting on was filthy, as was he. John took another sip of water.

He had never felt this much physical pain before nor had he ever felt this empty. He thought of Liz and the kids. The thoughts of yesterday threatened to overwhelm him and he tried to push them away. He knew he would be joining his family eventually and tried to take some comfort in that. The problem was he missed them now and so much it felt as if there was a physical hole in his chest. This wasn't the muscular pain from the digging or like the pain from his raw hands. This pain was much more intense and debilitating. For the first time in his life, he had absolutely no idea what to do. He had no family and no career. He had nothing to do and no one to do anything with or for. Reaching for the water bottle, he drained it. It no longer hurt his throat, but his head throbbed with each gulp.

Reaching down, John grabbed a couple of blankets from the floor and wrapped them around his body. It didn't matter they were soiled. It didn't matter they stank. John held on tightly to the blankets and slowly eased his way down on the couch again. He was asleep before his head hit the cushion.

෬

It was impossible to tell what time it was or how long he had been asleep. The room was still gray, and rain was still striking the windows with uncharacteristic force. John opened his eyes and just stared at the fireplace. They hadn't gotten around to unpacking pictures or putting anything up on the mantle. There were a small box of wooden matches and a piece of driftwood. The gray of the driftwood almost allowed it to blend into the overall grayness of the day.

John sat up, each movement reminding him of the day before. He welcomed the pain not because it reminded him he was still alive but, rather, because he treated it as a form of penance. The pain was both earned and deserved.

Slowly and stiffly, he stood up and wandered over to the kitchen. If he was going to die, he should at least be presentable. He grabbed another bottle of water and started to undress himself. Only after kicking off his shoes and pulling down his pants did he realize how cold it was. He needed to get a fire going in the fireplace and should have done that first.

Crouching down to build a fire was not an option, not with his muscles as sore as they were. Instead, he grabbed some newspaper and just threw it on the grate. He gingerly threw some kindling on top, followed by a couple of logs. Slowly, he lowered himself toward the ground. With his butt still a foot or more from the ground, he just fell backward. The mattresses cushioned the fall and he could feel the stiffness of the bedding beneath him.

As he struggled to sit up to light the fire, he realized he'd neglected to grab the box of matches off the mantle. "Fuck," he muttered.

Slowly and carefully, he rolled over and got on all fours. He then placed one knee on the mattress and straightened up. It was slow and painful and he was shivering uncontrollably from the cold.

Grabbing and holding the box of matches was easier than trying to actually remove a match and hold it in his swollen hands. It took four painful tries before the match lit and he tossed it into the fireplace to light the newspaper. The fire took instantly with the newspaper catching the kindling and the kindling igniting the logs. In only moments, the fire spread its warmth, with flickering light, all around the room, chasing the gloom to the edges.

The heat from the fire eased John's chills and he lay back down on the filthy mattresses. With the warmth, the fatigue returned and John forgot he had been getting ready to bathe. Staring into the flames, he whispered, "I'm ready, c'mon, I'm ready."

❧

It was totally dark when he next opened his eyes, with the sole light from the faint glow of the embers. Propping himself up on his elbow, John gingerly tossed a couple of logs on the embers.

136

They threw up sparks, but he didn't care. He didn't care if the sparks flew out of the fireplace and lit the whole damn house on fire. That would at least put an end to things. He knew he couldn't do it directly. He just wanted to be done with all of this but knew he didn't have whatever it took to actually do it himself. Whether that "whatever" was emotional strength or resolve, John knew he just couldn't take his own life. He wouldn't fight death, whether from the Curse or otherwise, but couldn't bring himself to actively do anything to get there.

The rain had stopped but it was dark outside, and John could hear the wind. It was a high whistling noise and it brought him some odd comfort. Maybe it was the souls of his family trying to communicate with him.

Leaning back against the couch, he sat and just gazed at the flames. He was mostly naked with the dirty blanket draping his shoulders. The light from the fire cast different shades of yellow and orange across the room. John watched the flames flicker and gradually engulf the entire logs. Sitting for what seemed like hours, his mind drifted and he got lost in his thoughts. Every once in a while, he would feel a chill on his shoulder and the blankets would be hiked up to cover the bare skin. Occasionally he would get up and drink some water. Gradually his urine began to take on the more usual pale yellow color.

Looking up at the windows, he was surprised to see it was getting light outside. John stood up, taking his time to stretch out his legs and allowing his arms to flail slowly about in order to loosen up his muscles. Unsteadily, he walked over to the sliding doors in the kitchen. John looked out on the deck and, just beyond it, was the square of wet dirt. He was too empty inside to cry and, instead, just stared at where his family was buried. Briefly the picture came to mind of what his family must look like under the dirt, wrapped in the sheets. Quickly he pushed that thought away and turned his back on the door.

The living room was a mess. He could smell the stench of vomit, urine, and feces. He would need to do something about that. First, however, he needed to get cleaned up and dressed. Liz and the children wouldn't want him to just lay in the filth. They would be disappointed if he just wallowed in self-pity and grief. He would not further disappoint them.

Gathering as many bottles of water as he could find, John stepped into the bathtub. With soap and shampoo, as well as a towel and washcloth, John started to clean himself up. While washing his hands, he could feel the dirt being dragged out of the scraps of remaining skin on the palms of his hands. His hands began to bleed again.

Slowly and painstakingly, John washed himself from head to toe. Looking down into the bathtub, he briefly marveled at the amount of dirt coming off his body. The dark brown liquid swirled down the drain. At last finished, he tossed the washcloth into the bathtub and gently dried himself off. Returning to the living room, he threw another couple of logs in the fireplace.

Grabbing a clean blanket, John wrapped it around himself and laid the towel down on the dirt-encrusted couch. Sitting down, he allowed the exhaustion to come. He had done enough to earn a nap. He felt a gnawing in his stomach but was just too tired to bother tracking down any food. The sleep came quick and easily.

This time when he awoke, the pain was still there but not as severe. He briefly wondered whether his body was healing or if he was just getting accustomed to it but decided it didn't really matter. He looked at his hands and noticed they were red and just starting to scab over. John reminded himself that it would be wise to put some lotion or oil on them to help the healing. Standing up, he tightened the blanket around him and headed upstairs.

The rooms were just as messy as the downstairs, albeit not as dirty. The frames for the beds were still there but the mattresses were downstairs. The dresser drawers were open and the clothes were disorganized. Picking up some underwear, clean jeans and a t-shirt, John struggled to get dressed and had to cinch his belt tighter. Every muscle and every joint barked at him as he got dressed. He really felt like he had been hit by a truck.

Finally dressed, John grabbed the warmest sweater he could find and headed downstairs. Going down the stairs was even more painful than going up so he stepped slowly and softly upon each tread.

Standing at the bottom of the steps, John surveyed the living room. Before he could do anything, he needed nourishment. He wasn't hungry, but he knew he needed to eat if he hoped to accomplish anything. Out of reflex, John opened the refrigerator, but Liz had cleaned it out. In the cupboard, he found some protein bars and a package of chocolate chip cookies. He started on the protein bars but quickly switched over to the cookies. The chocolate at least had some flavor and seemed to lighten his mood. Washing the cookies down with a full bottle of water, John walked to the front door and stepped outside. The air was cool and damp. It must have rained a lot because everything was wet.

Before putting on his boots, John poured some olive oil on his hands and wrapped them with gauze. He walked outside and around to the back of the house. There was water pooled on the grave. He pulled over a beach chair leaning against the house and sat down.

"Liz, what do I do?"

Resting his head in his hands, the tears came. He was so very alone and so very sad. This was like nothing he had ever known before.

"I don't know how to do this. I've never been alone before. What am I going to do?"

Sitting there, the sobs wracked his body and each time, the physical and emotional pain struck him hard. He noticed he was starting to shiver and felt the cold. As much as he was numb to life, the cold still got through to him. The shivering was even more painful because of the muscle pain so John got up and walked back inside.

Before cleaning the cabin, he needed to restock the firewood. He didn't expect to be going out much and wanted to at least be warm when the Curse came for him. Without Liz and the children there, the cabin didn't need to be quite as clean, but the current state was unacceptable even to him. The firewood had been stacked against the cabin, but he wanted it to be easier to reach now.

Heading to the garage, John found a pair of work gloves and carefully slipped them over the bandages on his hands. He also grabbed a couple of metal pipes and brought them back and placed them in the living room near, but not too near, the fireplace. Walking to the side of the cabin, he began carrying firewood, a few logs at a time, laying them atop the pipes. He built up the pile until it was almost two feet high and about ten feet long. He threw a couple of logs in the fireplace and watched as they caught.

Walking back outside, he gathered a couple more pipes and laid them in the middle of the driveway over the damp dirt. John then stacked the remaining firewood from the side of the cabin on top of them. Grabbing a bottle of lighter fluid he found in the garage, he lit a match and started the bonfire.

As the fire was building, John walked back into the cabin and picked up the stained and dirty sheets and blankets. He threw them on the bonfire, not even waiting to see if they caught. He knew they would.

Returning to the cabin, John grabbed the closest mattress and wrestled it outside before also tossing it onto the fire. This time he waited long enough to be certain it would burn. It did and a dark and acrid smoke began to rise up into the sky.

He repeated this process with the next mattress. This one threatened to smother the fire so John poured the remaining lighter fluid on it and watched as it went up in flames. The third mattress burned cleanly, and John could see the metal springs from all three mattresses glowing red amongst the embers.

As he walked back into the cabin, John looked for anything else needing to go. The couch was ruined but he knew it was too large for him to move out of the house by himself. There were some remaining clothes and small items laying around, so he gathered them up and tossed them into the fire.

The next step was to clean the living room. John got the remaining bottles of water, together with some liquid detergent and towels and began to wash the floor. He also did his best to wash the dirt off the couch. While not completely successful, it would be good enough. He threw a clean blanket over it and stood and surveyed his handiwork. Although it would not have been good enough for Liz, it was good enough for him.

With the floor and couch drying from the heat of the fireplace, John went back outside and watched the bonfire die out. He could just make out the corners of the mattresses. They still had some fabric remaining but were mostly just springs and wires.

John looked up at the sky and, as he did, the sun peeked out from the clouds and shone down on the backyard. He walked around the cabin and just stared at the light shining on the graves. He wanted to believe this to be a signal from beyond or a symbol of something. John was, however, just too tired to really be able to think of anything. He stood for a moment with his eyes closed and his face soaking up whatever rays the sun could spare.

What he needed now was some rest and more water. He had used up the last of it to clean the living room. It was time to go shopping and his first stop would be at Good Neighbor Ray's house.

ఇం

CHAPTER NINETEEN

The Air that I Breathe

Walking toward Ray's house, John stopped and sniffed the air. There was an odd mix of smells. The scent of the wet evergreen trees was mixed with a slight saltiness he attributed to the ocean. Underlying all of that, however, was a faint but distasteful odor of decay.

Looking over at Ray's house, he saw it was dark. He walked out to the street and every other house within sight was also dark. He looked up above the treetops in hopes of seeing smoke, which might lead him to other survivors. There was nothing.

He walked back to his car and fished the keys out of his jacket. It started right up and he turned on the radio.

"…under the guidance and supervision of Major Roger Boulden and his capable staff. Again, a state of martial law has been declared and all residents of Oregon and Southwest Washington are encouraged to come to Portland.

"We have established a safe community at the Oregon Health & Science University. We call this Camp Oregon and have food, shelter and medical care readily available. Our highly capable medical staff, working in conjunction with other laboratories throughout the nation and the world, is continuing to work on a vaccine for the virus. They are making progress on a daily basis and we expect a breakthrough any day.

"You may see military units in your community. These units are there to assist you in coming to the main camp. We encourage you to greet them and ask for their help. They are here to help you.

"Now, for a quick weather report, it is expected to be mostly dry throughout the western part of the state with only occasional small showers at the coast. Temperatures in the Portland metropolitan area will reach a high of 42 degrees this afternoon and down to the upper 30s this evening. On the coast, you can expect highs in the low 50s with chilly temperatures this evening.

"Again, this is Susan Giles with your afternoon news report. Martial law has been declared throughout the nation and the state of Oregon and southwest Washington has been placed under the guidance and supervision of Major Roger..." John turned the radio off.

The last thing he wanted to do was to join the other survivors at OHSU. He was going to stay here with his family. If...no, *when* the Curse claimed him, he was going to be close to them. In the meantime, he needed some food and water.

Climbing out of the SUV, John tucked his pistol in the back of his pants. He didn't expect to run into anyone as he assumed everyone was dead. The gun, however, was "just in case."

As he approached Ray's house he yelled out, "Ray?" As expected, there was no response. He thought back to his conversation with Liz and how she felt uncomfortable with the thought of moving into Ray's house in case he came back. John had no such issues. Ray wasn't coming back.

John walked up to the door and knocked loudly. He yelled out, "Ray, it's John Callahan from next door. Are you there? Ray?" John was startled by how loud his voice sounded and again noticed how quiet everything else was. There were birds chirping and a slight rustling of the trees. Other than that, there was nothing but silence.

After knocking again, John tried to turn the door handle but it was locked. Turning to his left, he started walking around the house. At every window, he would knock and again shout Ray's name. The inside of the house appeared to be clean and orderly although the furniture and fixtures were worn and dated. From their appearance, John guessed Ray was a long-time bachelor.

As John turned the corner to the back of the house, he took a closer look at Ray's generator. This was a "real deal" generator as John's father might have called it. It was about five feet long and sitting on concrete blocks. It wasn't working but it appeared to be hooked up to the house. With confidence this was a power source he might be able use, John continued his walk along the perimeter of the house. The back door was locked. There was a large pile of firewood beside it and John decided he would relocate this firewood over to the cabin. That would be just the type of mind-numbing work he would welcome. First, however, he had to find water.

Returning to the front door, John again knocked and called out Ray's name. With still no response, he took out his handgun and used the butt to break one of the windowpanes in the door. He carefully reached his hand in and unlocked the deadbolt, turning the knob on the inside of the door.

As he opened it, the first thing he noticed was the stench. It was a sickly-sweet smell instantly identifiable, even by John, as rotting meat. While he hoped it was just something from the kitchen, he knew it wasn't. Pulling his shirt up over his nose and mouth, John quickly examined the downstairs. It was much as it looked from the outside. He focused his attention on the kitchen.

He found a rack full of water bottles in the kitchen and grabbed as many as he could. He also opened cabinets and, much to his delight, found boxes of protein bars and canned meals like beef stew and soup. He grabbed a can of beef stew and headed outside, closing the door behind him.

John pulled down his shirt and took a deep breath, trying to clear the rancid smell of rotting flesh from his nostrils. The first order of business, after drinking some water, would be to carry some of the firewood over to the cabin. This would give him time to figure out what had to be done and devise a plan.

Moving most of the firewood took over an hour and, when done, John had broken a nice sweat. He got out a pan and poured the canned beef stew into it. With a couple of additional logs in the fireplace, he laid the pan on top. Using an oven mitt, he would occasionally stir the stew before pulling it out of the fire.

John sat on the couch and took a bite of the stew. It was the first warm meal he'd eaten in days, and it tasted awful. It was salty and the meat had little flavor, but he still ate it all. Just as he finished the stew, the grief returned—hard.

He barely made it out the door before vomiting over the stair railing. After rinsing out his mouth with water, he grabbed a bottle of Irish whisky and quickly drank himself to sleep.

❧

Waking up could only be described as ugly. The sun was shining through the windows with a brightness that sharpened the spike seeming to poke into his eyes. He could barely open his eyelids and, when he did, he started to look around. "Fuck," was all he could say. It came out more as a croak than as a fully formed curse. The pain brought with it the memories and he again rushed to the door and was able to get his head outside before whatever remained in his stomach erupted.

There was a sharp chill in the air, and he sat down on the stoop with his head in his hands. The cold helped cool him down a bit as his stomach settled. Stumbling back to the couch, he grabbed one of the water bottles from Ray's house and slowly drank it down. He staggered upstairs and downed some aspirin. John thought to himself that it didn't matter how long the rest of his life played out, he really didn't want to go through this again. He had never been much of a drinker and the hangovers weren't worth it. The whisky just wasn't going to help. The grief was going to be his dark and permanent companion and he needed to accept that.

He returned downstairs and nibbled on a protein bar. It tasted like cardboard, but John knew he needed something in his stomach. He started thinking about what he wanted to accomplish that day. He remembered Ray's generator and wondered whether he would be able to start it up. Then he remembered the plan he'd worked out yesterday while moving the firewood. Ray, or rather, Ray's corpse, was somewhere on the second floor. The house and the generator were pretty much useless with his body still there. As he thought about removing the body, John's stomach clenched, and he took deep breaths to try to calm himself.

Gradually the aspirin, the water and the protein bar started to work, and John was beginning to feel human again. He laced up his boots, walked outside and turned toward the back of the cabin. The grass was wet, but he didn't care. He even stopped at one point to lean against a tree and just let his face be bathed in sunlight. After this brief respite, John continued to the backyard. Looking over the grave, he noted that the ground was disturbed. Something had been digging there. Whatever it was didn't get very deep, but John was not going to allow his family to be bothered. He was going to have to find some rocks or some type of covering to discourage any curious animals.

Ray and the generator would have to wait. John needed to take care of his family before he did anything else. Walking into the garage, he spied a pile of tarps. It took two of them to completely cover the hole. He then walked through his yard, as well as Ray's and the other neighbors and gathered as many rocks as he could.

He worked for hours. It probably would have been easier to track down a wheelbarrow to carry the rocks, but John wasn't looking for easy. The labor, while exhausting, was deeply satisfying. This was for his family. His back hurt every time he bent over to pick up a rock. His hands started to bleed again but he barely noticed.

At last, he was finished. There were rock cairns on all four corners of the tarps and other rocks, of varying sizes, lined up around the edges. John went through the garbage and grabbed every glass container he could find, throwing them on top of the tarps. Returning to the garage, John found some old windows that had either been replaced or were intended for future use. That future use was now, and John tossed the windows onto the tarp.

With a substantial amount of glass piled in the center, he grabbed a sledgehammer and began to break it all up. John took an iron rake and spread the jagged glass all across the tarps. If any animal attempted to dig through, it would have to deal with jagged glass. John gave a weak smile as he surveyed his effort. Again, it wasn't pretty, but it should do the trick.

Now it was time to take care of Ray. Before turning on the generator, he needed to evict Ray from his now not-so-final resting place. While he had no desire to live in Ray's house, John knew that having a house with electricity might be a good thing.

With an old t-shirt covering his nose and mouth, John stood at the bottom of the stairs and looked up. There was light from the windows but no movement. He could hear a slight buzzing and knew Ray was up there somewhere.

"Fuck, I hope it's only Ray up there!"

The stairs creaked as he walked up them and the buzzing sound grew louder. At the top, John looked both ways down the hallway. To the right were three closed doors, presumably two of them would be bedroom doors and one either a bathroom or a closet door. To the left was a bedroom with the door ajar. In the light shining through the windows, John saw a swarm of flies. That was the buzzing.

Holding his breath as much as possible, John cautiously walked toward the open door. He nudged the door open with his foot. This was not just a swarm of flies; it was almost a solid mass. This is something he had never seen before. Where the fuck had they all come from, he wondered.

To the side was another open door and John instantly knew this was where Ray was—the master bathroom. There was light coming in through the window and the mass of flies seemed to emanate from there. They would fly out of the bathroom and then circle around the bedroom before returning.

John turned away and, holding his nose, took in a deep breath through his mouth. Keeping his mouth covered by the t-shirt, he took a couple of quick steps and looked into the bathroom. Ray's body was slumped against the bathtub, his bathrobe wrapped around his upper body. Around his legs were what appeared to be dried feces. John surmised Ray must have fallen off the toilet mid-defecation. The flies formed a blanket over his face, hands, and bare legs, making it seem like Ray was breathing.

"F-u-u-u-c-k-k-k-k!" John whispered and quickly turned away. Taking the steps two at a time, John rushed out the front door and vomited onto the lawn. This was not going to be easy.

☙

The plan was to just get Ray out of the house. John sure as hell wasn't going to dig a grave for him. No, he had a better, and simpler, resting place for Ray.

"I'm not touching that thing with my bare hands," he quietly said to himself. For a moment he wondered whether it was sane for him to be speaking to himself. Ultimately, he decided he would continue to talk aloud if he wanted. Who cared at this point? If he found any comfort in speaking aloud, so be it. It was just nice to hear a human voice, even if it was only his.

Returning to the cabin, John began rummaging around the kitchen, finally finding yellow vinyl gloves and duct tape. He also found some Pine-Sol cleaner and went into the laundry room to grab a container of bleach. He then grabbed his rain gear, both jacket and pants, from the front closet. Putting on the clothes and gloves, John wrapped duct tape around the bottoms of the pant legs, as well as around the sleeves at his wrists. He wanted to be absolutely sure no part of his body would have any direct contact with Ray and that there would be no way for the flies to get into his clothes.

While a mask of some sort would have been nice, John had no idea where he might find one. He did find some old ski goggles and put them on. He then grabbed a dish towel and, after searching through the kitchen cabinets, placed a liberal amount of peppermint oil on it. Wrapping it around his face, John inhaled. The scent of the peppermint started to bring back memories of his previous life, but John pushed them aside as he didn't have time. He strode outside and back to Good Neighbor Ray's.

The plan couldn't be to just grab Ray by the arms or legs and drag him out of the house. It would leave too much blood, mucus, flesh, and who knows what else, on the stairs and floors. That would be just as bad, if not worse, than leaving Ray where he was.

Back at the garage, John grabbed a couple more tarps and rolls of duct tape. With those in hand, it was now time to get to work. At the front door, he put a few more drops of peppermint oil on the dish towel and tied it tightly around his mouth and nose. He tightened the cord around the hood of his rain jacket and walked in. This time there would be no hesitation. The quicker this got done, the less time he would have to spend thinking about what he was doing.

The buzzing now seemed louder than just an hour before. Holding onto the banister with his left hand, John quickly walked up the stairs, taking two steps at a time. At the top, he immediately turned left and without even realizing it, began to hold his breath.

Fighting back the clenching of his stomach, John tossed the first tarp on the bedroom floor just outside of the bathroom and spread it out. At the sound of the tarp hitting the floor, the swarm of flies seemed to get more agitated and their buzzing louder. John could feel them crawling over him, looking for some opening in his clothes to attack him.

He walked into the bathroom and saw the flies lift off of Ray's body. For just a brief moment, John could see his face. It was blue and Ray's mouth was open. The flies were crawling around the inside of his mouth and then John saw a maggot sneak out between the lids of Ray's left eye.

John clenched his eyes closed, willing his stomach not to vomit.

"I'm a tax attorney, goddammit," he said loudly. "I'm not supposed to be doing this kind of crap."

Placing his hand against the doorjamb, he took a deep breath of the peppermint and walked into the bathroom. Ignoring the urge to gag, John bent over and grabbed Ray's legs. The skin was soft and almost mushy. John's fingers seemed to dig into it without any effort on his part. This wasn't like when you grabbed an ordinary person's leg. This was more akin to squeezing a marshmallow. John tried to clear his mind.

With his eyes closed, he pulled on the legs, perhaps a bit harder than was necessary, and felt the body shift and roll over. He could picture the body moving and then both heard and felt Ray's head strike the side of the toilet and then the floor. The sound was like an overly ripe melon being dropped.

John refused to look. Instead, he just continued to pull the body out of the bathroom and onto the tarp. Without hesitation, John let go of the legs and pulled the tarp so that it was completely under Ray and began wrapping one side over the other. He used the duct tape and sealed the edges. This required him to roll Ray's body back and forth. He could feel the sweat pouring down his body. Ray was not a small man. In his prime, he must have been well over 270 pounds. The term "dead weight" came to mind. Ray was heavy and while he wasn't raising any objections to being moved and wrapped in the tarp, the flies were furious. In addition to crawling all over John, the flies seemed to be almost attacking him. It almost felt like being pummeled by soft BBs. It didn't hurt but just knowing what it was raised the hair on the back of his neck.

Grabbing the second tarp and roll of duct tape, John wrapped the tarp around the body and taped it all around, starting around the head and working his way down to the feet. His work product wasn't going to be judged on aesthetics but rather, on functionality. The tarp had to be tied sufficiently so that neither Ray nor any of his bodily fluids would escape.

Standing up, John absently waved at the swarming flies and stretched his back. The worst was over. Now, all he had to do was to get the body outside. His goggles were fogging up, but John didn't dare to clean them. He could only imagine what the flies might do to him.

As he stretched his arms around in order to ease the aching in his back and shoulders, John felt a need to urinate, an urgent need. Clearly, Ray's bathroom wasn't an option, so John started to walk down the hall. Opening a door and then immediately closing it behind him, John found a bedroom with an attached bathroom. He grabbed a couple of bath towels and after soaking them in the toilet, placed them along the bottom of the bedroom door. While some flies had followed him in, the towels would keep the rest of them out for a while.

After first opening a window to allow some cool and fresh air in, John started to strip off the rain gear. His clothes were completely drenched in sweat but that was a matter for another time. Right now, he had to pee.

The urination was amazingly satisfying, and John decided to take a break before finishing his work. He looked around the bedroom. By the looks of it, it was a child's bedroom with a twin-sized bed, small dresser and desk.

Sitting down on the bed, John absentmindedly began to clean his goggles with the comforter from the bed. There were pictures on the wall across from him and John got up to look at them. He stopped and sat back down. He didn't want to see anything about what Ray had been. Whether or not he had been a husband or father was not something John wanted to think about now. Ray was a corpse wrapped in tarps and that was all he was.

Standing in front of the open window, John let his clothes dry a little and looked over to the cabin. Much of it was hidden but from what he could see, it seemed sad. He knew he would be returning there as soon as he finished with Ray and had a feeling it was not going to be a good night.

Eventually, he put his rain gear back on, wrapping duct tape around the legs and sleeves. Cinching down the cord around his hood, John applied more peppermint to the dish towel. With the dish towel and goggles in place, John opened the door and started walking down the hall, closing the bedroom door behind him. The flies were swarming throughout the hall and were crawling over the tarped body. It was almost as if they could sense their meal ticket in there somewhere but couldn't figure out how to reach it.

Without any further hesitation, John waved away the flies and, grabbing the bottom of the tarped body, started backing his way down the hallway, pulling it behind him. At the top of the stairs, John thought briefly about just rolling the body down but was concerned the tarps might tear. Instead, he descended backward, pulling it down with him. With each step, the body thumped, in particular where Ray's head was. The sound was wet and disgusting and John had to fight to avoid the image of it breaking open and scattering his brains around the inside of the tarp.

At the bottom of the stairs, John released his grip and threw the front door open. He grabbed the tarp again, not giving himself any time to think or rest. He was tired and the muscles in his arm, back and legs were really starting to burn but this was neither the time nor the place to think about that.

He dragged Ray's body out the front door and continued pulling it around the house. It was a good sixty or seventy feet to the fence at the edge of Ray's backyard. John was grateful the gate located along the south side of the fence wasn't locked. Just beyond the gate, not more than another ten feet, was the top of the cliff.

Getting as close to the edge as he could, John reached down and started moving the body, switching back and forth between the head and the legs. When it was finally at the very edge of the cliff, John sat down and, placing his feet against the side of the body, pushed forcefully. The body rolled over the edge. Jumping up, John watched the wrapped body as it tumbled and slid down the hill. He saw the tarp snag on a branch and start coming undone. An arm came out and started swinging around with every revolution of the body.

It finally stopped about thirty feet down, mostly under some brush. The arm was lying uncovered on the ground and sticking out. The palm was facing upward, and the fingers were contorted as if Ray was motioning to him to jump down the hill and join him.

"Not yet, good buddy, maybe someday but not quite yet," Ray quietly responded to the outstretched arm.

CHAPTER TWENTY

WE'RE ALL IN THIS TOGETHER

Sergeant Jeffrey Polits had mixed feelings about his continued deployment and the mission requiring him to go out and look for survivors. It wasn't just that by leaving the confines of the camp, he was at greater risk from the Curse. Mostly it was the fact he would see more dead and bloated bodies in a single day than he had in his whole life prior to the pandemic. It was also the make-up of his squad. In addition to a couple of green soldiers, usually too wet behind the ears to be of much use or company, the rest of the squad would be comprised of Class IIIs or, as most people referred to them, 'turds. As far as he was concerned, the 'turds were the dregs of the community. They were almost all alcoholics, addicts, and/or thieves. Many were psychopaths or sociopaths. Any attempt to institute any form of discipline was met with failure. Some of these cretins were living out their fantasies of death and destruction.

When he first started with these missions, he and his soldiers would interview all survivors and make an initial classification. The 'turds were generally assigned the responsibility of foraging for supplies. Over time, things changed. While initially survivors welcomed them, as time went by it became apparent that survivors were intentionally avoiding all invitations to come to Camp Oregon. This required greater diplomacy and persuasion on his part and more force and intimidation on the part of the 'turds.

At first, the missions were single day-trips with the squad leaving in the early morning hours and returning sometime in the evening. They were only traveling to the nearby suburbs, so this was easy to do. As the need for repopulation became more urgent, Major Boulden ordered the lengths of the missions to be left open-ended. The squads were advised not to return without a substantial number of quality survivors. They were given quotas although everyone did their best to inflate their numbers and keep Major Boulden from knowing the truth. It was, however, becoming harder and harder to locate survivors and they had to go farther and farther from Camp Oregon. Fortunately, and given they could forage for food and water, they did not require much in supplies.

The general routine for the squad would be to drive down the main streets of the various communities on the day's list. Driving slowly, Sergeant Polits would man the loudspeaker.

HELLO. I AM SERGEANT JEFFREY POLITS OF THE UNITED STATES ARMY. WE HAVE ESTABLISHED A SAFE HAVEN IN PORTLAND WHERE WE CAN PROVIDE FOOD AND MEDICAL CARE. IT IS SAFE AND WE HAVE A LARGE NUMBER OF PEOPLE WAITING TO GREET YOU. THERE MIGHT EVEN BE FAMILY AND FRIENDS OF YOURS THERE. IF YOU CAN HEAR ME, COME OUT TO THE STREET AND WE WILL HELP YOU TO SAFETY.

Any survivors who might respond were quickly rounded up and interviewed. Many of those were older woman and younger children. While he had his orders about unaccompanied children and feeble or disabled people, Polits took everyone with him. If

Major Boulden wanted to turn out defenseless children and the handicapped, knowing they would perish, he could do so but Sergeant Jeffrey Polits was not going to do that. He hadn't been raised like that.

After collecting whatever survivors would turn themselves in, the Class IIIs were then set loose to conduct a more invasive search. This involved inspecting each and every house—street-by-street, town-by-town. Any house with one or more corpses was to be burned to the ground. Their orders were to kick in the front door. If there were any survivors, they were to bring them to the sergeant. If they smelled rotting flesh, the house was to be torched.

The most efficient way to do this would be to use thermite grenades but there was no way Sergeant Polits or any other experienced military officer would trust the 'turds with that type of weapon. In lieu of military grade weapons, the Class IIIs were given cans of gasoline or kerosene and road flairs. This wasn't skilled work. The risk of a fire spreading from one house to another wasn't a concern.

Sergeant Polits knew once the 'turds were out of his sight, they were unlikely to look for survivors and, instead, would just torch the homes as quickly as possible. He assumed they would pillage the homes first, looking for alcohol and drugs. He wondered whether, if they did find survivors, they would actually bring them all back to the soldiers. Polits feared what these cretins might do with any women they found but, with only limited resources, he just could not closely supervise all of them.

From time to time, the squad would find a larger group of survivors and load them all up and bring them back to the camp. If the group was large enough, it would require him to leave a number of his Class IIIs behind. Often this would have to be accomplished by force, despite the promise that they would be back the following day. Unlike other squad leaders, Polits always went back to retrieve them. He could only remember three times when they were still there when he returned.

In the pre-dawn hours of this day, Sergeant Polits loaded up his trucks. He had a couple of buck privates who weren't even shaving on a daily basis. They were completely overwhelmed and he could see their fright as they put on their hazmat suits in the near darkness.

"Good morning, soldiers. What are your names?"

"Sir, my name is Kyle Jones, Sir," said the first one. He had an accent, but Polits wasn't sure where it was from.

"Sir, my name is Darnell Valentine, Sir," said the second.

"Don't worry, soldiers. I'll take care of you. Just be careful and do what I tell you. Also, make sure you never turn your backs on the 'turds.'"

Jones and Valentine knew to whom he was referring. On this mission, the six Class IIIs were particularly ragged and dirty and their hair was mangy. Even at this early hour and from a distance, the smell of alcohol was strong. Whether it was from the previous night or from that morning, or both, was impossible to tell.

"Gentlemen," he said forcefully, "we are heading to the coast today. We are going to drive due west on Highway 26 and will be searching through Cannon Beach and Seaside. We will be quick and we will be thorough. If anyone wanders off, they will be left behind. Does everyone understand me?"

Polits looked at the crew in front of him. The privates answered audibly and he could hear their voices as being high-pitched and quivering. The 'turds wouldn't even look at him. He heard them mutter under their breath and reluctantly nod their heads. There was no point trying to install either respect or discipline on these mongrels. Outside the fence, they would defer to him only because he and the two privates were better armed than they were.

"Let's go," Polits said.

Climbing into the passenger seat of the Humvee, Private Valentine took the driver's seat while Private Jones settled in the back seat. As Valentine started the vehicle, Polits pulled out his thermos of coffee and poured travel cups for both of the privates. With a wary eye, he watched the six 'turds climb into the cargo truck, start it up, and move out without even waiting for Polits' order.

They headed to the north gate and Polits could see a couple of soldiers step out of gatehouse. One stayed by the gate while the other walked past the truck and up to Sergeant Polits' vehicle.

"Hey, Sarge. What's the over/under today?"

"Willy, I'm betting we'll be back with a dozen or more. What do you think?"

"If I was a betting man," the soldier chuckled, "I'd be betting you come back with no more than seven or eight. I'm just hoping that however many you bring back, they are better than the six up there in the truck."

"You and me both, Willy, you and me both."

"Sarge, you be careful out there. I really don't trust those guys. I've heard some things."

"Me too, Willy. I'll be watching them the whole time."

The soldier tapped the hood of the Humvee and yelled out, "Open her up."

Another soldier opened the first gate and then slowly jogged the twenty feet or so to the next gate and opened that one too. Both soldiers waved as the vehicles passed. The soldiers noted the occupants of the cargo truck returning their waves with their middle fingers raised high.

After the vehicles passed through the gates, the two soldiers closed the gates behind them and retreated back into the warmth of the gatehouse.

CHAPTER TWENTY-ONE

Let's Get it Started

John stripped off the rain gear as he walked back to the cabin and felt the cool air against his soaked clothes. If he never had to touch another corpse, he would be fine with that. Grabbing a couple of beers from the cabin, he sat down on the chair by the graves.

"That was ugly, guys. I really hope I never have to do anything like that again. Hey, I wonder whether Hafez is still alive."

John's voice echoed in the silence, but he was getting used to talking to himself. Hearing a human voice, even if it was just his, sounded nice. Talking out loud helped keep the loneliness at bay, at least momentarily. He recognized that keeping busy, even if it involved disposing of a corpse, stopped his thoughts from going too dark.

He finished the first bottle of beer, tossed it on top of the grave, and opened the second.

"I'm not really sure what I'm doing. I can clean up Ray's house and hopefully get the generator going but what's the point? It's not like I can watch TV or get on the Internet. Even if I could get on the Internet, is there anyone really out there?

"I haven't seen a live person since the three of you. A couple of times I heard a truck engine in the distance but just couldn't convince myself to care enough to find out who it might be. What if it's someone dangerous? I'm not sure I even care enough to fight anymore."

John took another long pull from the beer.

"What I wouldn't give for a long, hot shower." He chuckled softly. "I wonder if I'll ever get another one—or a hot meal. Hell, I wonder if I'll ever see anyone again. Could I be it? Could I be the last person alive?

"What a fucking joke! If there is a God out there somewhere, what is He thinking? If He, oops sorry Liz, if *She* wanted to wipe out the human race, couldn't She have found a better way to do it? Where is the meteor or the super volcano? If I'm it, then the human race is going out with a whimper rather than a bang."

John finished the beer and tossed it beside the prior one. He reached for the iron rake lying on the ground and used it to smash the bottles and spread the glass around.

John walked over to the closest tree to pee. Silently he gathered his rain gear and went to the garage. There he found a pail with some Pine-Sol cleaner and bleach and headed back to Ray's house. While the corpse might be gone, John realized he would need to clean the house before it would be of any use to him.

Out of habit, John knocked on Ray's front door and waited a moment before opening the door and walking in. There was still the same sickly-sweet smell of rotting meat, but it did not seem quite as intense. The flies, however, were still buzzing all around the house, apparently searching for Ray.

Adjusting the goggles over his eyes, John applied the pepper-mint oil to the dish towel and again wrapped it around his face.

He first opened all of the windows downstairs to let some fresh air in. Then he walked upstairs.

It was now mid-to-late afternoon. John didn't bother wearing his Fitbit anymore, so he wasn't sure exactly what time it was. There was, however, still enough sunlight coming in the windows for him to see what he needed to do. He opened all the windows in the master bedroom and walked down to the bedroom doors on the far end of the hall. He opened the windows in those rooms and pushed the screens out, letting them fall below. He wanted a good cross flow of air to try to get rid of the stench and give the flies an escape route.

John took out the Pine-Sol and bleach and poured both liberally all over the bathroom floor. The flies fled the odor and John got down on his knees and started scrubbing. There was a closet in the bathroom, so he opened it to look for some towels.

There were more towels than John expected but there was also a surprisingly large collection of magazines. John picked one up and immediately realized these were cheap porn magazines. Flipping through them, he saw names like *Hustler*, *High Society* and *Juggs*. They were mostly dated from the 80s and the 90s and John shook his head and chuckled.

"Ray, Ray, Ray! Couldn't you just get your porn from the Internet like everyone else?"

He grabbed a couple of bath towels and wiped up as much of the fluid and detritus as he could. Even with the peppermint oil, John found himself breathing through his mouth in order to avoid the smell. Picking up the soiled towels, he walked over to the bedroom window and tossed them out. The bathroom looked better, but John could still see some streaks of feces and decay. With another towel, he wiped up the residue and again threw the towel out the window. Taking a close look, John was satisfied the floor showed no evidence of Ray being there.

Picking up the bottles, John poured more cleaner and bleach all over the bathroom floor and used a towel to spread it around. If he was going to spend any time at all in this house, he needed to make sure it was completely disinfected. Looking clean wasn't enough for him, at least not now. He needed this area to be "Liz" clean.

The floors would remain wet with the cleaner and bleach overnight. Normally this would be something he wouldn't do out of concern for the floors. But John didn't plan to use Ray's house long enough to have any such worry.

With the bathroom finished, John performed the same procedure on the hallway floor and the stairs. This was much easier as Ray had been wrapped in the tarp while he was being dragged outside, but John wanted to take no chances. If any of Ray had seeped through the tarps, John was going to disinfect it.

It was dark by the time he finished. John closed the windows throughout the house. Allowing Ray's house to dry overnight, John closed the front door behind him and walked back to the cabin.

He was exhausted but dreaded going home. It was the darkness that seemed to bring out the worst of the grief. The fire might warm his body and push the dark away, but it was only temporary. Before allowing the grief to fully return, John opened a can of chicken noodle soup and warmed it over the fire. Unlike the beef stew, he ate it slowly and tried to let his mind wander to better times.

While he might want to think about past holidays and vacations, his thoughts kept returning to the fact that his family was dead and the rest of the world was likely dead also. The loneliness came crashing in and, mixed with grief, he slumped on the couch and cried himself to sleep.

છ

As he struggled to open his eyes, John's head hurt. It wasn't a hangover as he'd only had those two beers.

"Perhaps this is the start of the Curse," he wondered.

It was cold and overcast outside and just as cold in the cabin. He quickly started a fire and silently allowed himself to revel in the warmth. Regardless of whether or not he was showing signs of the virus, John needed to do something. Sitting there and wallowing in his grief, waiting for virus to kill him, was just too painful and too slow. The first thing was to clean up the pan from the chicken noodle soup and then find more water. He only had six gallons of bottled water left from Ray's house and would have to find more.

He used up almost an entire gallon just cleaning up from dinner, drinking the rest of it. He bent his head over to smell his armpits and recognized the odor of the combined dried sweat and disinfectant. Grabbing the remaining gallons of water, John walked upstairs and into the bathroom.

This wouldn't be a hot shower and wouldn't be a pleasant bath, but it was necessary. Stripping off his clothes, he threw them in the corner.

"Yeah, I won't be using those again," he said.

Stepping into the bathtub, John took a big breath of air and poured the first bottle of cold water over his head.

"AAAAARRRRGGGGHHHH!" he screamed.

He was never a fan of cold-water showers or baths, and this reminded him why. He started shivering immediately and without wasting time, he grabbed a bar of soap and started washing himself from head to toe. He went quickly but thoroughly. Even if it was just for himself, he wanted to be clean.

When he was finished washing and without giving himself time to think, he lifted the second bottle of water over his head and poured it out.

"AAAAARRRRGGGGHHHH!"

He was short of breath but picked up the next bottle of water. He poured it on his armpits and then over his back and buttocks. The cold wasn't getting any easier to tolerate but he refused to stop until all of the soap had been rinsed off. He grabbed a towel and briskly and roughly dried himself off and wrapped it around his shoulders.

"God*dam*mit!" There was no pretense at being quiet or circumspect. John wanted to cuss and from now on he would.

Grabbing his dirty clothes, he threw them down the stairs and then found some replacements in his and Liz's room. With clean clothes in hand, John walked downstairs and stood in front of the fire. Throwing a couple of new logs in, he soaked up the heat, first on his front and then on his back. When he was finally dry and warm, John dressed.

His jeans were loose around his waist and John had to cinch the belt an extra hole tighter. Standing up, John felt his belly and realized it was flatter, noticeably flatter, than it had been for years. He started to yell out to Liz to have her come look but then remembered. Instead, he wandered into the kitchen and started to look through the cabinets.

What he really wanted right now was some bacon and eggs but that wasn't an option. Instead, he found some Fig Newtons and saltines. It was a good start, but he needed protein. There were a couple of small containers of a protein shake he used from time to time. It wasn't the breakfast of his dreams, but it was enough to wash away the gnawing hunger.

Sitting on the floor in front of the fire, John thought about what to do that day. The headache had dissipated and now he just wanted to do something. Ray's house should be dry and hopefully the smell, as well the flies, would be gone. He would try to start the generator although what he might use it for was something he wasn't sure about. It's not like he was going to move in. This cabin was his home. This cabin was where his family was, and he wouldn't leave it until the end.

He thought maybe the generator, and having a house with electricity, might provide him with at least a semblance of normalcy from time to time. Maybe Ray had some movies, other than pornos, he could watch.

With coat in hand, John stepped through the front door of the cabin and headed over to Ray's. He was pleased to find the house smelled clean although it was very cold. John walked upstairs and checked his handiwork. Everything was clean and he couldn't detect any scent of decaying flesh. There were dead flies laying in the windowsill and all across the floor. He returned to the kitchen, found a broom and dustpan, and quickly swept them up and threw them out the window. With the house secure, his mission now was to find out if he could start the generator.

Walking around the side of the house, he saw the generator, but he also saw the pile of soiled towels from the day before. There were flies, both living and dead, all around it. The flies seemed just as angry as they were yesterday. They were attracted by the smell of Ray's remains on the towels but repelled by the remaining scent of the Pine-Sol and bleach. Before he could take on the generator, he decided to dispose of the debris.

John walked back into the house and grabbed a pair of tongs from the kitchen. He found a large garbage bag and returned to the back yard. Carefully he placed the towels inside and tied it closed. Holding the bag at arms' length in front of him, John walked toward the cliff.

The grass at the edge of the cliff was still tamped down and muddy. He hesitated to look over because he really didn't want to see Ray's arm down there. Nonetheless, he did.

The brush looked the same but the spot where Ray's arm had seemed to wave to him the day before was different. There was no arm there anymore. John wondered if the body had just fallen further down the cliff overnight or if some scavenger had taken a liking to Ray. John thought the latter was more likely, but a part of his mind wondered if Ray hadn't somehow come alive again and started wandering the surrounding woods. Damn those Stephen King books!

Swinging the trash bag back and forth, John launched it far over the cliff and further into the brush. As a lifelong Oregonian, John felt a measure of guilt about littering but, at least intellectually, he knew there were limited alternatives. There would be no trash collection anytime soon and he couldn't keep rubbish nearby. He didn't want to encourage animals to come too close to the houses.

Turning around, John looked at the generator and began walking toward it. He had never used one before but assumed it would be relatively easy to start if it would work at all. The fuel tank was along the side and John unscrewed the cap. It was too dark to see into, so he grabbed a stick and dipped it into the tank. Checking, it appeared the tank was low on fuel.

"Well, that explains that mystery. Now I just have to figure out where Ray kept his fuel." Again, his voice sounded unusually loud, even though he was sure he was using an ordinary conversational volume.

Ray's garage would likely be the best place to look. The doors were unlocked, and John flung them open. As the daylight illuminated the garage's interior, John was amazed at what a packrat Ray had been. There were racks of what looked like tools and building supplies. In the center was a large item draped in a tarp. John pulled the tarp off and tossed it out into the driveway. The dust caused him to start coughing and only when it started to settle did John recognize a half-built 1963 Chevrolet Stingray. Beside it, he saw a drill press, a lathe, and various other types of woodworking and machining tools he couldn't readily identify.

Along the back wall, he spotted something and, directing the flashlight at it, saw a large tank on a pedestal. This looked like just the type of container someone would store fuel in. He took out the nozzle and opened it, pouring a small amount of fluid on the floor. Even to his untrained nose, it smelled the same as that from the generator's fuel tank. While he couldn't be sure, he assumed this was diesel, as he couldn't imagine what other type of fuel Ray would have stored. Gasoline for his truck was too readily available to require someone to maintain a large tank like this at home.

Continuing to look around the garage, John found a couple of five-gallon cans and filled them. Taking one in each hand, he walked back outside and around the house to the generator. The generator apparently took twenty gallons as it took John two trips to fill it up.

"Okay, that's done. Now, where's your on-switch, baby?"

There was no visible switch or key. There wasn't even a pulley like a lawn mower might have. What it did have were a couple of latches on both sides of the top, four altogether. John unhooked the latches and took the top of the generator off.

This was a control panel of sorts with four buttons. The small labels underneath each of the buttons stated, in turn, "auto," "manual," "off" and "enter." John pushed the auto button and listened for anything that might suggest the generator was starting to turn on. There was nothing, just the chirping of the birds in the trees. He pushed it again and, again, nothing happened.

He then pushed the manual button, and nothing happened. He tried pushing both the auto and manual buttons at the same time. He tried the manual and enter buttons at the same time and with the same result. He tried every combination he could think of, but nothing worked.

Turning from the generator, John clenched his fists and threw them to the sky, screaming "F-U-U-U-U-C-K!" as loud as he could. He kicked the side of the generator and, not surprisingly, nothing happened.

John turned away from the damned generator and started walking toward the cabin wondering what his Plan B would be. If he couldn't start it, Ray's house was of no real use to him and he would have to look at other houses. Certainly, out here near the coast, other people must have generators and maybe he would have more luck at one of those houses.

He had just turned the corner of Ray's house when a thought occurred to him. He was neither mechanically nor technologically inclined, but he knew that when his laptop or other computer froze, sometimes all he needed to do was shut it off and then restart it. Certainly, the generator must have some sort of computer in its darkest of dark hearts.

Returning to the generator, John first pushed the off button. Holding his breath even without realizing it, John pushed the enter button. Nothing.

He then pushed the off button again and then, after first counting to ten, he pushed the auto button, followed by the enter button. It seemed like nothing was happening and John was just about to hurl another expletive to the heavens when he was startled by the glorious sound of the generator starting. Looking up to the sky, John hooted and was then immediately shocked to hear Willie Nelson's voice behind him.

Blues skies, smiling at me,
Nothing but blue skies, do I see.
Bluebirds, singing a song,
Nothing but bluebirds, all day long.

John raced around to the front of the house and ran in through the front door. Willie's voice was coming from the stereo in the living room. John started to jump up and down and began singing along.

"Blue days, all of them gone; nothing but blue skies, from now on!"

The smile on his face almost hurt and John realized for the first time in over a week, he was happy. He had a vision of Tom Hanks' character in the movie *Castaway* dancing after "creating" fire. That was how John felt. He had "created" electricity and now had music again in his life.

The next song was *All of Me* and John sang along as he walked through the house turning lights off that had suddenly come on. He returned to the living room and sat on Ray's couch, closing his eyes and listening to Willie Nelson serenade him. His was a weary and worn voice but it was a human voice and John realized again how much he missed talking to Liz and the kids.

When the CD was finished, John shut off the stereo and walked into the kitchen. He needed water and found that Ray still had quite a bit stored in the hall closet.

After closing up the house, John shut off the generator and walked back to his chair beside the grave.

"Liz, you'd be proud of me. You were always better at figuring out stuff like this, but I did it. I got the generator to work. Did you hear Willie? I was never much of a fan before but now...I *love* me some Willie!"

He drank some water and looked around. The sky was becoming overcast, but the wind was still. The trees stood there. At first it felt like they were guarding his family but then he started to sense a degree of menace. The hairs on the back of his neck stood up. It was almost as if the trees, or something or someone hidden in them, was watching him. Involuntarily, he shivered and wondered if there was really anything to be concerned about or if his loneliness was triggering a measure of paranoia.

"That's enough for this morning. It's time to take a little walk. Liz, do you think someone might be out there? Brian? Cat?"

As he sat there and before he could get up, a wave of fatigue hit him and he slumped deep into the chair.

In a soft and resigned voice, he said, "Caffeine, my kingdom for some caffeine."

John slowly got up and retreated to the cabin. Closing the door behind him, he sat down on the couch, shut his eyes and, with the fatigue overwhelming his unease, fell solidly and peacefully asleep.

CHAPTER TWENTY-TWO

COLD, COLD, COLD

t was the shivering that woke him up. He was starting to get used to waking up to the cold, but this was exceptional—he could see his breath when he exhaled. He couldn't be sure but figured that it must be sometime in mid- or even late-February. He had been spending most days at Ray's, where he could listen to music and read whatever books he could find. Ray's modest library was supplemented by John's exploration of other neighbors' houses.

Today, the wind had begun to blow and the sound of the trees moving was loud. John straightened up, letting out a grunt as a back spasm forced him to hunch over. Slowly, he straightened up.

After putting some logs on the fire and helping them flare up, John grabbed his coat and walked out onto the deck. Looking down on the grave, he was pleased to see that it was still undisturbed. Looking into the trees, he watched as they shifted and swayed with the wind. John again felt a wave of unease.

"Ray? Is that you, Ray?" he said, recognizing his attempt at gallows humor was only causing him greater unease.

He turned back and walked into the house and drank a bottle of water. He grabbed a hat and a flashlight and went back outside. While he appreciated the relative comfort of Ray's house, what he needed now was to walk. John had always found relaxation in walking distances. When he was younger and before he hurt his knees, long distance running allowed him to relax and set his thoughts adrift. He wasn't a fast runner, but he could run seemingly forever. He had developed the ability to separate his thoughts from his body and think about whatever came to mind. This was what John wanted, and needed, now. He headed down the street.

The only sound was the trees swaying in the wind, and the occasional call of various birds, so there was nothing to distract him. The houses alongside the road were all dark. At some point he might have to explore them, if for nothing else than for food, but right now they held little interest. He really wanted to avoid any more corpses if he could. He wasn't sure how much more death he could handle.

Approaching the main road, John stopped and listened to see if he could hear anything. There was still nothing. To the left, the road headed further into the coast Range; to the right it headed downhill toward the ocean and Manzanita. He decided to walk downhill. There were some scattered neighborhoods and he figured he should at least check them out. As he walked, the thought occurred to him that Ray, or what was left of him, was somewhere in the trees to his right. "Damn," he whispered to himself, "I really need to stop thinking about him."

The wind was blowing from the south and John thought he could smell the scent of smoke in the air. Stopping at a clearing that gave him a view over the coast, John looked at the ocean in the distance. Most of the visible expanse was made up of fir trees with little movement. He could see a portion of Manzanita, but it was too far to walk. There was, however, another street just down a little bit and John decided to check it out.

This street was similar to his, with dark and silent houses set far back from the road and spread out. As he passed each driveway, John hoped to see tire tracks which might indicate someone having driven there recently. There was nothing—no tire tracks, no smoke coming out of chimneys, no sound, just nothing at all. While he hadn't expected to find anything or anyone, he still held out a measure of hope.

"Maybe I really am it, maybe I really am the last person alive." Then he heard the sound of trucks in the distance.

☙

Curiosity got the better of him and John looked for a perch where he might be able to see where the trucks were. Unfortunately, the trees blocked his ability to see that far. Nonetheless, he could see black smoke in the distance rising up into the sky. John stood there and listened, trying to figure out how many trucks there might be and what they might be for.

"Who would be using trucks?" he wondered. "If those were fire trucks, I'd be able to hear the sirens."

He knew he was going to have to explore this but wanted to make sure he could do so without being seen. John didn't quite know why but he knew he didn't want anyone to see him until, and unless, he wanted them to.

The SUV wasn't going to work. It was too big and, while in normal times it ran quietly, these weren't normal times. Now, with the only sounds being wind and birds, noise from the SUV would stand out. He needed something quiet, either an electric or hybrid car.

It took him a while, but he finally found what he was looking for—a black Prius. It was parked in a garage a few streets down. Breaking into the house was easy, and it was even easier to find the vehicle's keys, which were lying on a table near the front door.

John didn't linger because he could smell the owner and didn't care to meet him or her.

Driving back to the cabin, John worked on becoming as familiar as he could with the car. It looked like the battery was about half-charged, so he knew he was going to have to figure out how to charge it. The gas tank was also half-full, so he was also going to have to find gas. Without electricity, he wouldn't be able to just pump gasoline at a station.

"Okay, big guy," he said absently to himself, "we've got some things to figure out."

Back at the cabin, he got out the Prius' owner's manual. He then began to explore the car itself. Locating the fuse box, John began removing fuses until he figured out which ones controlled the lights. It took a while, but he was able to pull the fuses controlling the headlights and running lights, as well as the turn signals and the interior lights. The brake lights were more difficult as they also seemed to affect the power windows. Grabbing a hammer from the garage, John broke out the brake lights.

"I'm not going to be needing those anyway," he said quietly.

The only lights remaining were on the dashboard and he wanted to keep those. He wanted to know how much gasoline and battery power he had at all times. Using some cardboard and duct tape, he fashioned a flap covering the dashboard, but which could be lifted up when needed.

If he was driving at night, he might want the headlights, but he also understood that headlights would be visible from afar. John decided he would just need to drive slowly and rely upon moonlight and, perhaps, a handheld flashlight, for any night travels.

It was now early afternoon and John realized he hadn't eaten anything yet. Walking into the cabin, he grabbed a couple of protein bars and a sleeve of crackers, together with another bottle of water. Before tackling the owner's manual, John decided to tend to his hands. They were healing, but slowly. He continued to treat them with olive oil to keep the scabs from forming too thickly and restricting his ability to use his hands.

With his hands re-wrapped with gauze, John opened up the owner's manual and began to learn about the inner workings of his new car. By the time it was too dark to read, he was ready to call it a day.

John made some soup and tried to fall asleep as quickly as he could. He knew dreams were awaiting him and could only hope they would be nice ones—perhaps dreams of his family back then rather than now. He could hope but the more he thought about it, the more the dark dreams came and there was nothing he could do about it.

⁓

John longed for restful sleep and wondered if he would ever have it again. He certainly hadn't gotten one the night before. It was early and the sun hadn't yet risen. Even with the limited light, he could tell it was going to be overcast and wet again—but this day would still be different. Today, he was heading into town and maybe that explained why he woke up so early.

Moving sluggishly, John headed to the back deck. He hoped the crisp morning air would clear his mind. As he opened the sliding doors, he heard a noise down by the grave—it seemed to be a growling. John quickly grabbed his pistol and flashlight from inside the house, ran out the front door and around to the back.

Shining the light ahead of him and down on the ground, he saw a small pack of dogs of varying breeds. They were walking around the tarps, seemingly trying to get through without getting cut from the glass. With the light from the flashlight shining on them, they looked up at John and growled.

John yelled at them, "Shoo! Get out of here!" All they did, in response, was continue to stare at him and growl.

John leveled the pistol and aimed for a patch of dirt between the dogs. He fired once and the dogs all leapt backward. He could see them run into the woods and flashed the light in their direction. One dog, it looked like a particularly dirty Rottweiler, turned and stared at him. The dog didn't bark or even snarl. It was just staring at John with its mouth open. Even from this distance, John could see slobber dripping from its lower jaw.

"Fuck you, dog!" John yelled at him and pulled the gun up to aim at the Rottweiler. Before he could fire again, the dog turned and leapt into the woods.

After a few minutes, waiting just long enough to make sure the dogs weren't coming back, John walked back into the house and put on a warm coat and some boots. Walking outside again, he sat down on his chair by the grave with his shotgun on his lap and guarded his family.

"Come on back, pups," he whispered with a tone of unhidden menace, "come on back." He hated those dogs and, in particular, the Rottweiler. He used to love dogs, but these were different. They were wild and perhaps even evil. They wanted to disturb his family. They wanted to destroy him. John didn't know how he knew, but he did.

He sat guard for over an hour until the daylight was sufficient and the flashlight was no longer needed. Deciding that the dogs weren't coming back, at least not that day, John stood up and, with one last look toward the woods, walked back into the cabin. Doffing his boots and throwing his coat aside, John threw a couple of logs into the fire. He realized he was shaking although he wasn't sure if it was from rage at the dogs or from fear. Either way it was not something he relished. Closing his eyes, John forced his breath to slow and, surprisingly, quickly fell back asleep. When he awoke, he sensed something outside, something that wanted to do him harm.

❧

CHAPTER TWENTY-THREE

DOWN WITH THE SICKNESS

Mo heard the alarm sound and casually reached over to shut it off. She rolled back and returned her arms to their tight embrace of the pillow. She nuzzled her nose into it and in that moment, that moment when she was still at least partially asleep, she could almost smell Meghan. As the haze slowly cleared, the tears began to roll down her cheeks.

Why did Meghan have to die? Why hadn't she joined her yet? If she pushed her face further in, searching for that elusive scent, might she smother herself and finally find the freedom she so desperately wanted. She knew it wouldn't happen. Her medical training, if nothing else, had taught her that self-suffocation was not possible, at least not by merely sticking her face into a pillow.

Instead, she lay there, quietly crying for a time long passed and the person who truly defined her. What would Meghan think of her? That was a question she really didn't want to ponder because she knew the answer. Meghan would certainly be disappointed in her. That was the best-case scenario. If she really thought about it, she knew that Meghan would hate what she had become.

What she had become was a doctor who had foresworn her Hippocratic oath. She was a doctor who had abandoned her professional and personal ethics. She was a woman who had completely lost any sense of morality. Meghan would have hated her and Mo knew it.

Her experiments had been as fruitless as they had been brutal and inhumane. While she couldn't determine why some people appeared to be immune to the virus when virtually everyone else wasn't, she tried to determine how the immunity worked. She injected some of these survivors with higher and more concentrated doses of the virus to learn whether there was a limit to their immunity. She injected others with other viruses, including measles, smallpox, yellow fever, Zika and even Ebola, in an effort to see what effect, if any, the other viruses might have on the Curse. There was at least a chance that the Curse might be rendered less lethal through exposure to these deadly, but still less lethal, viruses. The camp did not have samples of these viruses, but Boulden was apparently very efficient at retrieving them from a number of different military facilities.

She knew all along, however, that she had neither the training nor the equipment to conduct these experiments in any sort of proper scientific fashion. She could not explore the genetic makeup of the virus, nor could she develop any sort of vaccine. Dr. Mo knew this from the moment Major Boulden ordered her to begin. Her experiments were merely shots in the dark; beastly and horrible in both their conception and implementation.

The survivors were involuntary and unwilling test subjects and suffered horribly from all of this testing. Perhaps most importantly, all of them eventually died. The only thing that Dr. Mo ultimately learned from this testing was that there was no silver bullet to defeat the Curse. Their only remaining hope was for it to die out naturally.

Viruses, by their nature, adapt to their environment and mutate. There were countless examples of viruses throughout history evolving from deadly to benign in just a matter of months. This virus, however, evolved continuously but never lost its lethal nature. Dr. Mo fought the urge to think of the virus as a sentient being, intent upon the complete obliteration of the human race. Still, that nagging thought remained.

If the virus did eventually burn itself out, they would try to rebuild society and she could actually do what she was trained for—help people. If it didn't, if the Curse didn't burn itself out soon, then the whole human race, including her, would cease to exist.

With this realization, she wondered why she couldn't have just stood up to him. She had some leverage. As the senior doctor of an ever-shrinking community, she was irreplaceable and that meant any threats from him were nothing more than that—threats. He wouldn't dare act on them.

Nonetheless, she had given in. Maybe it was the force of his personality or his increasingly irrational actions, but whatever it was, she had given in. She had never liked him. At first, he merely seemed full of himself—a classic narcissist with a thirst for power. Eventually, however, she came to recognize him for the monster he was. While she understood the immensity of the pressures he faced on a daily, if not hourly, basis, she also suspected he was using something. His anger and irrationality were likely caused by abusing various pharmaceuticals—over and above any inherent mental instability.

She feared for her life but decided it wasn't the idea of death that caused her to cede to his demands. She knew she would welcome death, even if there were only a sliver of a chance that she would be reunited with Meghan. No, what she feared was pain. She imagined once Boulden started, he would so enjoy inflicting pain upon her that he would figure out a way to extend it as long as possible. She also dreaded the look she saw in the eyes of her patients. The expressions of terror she witnessed while she was experimenting on these innocent souls was unnerving. She balanced terror against the fear of the pain she might receive from Boulden. The fact she chose to give rather than receive was evidence of her cowardice and she hated herself for it.

৽৵

Boulden strode out of his office and slammed his hand on his assistant's desk. Where the hell was he?

"THURBER! *THURBER*! Where the fuck are you?"

He turned as he heard a flush from the bathroom next door and PFC Robert Thurber skulked into the room, head bowed, and hands tucked into his pants pockets.

"How many squads are going out today?"

Thurber slunk over to his desk and picked up a file.

"We're scheduled to have five squads leave this morning."

"Why only five?" Boulden demanded.

"Major, the squads that came in yesterday have to go through the disinfection protocol and then they are scheduled for their two-day break. The squads from the day before are on the first day of their break."

"How many squads remain—all total?"

"We have three rotating groups of squads. Two of the groups have six squads and the one going out today only has five."

"We're down to seventeen total search squads?"

"Yes, sir."

"Goddammit! I thought we had four groups of five squads each," Boulden said, the irritation growing in his voice.

"We did, Sir, but we lost three squads. One got in a firefight down in Eugene and the other two just disappeared. We've been unable to make any radio contact. One of the groups was going east toward Bend and the other was out in the Columbia Gorge."

179

"GODDAMNIT! I want a message sent out to all squad leaders. Let them know that *anyone* who doesn't return will be deemed a deserter and subject to immediate execution."

Boulden was pacing back and forth, clenching and unclenching his fists. Thurber saw how red his face was and wondered how much more of this stress Boulden could handle.

"Sir, you gave that order last week and I believe the men all know it."

Boulden whipped around and stood directly in front of the now-cowering private.

"So, what do *you* suggest, Private?" His voice dripped with obvious hostility and Thurber felt, not for the first time, that Boulden could snap at any moment and pummel him into a bloody pulp.

"Sir, maybe we could require all squad leaders to maintain constant radio contact with us and to continually be updating their location. That way, if anyone deserted, we would know it almost instantly and would have a recent location. We could then send out another squad to locate and return them."

Boulden looked up and over Thurber's head. He turned and walked over to the window.

"Fine. You will be in charge of maintaining the radio communication and tracking locations. Don't fuck up, Thurber! I will hold you personally responsible should any further squads desert. Am I clear?"

"Yes, sir. I'll get it set up immediately."

Boulden turned to the window. The sun was just coming up but was quickly hidden by clouds. It was going to be another dreary fucking day in Portland. He didn't bother looking back as he heard Thurber's chair scrape on the floor as he got up nor when he heard Thurber's shoes scuffle across the room and out the door. The door closed behind him.

"Seventeen fucking search squads," he thought. That was not nearly enough. He walked over to Thurber's desk and dug out the last report on the number of survivors that had been located over the prior two weeks. On average, the squads were locating seven to ten survivors each day, but that average was down from fifteen per day just a month before. Worse yet, many of the survivors were older and required more medical care or were drunks and addicts and of little value to the camp. What he needed was more soldiers and policemen.

It wasn't just his camp that was suffering. The other camps across the country were also being affected by attrition. Not only were each of the camps being reduced in size, but three had gone completely silent. He'd lost contact with Boise, Yuma, and Colorado. Fort Bay, located in San Francisco, was still surviving but their commander, Captain Patricia Burke, had started to become increasingly hostile in their radio communications.

A few weeks before, Boulden suggested to her that perhaps Camp Oregon and Fort Bay should combine. While initially receptive, Captain Burke became increasingly resistant to the idea. Boulden momentarily considered using force to combine the two but wasn't confident he had a sufficient advantage in manpower and weaponry to be successful. Any such forced combination, if unsuccessful, would have resulted in the end of Camp Oregon. Boulden wasn't willing to accept that risk, at least not yet.

He looked at his watch and strode back into his office. Reaching into his top drawer, he grabbed the container and shook a couple of pills into the palm of his hand. He tossed them into his mouth and, without even bothering to drink anything, swallowed them.

It was time to make his morning rounds of the camp. He thought to himself how unwise if would be for anyone to *not* be manning their post this morning. He just wasn't in the fucking mood for that.

CHAPTER TWENTY-FOUR

We Didn't Start the Fire

There was no time to waste now. He wanted to get into town as quickly as he could. He thought about it for a moment and realized it would be safer to wait until the evening when he could better avoid being seen, but he was too impatient. He would just need to be careful.

With protein bars in hand, as well as a couple of warm diet colas, John set off in the Prius. The drive brought back memories of taking Brian to look for medical care.

"How long ago was that?" John wondered but he just didn't know. Time was passing by without notice and he couldn't tell if it had been days or weeks. He knew it had been too long but that was all.

Keeping the windows rolled down, John silently drove away from the cabin and toward town. He was listening for the sound of vehicles, as well as looking for any smoke.

The road was wet, but he didn't really notice or even care. He was looking constantly from right to left for any sign of life. His pistol was on the seat beside him with the rifle and shotgun in the back seat.

He drove first through Nehalem, a tiny town on the Nehalem River, and noted the small grocery store there. He turned onto Highway 101 and drove toward Manzanita. He had to stop once to allow a herd of elk to cross the road. They paid no attention to him, and he was surprised they had already adapted to the lack of humans in the area.

Turning off the highway he drove into Manzanita and tried to memorize the location of any store or business that might be of use to him in the future. Turning left on Manzanita Avenue, John headed toward the beach and parked a few blocks away. Putting his pistol in his coat pocket, John hung the hunting rifle over his shoulder, leaving the shotgun in the back seat. He started walking toward the beach, listening for any noises suggesting human life. He walked in the shadows as much as possible.

He passed between some motels, noting that, as expected, the beach was deserted but for seagulls and a couple of seals lolling on the sand. It was beautiful but overwhelmingly desolate.

The tide was about midway, either on the way out or in. He couldn't tell. The waves were large and he sat down on the soft sand, staring at the ocean and allowing his mind to drift. He found himself focusing on the sound of the crashing waves and the squawking of seagulls. He took his shoes off and dug his toes into the sand. It was warm, although the wind caused the air to be cool. John stood up and, brushing the sand off of his pants, started to walk south. He walked on the hard-packed sand nearer to the surf. It was nice as he measured his path against the incoming waves.

The memory came of him and Liz bringing Brian and Cassie to the beach when they were young. They would "chase" the waves out and then, in turn, be chased by the waves as they came back in. He could almost picture Cassie's hair flowing in the wind, turning into a tangled mess.

Looking onshore, he saw the hulking shapes of the beach motels. They looked dark and sad, more than foreboding. There were a few cars in the parking lots but, even from a distance, he could see the dried salt spray covering them.

As John walked along the beach, he focused on the seagulls flying all around. There seemed to be more than he remembered and wondered if the absence of humans allowed them to thrive. To his left, the beach motels gave way to houses of all different sizes and shapes. John stopped and picked up a handful of stones and began skimming them across the top of the water. It was relaxing to try to toss the stone to hit the crest of the front wave before skipping out to sea. For a moment, he could almost forget where he was and what was happening.

John was enjoying himself so much that he almost didn't hear the sound. A part of him finally seemed to register a new noise, something other than the waves and the birds. This was more of a constant drone that John eventually recognized as the sound of engines.

Running up from the beach and through the tall grass, John hid behind the closest house and peeked around the corner. The sound kept getting louder and John could tell they were trucks of some sort. Finally, the first one came into view between the houses. It was a military Humvee of some sort with four people, all wearing yellow hazmat suits. They had the helmets off and the suits were unzipped. John could see their military uniforms underneath.

The next vehicle was a larger truck with a tarp over the back. John saw three people in the cab, with others in the back, but couldn't determine their exact number.

The trucks continued down the street and shut their engines off somewhere in the distance. He figured they must have parked down by the motels. John wondered if they were looking for survivors like him and whether, if they discovered him, he would be able to convince them to let him stay here. He suspected they wouldn't.

John considered his options. He couldn't make it back to the Prius because he would have to walk right by the soldiers. He might be able to hide in one of the houses until they left and then go back. That seemed like the best idea when he heard a loud voice saying:

"HELLO. I AM SERGEANT JEFFERSON POLITS OF THE UNITED STATES ARMY. WE HAVE ESTABLISHED A SAFE HAVEN IN PORTLAND WHERE WE CAN PROVIDE FOOD AND MEDICAL CARE. IT IS SAFE AND WE HAVE A LARGE NUMBER OF PEOPLE WAITING TO GREET YOU. THERE MIGHT EVEN BE FAMILY AND FRIENDS OF YOURS THERE. IF YOU CAN HEAR ME, COME OUT TO THE STREET AND WE WILL HELP YOU TO SAFETY."

John froze. He reached into his pocket and gripped the handgun.

"Crap," he thought. "I can't outshoot these guys. They're soldiers. If I come out, they're going to take me away. Shit, if they *find* me, they're going to take me away."

Even hiding behind the houses, he was too exposed. There was no point in running back down to the beach and the sea grass wasn't high enough to hide in. No, his only chance was to hide in a house and hope they wouldn't look too carefully. The house right in front of him looked as good as any. It was a two-story older home, with a wooden deck in back. If he could find a closet or cabinet or something to hide in, he could just wait out the soldiers.

Quietly scrambling up to the deck, John tried to open the back door, but it was locked, as he knew it would be. Taking off his coat, John wrapped it around the handgun and broke one of the windowpanes in the door. While it was loud, he could only hope that the waves and the seagulls drowned out the noise.

Reaching in and unlocking the deadbolt and door lock, John opened the door and slipped in, closing it behind him. The kitchen was tidy and, in the sunlight streaming in through the windows, he saw dust swirling in the air. Outside, he heard a crash that sounded as if it was coming from one of the houses down the street. He heard yelling but couldn't make out what was being said. Standing still, he heard another crash, this one closer, and again voices which seemed to be shouting something.

John crept through the kitchen out to the hallway and found the stairs. Climbing up, he knew he had to make a decision quickly. There were two doors to the right and one to the left. Guessing the door to the left led to the master bedroom, John decided the larger room would likely be better to hide in.

As he turned to his left, John jumped a little at the sound of another crash, this one seeming to almost be next door. Opening the bedroom door and walking in, John closed the door behind him. Immediately he knew he'd made a mistake—the odor was obvious but not as strong as it had been at Ray's. Looking around, he saw a queen-sized bed with a large lump on it. It was clearly a body and the flies confirmed it.

The room spanned the width of the house and John could see windows facing both the front of the house and the back. He first went to the front window and looked around. He could hear the soldiers but couldn't see them. He then walked to the back window and looked out over the deck and toward the ocean. This window was broken, with a large hole in one of the panes of glass. Sticking his face as close to the hole as possible, he took a deep inhale of the sea air to clear out the stench accosting his nostrils.

Taking a deep breath and holding his nose, John turned around and surveyed the room further. The bed was along the side wall. There was enough space under the bed to allow him to crawl there. The problem was the uncertainty as to whether the smell might be worse there and whether the flies would come after him.

On the wall across from the bed, John saw a door slightly ajar.

He walked over to it and just as he grabbed the handle, he heard a loud crash. This time it was coming from downstairs as the front door was kicked in. Without any hesitation, John slipped into the closet and closed the door behind him.

"HELLO! Is there anyone here?"

John stayed silent.

"I'm with the US Army and we are looking for survivors. Is there anyone here?"

John waited silently for his eyes to adjust to the darkness. Unfortunately, there was absolutely no light in the confined quarters of the closet. He lowered himself onto his knees and felt along the wall. He could hear someone tromping around downstairs, but he also heard a softer sound. It was almost like a fluttering noise and much closer.

Suddenly, he heard footsteps coming up the stairs and John crawled toward what he assumed was the back of the closet. There was the sound of one door opening and a little more fluttering. He heard another noise and this time the fluttering was a little louder. No, actually it wasn't louder, but it seemed to be more pronounced, and it was very close. His skin seemed to be crawling but he wasn't sure from what.

The footsteps were approaching and John heard the door to the master bedroom open.

"JESUS CHRIST! I'm so fucking sick of this shit!"

The fluttering got louder. John reached up to grab whatever was hanging above him and as he did, a hanger fell to the floor. In those tight quarters, the noise was loud. Outside of the closet, the hanger falling wasn't loud, but it was noticeable.

"Hello? Is someone in the closet?"

John could hear the soldier walking toward the door and then rap loudly on the door. Cringing on the floor, John grabbed whatever clothes he could to hide himself. At this point, there was no point in trying to be quiet, all he could do was try to hide. As he did so, the fluttering became loud, both within the closet and outside of it. Furthermore, it was not just the fluttering. There were things moving all around John and they were bumping into walls and, more disturbingly, into him. Fighting the urge to scream and flee, John bit down on the side of his cheek. He could feel the coppery taste of blood in his mouth and tried to focus on that rather than the maelstrom unfolding around him.

"IF SOMEONE IS IN THERE, COME OUT NOW! I'M NOT FUCKING AROUND!"

John forced himself into as tight a ball as he could. The noise was everywhere and seemed, at least to John, to be deafening. He could hear the door being flung open violently and could also sense the fluttering of wings exiting through it.

"FU-U-U-C-K-K!" the soldier screamed. This was followed by gunshots. There had to have been at least a half dozen and John's ears were ringing. He felt the impact of a bullet hitting the floor next to his feet and another strike the wall just above his head.

More gunshots but this time they seemed to be going in another direction, almost as if they were being sprayed around the room.

"JONES!" This was a voice from downstairs. The shooting stopped. "JONES! WHAT THE FUCK IS GOING ON?"

John could hear another set of footsteps on the stairs. They were moving fast and getting closer.

"JONES! REPORT!"

Then there was another voice, this one just outside of the still open closet door. "It's okay, Sarge." The voice seemed to tremble and had a high pitch.

While John's ears were still ringing, he could hear the second pair of footsteps enter the master bedroom. "What the fuck happened? Who were you shooting at?"

"I'm sorry, Sarge. I heard something coming from the closet. When I opened the door, a shitload of bats flew out and it startled me. I guess the gun just went off."

"You *guess* your gun just went off?" the first voice asked. The anger in the voice was palpable. "How fucking stupid are you,

Private? The walls in these houses are paper thin and you could have easily hit one of us. Haven't you ever seen a bat before?"

"Yes, Sir, but they just startled me and there were a lot of them. I wasn't expecting them and they started flying all around the room before going out the window."

There was a pause and John could only wonder if either of the soldiers would decide to take another look inside the closet now that the bats were gone.

"Alright, let's wrap this up. Did you check the rest of the house?"

"Yes, Sir"

"Okay, burn this fucker down and let's get out of here. I want to get back to camp before it gets too dark. We've got five people already and that should be enough for this shithole of a town."

John listened as the two sets of footsteps walked out of the master bedroom. Through the walls, he heard one of the soldiers, presumably Sarge, mutter, "What a fucking moron, firing your gun all around like that. Jesus, I hate this fucking smell and all these fucking flies."

As the footsteps descended the stairs, John wondered what the one soldier meant when he said to "burn this fucker down." He could hear them outside and started to uncoil his body. His knees were stiff and his legs were tingly from being bunched up so long. Slowly standing up, John stretched his legs and then stealthily snuck out of the closet. He peeked outside the front window and saw a couple of soldiers talking.

"That must be Sarge and Jones," he thought.

They were talking but John couldn't make out what they were saying. It didn't look like Sarge was through berating Jones. He then saw Sarge walk away and Jones move over to a small pile of what looked like gas cans.

Another three men, all in hazmat suits, walked by Jones and seemed to say something. Even with their helmets on, it appeared that they were laughing at the poor guy. The only thing John could make out was "We'll show you how to do it."

The soldiers walked in front of John's window and down the street. Two of them were carrying gasoline cans. Looking back at Jones, John saw him looking in the direction of the other soldiers. John heard a crash and assumed they had kicked in the door of the house next door.

John craned his neck and could barely see the soldiers gather in front of the neighboring house. One of them held what looked like a road flare. He lit it with a cigarette lighter and then tossed it in the direction of the house. Immediately John heard a large "whoosh" and then an explosion. While he couldn't see the house, he could see the light glowing from a large fire.

"Shit, they really are burning houses," John thought. "I've got to get out of here."

John looked back at the soldier he identified as Jones and he was walking to the front of John's house with a gas can in each hand.

CHAPTER TWENTY-FIVE

Jumpin' Jack Flash

John stood in the middle of the room, frozen by indecision. It sounded like Jones was pouring something, presumably gasoline, on the floor downstairs. John didn't want to go with the soldiers; he wanted to go back to the cabin. That was his home now. His mind racing, John tried to play out his options. He could go with the soldiers or...what? The soldiers were not going to just let him go.

As much as he wanted to go home, he finally came to the realization it really wasn't an option. He couldn't go home and he couldn't stay there. The noise downstairs stopped momentarily, and John knew Jones was getting ready to light the gasoline. If he did, John would die. It wasn't the dying that bothered him; he could handle that. It was how he would die. John could only imagine how painful it would be to burn to death.

Running over to the bedroom door, John opened it and called out "WAIT!" Just as that word came out of his mouth, he heard a whoosh and felt a strong wave of heat come up the stairs and hit him in the face. He staggered back into the bedroom. The fire was not just hot, it was loud. He could almost feel it starting to devour the house. John slammed the bedroom door shut and threw some clothes down along the bottom of the door in hopes of keeping smoke from coming in.

He was now in full panic mode. Running first to the front window, John hoped to be able to call out to the soldiers, but they were nowhere in sight. Apparently, they had no interest in watching their handiwork. Quickly turning around, John ran to the window in the back of the house. The window had been shattered although he didn't know, or care, if it was from the bats, the bullets, or some combination of the two.

Sticking his head out the window, he first took a deep breath of the cool ocean air. It seemed to momentarily calm him until he looked down and saw how far below him the deck was. While he was only on the second floor, it would be at least a fifteen-foot drop and it looked like a lot more. Even if he survived the jump, John suspected he would end up with one or both ankles or legs broken. And unless the soldiers somehow saved him, he would die a miserable death from exposure.

The room was getting warm and when he looked back at the bedroom door, the doorknob seemed to be glowing. Tendrils of smoke snaked their way through the clothes piled at the bottom. There was little time to figure out what to do.

Running over to the bed, he grabbed a blanket off the top. As he did two things happened. First, the flies rose like a wave and filled the air. Second, the body started to move as the blanket was partially tucked underneath it. It rolled and toppled off the bed and hit the floor with a sickening thud. It was a woman, a large woman with blue, waxy skin. The body was bloated and as she hit the floor, she seemed to burst with internal organs flowing out of her.

John wanted to retch but couldn't allow himself that luxury. Freeing the blanket, John grabbed a bed sheet and tied them together. He bent down, holding his breath and, trying not to look at the oozing corpse, tied one end to the bedpost and gave it a tug. The bed did not move. He threw the other end of his makeshift rope out the window and saw that it only reached about eight feet down. It was still too far of a drop for him so he quickly looked around for anything else he could use.

Finally, he took off his jacket and tied one arm to the line and tossed it out the window. There would still be a small drop, assuming that the line would hold his weight, but it was at least possible. What he couldn't do was to hold on to his handgun. He tossed it out the window, making sure that it landed beyond the deck and in the sand.

Carefully, John put one leg out the window, holding tightly to the line. There was a small ledge just beneath the window and he was able to rest the toe of his shoe on it. Looking back at the bedroom door, the doorknob was now glowing a bright red. Even more disconcerting was how the door seemed to be bowing inward. Resting his weight on the ledge, John pulled his makeshift line tight and slowly eased his other foot onto the ledge. The line was taut and John gripped it as hard as he could. Slowly he started to walk his hands down the line, lifting one foot off the ledge and then the other.

John hung on the line, hoping it would hold him. Slowly he held on with one hand while moving the other a few inches below, all the time gripping as hard as he could and trying not to notice how the muscles in his arms were quivering. He wrapped his legs around the line and tried to dig the edges of his feet into it.

Despite his circumstances, John had a flashback to his grade school gym class when everyone had to climb a rope hanging from the ceiling. John was never able to climb more than five or six feet up the rope. This had been a constant source of belittlement by the gym teacher. John managed a dry chuckle at a memory he hadn't thought of for years, if not decades. "Fuck you, Mr. Duane!" he said to his long-gone gym teacher.

Refusing to look down, John shifted his gaze between straight ahead and looking up at the window now a couple of feet above his head. He heard a crash and assumed the bedroom door had finally given in to the force of the fire. Instinctively John knew he was running out of time. With the fire now in the bedroom, it would only be moments before the blanket and sheet burned through.

Picking up his pace, John felt his feet touch glass. This must be another window, one in line with the bedroom window he had just climbed out of. Releasing his right leg from the rope line, he pushed against the house, right beside the downstairs window. He didn't want to break the glass. Slowly and incrementally, John continued his descent. Now his waist was about even with the top of the downstairs window and he was coming up to the end of his line. The heat emanating from the window was strong and John decided to jump just as it suddenly blew out.

A blast of superheated air and shards of glass crashed into him. John was blown back and lost his grip. He landed on the deck on his right foot, as his left foot was still extended in the air. His body was twisting and he felt a sharp pain in his right ankle as he continued to spin. Tucking his head and shoulder, he rolled and his momentum carried him off the deck and onto the soft sand.

Looking up, John could see that the sky was starting to get dark but the area around was still lit and shimmering. The light from the fire was bright but, fortunately, the heat was flowing above him as the deck shielded him. John tried to slow his breath.

He then began a physical inventory. John first moved his head and arms and found both moved easily and without pain. He then moved his legs and felt an immediate stabbing pain in his right ankle. Gingerly he moved it in circles and was satisfied that it was not broken. As he began to sit up, John felt a sudden and searing pain in both thighs. In the light from the fire, John could see that his pants were shredded, and his legs were a bloody mess.

There were shards of glass, big and small, sticking out of them. The glass wasn't what hurt, it was the blisters he saw starting to form.

Suddenly a burst of uncontrollable shivering overcame him. Over and above the pain from his thighs and ankle, John could feel the cold blowing from the ocean. It wasn't this cold, however, causing him to shiver. It was a combination of the pain of his injuries and the relief from knowing he escaped. Adjusting his position, John sat up with his back against the edge of the deck. In that position, he could feel the cool wind from the ocean blowing over his face and legs. The burning house warmed his back.

Eventually the heat from the house became too much and John slowly stood up. It was difficult, as he couldn't put any weight on his right leg. There was a tree branch nearby, one someone had once turned into a walking stick. Using the stick to prop himself up, John looked around and found his pistol.

Placing the pistol in the back of his jeans, John stumbled around to the side of the house. He needed to be close to the house for warmth, but not too close. The houses to his right and left were all aflame, and the ones to his right were already starting to burn out. Looking across the street, he saw those houses were also on fire. He looked and listened for the soldiers but there was nothing and no one to see or hear.

John started walking along the beachside of the burning houses. Depending upon how close he could stay to them, they would provide enough warmth at least for a while. The only sound he could hear was windows breaking and walls and floors collapsing. He moved slowly behind the protection of the burning houses but tried to hurry across the gaps between them. He did not want to be seen, not at this point. Having made it out of the house, he had no desire to end up with the military now.

After four houses, John peeked out and saw the army trucks parked with the hazmat-suited soldiers milling around. The group by the larger truck appeared be drinking beer and laughing.

He couldn't hear them but just watched as he saw the one soldier, the one John had previously identified as Sarge, walk over to them. The soldiers took a final drink of their beers and tossed them aside before climbing into the truck. Sarge then walked back to the jeep and both vehicles drove away.

John ducked down and slowly advanced toward the street to watch the truck and the Humvee disappear. The houses on both sides of the street were in various stages of destruction but the fires were slowly dying out. John could no longer rely upon the heat from the fires to keep him warm. He needed to get to the Prius as quickly as possible. Only then would he be able to focus on what to do to his ankle and legs.

ॐ

CHAPTER TWENTY-SIX

MAMA HE'S CRAZY

Walking was difficult. With every other step, the pain from his ankle overwhelmed the pain from the glass slivers but still he felt them. It was also getting cold and John had no coat. Once he passed the burning houses, he knew it was still a mile or so before he would be back to the Prius. He wasn't sure if he could make it. Moving as slowly as he was, the cold was likely to get him first as the shivering was getting painful. While he needed to rest his ankle and treat the burns, the first priority had to be a coat of some sort. With everything happening, he didn't realize how thirsty he was.

Across from one of the beach motels, John saw a small house among some stores and decided to make it his first stop. He gave only brief thought as to why this house had escaped the soldiers' fire. Making no pretense of propriety, John used the walking stick to smash the sliding glass door in the back of the house. The noise was loud, but he didn't care.

John was shivering violently as he stepped across the threshold, picking his way through the broken glass. His sense of smell was dulled by all of the smoke. He tried to get a whiff of any rotting flesh, but he couldn't smell anything. If there was a corpse in this house, he'd just have to deal with it.

The house was dark and cold but, by feeling around, John determined he was in a kitchen. He found the refrigerator and fumbled through it, tossing things to the ground until his hands found what felt like a beer bottle. He twisted the top off and guzzled the beer as quickly as he had when he had been in college. It slaked his thirst—at least momentarily. Rummaging through the refrigerator, he felt a plastic bottle. Opening it, he took a sip and confirmed that it was water. He slowly poured the water over his thighs. The water was cold and he let out a loud grunt in spite of himself. After the initial shock, the pain subsided just a little.

John reached back into the refrigerator and found two more beer bottles. With the bottles in his hands, John looked around. He had been able to operate so far on pure adrenalin, but he knew an energy crash would be coming soon. He could feel fatigue rumbling in the distance like a freight train making its way back home. It was approaching and John realized he needed to get to the Prius and home before it all came crashing down.

Moving out of the dark kitchen, John felt along the wall, looking for a door. Sometimes kitchens had coat closets. He was still shivering and the beer bottles rattled in his hands. He didn't find a door, but he did find an opening. With one hand on the wall, he slowly followed the wall into the blackness.

"Bobby?"

John stopped dead in his tracks. The sound was faint and the voice raspy. John wondered if he had really heard someone or if it had just been the wind.

"Bobby, is that you?"

It was definitely a voice, like an old woman's voice, and it was coming from somewhere in front of him. Taking a breath to calm his nerves, John stared into the darkness and said quietly, "Yeah, it's me." He kept his voice soft and low.

"Oh good, I was worried." This *was* a woman and her breath was labored. John could tell she was struggling to even say that much.

"Bobby, I don't feel so good."

"I know," John responded. "This flu bug is a bad one." He could only hope, by keeping his voice soft, that she wouldn't recognize he wasn't Bobby. John didn't know why he was engaging with her, but he was.

"Bobby, can you get me some water? Your mom is so thirsty."

"Sorry, Mom, we're out of water. I've got a beer. Will that help?"

There was silence for a moment, as if the woman was trying to work up the strength to respond. John got down on his hands and knees and started crawling toward where the voice had been. His legs hurt but he figured he didn't dare risk walking into a coffee table in the darkness.

As he crawled, he began to make out shapes in the dark. In front of him was a large shape, which he assumed was the couch where the woman was laying.

"Mom, put out your hand."

As he said that, John opened one of the bottles of beer. In the darkness, he could see some motion and stretched his hand to it. The woman's hands touched his and they were hot and moist. One hand clenched his wrist tightly at first and then softened. John fought back an instinctual flinch.

"Can you hold the bottle yourself?" John asked softly.

The only response was "ugh ugh."

John crept a little closer and felt into the darkness. He felt the top of the woman's head; the hair was damp and coarse. Gradually easing himself alongside the woman, he held her head in one hand and slowly moved the bottleneck toward her mouth. He lifted the bottle up as he heard, rather than saw, the woman suck in, trying to drink the beer. It was impossible to tell how much beer was going in her mouth and how much on her clothes, but John figured it didn't really matter at this point.

Her breathing was mixed with slurping and she coughed and John felt spittle spray on his arm.

"Mom, where do we keep the flashlight?"

The woman slumped and John pulled the bottle away and set it on the floor. Her breathing softened.

"Mom? The flashlight?" John repeated softly.

"Aaarggghhh. Closssss."

The breathing started to calm, and John sensed the woman losing consciousness. Her head became heavy and slumped in his hand. Gently he placed her head down on the cushion. Resting back on his heels, John tried to make some sense of her final statement. Might it have been front closet? If so, that would make sense. The problem, of course, was that he had no idea where the front closet was.

Slowly turning himself around, John sat on the floor with the woman behind him. He could still hear her breathing, but it was becoming increasingly labored and intermittent. John tried to form a mental picture of the house's layout.

He had come in the back door and into the kitchen. After getting the beers, he had turned around and headed to his right, away from the kitchen into what was presumably the living room. The house hadn't looked very big from outside so he assumed that it couldn't have more than three or so rooms on the main floor.

He looked to his right and wondered if that would be the front of the house. But if it was, why couldn't he at least see some ambient light coming in? If it were the front of the house, he would expect a door and a window and at least some light from outside. There was nothing.

Perhaps, he wondered, there might be another room there. The only thing to do was to start crawling directly away from the woman until he found a wall. He would then follow the wall until he found a door.

While the house was warmer than outside, the air coming in from the broken sliding door was quickly starting to chill him again. The fatigue train was roaring down the tracks, much closer than just a few minutes ago. He was so tired and just wanted to sleep but knew that if he did, he would never wake up.

John didn't have to crawl far before feeling the wall. He started following it to the right, toward what he hoped would be the front of the house. He came across what felt like a chair and rather than going around it, John pushed it out of the way. He didn't dare lose contact with the wall.

He felt something. It was a protrusion from the wall that he recognized as the casement around a door. Getting up on his knees, John started feeling around until he found the doorknob. He stood up and opened the door. He figured if he felt fresh air, it was the front door. If it was anything else, it would either be a closet or bathroom door.

Feeling no rush of cold air, John carefully reached his hand in and slowly waved it from side to side. He didn't get far before feeling cloth, presumably coats. It *was* a closet. This would at least provide him with something to wear but first he needed to find a flashlight. Kneeling down, John felt along the floor. There were shoes, a vacuum cleaner, and what felt like an umbrella. Standing back up and ignoring the shooting pains in his thighs and ankle, John reached up and found a shelf above the coats and that was where he found it.

It was a cold metallic tube and John fumbled to turn it on. The brightness hurt his eyes and he quickly shut it off. Pointing the flashlight down toward the ground and keeping his eyes shut, John turned the flashlight back on. He could see light through his eyelids and slowly opened them. It was a closet with a number of coats. As his eyes adjusted to the light, John found a heavy woolen coat and slipped it on. It was a couple of sizes too large but that didn't matter, it was warm. There was a simple cane leaning against the wall and he took that also.

He also grabbed a Seattle Seahawks stocking cap from a hook and put that on. With at least some warmth, John turned the flashlight's beams on his legs. They were worse than he feared. There was blistering but he could also see the glint of glass sticking out of the skin. "Those are going to be a bitch to get out," he mumbled to himself.

Turning to lumber out of the closet, John staggered, overcome by another rush of fatigue. For a moment he considered just drinking the last beer and falling asleep on the floor of the closet. If he was going to die, and that was a distinct possibility if not a likelihood, he wanted to die by his family. He needed to get back to the cabin.

He eased out of the closet.

Keeping the flashlight pointed low and in front of him, John started toward the front door. He made the decision not to look at the woman on the couch. There was nothing else he could do for her and could only hope he had brought her a measure of peace in her final moments. As far as she knew, her son was home, safe and sound, with her. That had to be good for something.

Ahead of him, John saw why there had been no light coming in from the front of the house. The door was, in fact, solid wood and there were heavy curtains across what was presumably the window. John hobbled to the door, opened it and walked out. The wind had picked up and it was starting to rain.

With his flashlight as a guide, John headed back in the direction of the Prius. He counted his steps to try to distract his mind from the pain in his legs, as well as the post-adrenaline crash rapidly approaching.

"One...Two...Three...Four... One...Two...Three...Four..." he whispered. Over and over again he focused on placing one foot in front of the other and repeating the count. John only looked up to confirm he was on the right street. With every step, the glass splinters stabbed him over and over again. The cane helped but only with his ankle.

In normal times, there would be streetlamps to light his way and show him where the Prius was. Now he just had to rely upon his memory and the flashlight. "One…Two…Three…Four… One… Two…Three…Four…" John almost stumbled into the Prius. He was so tired and so focused on the count that he'd stopped himself a mere foot from the car. Throwing the cane on to the passenger seat, he climbed in the Prius and said a silent prayer as he pushed the ignition button. The lights on the dashboard lit up. He turned on the heat, put the car into gear, and slowly drove through the dark night.

It was only ten miles to the cabin. "One…Two…Three…Four… One…Two… Three…Four…" He really just wanted to sleep. "One…Two…Three…Four… One…Two… Three…Four…"

CHAPTER TWENTY-SEVEN

Raindrops Keep Falling on my Head

The drive back to the cabin seemed to take forever. The cuts on his legs kept bleeding with every bump and turn of the car. The pain kept him at least minimally alert and awake. His pants were wet, and blood was starting to pool around the seat. Without stopping to inspect his wounds, John wondered whether he might just bleed out. He returned his focus to getting back to the cabin.

Pulling into the driveway, John saw a large animal start to move slowly toward the cabin. Even in the dim light from the moon, he could see it was an elk. It didn't appear to be afraid of the Prius and as John came to a stop, the elk continued its slow saunter into the woods.

With flashlight in hand and fighting fatigue every step, John walked into the cabin, the pain in his ankle almost, but not quite, forgotten. The first thing to do was to light a fire. Despite the pain, he didn't want to continue shivering all night. Thankfully, he had enough firewood beside the fireplace and the fire started quickly.

He limped into the kitchen and found the first aid kit. There was ointment and gauze but first he needed to dig out as many glass shards as he could. Being back in the cabin and with a purpose gave him a burst of energy. Pouring himself a stiff drink of Irish whisky, John held the tweezers and slowly started the process of removing the glass. It hurt and, a couple of times, John thought he might pass out.

After about thirty minutes, John knew it was time to quit. His hands were shaking too much to grab the smaller pieces of glass. He dabbed antiseptic cream on the holes where he removed glass. He found some burn gel and started slathering it on his thighs. He went through two packs and realized there was no more.

"Damn it!"

John had an idea and uneasily stood up and walked back into the kitchen. Using the flashlight to search through the pantry, he found a container of honey. Years before when the children were still young, Cassie burned her arm on a charcoal grill. Before sending John off to the pharmacy, Liz poured cold water over the burn and then applied honey. She explained to him at the time how honey was a natural antiseptic and would help with the healing.

Pouring the honey on his burns, John used his fingers to spread it out. It was sticky and messy and, when done, he stuck his fingers into his mouth and sucked the honey off. He knew he hadn't eaten anything since the morning, but he wasn't hungry. The sweetness of the honey, however, gave him just enough additional energy to wrap his legs with gauze.

He lay down on the couch and tried to mumble a goodnight to his family but was asleep before the words could come out.

ଏ

He awoke to the sound of raindrops striking the window. He was huddled into his woolen jacket from the night before and his blanket. It was cold and the fire was mostly burned out. He pushed himself up and screamed from the pain in his legs.

Easing the blanket off his legs, he saw the blisters and blood. The remaining glass shards had drawn new blood just by him sitting up. Gingerly, he stood and worked to get the fireplace burning again. Then he walked into the kitchen and drank two bottles of water. John noticed a can of Sprite sitting on the counter and downed that. The sugar and carbonation were bracing and gave him a sufficient jolt to clear the remaining cobwebs.

In the morning light, John saw that the first aid kit was clearly not sufficient for his burns. He could only hope that Good Neighbor Ray might have more supplies. Clutching the coat around himself, John walked out the door and over to Ray's. His ankle hurt but he knew it wasn't broken so it wouldn't stop him. He had to treat his thighs before infection set in.

While the walk over to Ray's house was short, it was painful. His breathing was ragged, and his teeth were clenched. The cool morning air and rain felt good on his legs.

John didn't bother to turn on the generator. There was enough light between the morning sun and his flashlight to complete his search for a first aid kit. He found it quickly, but it was sorely lacking. There was a bottle of Bactine First Aid Liquid, an old container of Neosporin ointment, and tweezers. This wasn't going to be enough, but it was a start and would at least allow him to remove the remaining glass.

Back in the cabin, he lit a match and burned the ends of the tweezers to disinfect them. He took a towel, rolled it up and placed it between his teeth. Moving slowly, he carefully squeezed a glass shard with the tweezers and ripped it out. Each time he did, he bit down on the towel and screamed. John had no idea how long he worked on his legs, consistently pouring water over them to wash away the blood. Finally, they were too bloody and swollen to find any other shards. He poured the rest of the water over his thighs to wash away the blood before pouring the Bactine over them. It stung but he just kept on biting the towel.

Once the liquid was mostly absorbed or evaporated, John applied the remaining Neosporin on the worst-looking wounds and wrapped his legs in gauze. Taking a large swig of water, he lay back on the couch and closed his eyes.

As best he could tell, it was afternoon when he awoke. His legs felt even more painful than that morning. The gauze was soaked with blood, so he unwrapped it and reapplied new gauze with barely enough to complete the job.

There was no doubt that resting was not an option. He had to go back into town and get more medical supplies. Walking slowly to the Prius, he started the long, slow drive back to Manzanita. The pain was causing him to sweat and he barely acknowledged a family of deer he passed on the way.

Driving first through Nehalem, John spotted Hal's Emporium and stopped in front. Without even worrying about noise or propriety, he hurled a rock through the front door and walked in. Hal's was basically a small general store and he was able to find gauze and several boxes of Neosporin. There were also antiseptic wipes and a few containers of burn dressings with lidocaine. John grabbed a bag and threw everything in. As he headed back to the door, he grabbed a bottle of Sprite and a handful of candy bars.

Sitting in the driver's seat with his legs out the door, John pulled the bloody gauze off his legs and applied the burn dressings. The gel on the dressings was cool and seemed to ease the pain a bit. Tossing the used gauze and packaging on the road, he wrapped his legs in fresh gauze and pulled his legs back into the car.

Nehalem was too small to have a full pharmacy, so John headed for Manzanita. Between the Sprite and the candy, the drive went by quickly. His eyes were constantly scanning for a pharmacy.

Eventually he might need to head up to the hospital, but John wasn't sure he had the stamina for that yet.

Driving past dark and empty streets, John saw restaurants and pubs, small stores that catered to tourists, and more than a few marijuana outlets. None of these were going to provide the medical supplies he so desperately needed. He was also on the lookout for the soldiers and realized he was exposed. John tried to think whether there might be any pharmacies in the towns to the south. Tillamook was in that direction, but he had no idea how far away it was and he would have to travel on Highway 101, which would likely be the road that the soldiers were using. He remembered some smaller communities along the way but had no idea if any of them would have a pharmacy.

Finally coming to the conclusion his need for medical supplies outweighed the risk of detection, John decided to take his chances with the smaller communities to the south. He headed back through Nehalem and continued the winding road south.

John passed the Nehalem Food Mart. He decided to stop there on his way back to see if there was any food to scavenge. He also saw a veterinary clinic and briefly considered stopping there. Ultimately, he decided not to because he didn't know whether they would have anything helpful for the pain and, even if they did, he wasn't sure whether he would be able to determine the proper dosages.

Driving quickly on the straight portions of the road, he would always slow down around the corners. This allowed him to avoid the multiple abandoned and crashed cars and trucks blocking the road. A highway sign announced the next town as Wheeler and, as he drove, he saw a sign for "Hospital Road." Slamming on the brakes, John turned down this road. He wondered how it was he didn't know about a hospital to the south of Manzanita. He considered briefly whether there might be someone there and, if there was, whether they could have helped Brian.

Hospital Road turned into First Street and wound around until it became Second Street. As he came around a bend, he saw a sign for Rinehart Pharmacy. He continued past it and pulled into the parking lot. Right behind the pharmacy was the Nehalem Valley Care Center. This was the hospital. The building was dark and most of the windows were broken. There would be no one there to help him now and likely no one who could have helped Brian before.

While the hospital might have necessary supplies, John realized it would be easier to search a pharmacy than the larger facility. He drove up to the front door, which was intact and locked. Rather than throwing a rock, John slowly nosed the front end of the car through the glass doors. There was only a small jolt to the vehicle, but the noise of the crashing glass was jarring.

Backing the Prius out of the doorway, John eased himself out of the car and walked in. The front of the pharmacy had various items holding little interest for him. He found a section for burns and filled a large shopping bag with every type of burn cream, ointment, and bandage he could find.

John grabbed another bag and filled it with gauze, four different types of ankle braces, toothpaste, and a couple of bottles of mouthwash. He then walked behind the pharmacy counter and started to look at the various bottles and containers there. He hoped to find two things. First of all, he wanted an antibiotic like penicillin in case any infection might be starting in his legs. Secondly, he wanted a pain killer. He was well past the point of wanting aspirin or Tylenol. He wanted to find something that would knock him out while his body healed. The problem was he didn't know where to look.

Along the back wall, he saw shelves full of bottles. These were prescriptions waiting to be picked up. John walked over to them and started reading the various bottles. Those he didn't recognize or which didn't interest him were thrown on the floor. Ultimately, he was successful in finding bottles of amoxicillin and doxycycline. He also found varying doses of both Vicodin and oxycodone and threw them all in a bag.

After putting the bags in the Prius, John went back and grabbed as many bottles of water and juice as he could. Leaning against the car with a light rain coming down, he downed three tablets of amoxicillin. He wanted to also take the Vicodin but decided to wait until he was back at the cabin. With one last trip into the pharmacy, John loaded a bag with all of the protein and candy bars he could find. Now was not the time to worry about his diet. John just wanted to rest and recuperate without having to worry about hunger.

With a sense of accomplishment, John headed back to the cabin. Driving through Nehalem, he decided to stop at Hal's Emporium once more. He needed clothes and picked up a couple of t-shirts and sweatshirts. He also found a couple of bathing suits, which, he decided, would be more comfortable than pants.

Walking out of Hal's, he could see smoke rising up from the west. The soldiers were back and obviously continuing their search and destroy mission. John wondered how long it would be before they worked their way up into the hills and to the cabin. That was something to think about later. Right now, he needed to get back home and start the healing process.

As he pulled onto his street, John decided to head to Ray's rather than the cabin. It would be easier to regulate the heat by using the generator rather than having to keep feeding the fire. Then he realized that he couldn't use either Ray's generator or the cabin's fireplace. Whether through noise or smoke, he would be calling attention to himself and allow the soldiers to realize he was there. Nonetheless, he decided that Ray's house would be warmer at least during the day.

After his customary and cursory knock, John walked in through the front door and immediately went upstairs. Rather than use the master bedroom where the image of Ray's body would be forever seared in his mind, John went to the second bedroom and laid down on a twin bed. While he wanted to treat his legs, he needed sleep. Pulling the blankets off the other bed, John pulled his wool coat tight and quickly fell into a dreamless sleep.

ɞ

CHAPTER TWENTY-EIGHT

You've Lost that Loving Feeling

B oulden reminded himself that difficult times required difficult decisions. What bothered him was so many others didn't seem to understand that simple reality. He was able to keep most of the Class I and Class II residents busy and motivated, even if they weren't happy. Many of these people had been Type A personalities in the past and were looking for something to distract them from their grief. He held out at least some hope for a future, which was the carrot so many of them needed. Boulden would provide them with privileges including movies, games, and, to a limited extent, alcohol and marijuana. It was these residents who received the best housing and first selection of clothes brought in from scavenging trips.

The real problem was with the 'turds, as everyone was now calling them. They were unmotivated, slovenly, and unaffected by all but the most violent of encouragement. They were resistant to all forms of order and discipline. Boulden tried using rationing with alcohol and marijuana but the 'turds ignored this process. They would find their contraband while on patrol and cache them. Despite periodic sweeps, Boulden knew that the 'turds were stocking and using the camp's black market. They didn't need him for their vices, which only caused Boulden to become more frustrated with them.

While the 'turds were of limited use, they still had value. If they didn't, he would have banished them from the camp long ago. As it was, he already banned and banished people who proved to be too difficult to care for or who used too many resources. This included those with physical and mental disabilities, as well as those with any serious illnesses. This world was no place for the weak of heart, body or will.

Boulden's most recent strategy was proving to be more successful with the 'turds and even some of the other residents. He hand-selected a group of men who were known to have a violent streak. He bribed them with whatever they might want and, in exchange, made them responsible for maintaining order throughout the camp. The soldiers were too bound by honor and morality to do what sometimes needed to be done. By keeping his involvement with these goon squads a secret, Boulden could disclaim any knowledge of, and responsibility for, their brutality. These squads were small but incredibly effective at motivating the other 'turds to perform their duties, as well as keeping other residents from raising too many questions about Boulden's administration of the camp. Of course, he had to keep a close eye on them as he recognized they would turn on him if they suspected any vulnerability. This required him to perform a balancing act between bribery and vigilance.

Fortunately for him, he controlled the leaders of these squads with narcotics. First, Boulden had his soldiers locate and stockpile all opioids, especially heroin, as well as all syringes. He then seduced the leaders with some prostitutes and got them hooked on heroin. To the extent he could control the supply, he could control the leaders. He also had his close group of rabid and loyal soldiers who, when necessary, eliminated those members of the goon squad who became too troublesome.

Despite his efforts, there continued to be violent crime, mostly, but not exclusively, by the 'turds. In just the prior three months, they experienced three murders, five sexual assaults and countless fights.

He could live with the violence—the real problem was still with the population level. The camp remained at about three thousand residents but that was only through new residents being located and brought to it. He was troubled by the fact he could only send the squads so far away before they just didn't return at all.

Also bothersome was the fact that other camps continued falling off the grid. He was still able to maintain communications with camps in Florida, Tennessee, and Maine but lost contact with all other camps within the borders of what had been the United States. There was still a camp near Toronto, but they were in distress. Fort Bay was one of the camps that had gone dark.

There were occasional communications with foreign camps. With the use of a translator, Boulden was able to communicate with a camp somewhere in what had been Argentina, as well as a camp in Brazil. Other foreign camps attempted to communicate in a language Boulden recognized as Asian, but he had no idea whether it was Chinese or Vietnamese or something else. He didn't have any translators who could help him, so he ignored them.

Assuming the other North American camps were similar in size to Camp Oregon, Boulden figured that the entire continent was likely comprised of less than fifteen thousand people in organized communities. Certainly, there might be survivors outside of the camps, but he doubted there could be more than another twenty thousand people at most.

This meant that on the entire continent, a continent that once housed almost six hundred million people, there were thirty-five thousand people. The sheer numbers boggled his mind and he had visions of corpses being eaten as carrion by all sorts of creatures. From time to time, Boulden wondered if he should just give up and walk out of there. Getting away from all the burdens of running the camp would be simple. There would still be enough food and water in Eastern Oregon but, deep down, he knew he could not do that. Even if he could somehow survive the Curse, he recognized that the crushing loneliness would strain the remaining shreds of his sanity.

No, he needed to stay. Here he had at least a measure of control. Here he had at least a semblance of companionship and never had to look far to find a woman willing to exchange sex for favors. He was responsible for ensuring the survival of the human race. He would be responsible for repopulating the world, just as soon as the virus burned itself out or Dr. Mo finally came up with a cure.

Just ruminating about all of his responsibilities, Boulden started to get angry. He had provided that fucking doctor with everything she asked for and still there were no results. If she weren't one of the few medical providers left, he would have broken her little dyke neck by now. In the past, he welcomed seeing the fear in her eyes whenever she was summoned to his office. Now, however, he started seeing something more akin to disdain. Maybe it was fatigue or maybe it was just complete insolence. He might just have to beat the fear back into her.

Without even being aware of it, Boulden was now pacing around his office with his fists clenched and his teeth grinding.

"That fucking bitch!" he snarled.

⁖

Dr. Mo was worried. She never expected to achieve any real progress and, in fact, had long ago given up any hope for a cure or vaccine. She had finally given up the inhumane testing, as it served no conceivable benefit. Now she was playing medical games by injecting new test subjects with placebos and even placing them in chemically-induced comas to give the appearance that she was continuing the testing.

She knew, however, that she had to give Boulden something. She created reports with falsified information that was intended to provide a glimmer of hope without making any real promises. Dr. Mo knew that Major Boulden wasn't smart enough to understand most of the medical jargon she used, or even misused, in her reports. All she needed to do was to include a conclusion that suggested that *some* progress was being made.

Looking out the window, she watched the rain splatter against the glass. It was dark outside except for the light coming out of various windows to the side of her. She wondered what day it was, knowing full well it didn't really matter. There were no normal workweeks anymore nor were there any such thing as vacations. Dr. Mo worked from the moment she awoke until she was forced to rest by the fatigue. There were so many things to do.

The OHSU library provided her with all sorts of research material and she poured over the books trying to find anything new to try. When she finally allowed herself to go to bed, sleep was always devoid of dreams and never restful. She awoke tired and relied upon coffee and occasional stimulants, to function. It wasn't healthy but she couldn't concern herself with that. She was a doctor and would do what she had to.

CHAPTER TWENTY-NINE

Run Run Run

He could hear the rain before he could see it. It was still dark outside but at least he was warm. Even with the generator off, Ray's house seemed to be insulated well enough to retain whatever heat John's body was generating. He stretched his legs and moved his ankle around. The ankle felt a little better but was still sore. There was some stinging in his thighs and he slowly sat up to take a look.

With the flashlight in hand, he pulled off the blankets and opened his coat. It was not good. The gauze wrapped around his legs was damp and red with blood. The bleeding may have slowed but it hadn't stopped.

Rather than trying to peel off the partially dried gauze and risk tearing off any scabbing that might have started, John headed downstairs. With each step, he could feel the scabs stretch and break. He took a quick walk out the back door, started the generator and returned to the kitchen, turning the thermostat up to eighty degrees. Grabbing as many bottles of water as he could, he placed them on the kitchen table and went looking for pots and pans. They were exactly where he expected them to be and John started filling them up and placing them on the electric stove. He turned the burners on and while the water was warming, he went up to the bathroom. Laying out some towels, he organized all of his burn medicine.

Over the following thirty minutes, John made repeated trips between the kitchen and the bathroom to fill the tub with water. It didn't need to be hot water and would probably be better if it wasn't. He did, however, want the water to be warm so he could soak his legs.

When the bathtub was finally ready, John turned off the generator, returned to the bathroom and took off his clothes. He lowered himself into the water with teeth clenched. The water, while lukewarm, still burned his legs. Nonetheless, he lay there and let the gauze bandages soak up the water. The water in the bathtub quickly turned a pale red.

Carefully, John began to unwrap the gauze from his legs, taking his time so as to not damage any healing that might have already begun. He tossed the soaked bandages on the floor and took a good look at his legs. With the light from the flashlight, he could still see a few glass shards and quickly and painfully, plucked them out.

He wiped the remaining blood from his legs and washed his hair. He didn't even notice that he was using bloodstained water. John's focus was on minimizing the pain in his legs, but he knew he needed to wash off the sweat, dirt, and smoke from the last couple of days. When he was finally finished, he eased up to his feet and stepped out of the tub. Sitting on the toilet, he dried his upper body and gently patted his legs dry.

There was still some bleeding from where he removed the final glass splinters, but it was relatively minimal. His thighs were red and slightly puffy with no evidence of obvious infection. He gently applied the burn cream and loosely wrapped his legs with gauze. He downed another three tablets of amoxicillin.

John needed some fresh clothes but hadn't brought them in from the Prius. Putting the wool coat back on, as well as his muddy shoes, he headed over to the car, grabbed the bags of clothes and returned to Ray's house.

There was no place left in the world for fashion. At least that's what John told himself as he slid on a pair of plaid swim trunks and then pulled on a bright blue t-shirt that said, "Life's short; surf naked!" On top, he added a hooded sweatshirt. Liz would be embarrassed to be seen, in public *or* private, with him dressed like this but it was the best he could do.

Between his body heat and the heat remaining from the electric floor registers, Ray's house was comfortably warm. John sat down on the couch. He needed a plan. Assuming he might need to leave in a hurry sometime soon, he would stock the Prius with enough supplies to allow him to live in the car, if necessary, for at least a couple of days. It would likely be a while before he could return to the cabin, so he had to take everything he needed with him.

Over the next several hours, John loaded the Prius with whatever remaining clothes were clean enough to still use, as well as water, protein bars, and candy. He figured it shouldn't be too tough to find another house and scavenge additional canned food. The most important possession for him was his computer backup. That was where he had all the family photos and he could not and would not ever leave those behind. He put the computer drive in a small duffle bag that he thought of as his "go" bag.

He put the shotgun in the back seat but held onto the handgun. He felt more secure having it with him at all times, just in case.

The packing of the Prius took most of the rest of the morning and John could occasionally see smoke rising in the west. He couldn't tell how close it was, but he knew he would have to be very careful.

On a trip over to the cabin to pick up toiletries, John noticed how cold it was getting. The sky was a dull gray and it felt almost cold enough for snow. The Oregon coast didn't get a lot of snow, but it happened. He couldn't help but wonder if, and when, it might start. He worried that his tire tracks might give him away.

With that thought in mind, John completed packing the Prius and drove to the far end of the street. While the street was technically a dead end, there was a dirt road leading up the hill to the next street. He removed a few branches that had fallen across it. Hopefully the soldiers wouldn't know about it and he would be able to make a clean getaway. He assumed the soldiers would come up the hill using the main street and then branch off to the various side streets. With the car parked away from the main street and around the corner, he would be able to drive away from the soldiers and take the back roads to escape. If it did snow, any tire tracks would be far enough away that they might not be noticed.

He thought it was mid-afternoon, but he wasn't sure. Now would be a good time to have some food and remove the bandages and let his legs breathe. It was obvious his wounds were still bleeding but not nearly as much as the day before. John opened a can of beef stew but didn't dare start the generator. The food was cold and tasteless, but it was at least some nourishment. Downing a couple of sodas, John swallowed two more amoxicillin tablets and reminded himself to take them more regularly.

Walking over to the cabin, John turned and headed toward the back of the house, where the grave was. Sitting down in the lawn chair, he clenched his coat around him.

"Liz? Brian? Cassie? I'm going to be leaving soon but I promise I'll be back.

"I'm not sure what happens next. Maybe I shouldn't try running from the soldiers. Given the condition of my legs though, maybe I should go with them and get some medical treatment.

"Shit, I just don't want to be around other people. When the Curse gets me, I want to be here with you guys, not with a bunch of strangers."

With a deep sigh, John got up and walked around the grave, inspecting his handiwork. The tarp was still stretched out, but it was clear that something had been sniffing around as he saw some dried blood. Whatever it was hadn't expected the broken glass. He silently congratulated himself.

"Damn, it's getting cold!" he muttered as he wrapped his coat tighter around him and noted the goose bumps on his legs.

Sitting back down, John gazed vacantly toward the woods. He wondered what was next. He wondered how long it had been since the New Year's Eve when Brian first coughed. He wondered what the hell he was doing and why he was still alive.

"I'm miserable, Liz. I'm fucking miserable and I miss you and the kids so much."

He buried his face in his hands and let the tears come. A soft but primal wail escaped his lips and he was powerless to stop it. His body convulsed with spasms. There was no point in being a rock anymore. Slowly the spasms slowed and finally stopped. John wiped his nose on his coat sleeve. Standing up he looked over the grave.

"I wish there was something I could say. I don't even know what kind of prayer I could say…it's been too damn long. I can only promise that somehow and some way, I *will* see you again. I have to. If you can pull any strings from over on your side, pull them so I can join you sooner rather than later.

"Jesus, it's fucking cold!"

Starting to walk back, he stopped and turned once more, "I love all three of you with every fiber of my being. I truly hope that you can forgive me for failing you so miserably."

With that, John walked back to Ray's house.

එ

While John wasn't interested in Ray's porn magazines, he did enjoy his collection of paperbacks. Apparently, Ray had been a big fan of Louis L'Amour. Flipping through the various books, John found *The Quick and the Dead* and settled down on the couch. He would read a couple of chapters in the light coming through the window and then doze. Upon awakening, he would read a couple more.

The books were easy to read and it allowed him to escape from the emptiness of his life. Rather than eat the rest of the beef stew, he ate some Fig Newtons and half a sleeve of crackers.

As it was starting to get dark, John re-applied the cream to his legs and wrapped them with gauze. He stood up and walked to the window. It was starting to snow. In normal times, this would have made him happy. There was nothing more beautiful to him, other than his family, than seeing falling snow.

He thought about having survived another day. The soldiers hadn't bothered him, so that was good. He took some more amoxicillin and lay down on the couch.

John looked up and saw that he was sitting on the beach watching Brian flying a kite. Cassie was lying down on one side of him reading a book and Liz was on the other side just soaking up the sun. It was a gorgeous day and John was surprised by how comfortable it was. The Oregon beaches can often be windy and cold even in the summer, but this was perfect—no wind, no clouds. It was just him and his family having a lazy afternoon together.

He leaned over to give Liz a kiss and she jumped up without saying a word. Extending her hand, John grabbed it and let her pull him to his feet. Her hands were warm and soft, making him smile.

Together, they started walking toward the water. Delirious with joy, John lifted up Liz's arm and twirled her about. He could see her laughing but couldn't hear her laughter. Her smile was dazzling and just as he remembered. Suddenly Liz stopped and looked out over the ocean. There was a dark cloudbank in the distance and John saw flashes of lightning.

The storm seemed to be approaching but John knew it would be at least an hour before it would reach shore. He reached to put his arm around Liz's shoulders and pull her near, but she pushed him away. John looked at her and her stare was intense. She seemed to be saying something to him, but John couldn't hear over the noise of the ocean.

Suddenly Liz grabbed his face with both hands and started to yell. John still couldn't hear what she was saying. She was shouting without making any sound when, suddenly he heard her voice. "GO! GO! GO!"

John sat up with a start just as the headlights splashed across his face.

CHAPTER THIRTY

LET IT SNOW

"Sarge! Sarge! Come over here!"

He was never happy when one of the privates called him over. Too often it was to see something which, in a prior lifetime, might have had some value or that now served some sort of morbid fascination for the younger generation.

It was cold and the snow was coming down. It was the wind, however, that bothered him. It seemed to blow right through his hazmat suit, then through his fatigues and, finally, right into his bones. When the order came to start extending the search missions for days at a time, he understood it made sense, but it didn't make it any easier to accept. Sergeant Polits knew he needed to find more survivors. It didn't take any great insight to understand that Camp Oregon was, at best, stagnant in size and, more likely, starting to shrink. That was not a good thing.

If the Curse just passed from human to human, perhaps he could leave the camp and hide out somewhere. If he didn't have any contact with other humans, maybe he could survive. Of course, that assumed that life without any human contact would be a life worth living. That was an assumption that he didn't really want to address at this point.

As he approached the house, he could see Private Valentine standing inside the front door with his flashlight sweeping all around.

"Okay, Valentine, what is it?"

"Sarge, when I broke in the front door, I noticed the house seemed warmer than the others we've been through. My initial thought was that it might have a generator or a propane-furnace still working."

"As I started to look around, the place looked more lived in. I mean lived in recently, more than the others. I went to the back door to look for a generator and look."

Valentine was walking toward the back of the house and was motioning for the Sergeant to follow him. With his curiosity piqued, he did.

As Valentine opened the back door, he shined his flashlight on the snow-covered grounds. The footprints were obvious and, given how it was still snowing, they appeared fresh. The tracks led toward the north where he saw the outline of another house.

"Okay, Private. Grab a couple of 'turds and follow the tracks. Have them walk ahead of you though and be very careful."

Sergeant Polits walked up closer to Private Valentine and said quietly, "This guy may be bat-shit crazy by now which makes him particularly dangerous. If he is going to start shooting at you, I want him to hit the 'turds first. Do you understand?"

Valentine nodded and walked back through the house to locate a couple of the others to help him conduct the search.

⌒

John was out of breath by the time he got to the car and realized how cold it was. He had thrown on his shoes, without tying the laces, and grabbed his coat but was still wearing the bathing suit, t-shirt, and sweatshirt. He looked back and could see traces of flashlights shining from around the corner.

Wasting no time, John climbed in and started the Prius. He would need to go slowly in order to keep it operating on the battery and not trigger the engine starting. He held the flashlight in his right hand and pointed it straight ahead. The tires slipped when he first put it into gear and a momentary feeling of dread hit him. What if the car was stuck in the snow?

Without allowing himself to wallow in the uncertainty, John again slowly pushed down the accelerator pedal. With a lurch, the tires grabbed the dirt road and the Prius began moving forward. Even at only twenty miles per hour, he would be going faster than any soldiers on foot. Nonetheless, he split his time between looking forward to see where he was going and looking in the rearview mirror to check whether he was being followed.

It seemed like at least ten minutes before he could breathe again. With some distance between him and the soldiers, John had to decide when it would be safe to pick up his speed. He didn't want to tip off the soldiers but, then again, with the snow, anyone looking for him would just have to follow his tire tracks. He needed to get beyond the snowstorm and do it quickly.

In Oregon, it was very common to have snow in the Coast Range but, once you were back on the valley floor, the snow would likely turn to rain. From memory, John knew he had about twenty miles or so before he would be completely out of the mountains. Even with only the light from the flashlight, John confidently picked up speed. With a comforting hum, the gas engine kicked in.

℘

Valentine was out of breath by the time he got back.

"Sarge, he got away. We couldn't see what kind of car he's driving but we saw the tire tracks. What do you want us to do?"

The sergeant looked into the darkness, trying to will himself to be able to see who had just gotten away and what he might be driving. If this guy, assuming it was a guy, was good enough to get away that quickly, he had to be smart and would likely be a good resource for the camp.

"Let's load up and go after him. Tell the 'turds to keep working this street and the next one and that we'll be back as soon as we get this guy."

The sergeant jogged over to the Humvee and got out his map. The roads through the Coast Range were winding so this guy wouldn't be driving too quickly. Unless the snow started coming down really hard, they could just follow the tire tracks and would only need to go slightly faster than him to catch up. Rather than leaving the driving in these conditions to the privates, Sergeant Polits climbed behind the wheel and started up the Humvee.

ɛ⌂

John felt the back end of the Prius slip from time to time, but he was able to keep the vehicle in control. In his prior life, he would have driven on the right side of the road and been concerned about oncoming traffic with every curve. Now, he didn't have that concern. John could confidently drive in the middle of the road without fear of any traffic. The only thing to worry about might be an animal but it would be safer hitting it in the middle of the road than on either lane.

It was an odd sensation to be driving at night with only the single beam of light from the flashlight guiding the way. There was almost no light from the moon as it was hidden behind the clouds. While he could see the road ahead of him and at least some of the roadside as he passed, looking to the right or left, all he could see was blackness. He couldn't even make out the shapes of the trees he knew had to be there.

As he came around a sharp curve, he put his foot on the brake to slow down. As he did, he felt the backside of the Prius start sliding to the right. Turning the wheel, John tried to steer into the skid. Unfortunately, he overcorrected, and the car started to spin the other way. He no longer had any control of the car and dropped the flashlight. He could only hope that whatever he hit next would be soft. It wasn't.

It is often said that in moments of high stress, time seems to slow down. Whether that was true or not, John had a heightened sense of everything going on around him. He felt the front of the car bump something and then start falling.

"I'm heading down an embankment," he thought as he tried to remember how steep and deep the drop offs in this part of the Coast Range were. Was there a river down there?

The car bounced off a tree and John was thrown to the right. He heard a crash as the windshield exploded and something roughly brushed his face. He felt a sharp pain on the right side of his chest.

The car continued sliding downhill before smacking into a large tree, stopping instantly. John was thrown forward, his head hitting the steering wheel. Just before blackness enveloped him, he wondered why the airbag hadn't deployed and whether it had something to do with the fuses he'd removed.

ↂ

John slowly came to as the cold wind battered his face. With no idea as to how long he had been unconscious, he needed to determine the extent of his injuries. His head hurt but he could move his arms and legs. He reached up to his forehead and could feel wetness. His chest was stinging and when he touched his sweatshirt, it was wet and very tender.

Reaching down to the floor, John moved his hand about before finally feeling the flashlight. Turning it on, he looked around.

The car was resting at an angle with the driver's side door lodged against a large tree. Pointing the flashlight upward, John saw the steep embankment but couldn't see the top.

Wind and snow were coming in through where the windshield had been. John understood he couldn't stay there much longer or he would freeze or bleed to death. Unbuckling his seatbelt and carefully turning in his seat, John reached up and tried to push the passenger side door open. It wouldn't budge. He would need to climb out of the window.

John turned his head as he swung the butt of the flashlight against the passenger side window. It shattered and safety glass fell all around him. Between the pain in his neck and chest, it was a slow and tortuous process, but John was finally able to turn himself around and stand on the driver's side door. He slowly straightened his legs, allowing his head to emerge through the passenger side window. Pushing his hands out, he slowly pulled himself up and out.

The side of the car was slippery and wet from the snow and John wondered where his gloves might be. His upper body was now out of the car and with a quick push, he found himself seated on the side of it. Using the flashlight, he could see the top of the embankment about twenty feet above him.

He grabbed a small tree with one hand and worked to get his feet out, bracing them between another tree and the side of the car. He shone the flashlight back into the car and saw his entire stock of food, clothes, and other supplies were completely disorganized.

He reached down for his go bag but it was stuck behind one of the seats. After numerous attempts, he realized it wasn't coming loose. He grabbed another bag containing clothes and pulled it out, wrapping the strap over his shoulder. He saw the barrel of the shotgun and pulled it out too, placing the gun around his back. This was enough for the first trip to the top. He would have to come back for a second trip to get the go bag and more of his supplies. He started to work his way uphill. This required him to brace one foot on a small tree and then grab another tree or branch above him and pull himself up. More than once he slipped but, slowly and surely, made progress.

Just below the lip of the road, there were no trees to hold onto so John held tight to the dirt and small plants beneath him. Leaning into the hill, he was able to work his way back to the top.

With the flashlight, he could see the tire tracks leading off the road. John was surprised he really hadn't travelled very far once the skid had begun. Standing up, he opened up the bag and pulled out a sweater and another jacket. Before putting them on, he looked down. His sweatshirt was now bright red and the material had begun to freeze. He could put clothes on top, but the blood would then soak through them and he would eventually freeze to death. His legs were uncovered and starting to bleed through the gauze.

After all he'd been through, John needed to at least try to survive. He owed it to Liz and the kids. He didn't have the strength for another trip to the Prius. He needed to find some shelter. If he went east, the direction he was headed when he went over the embankment, he would have to hope he might find a house nearby with medical supplies. If he didn't find a house quickly, he wouldn't make it.

The other choice was to head west, back toward the cabin, and hope the soldiers were following him. As much as he hated the idea of being taken away from the cabin and his family, he likely wouldn't make it any other way. With his luck, even if he somehow got all the way back to the cabin, it would probably be burned down.

No, he would walk west, as best he could, and hope he would be found.

"One, two, three, four…one, two, three, four…"

Driving a Humvee in snow wasn't a problem for Sergeant Polits. The tires on the Humvee were wide and had good tread. As long as he didn't push it too hard, he should be able to continue following the tire tracks. Even if this guy somehow eluded them, they were heading back in the general direction of the camp and he would just continue all the way back. He could always come back for the 'turds the next day and right now he just wanted a hot shower.

Noting the tire tracks occasionally showed some slippage, the sergeant knew he would catch up to this guy eventually. Those tire tracks were narrow, so he was driving a small passenger car. Polits just needed to be patient.

Coming around a corner, Sergeant Polits slammed on the brakes forcing the Humvee into a skid. Taking his foot off the brake, he compensated for the drift and again applied the brakes, this time more slowly.

Ahead of him was what appeared to be an apparition. It was a white man but with red splotches all around his face and chest. He was wearing swim trunks and it looked like only one shoe. He was shuffling toward them with a pack on his front and what looked like a shotgun on his back.

With the headlights illuminating the ghost-like figure, Sergeant Polits climbed out of the car. Standing behind the driver's door and with his handgun aimed at the figure, he called out.

"Stop where you are!"

The figure did.

"What weapons do you have on you?"

Sergeant Polits could barely hear what the man said. In normal situations, he would have had the man lie on the road and then just handcuff him. This poor sap, however, appeared too feeble and injured to be of real risk. Deciding there was no immediate threat, Sergeant Polits ordered the privates to go out and carry the man in. He offered no resistance and was placed in the back seat with Privates Valentine and Jones on either side of him.

They placed a blanket over him and tried to clean the blood off in order to determine the extent of his injuries. Sergeant Polits started the Humvee, turned the heater on full blast, and decided to head back to camp. He gave no further thought at all to the 'turds. He was now focused on the injured person in back and the road ahead.

"How's he doing?"

Valentine caught the sergeant's eye in the rearview mirror and just shrugged.

Once they were out of the snow, Polits drove faster. The passenger was shivering and could only communicate with brief grunts. The privates refused to allow him to lose consciousness. As it was crowded in the back seat, both Valentine and Jones took off their Hazmat helmets in order to more easily provide the passenger with first aid. Polits thought about chastising them but ultimately took his helmet off too. It was too warm with it on and they would be home soon.

Arriving at the camp, they approached the gates. Polits put his Hazmat helmet back on and instructed both privates to do likewise. There was no use in causing any further concern to Dr. Mo or Major Boulden.

Stopping, Polits motioned for the guards to quickly open the gates.

"What's up, Sarge?"

"I'll fill you in later, boys. Right now, we got a guy who needs to see the doc—quick!"

They sped through the gates and carried John Callahan into the camp.

CHAPTER THIRTY-ONE

GAMES PEOPLE PLAY

He didn't even try to open his eyes. The first thing was to try to figure out *how* he was. That was more important than *where* he was. He could sense something around his head, as well as across his chest. Around his neck was what felt like a brace. John could move his hands and feet but couldn't raise either. It wasn't a muscular limitation but, rather, straps of some sort holding his arms and legs down.

There was also something in his left arm. When moving it, he could feel tape pulling at his arm hair.

Slowly he opened his eyes. Even just doing that seemed to fatigue him. He told himself the fatigue was why he didn't recognize anything. Straight above him was a white-paneled ceiling and he could see the IV and heart monitor beside him.

Rather than try anything more, John just closed his eyes and drifted back into the darkness.

ↀ

"I know you can hear me so let's stop playing games. Open your eyes."

The voice was both female and soothing although he could sense impatience. Without opening his eyes, he said, "Where am I?" His voice was raspy and more a croak than anything else. John tried to clear his throat.

"Okay, so your mouth is dry. That is completely normal. How about some water?"

John slowly shook his head and again whispered, "Where am I?"

"There will be time for your questions later, but you need to answer mine first. Would you like some water?"

John opened his eyes and was looking at a woman in a full Hazmat suit. He tried to nod "yes" but when he did, he felt a sharp pain. The grimace was obvious.

"Yeah, your neck is going to hurt for a while. Don't worry though; it's just a bad sprain. It's what you would probably call whiplash. It may take several months before you are completely pain free, but you'll get there eventually."

The woman leaned in and placed a straw on his bottom lip. John closed his mouth and started to suck.

"Slow down, cowboy! You only want to take little sips. If you start choking, it's going to really, really hurt."

John took a breath of air and then a series of small sips. The water was cool and tasted better than anything he could ever remember drinking before.

"Where am I?" This time his voice sounded more normal.

"I know you have a lot of questions and I promise I'll answer them in time. First, I need to ask you a series of questions. You've got some significant injuries and we've been flying blind because we don't have your medical history. Trust me, after all you've been through, it would really be pity if you died because we didn't know of an allergy to a particular medicine. Will that work for you?"

John nodded yes but when the pain hit, he decided it would be better to use words.

"Yes," he croaked.

"Good," the woman nodded. "The first thing I need is your name."

"John," he replied.

"John, that is a good start but let's not play games. I need a lot of information from you and really don't want to waste time, either yours or mine. Now, let's try again. John, what is your name?"

"John Thomas Callahan without a g."

"That's better." She leaned her head down and started writing on a notepad. "By the way, are the pain drugs starting to wear off? I can see you grimacing a little."

"They are, can I have some more?"

"Absolutely but let's get some information first. Where do you live?"

"Wilsonville."

Through the visor of her suit, he could see her frown.

"John, what did I say about wasting time? I have no reason yet to dislike you but if you are going to waste my time, well, let's just say it might affect the quality of the medical treatment you receive. Now, I am going to ask again—where do you live?"

"6 Adams Road…in Wilsonville."

"Good, John, now let's keep this going. When you were found, you were on Highway 18 in the Coast Range. That is a long way from Wilsonville. What were you doing there?"

"I rented a house outside of Neskowin and was going back to Wilsonville when my car ran off the road."

"Yes, your car. We found it and I'm going to have some questions about that, but we'll do that later. John, was anyone staying with you in the house outside of Neskowin?"

"My family…but they died."

"Yes, I'm sure they did. A lot of people have died...but not you." She stopped writing on her pad and stared at him. Her eyes were bloodshot and she looked tired. "That's what we need to find out, John. Why did your family and so many others die, but not you? Do you have any ideas?

"My head is really hurting. Can I get something for that?"

"I can do that for you, John, because you are cooperating." She stood up and he watched as she inserted a syringe into the IV drip line. "One last question, John. What is your date of birth?"

"November 1, 1968."

"Thank you, John. You're going to fall back asleep for a while and when you wake, we are going to talk a bit more. Is that all right with you, John?"

"Yes," he murmured as the edges of his vision started to darken and close up. His last thought was that he wasn't sure whether or not he liked this woman. Were her persistent and veiled threats intended to be intimidating or was she just tired?

❧

Over the next several days, they established a routine. The woman, who finally introduced herself as Dr. Moira Kessel, would ask questions but rarely, if ever, answer any. She told him to call her Dr. Mo and that he was in a quarantined facility.

Over the course of what seemed like countless hours, they would discuss John's past. First, Dr. Mo focused on his health history, which was mostly unremarkable, and then a detailed rendition of the past six months. Once that was completed, Dr. Mo would provide some minor information and then go back over John's complete history again. He knew she was looking for any inconsistencies to determine his credibility. Knowing this, however, didn't make it any less annoying to John.

Over the course of the first week, John learned the extent of his injuries. The burns to his thighs were mostly first- and second-degree burns. Dr. Mo had been required to remove a small number of remaining glass shards and infection had just started. Fortunately, antibiotics knocked the infection out quickly and the burns were healing well.

The lacerations to his forehead and chest from sliding off the road resulted in twelve stitches to his forehead and thirty-four to his chest.

Every time John needed to use the restroom, he would be unshackled from the bed but then placed in handcuffs and escorted by two armed guards. These guards had both handguns and Tasers. The bathroom door was left open at all times and John felt a complete lack of privacy. John asked but Dr. Mo ducked all questions about the necessity for such measures.

"Doc, you're going to have to let me out of these restraints sometime. I haven't committed any crime that I'm aware of."

"No, John, you haven't," she responded.

"Then why am I always restrained? I know my rights."

"John, I know you're a lawyer and I'm not, but you need to understand that you have no rights, none of us do." With this, Dr. Mo looked down in her lap for a moment before looking back up at him.

"With the declaration of martial law, Major Roger Boulden is now in charge. He is the judge, jury, and sometimes, even the executioner." Dr. Mo stood up and walked over to the window. "I'm under strict orders to keep you restrained until we deem you to not be a threat to the camp."

"Doc, you've known me now for over a week now. I'm not a threat to anyone."

"There are...issues, John, and we need to be careful. I'll see what I can do. You'll have to remain in quarantine for a while yet, but I'll see if we can't at least let you get up so you can take a shower and use the bathroom without restraints."

"Thanks, I would really appreciate that. I'm going a bit stir crazy. What's it really like out there?" John nodded his head toward the door.

"We are a functioning community. I don't know if you ever came up the hill to OHSU back in the day, but it looks a lot different now. Many of the buildings are gone and others have been repurposed. Let's just say...we are surviving."

"What about the Curse? Has any progress been made on a cure?"

"The short answer is no. Unfortunately, our best hope is that the virus will burn itself out. The Curse is a particularly ugly little bastard that keeps mutating before we can figure out a vaccine. Right now, we are just waiting."

Dr. Mo's hand was resting on John's bed and he reached over and placed his hand on top of hers.

"Waiting for what?"

"Just waiting for it to either burn itself out or..." her voice trailed off.

John looked in her downcast eyes through the visor. "Or what?" he asked.

Dr. Mo looked at John and as she pulled her hand away from his, she sighed and said, "...or the complete extinction of the human race."

☙

It was early one morning, about three weeks in, when John found himself reading a three-year-old copy of *Sports Illustrated*. The door thudded open and four people entered, all fully shielded in hazmat suits. Two of them had rifles and they took up a position by the door. John recognized Dr. Mo but didn't recognize the others.

The man without a rifle was tall, and John could see intense and bloodshot eyes staring at him through the visor.

"So, you're Callahan?"

Looking at this man, a feeling of dread crept over John and he sat up in the bed, nodding.

"Do you want to tell me why you didn't turn yourself in months ago?"

John stared at him and, with false meekness, said, "I didn't know I was supposed to."

Through the visor of the hazmat suit, John could see the man's face start getting red. Leaning down toward John, the man placed his hand on John's chest, right over the sutures, and pushed him down on the bed, hard.

"Don't fuck with me, Callahan. You aren't a guest here. You are getting medical treatment because I allow it. You are getting food because I allow it. You are still alive because I allow it. I'm allowing all of this because you may have some useful information. If I find you are no use to me, you will no longer be welcome here and we'll make other arrangements for you."

From the look of his face, John found no comfort in the reference to "other arrangements."

"Dr. Kessel, is Callahan cooperating?"

"Yes, sir."

"And are you getting useful information?"

"We're doing daily blood work and running as many tests as we can."

"Very well," the man said. "Keep me advised."

He turned quickly and strode out the door. The two soldiers, however, remained where they were.

"So, is this someone I should know?" John said.

In one single movement, Dr. Mo allowed her shoulders to sag and let out a deep sigh. John noticed she was holding a paper bag.

"You want to be very careful around Major Boulden. He's…" She paused as if searching for just the right words. "He's under a lot of pressure and can sometimes act erratically. That makes him a danger to you."

It was then John noticed that Dr. Mo had keys in her hand and she unlocked the restraints holding him to the bed.

"You will be allowed to get up and shower, but the door will remain open at all times. I've got a small bag with electric shears, an electric razor, and various toiletries. John, you need to move slowly and when you are done, I will need everything back."

"Thanks, Doc. This is at least a start."

John stood up and rubbed his wrists. Putting first one and then the other foot down, he steadied himself by holding onto the bed. The soreness from his wounds was one thing but John was surprised at how weak he was.

Slowly he stepped to the window and looked outside. It was daytime but overcast.

He asked, "Doc, what's it like out there?"

"I'm not really sure. As you know, the virus has become a cataclysmic event the likes of which is unprecedented in recorded history. Society as you knew it is gone. It isn't just your family who died. Essentially everyone has. We've got the people who live here in the camp but beyond this, we have little information.

"There has been some communication with a few other camps, but we aren't told any details. Most of us assume this means everyone else is in the same condition we are…desperately trying to stay alive as long as we can."

With his back still to her, John said, "So why are they out there burning houses?"

"We need people, John. With the ordinary rate of attrition—and there is nothing ordinary about any of this, the camp won't last the year. Major Boulden is out looking for people. All able-bodied people are brought back to offset the deaths and desertions we experience. Any houses in which corpses are found are promptly burned for hygiene purposes."

John started to turn around to ask another question when something caught his eye. Leaning into the window, John strained to look.

"What the fuck? Is that a polar bear?"

He actually heard Dr. Mo softly laugh and it was a sweet, albeit tired, sound. "That's probably Duke. Was he outside of the fence?"

"Yes, and who or what is Duke?" John asked, this time looking right at Dr. Mo.

"Duke, along with a bunch of other animals, was released from the Oregon Zoo. The fence keeps most of them out, well, not the monkeys, but the other animals. As long as we're inside of the fence, we are safe from them. Outside of the fence, we need to be very careful. The few times I have been out there, I've stayed in a truck as much as possible and always had an armed guard."

"Why Duke?"

"One of my assistants had a Great Pyrenees with that name. She named the bear Duke in memory of her dog, and it just seemed to stick. Occasionally you'll see an elephant. We all suspect there are various types of big cats too, but we rarely see them.

"It is literally a jungle out there now and I'm not sure I'd ever want to face Duke or any of the other animals face-to-face."

John softly shook his head while smiling. Reaching over, he took the bag from Dr. Mo's hand and headed into the bathroom.

"Remember, John, don't try anything stupid. When you are done, let the soldiers know and they'll call me."

Turning away from him, she left, leaving the guards at the door. John nodded to them as he stepped into the bathroom. The first thing to do was to look at himself in the mirror. This is something he hadn't done in months. Back at the cabin and at Ray's house, he avoided mirrors. His reflection would just remind him of his failures. Things were different now. He was here at Camp Oregon and it was time to face his failures head on.

Walking in front of the mirror, John almost didn't recognize himself. His hair was long and unruly. It hadn't been this long since high school. He also had a ratty beard. He bent forward and examined the wounds on his forehead and then down at his chest. Both wounds were red but obviously healing.

His legs were also better. The burns were scabbed over and there was no trace of infection.

Most surprising was that John could see his ribs. There was no trace of a beer belly and in its place was just loose skin.

"Jesus, this is one hell of a diet," he whispered to himself.

Stepping onto the scale in the corner, John let out a soft whistle as the number came up—164 pounds. As much as he tried, John couldn't remember the last time he had weighed so little. He thought back to when he and Liz got married. Even back then, his weight fluctuated between 180 and 185 pounds.

Plugging in the shears John wasted no time in trimming his hair and beard down to stubble. Then he took the razor and shaved his face before stepping into the enclosure for his first hot shower in over four months. It was a long, long shower.

CHAPTER THIRTY-TWO

Another One Bites the Dust

The next morning, Dr. Mo arrived and gave John a warm smile through her visor. This was not a sad or a tired smile but, rather, a genuine smile of joy.

"John, welcome back to civilization. Is it safe to assume you are feeling better today?" She seemed truly pleased by his appearance.

"Doc, that shower breathed new life into me. I can only imagine how bad I must have smelled and I apologize for that. I'm just glad I couldn't smell myself. Now tell me, what can I do to help you with your research?"

Dr. Mo explained how she was going to continue to draw blood regularly and he would remain in quarantine for the foreseeable future.

"Can I ask a couple of questions?" he inquired.

Sitting down on a chair by the window, Dr. Mo allowed a bemused smile to form.

"Certainly, John. I can't guarantee I'll answer all of them but let's see what you've got. What would you like to know?"

"Well," he began, "I assume the power grid must be down. How do you have electricity here?"

"Everything here is run on generators. We've got some very good mechanical engineers and electricians who keep things operating smoothly. We have occasional blackouts but not very often. There is a fleet of tanker trucks bringing fuel up every day. As you can imagine, there's not a lot of demand for fuel other than here and we have trucks going down to the fuel tank farms just north of here."

Standing up and walking to the window, he said, "So I assume you also bring food from grocery stores up here?"

"That's right, that and distribution centers. There is no shortage of food although we don't have much fresh food. We've got some fresh meat but only canned and dried fruits and vegetables. The hope is to set up some farms and orchards this summer assuming..." She left the rest unsaid although John knew what she meant to say.

"So why hasn't the Curse burned itself out yet?"

When he got no response, he turned and faced Dr. Mo. She had an odd look on her face, one that John couldn't decipher.

"I've got some theories but I'm just not sure."

"What are your they?"

This time it was her turn to walk to the window beside him and look outside.

"John, that is one of the questions I can't answer just yet. Until I have greater certainty, I'd rather keep that to myself. I'm not even going to mention these theories to the major."

For some reason, this made John feel uneasy and he sat down on the bed. "So, how many people are left?"

Dr. Mo turned around and faced him again. "Do you mean here in the camp or in America or in the world?"

With a slight grin, he responded, "Yes."

This, in turn, made Dr. Mo smile. It quickly faded as she said, "A year ago, the population of the world was probably about seven and half billion people, with maybe three hundred and twenty-five million in the United States."

She walked back to the chair, sat down again and continued, "I'm not sure if there are a million people left in the whole world and likely well less than a hundred thousand on the entire North American continent. Of course, we don't know for sure. The major rarely gives us any real information but I hear people talk—especially people close to him."

Her shoulders slumped and as she placed her head in her hands, a quiet sob escaped her lips.

"I'm sorry, John. It just gets so overwhelming sometimes and then these damn hazmat suits won't even allow me to wipe my eyes or blow my nose."

"Do you still need the hazmat suit? I mean, surely I'm not contagious anymore."

"Oh, John," her voice visibly cracking, "you seem to have some immunity to the virus and we're not sure why."

She abruptly stood up and walked toward the door. The guards opened and closed it behind her.

John stood there, not really sure what had just happened. The thought he might be infected with the Curse was not entirely unwelcome but the thought he might be immune was really puzzling.

෩

Over the next week or so, Dr. Mo would come several times a day, draw blood, and, occasionally, give him injections. She was not, however, the same. Her answers were short and any attempts at small talk were shrugged off. John wasn't sure whether he had somehow offended her.

The soldiers now only stayed in the room when Dr. Mo was there. This allowed John to start stretching and even do pushups. The discomfort from the wounds was diminishing on a daily basis but John was still shocked by his overall physical condition. While never much of an athlete, he couldn't remember ever being this weak. Initially it was difficult to even do a single pushup.

With an abundance of time and a desire to regain some strength, John began doing stretches and calisthenics throughout the day.

One day, Dr. Mo came in and asked him to sit on the bed so she could take some more blood.

"John, I want to apologize for my behavior over the past couple of weeks."

"Doc, no apology is necessary."

"Yes, John, it is. I acted unprofessionally. We live in difficult times and I can't allow myself to be weak."

"Doc, I understand but don't be so hard on yourself. You are still human and, as you say, we are living in difficult times. No one expects you to be able to keep it together all the time."

"Thanks, but I expect more of myself...I have to. Now, let's get started."

Taking his wrist in her hand, she briskly and wordlessly took his vitals and examined the lacerations to John's forehead and chest.

"Hmmm, these are healing nicely. You'll still have some significant scarring, but I'm really pleased with how they are healing. I'm also pleased that you seem to have regained full mobility of your neck. How does it feel?"

"The neck only hurts now if I turn sharply or if I try to turn it too far. Other than that, it feels pretty good. How are the burns doing?"

"I was just going to say that they are doing very well. You are always going to have a heightened sensitivity to heat on your thighs and you will need to make sure you never get sunburned there. The skin is much more susceptible to the UV rays so you should plan on always wearing pants while outside."

"So, I shouldn't wear my speedos anymore?" John said with a grin.

Dr. Mo looked at him without any sense of mirth and said, "John, this is serious. You suffered first and second-degree burns, bordering on third-degree burns. Your self-treatment was pretty good, but you were very fortunate to have been captured when you were. The infections when you first came in were just at the beginning stage and we were lucky to be able to knock them out."

John could sense that she felt the weight of the world on her shoulders. "Doc, I don't think I've said this yet so let me do so now. Thanks for everything. You've saved my life and I will be forever grateful."

Dr. Mo looked down at her gloved hands and began gathering up her notepad, blood pressure cuff and other supplies.

"I heard another base went dark yesterday. I'm not sure which one but I think it was one of the bases in southern California."

The tone of her voice was somewhat detached as if she were telling him that the mail hadn't arrived yet.

"John, you never answered the question as to why you didn't turn yourself in. Why were you running from the soldiers?"

Knowing this was a loaded question, John took his time to formulate a response. The sun was now well up in the sky and there were only a few white clouds drifting by. He thought about how this was the type of spring day when he should be on a picnic with Liz or taking the kids rafting. Generally, however, this was the type of day he would truly notice only if he thought to look out his office window.

"Doc, do you have a family?"

She paused for a moment and then said, "No…not anymore. No kids, though. I work long and unusual hours and that is apparently not conducive to raising a family. I wanted…" She stopped and gathered herself. "I guess, given all that has gone on, I was fortunate not to have kids.

"Well, I was fortunate, incredibly fortunate. Despite the hours I worked, I found the love of my life. My wife really was a remarkable woman. It wasn't just that she was beautiful and smart, she was kind and forgiving and tolerant of my work schedule. If I'm being honest with myself, she really was the main parent to our kids.

"She was the one who would schlep them to most practices, games and recitals. She was the one who would help them with their homework and projects. She was the one who would treat their scraped knees and bruised emotions.

"Liz was a wonderful woman and much more than I ever deserved. I would have sacrificed my life for her or either of the kids. Brian and Cassie were funny and smart and just great kids. Most importantly, they had their whole lives ahead of them... then they didn't.

"When they died, I didn't know what to do or how to feel. I'd never been alone before. Liz and I met when I was in law school and she was always there for me. She was a part of me and suddenly she was gone too.

"Obviously I knew the Curse was impacting other people but, to tell you the truth, I really didn't care. The Curse took my wife and kids from me. I had nothing left. The last thing I wanted was to be around other people, let alone join a community.

"I didn't care what happened to the rest of the world because I really didn't care what happened to me. I survived but it was more out of instinct than anything else. I survived because it was something to do, something to distract me from the fact my whole life was fucked over."

He walked to the bathroom and blew his nose using toilet paper.

"I'm sorry, John."

"Oh, Doc, don't be sorry for me. Be sorry for my wife and kids, not for me. I failed them. I had one job to do, one *fucking* job. I was just supposed to take care of my family and I completely and utterly failed.

"Do you know why I've never complained about the burns or the lacerations or the scars or any of this? Do you?"

She bowed her head and shook it back and forth.

"I don't complain because I deserve all of this and so much more. What I don't deserve is sympathy. I would love forgiveness but the only three people who could possibly forgive me are all dead. So, Doc, the short answer to your question about why I didn't turn myself in is that I am a bad person. I have always been selfish and focused on myself rather than anyone else. When all of the chips were on the table— when my family's life was at risk, I couldn't figure out how to save them. That is why I didn't volunteer to come here, I didn't deserve it."

The room was silent except for the soft sound of Doctor Mo's breathing through her hazmat suit.

Standing up she said, "John…" but it was as if she couldn't finish her thought. She turned toward the door and walked out.

CHAPTER THIRTY-THREE

WAKE ME UP BEFORE YOU GO-GO

He'd just completed a second set of twelve pushups and was sitting on the floor trying to catch his breath when he heard the door unlock. Slowly standing up, John sat on the edge of the bed.

"Good morning, Doc."

Doctor Mo nodded hello and sat down on the chair opposite him to start taking his vitals. She avoided looking him in the eyes.

"Your heart rate is slightly elevated. Do you know why, John?"

"I've been doing some pushups to try to build some strength back up."

This time, she looked up and, through her visor, took a close look at him.

"That's all right, isn't it?" he asked.

"Yes, John, that is fine. In fact, you should be trying to get stronger."

She stood up and walked to the window.

"How familiar are you with the OHSU campus?"

"Well, I've been up here a couple of times, usually to visit someone. I even remember back when I used to run, I would take the road up here and just run through the campus. Mostly I remember how crowded and confusing it was. There were so many different hospitals and buildings, and the roads seem to be constantly curving around each other."

Without looking back at him, she said, "Well, it's different now. Many of the buildings were torn down. The entire camp has been fenced and the only real way in and out is through a gate on the north side. It leads to Sam Jackson Park Road."

John looked at the back of her head, wondering why she was telling him all this.

"Yeah, it was Sam Jackson that I used to come up on. I only ran up here a couple of times because the drop off was so steep and there was no sidewalk. I was always concerned that a car coming around a corner might clip me."

"The gate is actually a double gate with armed guards." Her voice sounded affected and even had a sense of defeat in it.

"This campus used to be beautiful, at least to those who worked up here. Now with so many buildings just rubble, it is sad. They've replaced the torn-down buildings with parking lots for trucks and military vehicles.

"I remember how surprised I was to find out that they leave the keys in all of the vehicles. I guess they figure no one would be stupid enough to steal one. I mean where would you go?"

John was content to let her ramble, as he was not really sure what was going on. Just then, he heard another key in the door. Turning around, he saw Major Boulden stride in. Two soldiers, both of whom, again carrying military rifles, followed him.

"Okay, it's time to finish this farce." This was Boulden talking and John was somewhat startled by his eyes. Even through the faceplate of the hazmat suit, John could see that they were even more bloodshot than before and slightly bulging. Whatever he was on, it was obvious he was amped up on something.

"Major..." Dr. Mo began.

"Shut up, bitch. I've given you enough time. This fucker is not an answer to our problems; he is a cause."

Boulden strode toward John and barked, "Get up!"

Sensing this was not a time to be cute, John thought he might try to calm him down and asked, "What is going on, Major?"

"What is going on?" Boulden's voice was louder than normal and slightly higher pitched. "You're what's going on! I've given the doc here the chance to see if you could be of some help to us. She told me you might be the key to figuring out how to beat the Curse. Isn't that right, Doc?"

He looked at her and John couldn't help but note the look of scorn as well as the overall tone of disgust.

"I found out what is really going on. Callahan, you're not the fucking key, you're not the fucking cure. You are one of the reasons this goddamn virus keeps killing everyone."

"What do you mean? I thought I was immune to the Curse," John said with a quizzical look. He was working his mind feverishly to keep up with what Boulden was saying and what it all meant.

"Oh, so she hasn't told you yet? Well, that is *so* interesting." His voice dripped with sarcasm.

"Let's see if I can make it simple for you, Callahan. You're not immune to the Curse. You *are* the fucking Curse. Apparently, you are some sort of host allowing this goddamn virus to survive and even thrive. For some reason even our esteemed doctor here hasn't been able to figure out why. You and the Curse are one and the same. You have some sort of sick and twisted symbiotic relationship with the virus. It keeps you alive so it can stay alive.

"That means that you carry the virus with you everywhere you go and infect everyone you come in contact with. Remember those nice soldiers who brought you in. You know, the ones who saved your life out on that snowy night at the coast?"

John looked at Boulden warily and said, "Yeah, I remember them."

"Dead! All of them! You killed them. Yup, they assumed you were probably safe and got sloppy. When they took their masks off on the drive back, you infected them.

"That's quite the little thank you, you gave them, don't you think?"

John sank down on the edge of the bed and allowed his gaze to turn toward Dr. Mo. He wanted some confirmation Boulden was wrong, but her eyes were just cast down.

"I'm sorry," John said, his voice breaking. "I'm so, so sorry."

"Yeah, Callahan, fuck lot of good that does! Those soldiers were among my best and were a hell of a lot more important to our survival than you. In fact, as long as you are alive, you are the most significant threat to our survival. Maybe with you dead, the Curse will finally burn itself out.

"What do you think Callahan? Doesn't that make sense? I mean if you are a host for this virus and it somehow feeds off you, taking away its food source and its home environment might just kill it. It seems pretty logical to me. What do you think?"

John turned back to Dr. Mo. "Doc, you gotta tell me. Is this true? Am I responsible for those soldiers' deaths?"

Just as Dr. Mo raised her gaze and opened her mouth to speak, they both heard Boulden start laughing.

"Callahan, you really must be a fucking idiot. You haven't figured it out yet? Jesus, what the hell is wrong with you?"

John could tell Boulden was getting even more excited. Through the visor, John saw his face reddening.

"You shouldn't be so concerned about the soldiers. I mean, after all, they weren't the only important people you killed."

John felt himself starting to flush and get warm. Standing back up, he said, "What are you talking about?"

"Your fucking family, you idiot! Jesus, you haven't figure that out yet? You killed your fucking family. You are the one who exposed them to the Curse. Maybe they were immune to some of the early mutations you carried with you but eventually you allowed the fucking virus to mutate to a strain your family *wasn't* immune to. Congrats, Callahan! You killed your wife and kids!" He started maniacally laughing again.

John could feel the rage coming over him and balled up his fists. A quick look at the guards by the door showed they anticipated this emotion and they both raised their rifles.

Boulden was still laughing but John didn't notice anymore. Looking back at him, John saw Boulden had his handgun out and was pointing it at him.

"Time's up, Callahan. Slowly walk over to the soldiers and put your hands behind your back. We're going for a little walk."

Boulden was positioned between John and Dr. Mo, with his handgun in his left hand. Suddenly Dr. Mo reached over to grab Boulden by the right arm.

"Major, you can't do this. This isn't right."

Boulden violently swung to his right and effortlessly threw Dr. Mo to the corner. She flew over a chair and hit the wall with a loud thump.

For as long as he would live, John Callahan would never understand what happened next. The last time he had been in a physical altercation, *any* physical altercation, was in sixth grade. Even that fight ended with a single punch to his stomach. John had barely gotten his fists clenched before he doubled over and went down. He never received any training in any form of martial arts and was never in the military. Nonetheless, in one burst of energy, John reached out with his left hand and grabbed Boulden's wrist, extending the left arm fully.

Boulden was turning his head back around but not quickly enough. With Boulden's left arm fully extended, John took the base of his palm and drove it like a piston through the elbow joint of Boulden's arm. The human arm is designed to bend in one direction. John both felt and heard Boulden's entire left elbow joint explode in the wrong direction.

For just a brief moment, John saw Boulden's eyes widen and then a piercing scream erupted from his mouth. John wasn't thinking. This was an instinctual action, as was his next action. John reached down for Boulden's gun and quickly positioned himself behind the slumping major.

Looking at the two guards, they were moving around, trying to get a clear shot at him without hitting their commanding officer.

"Put your guns down now or I will blow his fucking brains out!" John screamed.

The soldiers looked at one another, unsure of what to do.

"Put the guns down NOW! He's not dead but he sure as fuck will be if you don't put your guns down right now."

Looking back and forth between each other and this obviously demented and dangerous man, they slowly lowered their weapons and put them on the ground.

"Okay, here's what is going to happen. Open the door and slide your guns outside and I don't just mean the rifles. I want to see your handguns and the Tasers go too."

One of the soldiers said, "How do we know you won't just kill us?"

"I have no desire to kill anyone." John was simultaneously trying to lower his voice and hide his shaking. He was pushing the handgun hard into the side of Boulden's head, not so much to hurt him or to scare the soldiers but to hide the fact that his entire body was trembling.

"Once you have your guns outside…oh, and your radios too, you're going to walk into the bathroom and close the door behind you. I'm then going to leave and I'll lock the door behind me." In his mind, he was trying to figure out how this plan would work. John had no idea what he would do once he was out of the room, but this at least gave him a chance to survive.

The two soldiers looked at each other again and both nodded. It took a while for them to put their weapons on the floor and slide them out to the hallway. John could only hope they didn't have any more weapons underneath their Hazmat suits.

As they started to walk toward the bathroom, John said, "Where are the keys?"

One of the soldiers threw them on the bed. An idea then came to him.

"Before either of you decide to be too brave and try to come after me, I'm taking Dr. Mo with me. If anyone tries to stop me, I'll kill her. Do you both understand?"

Both soldiers nodded and walked into the bathroom. John released Boulden and he slumped to the floor, unconscious. Quickly frisking him, John took a set of keys and a radio and tossed both of them out the open door. He shut the bathroom door and propped a chair against it. He then turned to where Dr. Mo was slumped in the corner. She was staring at him wide-eyed.

"Doc, are you okay?"

She nodded yes and slowly reached her arm out. John grasped it and slowly helped her stand.

"Don't worry, Doc. I would never hurt you. You are the only one here who has been nice to me. I just need you as a hostage so I can get out of the camp."

"John, are you sure that's the best thing? I mean, you *are* a host."

"Doc, I have no reason to doubt you. If I'm a host than I'm a host. I'll just disappear and never have contact with any human being again. Maybe I'll go back to the coast and just wait until my time is up. It's possible, isn't it, that the virus might mutate again and kill me? It's possible, right?"

"With this particular virus, anything is possible."

She was standing now, rubbing her shoulder where it had hit the wall.

"Let's go, Doc. I'll be behind you but if anyone comes after us, I'm going to point the gun at your head. I promise, however, I will never fire it. I'll shoot myself before ever hurting you. Do you believe me?"

"I do, John. I do."

John gently put his arm around Dr. Mo's waist and they walked out the door. Closing it behind them, Dr. Mo locked it without even being asked. The hallway was mostly dark and completely deserted. John tried a couple of doors before finding one that would open. Tucking one pistol into the back of his pants, he tossed the rest of the guns and radios in and then shut the door.

"How do we get out of here?" John asked.

"It's down this hall. We're on the second floor of the building so there will be a single set of stairs right through the door."

They walked and at the bottom of the stairs, John pushed the door open and was immediately blinded by the sunlight.

❦

CHAPTER THIRTY-FOUR

Truckin'

As soon as his eyes adjusted, John was shocked by how different the OHSU campus looked. He recognized instantly that buildings were missing, even if he couldn't remember what they had been. Rather than a labyrinth of hospital and medical buildings, it was now apparently down to six or so. Some structures lay in rubble while others had been cleared and turned into parking lots.

Looking to his left, he saw a lot full of trucks of all different types. There had to be more than twenty tanker trucks, together with flatbeds, semi-trucks and trailers. Over to his right was a large lot containing all sorts of military vehicles. John recognized the Humvees and the tanks, but the others appeared to be vehicles he wasn't familiar with.

John noticed people walking around, some in hazmat suits and a few in just ordinary clothes. Most seemed to be walking with a purpose and no one seemed to take any notice of them.

With Dr. Mo mostly leading the way, they started heading to the lot with the military vehicles. John stopped and tugged her the other way, toward the truck parking lot.

258

"Where are we going?" she asked.

"I've got an idea. Have you ever driven a large truck?"

"No," she responded.

"Yeah, me neither. This may, however, be as good a time as any to learn."

Without knowing how much time he had, John quickly pulled Dr. Mo along with him as they walked to the lot. He felt very uneasy and exposed being out in the open, so he took their first opportunity to walk between the trucks. He was looking for a tanker truck that gave him the straightest possible path out of the parking lot.

"The gate is over there, right?" he said, pointing toward the north.

"Yes, it's right around that building there."

"Okay, Doc, let's give this a try. Climb on up into the cab and let's see if I can start this beast."

John wasn't worried about Dr. Mo running away. He knew she wanted to help him and that, without understanding why, she had already done so.

Opening the door for her, he watched as she clambered up into the cab of the truck. He then walked around the front and climbed into the driver side. While he had driven small rental trucks before, the instrument panel on this vehicle was completely foreign to him. There were multiple gauges, but he knew there was no point in trying to figure them out. He wouldn't be driving far enough for any of them to be a concern.

As he had hoped, the keys were in the ignition. Putting his left foot on the clutch pedal, he pushed it fully down. He then placed his right foot on the brake pedal and turned the ignition key. The engine started right up and it was loud.

John knew that now was the tough part. The first thing he needed to do was to find and release the emergency brake. This only took seconds and he kept his right foot fully down on the brake.

There was the stick shift with a couple of buttons both on the left and the backside of the knob. He had no idea how many gears there might be or how fast he would be able to go, but there was no time to worry about that. When he was young, John's father insisted he learn how to drive a standard transmission. He learned how to shift gears on an old Opal Cadet and a Toyota Corolla. The basic shape for every manual transmission he'd ever driven was an H, with reverse usually over and up.

John knew that trucks like this had more than just four gears but all he needed was to get up to a decent speed. Hopefully he could do that in the four gears he knew without having to figure out what buttons or levers to push to get to the next set.

Putting the truck into what he hoped was first gear, John slowly let out the clutch while pushing down on the accelerator. The truck shuddered and John pushed harder. The engine started racing loudly and John let the clutch fully out as the truck inched forward.

He was looking out the window and people starting to turn in their direction due to the sound of the engine racing. With the truck moving, albeit very slowly, John put the truck into second gear and it picked up a little speed. This time the shift was smoother as he was starting to figure out how quickly he could let the clutch out while pushing down on the accelerator. He took a glance at the speedometer and noted that he was still going less than five miles per hour. He needed more speed. The engine was still loud and racing. More people stopped and stared.

Shifting the truck into third gear, John started steering it out of the parking lot and onto the road. The speedometer was starting to creep up to ten miles per hour. He shifted into fourth gear.

To his right, he saw a group of men running toward the building they'd just come out of. Apparently, Boulden and his soldiers had figured out a way to call for help.

Looking ahead, he saw people were starting to gather in groups and point at them. The engine was making a lot of noise, but John didn't really care. He put his foot on the clutch and tried everything he could to find a higher gear, all to no avail. Putting it back into fourth gear before he lost any speed, John just pushed the accelerator as far down as he could. He looked at the tachometer and it was in the red zone. Now the truck was moving at almost fifteen miles an hour but, more importantly, it just crested a small hill and would now be travelling downhill and directly at the gates.

"John, what are you going to do? JOHN? JOHN?"

He didn't bother to respond other than to say, "Hold on, Doc!"

The guards were only 100 or so feet ahead of him and they were both standing in front of the gate motioning for him to stop. He ignored them and kept pushing down on the accelerator.

Every fiber of John's attention and strength was focused on holding the truck in control. He briefly looked over at Dr. Mo out of the corner of his eye and saw her curled up on the seat, seemingly trying to make herself as small as possible. Just moments before he crashed into the first gate, John took a deep breath and closed his eyes.

The gate was made of wood and metal and was no match for the momentum of the heavy truck. It collapsed with one of the panels flying over the truck cab and the other attaching itself to the top of the engine compartment. John didn't even notice the noise as he was gearing up for the impact with the second gate. This gate was no better than the first at stopping the truck. They cruised right through and onto Sam Jackson Park Road.

For the first time, John took his foot off the accelerator and started to push down on the brake as the first sharp turn of the road was quickly approaching. He had a plan but couldn't afford to lose control and drive off the edge of the road. The drop-off was steep enough and if they went over, they would not survive.

Pushing harder and harder on the brake pedal while downshifting, he felt the truck start to slow just as he came around the first corner. A quick look at the speedometer showed that he was only going twelve miles an hour but if felt much faster. He continued braking as the road became a series of switchbacks. The truck continued to slow.

"What now, John?"

He ignored her. It took all of his concentration to be able to handle this truck and right now his focus was on bringing it to a stop.

"Why are you stopping?"

As the speedometer continued to slow, John steered the truck into the right-hand lane and then, just as it was coming to a complete stop, he took a sharp left and turned the truck so that it was totally blocking both lanes.

"C'mon, Doc."

John jumped out of the cab and crawled under the tanker. Then he helped Dr. Mo step down from the passenger side of the cab.

"I don't understand, John."

"Doc, I needed the truck to get through the gates but there is no way I can outrace other vehicles out here. By blocking the road, the bad guys are going to have to go all the way around. I figure I've got at least thirty minutes before they can get here."

John then took out the gun he had taken from Boulden. As he pulled it out, Dr. Mo flinched.

"Don't worry, Doc. This isn't for you. Cover your ears!"

John then bent down and fired a shot through the rear tires of the tanker. The truck tilted to the side. He then took another shot at the tires on the other side and the tanker settled down on the road. He then used a final shot on the left front tire, tilting the truck slightly uphill. The gunshots were loud and reverberated against the walls of the hill. John reached into the cab of the truck, grabbed the keys and threw them down the embankment as far as he could.

"This truck isn't going anywhere for a while. Now, let's go."

"John, I can't."

"What do you mean? If you go back, you know Boulden will

blame you for all of this. He's batshit crazy and who knows what he'll do."

"I'm not going but I'm also not going back. John, I'm tired. I'm tired of fighting this virus and losing. I'm tired of seeing all the death. I'm tired of seeing what we, the surviving members of the human species, are turning into.

"I miss my wife." Her face was turned to the side but John saw tears in her eyes.

"I don't know if this is God's way of saying that His children have failed so miserably that, instead of a Noah-style flood, he is using the Curse to wipe us out. Maybe it is just Mother Nature deciding to strike back at the pestilence—us, who have done so many evil things to this planet.

"Whatever it is, humankind as a species is going to be extinct for all intents and purposes. I have no reason to think anyone is going to find the magic bullet for the Curse. I heard two more bases went dark this morning. That means, at best, there are three bases still in existence throughout the entire continent.

"Over the coming weeks, or months at best, we are all going to die. You might survive but you will be one of the very few. I'd be surprised if there are more than a couple of thousand like you throughout the whole continent. Even if you survive the virus, it will be a very isolated and lonely experience. Most of the survivors will not last long whether due to an inability to adapt or untreated medical conditions.

"I'm not going to survive, John. Without a vaccine, it is only a matter of time before I am infected and die. What is the point of continuing to fight a battle I can't win?"

John tried to position himself to be able to look her in the eye. She continued to avoid his gaze.

"Can I ask you a question?"

This time, Dr. Mo turned and looked right at him.

"Am I really responsible for my family's death?"

Shaking her head, she asked, "John, have you ever heard of Mary Mallon?"

This time it was John's turn to shake his head no.

"You might know her by her nickname—Typhoid Mary. Mallon was an Irish immigrant working as a cook for a number of families in New York City. When her employers kept dying from Typhoid Fever, it was determined she was the cause. Mallon was the first known person identified as an "asymptomatic carrier." She was infected by the pathogen associated with Typhoid Fever but didn't experience any of the symptoms.

"She, like you, spread the disease without suffering herself. What we don't know about you, however, is when you became an asymptomatic carrier. It is possible that you and your family were all carriers to a certain degree but that the virus, at some point, mutated and became deadly for your family. I have no idea why it didn't turn deadly for you also.

"I wish I knew for sure but I'm only guessing at this point. Let's say it's just as possible that one of your family members first infected you as it is that you first infected them."

Now it was John who turned away as the tears started rolling down his cheeks.

"Think of it this way, even if you hadn't been a carrier, it is likely that the Curse would have gotten your family at some point. It is showing no signs of burning itself out so, at worst, you just sped up the inevitable."

John wiped his eyes with the bottom of his scrub shirt. Out of the corner of his eye, he saw Dr. Mo's hands move up to the helmet of her hazmat suit and she started taking it off.

"NO! DON'T!"

Before he could reach out to her, she had the helmet completely off and was taking a deep breath. With her eyes closed, she let out a slow sigh.

"I've really missed the smell of fresh air. Can you smell the trees and the flowers out there, John? Can you?"

"Doc, doesn't this mean…"

"Yes, absolutely."

She reached out and took his hand.

"I'm going to miss the smells, John. More than anything else, I'm going to miss being able to just stand and smell the flowers and trees on a warm spring day. I'm going to miss the feel of the wind and the warmth of the sun on my face.

"I've been very fortunate. We, as a species, have been very fortunate. The dinosaurs had the comet that wiped them out and we've got the Curse. Take care of yourself, John. I'm not sure that I'd trade places with you even if I could."

With that, she took a step toward him and lifting up on her toes, she first put her face right up to his and took a deep breath in. She then exhaled and kissed him on the cheek.

"You had better get going. If you are right, you only have another twenty minutes or so before the bad guys, as you call them, get here.

"I'm going to just stay here, John. I'm going to sit right against that rock over there and let the sunshine on my face. It is only a matter of time before I start feeling the effects but until then, I'm going to enjoy the feeling of freedom for the first time in a long, long time.

"Goodbye, John Callahan. I wish you well no matter where your journey takes you. You are a good man and you deserve whatever remaining vestiges of happiness may lie out there for you to find. Be well but, even more importantly, be good."

Turning around, she walked over to a large rock and sat down on the ground with her back against the rock. The sun bathed her entire face and she looked almost beatific. John turned without a further word and began walking down the hill.

CHAPTER THIRTY-FIVE

Ain't Wastin' Time No More

The road was steep and as soon as he rounded another corner and was beyond the view of Dr. Mo, he started jogging down the hill. She was right. The soldiers were coming and it was only a matter of time before they got there. He was barefoot but the warmth of the asphalt was comforting.

At the bottom of Sam Jackson Park Road, John turned south on S.W. Terwilliger Boulevard. This had a slight upward slope, but John knew that by backtracking just a little bit, he might be able to throw off his pursuit. He hoped they would assume he would try to get as far away as quickly as possible and would bypass looking for him close to the camp.

One of the fortunate aspects of living in the Portland area was that there seemed to be walking and hiking trails everywhere. John quickly found a trailhead on his left and ran into the woods. This trail was both good and bad. On one hand, it provided him with cover so he couldn't be seen by anyone driving on the nearby roads. On the other hand, his bare feet began getting poked by roots and small rocks.

Continuing downhill, John carefully and quickly arrived at a large road. Perched in the bushes beside the road, he listened for any traffic. He was startled to hear a gunshot, but it was in the distance and sounded like it was from up at the camp. He crossed the road and found he was now in the middle of a residential neighborhood. He looked at the street signs but didn't recognize any of the names.

While the sun was out, he kept mostly to the shadows where the air was cooler. John shivered involuntarily. He could feel the adrenaline dump approaching again and knew fatigue would soon overwhelm him. Looking at the houses around him, some burned and others not, John noted the windows were all dark. He imagined people inside looking out at him. He knew he'd used up at least a week's worth of adrenaline in just a little over an hour and needed to find shelter soon. Exhaustion was affecting his ability to think clearly.

One of the benefits of Major Boulden's program to locate survivors was that John didn't need to worry about encountering rotting corpses. The houses containing the dead had been torched. All he needed to find was a house, somewhat secluded, which was still whole.

He walked by a couple of houses knowing that if the soldiers decided to look for him in this neighborhood, he wanted some warning. He didn't want to be in the first house they might pull up to. About six houses down, he found a bungalow-style house. The front door was kicked in but, other than that, it was just dark and untouched.

Walking in he noted that the house smelled musty. He could live with that. With daylight streaming in the windows, John began his search of the house. The first place he went was the front closet where, as he hoped, there was a flashlight. He also grabbed a large coat, much too large for him, but still a coat and it slowly stopped the shivering.

The kitchen was his next stop. He held his breath as he opened the refrigerator door. Even without breathing, John could sense the stench of rotting food. Nonetheless, he saw a couple of cans of cola and bottles of water. He went back to the front closet and found a small backpack. Returning to the kitchen, he filled the backpack with all of the drinks he could find, together with crackers, cookies, and peanut butter. He turned and walked back to the front of the house and up the stairs.

There were three bedrooms and John ransacked all of them until he found some clothes he could wear. The jeans were too short and too baggy, but he fixed that with a belt. He put a fresh Nirvana t-shirt on, with a University of Oregon sweatshirt over it. Chuckling, he put some Birkenstock sandals on and looked at himself in the mirror, marveling how he was the stereotype of a pre-Curse Portlander. He put the coat back on and sat down on a bed. He drank down a full bottle of water.

Giving into the fatigue, John lay down and in only a matter of moments, was in a deep, dreamless sleep.

༄

He had no idea how long he slept but it must have been a while as it was now dark outside. It took a moment for him to remember where he was. Picking up the flashlight, John sat up and drank another bottle of water. He needed a plan.

It would only be a matter of time before the soldiers came to check out these houses. He didn't know Boulden well, but he didn't seem like the kind of guy who would just let someone get the better of him. Boulden would have everyone possible looking for him and it would only be a matter of time before they started searching the near-in neighborhoods. John could hear the sound of a lot of vehicles, though not like before the Curse, driving in the distance.

"Damn it," he cursed quietly and then wondered why he hadn't grabbed one of the radios Boulden and his goons were using. A radio would have allowed him to at least understand what was happening at the camp.

Standing up, John worked his way into the hallway and down the stairs. He had a gnawing in his stomach and needed something to eat. Suddenly he heard a loud noise and jumped back, holding the flashlight in front of him.

On the floor he saw a can of soup rolling in his direction. He pointed the flashlight in the direction the can had come from and saw the largest raccoon he had ever seen in his life sitting on the kitchen counter.

The raccoon looked at John and they just stared at one another for what, to John, seemed like an eternity. After a while, the raccoon opened its mouth, showed its sharp teeth, and hissed. Convinced that this was not a fight he wanted, John reached down and slowly picked up the backpack. He then backed out of the kitchen. Once in the hallway, he walked outside the house. In the distance and up the hill, toward the camp, John heard more gunfire. He could also hear the sound of vehicles but couldn't tell how near or far they might be.

The night air was cold, but the moon was out and shone its light all around. The world, when just lit by moonlight, was a tapestry of shade and shadows rather than one of color. He could distinguish the trees from the houses but not the trees from one another or the houses from one another. He began walking.

Instinctively, he looked down at his wrist where his Fitbit normally sat. He hadn't thought about time for quite a while but now, wondering what time it actually was, it seemed natural to look at his wrist. He began to ponder the concept of time. Time really didn't apply to him anymore and hadn't for quite a while. There was no longer a need for any specific hours in the day. He would try to eat when he was hungry and sleep when he was tired. There were no hours in the day, merely sunrises and sunsets—daylight and darkness.

It was the same with the calendar. He could guess that it was April or May but didn't really know. Days and months were irrelevant. It was the seasons that were of import.

What would life be like, he wondered, without the structure of time and calendars? John's life had always been structured, first with school and then his career, intermixed with familial obligations. Now the term "footloose and fancy free" sprung to mind although he knew it didn't really apply. It was, however, one more reminder of how different this new life was from his past.

With his sight limited by what the moon illuminated, John listened. The sound of trucks became fainter and more intermittent. In their place, he began to hear the sounds of nature.

First and foremost was the steady hum of the river. It was less than a mile away and created a very distinct, low drone. Next, there was the wind rustling the leaves in the trees. He could hear it as it flowed around the houses. The frogs and crickets were out in force but, other than those, it was quiet. No sound of traffic or hum of voices; no televisions or radios; no telephones.

Walking up to the next house, John knocked on the door. He did this not out of some instinctive habit but in order to alert any wild animals to his presence. Like the previous house, the front door was smashed in and the interior of the house was musty.

Conducting a quick but thorough search, John was satisfied there were no animals in the house that might cause him concern. He closed the broken front door as best he could and slid a dresser in front of it. By doing so, John would at least know that no raccoons or other animals would come in and surprise him.

Walking into the kitchen, he panned the flashlight across the room. The refrigerator would be horrible, but he needed to see if there might be anything to drink. He almost let out a loud whoop when he spotted a six pack of beer.

There was a pantry to the side and John discovered a wide range of food. Unfortunately, much of it required cooking but there were still cookies and Wheat Thins. The bread was moldy, but he did find another jar of peanut butter. Grabbing a knife from a drawer, John sat down on the floor and, bite by bite, devoured the entire container.

Between the beer and the peanut butter, John felt momentarily relaxed. The headache that he'd carried with him since his escape was easing away. He was still tired and his feet were sore. Nonetheless, he had to keep moving. The question now was what to do next. He was too close to the camp to stay there. It would only be a matter of days, if not hours, before the soldiers would come looking in this neighborhood. He needed to put some distance between him and them. The best way to accomplish that would be to cross the Willamette River. At least on the east side of the river, he would have a little more distance and hopefully more warning if the army got close.

Standing up, John walked back outside and drank a full can of cola before urinating into some bushes. He began walking east toward the Ross Island Bridge.

CHAPTER THIRTY-SIX

PEARL OF THE QUARTER

I f he had to guess, John would say that it was maybe one o'clock in the morning. There were clouds, but the moon still peeked out from time to time and was high in the sky. He stayed hidden in the shadows while walking down S.W. Kelly Street and turning onto the onramp for the bridge. Looking back and up the hill, the camp was lit up. Beams from headlights moved up and down, as well as across, the hill above him while the other side of the river was dark with few shapes discernible.

John knew the Ross Island Bridge turned into S.E. Powell Boulevard as it wound its way toward Mt. Hood. There would be some residential neighborhoods directly to the south and a few blocks to the east. To the north would be primarily warehouses and mostly older commercial buildings.

His plan was to hole up during the next day in one of the houses just to the south and then figure out what to do next. The most important thing was to make sure that the soldiers didn't find him as he could only imagine how painful a reunion with

Major Boulden would be. John got lucky once to surprise him but didn't anticipate that he would be given a second chance.

Approaching the bridge, John could hear, but not see, the river rushing beneath him. The moon only provided enough light so that he was able to avoid tripping over any debris that might be on the sidewalk. He could see the shapes of various vehicles strewn across the width of the bridge. The empty vehicles started on the approach to the bridge and continued as far as he could see. There wasn't enough light to see the end of the bridge and he could only estimate when he was halfway across.

In the distance, John suddenly heard a sharp but soft noise and then instantly felt something strike the concrete at his feet, spraying cement chips up and into his legs. Letting out a sharp cry, John immediately clapped his hand over his mouth and fell to the ground. He nudged his body as close to the bridge railing as possible in order to minimize his size.

Holding his breath, John listened. Despite being positioned up against the railing, he knew he was exposed. He wasn't even sure where the gunshot had come from. John slowly let out his breath and began to regulate it so as to be as quiet as possible. He tried to hear if there were any footsteps, which might tell him where his attacker was and which way he had to run to escape.

He started counting and after he hit 30, there was still nothing—no footsteps and no additional gunshots. Struggling up to his hands and knees, John started crawling across the bridge. He knees hurt on the rough concrete, but he barely noticed. He was focusing all his attention on his hearing, the only sense that might help him at this point.

He heard another sharp noise and before he could fling himself against the railing, he was again sprayed with concrete chips. This time he didn't make a sound but, instead, just stayed as still as he could.

"Who are you?"

It was a hard but low voice and John couldn't tell where it was coming from.

"Are you fucking deaf? I said who are you?"

Without being able to see in which direction to face, John just looked away from the railing and said "John Callahan. My name is John Callahan."

For at least thirty seconds there was no noise other than the hum of the river down below.

"Are you a soldier?"

"No, no. I'm trying to get away from the soldiers."

This time he heard what sounded like a slight, guttural laugh.

"Ah, you must be the reason for all the ruckus."

John had no idea how to respond or even if he should respond so he just waited. His breath and heart rate both slowed and John reached down to his legs. He was able to pull a few small concrete chips out of his leg and could tell that there was no substantial damage.

"Do you have any weapons?" It was the voice again, only this time it sounded closer.

"Just a revolver," John quietly responded.

"What kind of revolver?"

John was surprised by this question and tried to figure out how to respond. He reached into his pocket and started to take the handgun out.

"I wouldn't do that if I were you."

John stopped drawing the gun out and placed his hand back on the concrete.

"What kind of revolver do you have?"

"I don't know, a nine-millimeter, I think."

This time, John heard another dry chuckle and was startled to feel a hand on his shoulder grabbing him and pulling him to his feet.

"Get going."

He was propelled forward and guided around the various vehicles in the road. John looked over his shoulder but couldn't get a good look at the person. He heard the sound of the river decrease slightly and John recognized that he was no longer over the river but, rather, across the bridge. In the darkness ahead, he saw what looked like a large wall and before he could stop to try to figure out what to do, he was pushed to his left and then to his right, through an opening. Once past the wall, the hand on his shoulder lifted. John looked for someplace to get off the road and made out a couple of trees on the north side of the road. He scrambled across the road and stopped by the trees, leaning against one of them.

While catching his breath, John peered through the darkness looking for the man but still couldn't see anything.

"I'll give you twenty minutes to catch your breath and then get out of this zone. If I see you after that time, I will shoot you and there will be no warning shots for that."

It was unnerving to not just hear this threat but to not be able to identify where the voice was coming from. Briefly he wondered if the man had night vision goggles but decided it didn't really matter. Rather than spending his limited time trying to figure out who this guy was, John tried to remember what this part of town looked like.

John decided to try to buy himself some time and maybe get some helpful information as to where to go.

"Who are you?" he asked.

John waited for a response but got none. He wondered if that was because the man was just not going to talk to him any further or if he might no longer be there. He hoped for the latter but suspected that the former was a more likely explanation.

Finally getting his bearings, at least as best he could, John decided to cross the road and head to the residential neighborhood just to the south. As he stepped foot on the road to cross it, he heard the voice just say "Nope!"

"Goddammit, where do you expect me to go? I need some place to stay until I can figure out where to go next."

Again, there was no response.

"Fuck you!" John said and he recognized that he spoke it loud enough for his voice to carry but he didn't care. He turned around and walked back to the trees and down a small hill. At the bottom was a road and John, staying to one side, started walking north.

In the dark, he could make out open spaces alternating with large dark shapes that he assumed were buildings. He walked about two blocks and then turned a corner and sat down with his back against a building. He reached into one of his coat pockets and pulled out a can of cola.

It was warm but it gave him a small jolt of energy.

"So, you met Tex, huh?"

John jumped to his feet and pulled out his handgun. He was getting tired of the voices coming out of nowhere and startling him. This time, however, he recognized it as a woman's voice.

"Where are you?" John's voice was soft but urgent.

Off to his left, he saw a flashlight turn on and shine out toward his feet. The beam travelled up his body and into his eyes. He shielded his eyes from the bright light.

"Who are you?" he said and pushed himself against the wall with his gun outstretched in front of him.

"Don't worry, I'm not a threat. Put your gun down and follow me."

John both saw and felt the light travel away from him and point toward an opening to the building just ahead. The light and the person holding it disappeared inside. In the dim glow of the flashlight, he could see her wheelchair. John reluctantly followed.

Calling out, "Wait!" John saw the flashlight beam and a head come back out.

"I've got the Curse."

"Wow, that's something I never would have expected." The sarcasm in her voice was clear.

"No, you don't understand, I'm some sort of carrier. It's not just that I am somehow immune but I'm like a Typhoid Mary or something."

"Okay, that's something different but I don't really care."

"How can you not care? I may have some version of the virus that could kill you."

There was a momentary pause and then the women responded, this time sounding a little more tired. "Look, buddy, I'm scared of a lot of things. I'm scared that I may end up being the last person in the whole world. I'm scared that some wild animals might attack me. I'm scared that I might fall out of this fucking wheelchair and not be able to get back in it and then die a slow and miserable death. What I'm not scared of is the fucking Curse. If the Curse gets me, at least I know I'll die a fairly quick death. I can handle that. Now get in here before someone sees or hears us."

With the light shining dimly outside of the door, John walked inside. While he couldn't see what the interior looked like, he could hear his footsteps echo and recognized that the building was cavernous.

Over to the right was a small area lit with what looked like a nightlight. He could see the person with the flashlight roll over to it and then shift out of her chair and onto a small couch.

"C'mon, I won't bite."

John cautiously walked over. He still had the gun in his hand but had it pointing to the ground rather than ahead of him.

"Who are you?" John asked.

"Yeah, we don't really do that around here, but you can call me Lisa if you want."

"What do you mean 'we don't really do that around here'?"

"There aren't many of us around here and we've found that it is best to share as little information with one another as possible. You never know when someone might try to use information against you. Plus, there's no point in getting to know someone when they will likely just die soon enough."

As John sat down on the floor across from the couch, Lisa explained that she had been living in this warehouse for a couple of weeks. It wasn't much but it kept her out of the elements and relatively safe. There were a few others living in here, but they weren't as social as she.

John listened intently and then asked, "Who is the guy out there?"

In the pale light, John could see her smile as she said, "Oh, that's Tex."

"What is his real name?"

Lisa stared at John and said, "Does it really matter?" She then reached down and pulled out a hot plate and plugged it into a small appliance that John didn't recognize.

"You have power?" John asked incredulously.

"I have a solar powered generator. I charge it during the day and then use it at night. It gives me a little light and lets me use a hot plate to heat up my food."

Lisa explained to John how the generator worked. As she poured a can of soup into a pan and started stirring it, she also explained that Tex was some sort of military guy, probably a combat veteran, and that he guarded the east side of the bridge. Tex, for some reason, hated Major Boulden and the military and shot at them any time they tried to cross the river.

Tex established a small zone that he controlled and he only allowed certain people to stay there. Mostly it was people with various handicaps or young children; many of whom had been tossed out from the camp. The military didn't dare enter the zone because Tex was well-armed and turned back various attempts to attack him. Apparently, they had established an effective truce whereby the military left Tex and his little zone alone and he left them alone. There was no point in attacking someone who could kill or injure enough of them to result in a net loss of people.

Pouring a serving of soup into a small coffee cup, Lisa asked John where he came from. He quickly summarized that he had come from the camp but left out specific details other than the fact that he had to destroy the gates to get out.

"So, you're the one who stirred up the hornets' nest."

Taking a spoonful of what tasted like vegetable soup, John asked, "What do you mean?"

"Well, I've gotten somewhat used to how the folks at the camp operate and follow their comings and goings. Over the last 24 hours or so, there's been a frenzy of activity up there. There have been a lot more vehicles coming down and they seem to be spreading out everywhere. Well, everywhere but here. They've still left us alone."

That confirmed John's fear that Major Boulden wasn't about to just let him go. He was going to have to get far away and quickly, but the question was how.

"If you're thinking about leaving, I wouldn't do it," Lisa said as she stared at him and could see him trying to work out his next step. "They've got roadblocks on all the major roads and foot patrols looking for…well, I guess looking for you."

"How do you know?"

"Tex has a radio and has warned me to stay close. I'd recommend that you do the same, at least for a while."

"But Tex told me to go."

"Yeah, he does that. He probably figured that either you could fend for yourself without his protection or that you are more trouble than you are worth. Either way, you can at least stay the night and get some rest."

They finished their soup and then Lisa cleaned up by tossing the rubbish into a garbage can and tightly sealing the lid. The plates were submerged in water that she kept in a basin. She explained that she didn't want to attract any animals into the building with the smell of food.

They agreed that John would sleep on the floor and she provided him with both a pillow and a heavy comforter. He wasted no time in falling asleep.

CHAPTER THIRTY-SEVEN

Dogs in the Yard

John awoke with an urgent need to pee. Slowly getting to his feet, he noticed that Lisa was gone. Walking toward the door he had come in the previous night, he pushed it open and took a deep breath. The air was cool but seemed so incredibly fresh. For a moment he wondered if the lack of exhaust from the cars, trucks and busses that normally swarmed throughout the area would really make such a difference in such a short time. Whether it did or not, John loved the scent of the fresh air.

As he was urinating against the side of the building, he looked around. It was going to be a glorious day. The sun was still low in the sky but there were few clouds. This would be the type of day best spent hiking in the Columbia Gorge or up on Mt. Hood.

Zipping up his pants, John walked back inside the building and found Lisa hunched over the hot plate. From the smell, he could tell that she was heating up coffee. There was now enough light for him to get a look at this woman. The problem was that with her bulky clothing and the hat she was wearing, he couldn't tell much about her. She could be anywhere from thirty to fifty years old. Other than that, however, she was just another fellow survivor.

"I…well I confirmed with Tex. You can't stay here."

She wasn't looking at him as she poured him a cup of coffee. John didn't respond.

"Look, I'd like to help you, but Tex thinks you create too much of a risk. I thought they were busy looking for you yesterday, but it looks like they have really increased their hunt. Trucks and cars have been swarming down from OHSU since before dawn.

"I don't know what the hell you did to them or why you might be so valuable, but they want to find you…badly."

This was not what John wanted to hear. He was tired of running and just wanted to find somewhere he could rest with some measure of safety. The way Lisa described it last night with Tex creating some sort of safe zone, John thought he might have found at least a temporary sanctuary. Now it was turning out to be way too temporary.

"I can't go out now, not in the light of day. They'll see me."

"I know. You can stay here until dusk and then you'll have to leave."

"Where am I supposed to go?"

"You might want to go up to Next Adventure, it's a couple of miles up the road. It's an outdoor store and you'll be able to pick up some camping supplies. They might even have some pouch meals left."

John stood up and started to pace back and forth. He needed to figure out what to do. He needed to find someplace where he could wait out the military. Dr. Mo told him that the virus was going to get everyone anyway so all he needed to do was to hide out long enough for the Curse to finish its work. Slowly an idea came to him.

"Where did you say this outdoor store is?" he asked.

Lisa looked up, somewhat surprised by the tone of his voice. She expected him to be dejected or defiant, but he was neither.

"It's up on Grand Avenue, just a couple blocks north of the Morrison Bridge. What are you thinking of?"

John looked at her and said with a bit of a smirk, "I thought we weren't supposed to share information."

This time it was Lisa's turn to smile and say, "Fair enough. It'll take you about an hour or so to get up to there."

Over the next several hours, the two of them talked about trivial matters such as sports and music. Lisa pulled out a small CD player and started playing some Metallica. John had never been a huge fan of the band but as he was working out his plans, the music seemed to be an appropriate backdrop.

John tried to get some sleep. He dreamed of playing catch with Brian and watching Cassie play soccer. It was really nice to see them again but then he was awakened by Lisa shaking his shoulder.

"It's time. It's not quite dark out but you should be able to hide in the shadows most of the way. I need to warn you about some things out there. The military is not your only threat. There are packs of dogs that have gone wild and really turned vicious. Be careful with them. They have no fear of humans and actually seem to be working out some hostility for who knows what—maybe for centuries of domestication. There are also other animals out there. I don't know what they are, but they lurk in the shadows and it almost looks like they are hunting those of us who remain.

"I don't know if your gun will be enough to protect you so be careful. Here's a flashlight. I recommend that you use it as little as possible. You won't want the bad guys to see it."

John thanked Lisa and even gave her an awkward hug. Putting on his coat, he began walking north, hiding behind buildings and trash containers anytime he heard a vehicle in the distance.

Crossing S.E. Morrison Street was difficult because of a large barricade stretching across the road. With his flashlight and the faint light from the moon, John could see various cars and trucks piled up, as well as concrete barriers. Scaling the barricade, John stepped out of Tex's safety zone and into the unknown.

For most of the thirty-plus years that he'd resided in the Portland area, there was little time spent in the inner eastside. He had always lived in Southwest Portland and only came across the river for business and some of the newer restaurants in town. In other words, he was in unfamiliar territory, even more unfamiliar in the dark.

He could hear vehicles, some close and some far, and knew that the search for him was still on. They apparently weren't going to quit for the night.

In the darkness, it was difficult to judge how far he'd walked and John was starting to worry that he might have passed the outdoor store. Vowing to walk just a couple of more blocks and then double back, John looked up and saw the sign, "Next Adventure."

The front door was shattered. Reaching into his pocket, he drew out his gun, with the flashlight still in his left hand. He turned the flashlight on only long enough to take a quick glance at the layout of the store. It was a shambles, but he could see that hiking shoes were on the far wall; tents were off to the left, along with some kayaks. There were stairs leading up to the second floor.

Turning off the flashlight, John slowly walked to the back of the store. While the hiking shoes on display might fit, he knew that he would have better luck going into the backroom where they, presumably, would be stored. He turned the flashlight back on but only long enough to find a set of double swinging doors that headed to the shoes.

Pushing through the doors, John quickly ransacked the shelves until he found a pair of hiking boots that were his size. Staying in the stockroom, he also located a large backpack. He was going to need some clothes and the backpack would allow him to carry them with him.

Walking back to the front of the store, John decided to see what was upstairs. He slowly walked up and used the flashlight to quickly assess the second floor of the store.

There was a glass counter that had various knives, Leatherman tools, ice axes, and hatchets. John threw a couple of knives and a Leatherman tool into the backpack. He undid his belt and threaded it through a holder for a hatchet and then placed the hatchet on his hip. It was heavy but it felt good. John then turned to see a wall filled with pouches of freeze-dried food. He filled up the rest of the backpack with these pouches, as well as some cooking supplies, and then walked downstairs. He dropped the backpack just inside the front door.

On his way back up the stairs, John grabbed another large backpack. This time he filled it with more food but also different brands of water purifiers. Never having used one before, he grabbed various kinds in the hope that he'd be able to figure out how to use at least one of them.

John saw a display of protein bars and, as sick of them as he was, threw a couple of boxes into the backpack. Before heading back downstairs, John flashed the light one more time around the room. He saw some small LED flashlights and put a handful into the backpack. He would need to organize his stash eventually but right now he needed to move quickly.

Dropping this second backpack by the first, he grabbed a third and started going through the clothes. He tossed underwear, socks, shorts and various shirts and light jackets into this third back-pack. He realized that he was basing the size of the clothes on his old weight. It was unlikely that his waist was still 34 inches. He quickly dropped his pants and tried on some shorts. The 32-inch waists were still too large, and he settled on 31-inches. For just a moment, he tried to remember the last time he had worn anything with a 31-inch waist and guessed that it must have been high school. He then swapped out all of the shorts and pants for ones with the 31-inch waist.

As he walked back to the front door, he saw a couple of wide brimmed hats. Liz always hated that style of hat, at least on him, and would never let him wear one in public. He was well past the point of trying to impress anyone anymore and he knew that the hats would be necessary with the amount of time he anticipated spending outside.

Dropping the third backpack by the front door, John looked around and grabbed a sleeping bag, a small tent, and a lightweight hammock and stacked them by the backpacks.

By this time, John had worked up a bit of sweat and he decided to sit and have a drink. As he was resting by the front door, he heard a truck engine nearby and backed up into the darkness. He saw the headlights well before he saw the truck and hid himself in among the racks of clothes.

Peering out through the front window, John saw the truck slowly pass by. It was a Humvee with spotlights on each side. The soldiers in back were shining the spotlights into every doorway and storefront as they passed. John was momentarily blinded when the spotlight lit upon him. Fortunately, the spotlight did not linger. Silently he congratulated himself on stashing the backpacks inside of the front door rather than on the sidewalk.

As the sound of the Humvee's engine faded into the distance, John recognized that he needed to get going. He did not want to be there when the sun came up. To his left was a display of kayaks. John lifted various models until he found one that was light enough for him to carry. He then grabbed an oar and some bungee cords.

Putting on one of the backpacks, John hoisted the kayak up on his shoulder and walked outside. He knew that he was only a few blocks from the river and immediately headed down S.E. Oak Street. He walked as quietly as possible and tried to stay in the shadows. While constantly listening for cars or trucks, John quickly made it down to the end of Oak Street and crossed the railroad tracks. This section of town offered John a lot of cover but also presented a physical challenge. He would need to cross under I-5, but that area was blocked by chain-link fences. The first was on the east side of I-5 and the other was on the west side. In the middle, between the northbound and southbound lanes was a concrete barrier he would need to climb over.

Walking up to the first fence, John looked to see if there might be an opening but found none. There were some bushes and he tucked the kayak and the backpack behind them.

Rather than walking back up Oak, John walked down a block and walked up S.E. Washington Street. He hoped that he could find a store or mechanic shop that might have a bolt cutter or something else he could use to cut through the fencing.

He'd only gone a couple of blocks when he noticed a store with bars in the windows. Using the flashlight to peer in, he saw it was a hardware store. With a big smile on his face, he walked up to the front door. It was still intact and locked. After pausing for a moment to listen for engine noises, John quickly broke the front door window with his flashlight, unlocked the deadbolt, and walked right in.

While he knew that this store could be a great resource for him sometime in the future, the only thing he really needed at this point was something to cut the chain-link. It didn't take him long to find a bolt cutter and he quickly left and headed back to the outdoor store. He did notice, about a block further up, the Portland Music Company and resisted the urge to grab a guitar. Like the hardware store, there would be things there that he would like but none that were absolutely necessary at this time.

The second trip down to the river involved a second kayak and another backpack. He was getting tired but knew that he only had limited time to accomplish what needed to be done.

As he headed back to the outdoor store for his final trip, he noticed what looked like a convenience store across the street. Deciding that he might be able to find some additional supplies there, John picked up the last backpack and then headed across the street. As with most others around, the store's front door was smashed so he could walk right in.

Laying the backpack inside the front door, John quickly filled a grocery bag with nail clippers and tweezers, as well as aspirin and Pepto Bismol. In another grocery bag, he stashed cookies and various containers of ramen noodles. Picking up his backpack and placing it over his shoulder, and holding the two grocery bags, John walked out the door. Distracted by his thoughts, he didn't notice the growling at first.

In the darkness, he stopped, slowly putting the bags on the ground, and reaching for his flashlight. The source of the growling was obvious, and he could see at least ten dogs only 20 or so feet away. When the flashlight turned on, the dogs all jumped backward slightly but then began to growl even louder. This was a wide variety of dogs. In the middle, and presumably the alpha dog of this pack, was a large Rottweiler similar to the one he'd seen at the cabin. On either side were some pit bulls, as well as another six medium-sized dogs of indistinguishable breeds.

John stood as tall as he could, hoping that his size, especially with the large backpack over his shoulder, would scare off the dogs. It didn't. They started to growl louder and slowly approach. Lowering his right arm, John felt for his gun but realized that it was in his left pocket. The dogs continued their snarling approach.

Reaching to his belt and unclipping the clasp, John gripped the hatchet just as the pit bulls leapt at him. Swinging the backpack in front of him, the dogs first latched onto it. They wouldn't be fooled for long but there was just enough time for John to rear back and plant the blade of the hatchet behind the left ear of one of the dogs. The dog let out a shriek and John pulled the hatchet back as the other pit bulls raised their eyes to focus on him again.

Wasting no time, John threw the backpack in the direction of the pit bulls and quickly turned and ran into the store. Being outnumbered, John realized that he needed both protection and time, so he ran to the back of the store. Perhaps it was the stress of the situation, but John seemed to be able to see better in the dark than he expected. Just before reaching the back wall, John saw the door to the cooler and, with the dogs running after him, pulled the door open and leaped in. As he tried to it behind him, one of the dogs got his head in and grabbed his pant leg. John briefly opened the door and then slammed it with all of his might, striking the side of the dog. With a yelp, the dog let go of the pant leg just long enough for John to kick it in the snout, pushing it backward, and allowing him to slam the door shut.

John leaned against the door and took a deep breath, only to start coughing as he was overwhelmed with the odor of sour milk. The cooler was cramped and with a horrible stench but at least it was safe. He could hear the dogs rampaging throughout the store, snarling, and scratching at the cooler door.

He hoped that they would grow bored and leave quickly but John wondered what might happen if they didn't. It was only a matter of time before the military would drive by and see the backpack and the dead dog. He was trapped and he needed to figure out how to get out.

While John's main worry was getting caught, he quickly realized that he had a greater, and more immediate, concern. While leaning against the door considering his options, he was startled when he heard a loud thud against one of the glass doors. Immediately, another one sounded, and John turned his flashlight on.

Looking out, John saw two dogs stumbling around but suddenly a third dog took a running leap at one of the glass doors and struck it with his forehead. He bounced off and quickly fell to the ground, shaking. John noticed, however, that a small crack had appeared in the glass. Just as he was noticing this, one of the other dogs took a run at the same door and smashed into it. This time the crack expanded and turned into a star shape.

The dogs must have figured out that by concentrating their efforts, they could weaken and eventually break the glass. John could only watch as dog after dog ran full speed into the glass. With every impact, the glass would push further inward and the cracks would grow. Realizing that it was only a matter of time before the dogs were successful in breaching the glass door, John shut off his flashlight and waited.

Within only few minutes, glass started falling inward and a hole appeared in the door. One of the dogs stuck his head through it. He was snarling and barking as best he could through the small hole. Taking out his handgun, John placed it in the dog's mouth and immediately pulled the trigger.

The explosion was immediate and stunned John. The dog fell backward and slumped on the floor. The other dogs drew away from the door. Any hope that John had that this might scare them away was quickly extinguished. As soon as he turned the flashlight on to see if the dogs had left, another one, this time a black Labrador mix stuck his head in. He was snarling and spittle was flying all around. John again placed the gun in the dog's mouth and felt it trying to bite the metal. Without any hesitation, John pulled the trigger and again the explosion knocked the dog backward.

Turning the flashlight back on, the other dogs were still there and they remained agitated and undaunted. One of the pit bulls leaped into the hole, desperately trying to breach the door and kill John. The dog's shoulders were pushing the glass further in and it would just be a matter of time before the hole would become large enough for the dog to enter the cooler.

John had a couple of problems. The first was that he didn't know how many bullets were left in the gun. Secondly, with each gunshot, he risked alerting any passing patrols. He needed to get out and quickly.

As the dogs continued their assault, John started lining up the cases of beer and cases of rotten milk to create a room within the cooler. Behind the stacks, he rearranged the shelves to provide support. He waited but didn't need to wait long.

Within minutes, the remaining dogs had created a hole large enough to leap inside the cooler. One after another, they crawled in, only to find themselves trapped in John's makeshift room. Without waiting for them to figure out that they could leap back outside through the same hole they entered, John opened the door to the cooler.

With his gun in his right hand and his flashlight in his left, John turned it on and swept the light across the floor of the store. As he swung his left arm in an arc, he saw what he feared most. The Rottweiler was standing in front of him. The dog's back was hunched and his ears were pinned back. His mouth was agape and John saw slobber drip off its fangs. Slowly the dog began to approach with his head down low and his butt in the air. At this point, John couldn't even hear the dogs trapped in the cooler.

He raised the handgun and just started shooting. He was still pulling the trigger long after the gun stopped firing. The dog had fallen to the ground but was struggling to get up. It finally got to its feet but then fell back over. John could hear its growl and the dog kept snapping its mouth, hoping to latch onto any part of John.

Stepping wide of the thrashing dog, John sprinted for the front door and without missing a step, grabbed the bolt cutter and scooped the backpack up and slung it over his shoulder. He tossed the now empty gun aside and kept running down the street toward the river. He could hear the sound of trucks approaching and stayed off to the side of the road and in the shadows.

Briefly he looked back over his shoulder and saw the beams of headlights converging on the convenience store. This was followed by the sharp sound of repeated gunshots. John could only imagine that the remaining dogs finally escaped from the cooler and were seeking vengeance on the soldiers.

❧

CHAPTER THIRTY-EIGHT

Mannish Water

There was little time to worry about anything other than getting away from the area as quickly as possible. It wouldn't take long for the military to figure out who shot the dogs. As soon as that happened, the chase would be afoot and unless he got distance from the convenience store, John would quickly be discovered. Finding the fence and his cache, John pulled aside the piece of fence he had previously cut and carried everything, in two trips, over to the chain link fence on the west side.

The second was as easy to breach as the first and John worked so fast that he almost didn't notice that he was shaking. Dragging the kayaks down to the river's edge, John tied them together with a length of rope. He positioned the backpacks on the kayaks and secured them with the bungee cords and ropes.

Walking alongside the front kayak, John stepped into it as soon as the water got above his knees. As quietly as possible, John started paddling south. Progress was difficult for various reasons. First of all, he was paddling upstream. Fortunately, the current wasn't too strong, but it meant that he couldn't stop to rest without floating backward.

More importantly, he had very little experience with kayaking and struggled to keep moving forward while staying as close to shore as possible. There was some moonlight, but it was too dark for him to be able to make out any small obstructions in the water. Once John ran into a large tree branch that was sticking out of the river and became entangled. He scratched his head and arms while extricating himself.

Another time he bumped into something, which in the faint moonlight, he discovered was a bloated corpse. He slowly pushed the body out further toward the middle of the river to let the current continue taking it downstream.

In the darkness, it was difficult to track his distance. John knew that he had to paddle under a number of bridges but wasn't sure how many there were until he got to his destination.

With the first bridge, he stopped along a piling and drank a cola. The combination of carbonation, sugar and caffeine gave him the energy he needed to continue. His arms were aching and his lower back gave a sharp twinge with every stroke as he approached the Hawthorne Bridge.

This was a bridge he recognized even from the river. It had always been one of his favorites and the main one he used to drive across the river. Looking up, he could see headlights and hear trucks as they crossed right above him

After paddling for another thirty minutes, John ran into a pier. The noise startled him and he grabbed onto it and tried to stop the second kayak from bumping into it also. Even the little noise seemed to carry. John was convinced anyone on shore or on any of the bridges must have heard it and would begin looking for him.

As much as he knew he needed to keep going, he also knew that he needed to rest. Between his legs and his back, he had to get out and stretch. The pier was level with the top of the kayak and John eased himself out. Tying the lead kayak to a post, John lay down and stretched his entire body. It was times like this, he thought to himself, when he really wished he knew yoga.

The pier was made of metal and felt cool against the back of his head and his hands. John was exhausted but knew he could only rest there for a short while without being discovered. Closing his eyes, John focused on his breathing and just tried to let his muscles relax. Slowly the kink in his back seemed to melt away. He sat up and opened another soda.

Taking a moment to look up at the hill where Camp Oregon sat, he noticed it was lit up and he could see the vehicles traveling both up and down the road to the camp. Headlights crisscrossed the hills. There were a lot of them. Callahan thought that Boulden must have had everyone in the camp looking for him. In parts of the hills, there was a shimmering light he identified as fire. The military was burning as many buildings as possible in their search for him. This was no longer an effort to just burn houses with corpses. They were burning anything and everything they could. It was a scorched earth strategy with the obvious hope of driving him out of hiding.

With the soda drained, John reached over and filled it with water from the river. With teeth gritted, he poured it over his head. It was cold and caused a reflexive shiver as it trickled down his back. He slowly clambered back into the front kayak.

The fires in the West Hills were a double-edged sword. On one hand, the light from the flames gave him some improved ability to see where he was paddling. However, it also created enough light to expose him. With no further time to waste, John put his paddle in the water and continued heading south.

Crossing under the Marquam Bridge, John felt small as the bridge towered above him. This was the bridge that carried I-5 across the Willamette River. It was always crowded, going both north and south on the highway, regardless of time of day. Now, however, he could hear a number of vehicles crossing but nothing like the noise of ordinary traffic.

Continuing his journey and ignoring the fatigue and pain, John saw a large object in the river. He swung wide and realized it was a submarine. The Oregon Museum of Science and Industry had moored this submarine in the river years before and opened it for tours. John thought briefly about climbing into the ship to hide but decided it would be too noisy to load all of his gear in there. Also, if he were discovered, he would have no way to escape. He kept paddling.

The next bridge to cross under was the city's newest—the Tillicum Bridge. This was intended solely for pedestrians and light rail trains and was the most visually attractive of all the city's bridges. Its design involved cables supporting the deck and, even in the dim light cast by the fires, was a beautiful and welcome distraction.

John knew he was almost done. There was one more bridge to cross under and this was the Ross Island Bridge he had previously walked over. Had it really just been the prior evening?

Just south of the bridge was the island for which it was named— Ross Island. For years, a gravel company owned the island and used it to dredge gravel that built much of the city. Over the previous 15 years, the island was donated to the City of Portland in stages for use as a nature preserve. It was shaped somewhat like a fishing hook with the northern part of the island being heavily wooded. The southern part was widely open with buildings involved in dredging the island and the river.

Fortunately, John was aiming for the heavily wooded northern part. Travelling about 100 yards past the tip of the island on the eastern side, John pulled into a small cove. He stepped out of the front kayak and pulled it all the way onto land before untying the rope and dragging up the second.

With both kayaks securely on land, John took out his hatchet and started cutting down small branches and placing them on top and around them. Once that was accomplished, he dragged the backpacks further into the woods. There was a small clearing barely big enough for him to lie down. Most important, however, was that he couldn't see either shoreline. If he couldn't see the shorelines, he figured people on the shore wouldn't be able to see him.

John opened the tent and stretched it on the ground. He then placed one of the backpacks on one end and, using it as a pillow, lay down. He pulled the sleeping bag on top of him and fell asleep.

ея

CHAPTER THIRTY-NINE

SHOWDOWN AT BIG SKY

The sun was up and warm well before John awoke. Moving his arms and legs slowly, he felt the aches and pains. The warmth of the day would help but he would still be sore. His hands were blistered and raw and his lower back and shoulders caused him excruciating pain whenever he moved. John eased his way up to a sitting position and looked around. He could barely see through the trees to either side of the river and was comfortable knowing it would be difficult for anyone to see him. To the east, the shore was only about 100 yards away. To the west, it was not much further.

High above the western shore, Camp Oregon dominated the landscape. Much of the area running from the camp down to the river, and then both north and south, was covered in smoke. Looking closely, John saw large earthmoving equipment, and even tanks, seemingly knocking down whatever buildings they could.

One tank seemed to be positioning itself to aim at one of the high-rise buildings down at the OHSU waterfront campus. John saw a flash of light first, then heard a loud boom. Dust and debris erupted. Watching with complete fascination, John saw the tank line up again and fire another shot. From the north, another tank started to roll toward the damaged structure.

The tanks fired shot after shot until, finally, the building collapsed in a huge plume of dust. The tanks then turned and focused on the next building. John was amazed at how crazed Boulden must be if he were using artillery to try to flush him out.

It was time to get up and stretch his legs. Moving slowly, so as to not attract any attention, John pulled the kayaks a little further from the water and placed more branches and boughs around them. Assembling his backpacks on top of the tent floor, he began to organize his supplies.

He piled his clothes in one area, food pouches in another, with cooking tools and water purifiers in another. He opened one of the water purifier packages and took out the directions.

Sitting down with his back against a tree, John absently opened a bottle of water while reading the instructions. He also downed a couple of aspirin and snacked on some stale cookies.

The freeze-dried food packets required heat, but he didn't dare start a fire. With a craving for protein, John poured some of his bottled water into a packet of chili and shook it to let it mix. He then tipped the bag and ate the cold and uncooked meal. It wasn't the taste and it wasn't that it was no better than room temperature that repulsed him. It was the texture. There were nuggets of something, whether beans or meat, which were dry and hard. Nonetheless, he ate the whole bag. Wiping his mouth with his forearm, John placed the empty bag into a trash bag and tied it off. He then lay down again and resumed reading the instructions for the water purifier.

When John awoke, he saw that the sun was setting over the West Hills. He was still sore and took a couple more aspirin and slowly stood up. Winding his way through the trees to the west, he saw most of the buildings along the river were now just piles of rubble. What had awakened him was shouting. It sounded like bullhorns. John stood and crept through the trees toward the northernmost point of the island. There, in the faltering light, he saw a Humvee on the west side of the Ross Island Bridge. Alongside it was a large, yellow bulldozer. Someone was standing up and calling over toward the east side of the bridge.

"Warrant Officer Dutile, we need to come across."

John recognized Major Boulden's voice although it seemed hoarser than he remembered. From the other side of the bridge and somewhere behind the barricade, a response came, "Sorry, Sir, but I can't allow that."

"This is the United States Military, under my command. Pursuant to Executive Order No. 14132, martial law has been declared. Under that presidential authority, I am advising you that we are coming across. We believe you may be harboring a fugitive and I have issued orders to locate and arrest this man."

"I'm sorry, Sir, but you and I both know the Executive Order lost all force and effect with the downfall of the United States government. I don't doubt your command but deny the validity of it."

"Dutile, I wasn't asking for permission. I'm telling you that we are going to inspect the vector of the east side of this bridge, which you claim to control. If you want to avoid this confrontation, I goddamn well suggest you turn over Callahan."

There was silence for a moment then came the response, "Sir, I have warned you. No one crosses this bridge without my permission and unfortunately for you, I'm not granting you permission."

John saw Boulden sit down in the Humvee and make a motion with his right arm. The bulldozer immediately began moving forward, pushing vehicles out of its way. The bulldozer wasn't even halfway across the bridge when John heard a loud whoosh and saw something streaking toward it. With a loud explosion, the bulldozer seemed to buck and rear up before toppling onto its side.

John assumed that Tex must have some sort of rocket-propelled grenade or even a bazooka. He wondered who the hell this guy really was.

Gunfire erupted from the west side and John could hear bullets ricocheting off the barricade on the east side.

"Dutile, you have fucked with the wrong fucking guy. I tried to give you a chance, but you have now declared open hostility upon the United States of America and we will put down this insurrection."

Behind the Humvee, a rumble arose and a tank slowly appeared. It passed the Humvee, crushing the abandoned vehicles in its path. Just as it reached the apex of the bridge it stopped. Slowly the barrel of the tank lowered. With a loud boom and a flash, both simultaneous, the barricade on the east side of the bridge exploded.

Cheers erupted from behind the tank. Slowly it began to move forward.

The tank advanced with the barrel of its gun pointed directly at what remained of the barricade. With the tank only 100 yards from the remains of the barricade, John heard a popping sound and small flashes down below the bridge, amongst the metal supports. Although it was dusk, there was still enough light for John to see the tank shift forward as the road in front of it disappeared. It dropped quickly, hitting the water with a large splash. Briefly it righted itself and seemed to float on the river and then, just as quickly, the back of the tank sank and disappeared with only the barrel breaking the surface of the water.

"What the *fuck* was that?" yelled Major Boulden.

The response came. It sounded as if it was still behind the destroyed barricade, albeit from a slightly different location.

"I warned you, Major. No one crosses my bridge without my permission."

"FUCK YOU, Dutile. I'm going to fuck you up so badly. We are going to send everyone over and wipe you the fuck out. I don't know if we'll find Callahan or not but at this point, I don't care. We're coming for you now, Dickhead."

This time, Tex's voice was just as commanding but much softer, "With all due respect, Sir, how do you plan on doing that?"

"Dutile, you just fucking wait and see."

This time, John saw the flashes a full second before he heard the booms. They seemed to come from the bridge to the immediate north—the Tillicum Bridge. The flashes were above and cut through the cables running across this suspension bridge. Half of the flashes came around the cables on the southeast side and the others were around the northeast side. The headlights of the vehicles crossing it seemed to waver and then the bridge just twisted. John watched as the vehicles were tossed off the bridge and disappeared into the inky black water. The towers holding the cables seemed to bend and one of them broke. The twisting continued until the bridge span collapsed into the river.

"Dutile, what are you doing?"

"Sir, I warned you. You have now expressed open hostility toward me and I have no choice but to defend myself...and anyone who might be seeking sanctuary with me."

"So, you do have Callahan! Okay, Dutile, I'll give you one last chance. Give us Callahan and we'll leave you alone. If you refuse, we'll finish what you've just started."

"Sir, with all due respect, I don't believe I started anything or that you are in any position to make demands."

John heard and saw another explosion, this one from the Marquam Bridge, the tallest bridge in the city and the one used for the I-5 highway. It had two levels. He could see a stretch of the upper deck collapse upon the lower. There was another explosion and the middle of the lower deck of the bridge lifted slightly before disintegrating and toppling into the river.

"Dutile, don't do this!"

"I'm sorry Sir, but there is now a distinct lack of trust between us. Given your threats, you have left me no choice but to ensure a measure of protection from your aggression."

In the distance, John saw lights appear in the sky as the sound of explosions echoed up and down the river. John could only assume the bridges north and south of him, including the very ones he had kayaked under the previous night, were being destroyed.

It would be more than a week before John understood the extent of the damage that Tex Dutile wrought. All twelve of the bridges crossing the Willamette River, running from the I-205 Bridge to the south and the St. John's Bridge to the north were destroyed. There was no effective way for anyone from Camp Oregon to now drive across the river and any troops already on the east side would have no way to get back.

John retreated to his bedroll and sat down. What would this mean for Boulden and his hunt for him? Why did Dutile imply he was with him? Was he baiting the military or did he know that John was on Ross Island already?

With no appetite for another cold meal, John tore open a protein bar and quietly ate it, all the while trying to figure out what just happened and how it affected him. In the dark, voices of men and women crying for help echoed across the water, and then stopped. Quiet fell on what was left of Portland.

ᴇᴏ

CHAPTER FORTY

Guns of Umpqua

T he Pacific Northwest has always been a geographical area of contrasts. To the west is the Pacific Ocean with all its beauty and fearsomeness. Just inland are lush forests and a moderate climate with plentiful rainfall. The rain comes in various measurements, forcing local weathercasters to use a thesaurus to differentiate them. Their descriptions include showers, mists, rain, downpours, drizzle, sprinkles, and the like. Despite the frequency of precipitation, most true denizens of the Pacific Northwest would scoff at the idea of carrying an umbrella.

To the east is high desert with colored and varied rock formations and a greater range of temperatures.

In between is the Cascade Mountain Range and, between the coast and the mountains, is some of the lushest and most productive farmland in the country.

Politically, the contrast was just as pronounced. The western parts of Oregon and Washington were notoriously liberal while the eastern parts of both states were conservative and much more aligned with states such as Montana and Wyoming.

It was an environment requiring a tolerance of differing personalities and beliefs that fostered innovation and growth. In the Seattle area, businesses such as Microsoft, Amazon and Starbucks originated and grew exponentially. What Portland may have lacked in technological innovation, it excelled with businesses involved with an active lifestyle. Nike, Pendleton Woolen Mills, Columbia Sportswear and Keen Footwear called the Portland area home and attracted other sports-related companies, including Adidas and Under Armor. Perhaps more importantly to many was the fact that Oregon became a leader in the micro-brewing industry, as well as ice cream and even donuts.

John loved the fact that in less than two hours, he could drive from his home to Mount Hood to ski or snowboard or, within the same time span, drive to the coast and surf. Of course, he hadn't done any of those things. John's pursuits were more sedentary. He loved sampling local micro-brews and spending his limited off-time with his family.

As he lay in his sleeping bag looking through the trees at the blue sky, John thought about all these things. Having lost complete track of time and dates, he thought it might be June. This meant that, in the course of slightly more than a year, everything he knew was gone.

The concepts of family, career and even leisure were now unimaginable. Any hope of mankind somehow reorganizing and reestablishing itself was dashed. The events of the prior night had proven that. Even when facing a cataclysmic event, mankind could not put aside its petty differences and egos to work together.

There was no blame to be assigned to one side or the other. Perhaps it was just an inherent weakness in the species—this individuality, this inability to truly understand and coordinate life at both a macro and a micro level. Certainly, the Curse brought all of this to a head, but it might just as well have been a nuclear war, manmade biological weapons or even abuse of the climate.

Mankind was doomed, perhaps from the start. Perhaps this was just mankind's expiration date.

John sat up and drank a diet cola. Slowly standing, he wound his way through the trees to a point where he could look northward while remaining hidden. Most of the Ross Island Bridge was still standing, except for a span of forty feet where there was just open air. Beneath that and sticking out of the water was the barrel of the tank. A shimmer of oil surrounded it and the river's current took it north leading, eventually, to the Columbia River and then the Pacific Ocean.

On the east side of the bridge, there were large gaps in the barricade where the tank's projectile had exploded. With the bridge breached, there was likely no point in trying to rebuild it.

Further to the north, the remains of the Tillicum Crossing Bridge and the Marquam Bridge could also be seen. The first bridge was effectively gone with only portions dangling into the water, restrained by the few remaining cables that hadn't been destroyed by the blasts. The second bridge appeared at first glance to be intact but, upon closer examination, a large span of both the upper and lower decks was missing.

None of those three bridges would ever be used again, at least not in his lifetime. John could only assume the remaining eight bridges within the City of Portland were similarly useless.

Never again would anyone drive a vehicle across the Willamette River within the city limits. Whoever was on the east side of the city when the bridges were destroyed would be stuck there. In reality, though, that is not what had happened.

With the destruction of the bridges, those from Camp Oregon who were on the east side scattered and disbursed. Those who had been categorized as Type I or II recognized the events as releasing them from Major Boulden's bondage. He could not chase them. He could not order them to do anything. He was no longer a factor in their lives and so they disbursed. Some wandered back to their homes only to find them empty or torched. With no electricity or water, there was no point in staying there. Whatever life they had previously led was gone forever.

The 'turds rampaged and looted but soon lost interest. Many took comfort in whatever pharmaceuticals and alcohol they could find and drifted off into oblivion.

The one constant among all these refugees from Camp Oregon was that they were no longer afraid of the Curse. They threw off their hazmat suits and breathed the fresh air. The understanding was that the Curse had won; it destroyed mankind and it was only a matter of time before it would destroy them too. It wasn't that they gave up, at least not most of them. They were just tired of fighting an invincible and invisible foe. They would live whatever remained of their lives with whatever dignity and grace they might be able to cobble together.

When looking eastward, John could hear vehicles, but the noise was diminishing as people fled east. Picking his way through the woods to the western side of the island, John could see that Camp Oregon was still active. What he didn't notice at first was how most vehicles seemed to be descending from the camp and very few were heading back up. From this distance, it reminded him of rats deserting a sinking ship.

John assembled his small dome tent and put his bedroll and sleeping bag inside. He cut and laid branches from nearby trees against the tent. He also organized his clothes between new and dirty. Nearby, he tied the ends of a hammock to two trees. It was difficult to climb into, as he was still sore from all of the kayaking. He needed time to think but first he needed more sleep and to heal. Sleep came quicker than healing.

The rumbling of his stomach awakened John and for the first time in days, he was hungry, truly hungry. Since escaping Camp Oregon, he had eaten more from an instinctive understanding of his body's need for fuel than from desire. Even though the afternoon was still warm, John craved a hot meal. While he would not be able to barbecue a steak or grab a burger somewhere, he knew that he might be able to start a fire to heat up one of his dehydrated meal packets. It wasn't a perfect solution, but it was still better than either eating more protein bars or eating a cold meal packet.

The problem was how to start a fire without being seen from Camp Oregon. Grabbing a small backpack, John loaded it with a couple of cans of beer, a few water bottles, and two packets of freeze-dried food. One packet was lasagna with meat sauce and the other was a breakfast scramble.

John started picking his way south on the island, staying in the woods at all times and keeping as close to the east side of the island as he could. Upon reaching the lagoon that bisected the island, he followed the shoreline to the west. At this point, the island was only fifty feet wide but, fortunately, trees ran the length of this thin stretch. By staying within the trees, the route to the southern part of the island was much slower but it allowed him to remain mostly hidden.

As the coastline of the island hooked to the east, John shifted further into the trees. Taking a moment, he crept on his hands and knees and gazed up at Camp Oregon. It was unnerving how large and how close the compound seemed. John almost felt as if he could reach out and touch it. He backed into the woods and continued his slow journey.

The island continued to hook its way around and John could finally see the buildings he was looking for. They would provide him with shelter, but he would be briefly exposed while sprinting over open ground to them. To minimize the risk of being seen, John decided to wait until the sun set. This would take several hours but he could be patient. He had time; time was the only thing he seemingly had a surplus of. Sitting down deep within the woods, John ate a protein bar and settled in. He listened to the birds and the insects, as well as the gentle hum of the river.

In the distance he could hear some vehicles but not as many as in prior days.

When the sun finally set behind the West Hills, John stood up and continued in the shadows. Creeping up to the edge of the forest, John looked up at Camp Oregon. Some lights were starting to come on but there was a noticeable lack of vehicles crisscrossing the area.

Holding his breath, John spied a pile of gravel, about fifteen feet high and approximately thirty feet away. He sprinted to the gravel and lay down behind it. There was no way he would be able to tell if he had been spotted but thought it best to wait before the next sprint.

Slowly counting to 100, John looked around the side of the pile of gravel and saw his next target. There were a few large dump trucks another 50 feet away and, again, John sprinted to them, keeping as low to the ground as he could. He then began to count to 100 again.

Even at dusk, he had to believe that if he could see, he could be seen.

By the time John reached the first building, he was winded. The door on the east side of the building opened easily and he peered inside. There were a few offices but mostly bays for working on equipment and vehicles. There were also five trucks and some larger machinery, all in various stages of disassembly. The offices were on the east side of the building and John was relieved to see there were no windows facing to the west. This allowed him to explore the building without fear of being spotted from Camp Oregon.

Two vending machines were positioned beside the first office. With the butt of his flashlight, John was able to retrieve a couple of warm bottles of water, together with a variety of chips and candy. The offices were relatively non-descript, but John went through every drawer and file cabinet. It wasn't that he was looking for anything in particular but, rather, looking for anything that might be useful. In the bottom drawer of one desk, he spotted a pistol.

It was a 9mm pistol and it took a little while for him to figure out how to eject the magazine.

Much to John's chagrin, the magazine was empty. He looked through the rest of the office for bullets but was unsuccessful. The gun, however, felt good in his hand. Holding it up and pointing it at some of the equipment on the far side of the building, John started thinking about the dogs that had attacked him at the convenience store. A slight shudder ran through his body as he pointed the gun and slowly pulled the trigger.

The noise was both loud and instantaneous. John jumped back and dropped the gun. The sound of the gunshot was still echoing within the building as he ran to the door and started to peek out to see if he had alerted anyone. Just then, gunshots erupted from the east side of the remains of the Ross Island Bridge.

It was impossible to tell where these new gunshots were directed but, nonetheless, John stayed hidden inside the building. He wracked his brain trying to figure out how the gun had fired. With the magazine ejected, it should not have had any bullets in it. He wondered if there might be another one in there. Walking over to the gun, John put it back into the drawer. While he desperately needed one, it was readily apparent that he still knew too little about how they work. This, however, was not the time or place to try to figure out the gun. He could only hope the subsequent gunshots from the east side of the river, presumably from Tex, had hidden his shot.

John stood very still and listened. His ears were still ringing from the gunshot but, other than that, all he could hear was the rushing of the river and some birds calling out from the trees.

After a five-minute wait, John resumed his search of the building and found a half-full bottle of Pendleton whiskey and a hotplate with a small pan on it. The hotplate was useless without electricity, but the pan could be used and the whiskey was just what he needed to calm his nerves.

It was starting to get dark as John began grabbing wooden drawers and dragging them back to the door. Just inside of the door, John built a small bonfire. Using paper and breaking the drawers up, he lit the blaze and kept it burning slowly. Much of the smoke stayed in the building but John wasn't worried about that. In fact, with the smoke mostly *in* the building, he hoped it wouldn't be visible from Camp Oregon. Any smoke that might escape the building would likely be undetectable in the darkness of the evening.

He poured water into the lasagna packet, mixed it and then put it into the pan. He rested the pan on the embers and occasionally mixed the concoction with a ruler he'd found. Once it was warm, John poured water over the fire to put it out and sat down, just outside of the door. With a bottle of water and occasional sips of the whiskey, John enjoyed his first warm meal in a while. The lasagna was much better than the vegetable soup he shared with Lisa back in the warehouse. He briefly wondered if she were still alive. He then thought of Dr. Mo, but he knew she was dead.

The question now was what to do next. Staying on the island wasn't really an option. John figured it would only be a matter of time before Boulden commandeered some boats and again attempted to cross the river and maybe explore the island. Getting back on land put him at risk of not just Boulden and his goons but also dog packs. He needed a gun for protection but really had limited ideas as to where to find one.

The east side would certainly have any number of gun shops, but John had no idea where they might be. Born in Tualatin, a suburb to the southwest of Portland, and spending most of his life in that part of town, John only went to the east side for specific reasons. He could locate various favorite restaurants, as well the offices of some of his clients, but had no idea where a gun shop might be. It wouldn't be safe to just wander around, hoping to be lucky enough to stumble upon a store.

While there were undoubtedly gun stores on the west side, John only knew of one. He remembered going to Cabella's and buying his little arsenal of weapons last fall. It was in Tualatin and right off Interstate 5. It was only ten miles from downtown.

The risk, of course, was that Boulden and his goons were on the west side. John would have to be both stealthy and lucky to get there undetected. All things considered, the choice was pretty easy. John would go to where he was comfortable with the lay of the land and hope the Curse got Boulden before Boulden got him.

CHAPTER FORTY-ONE

The Lion Sleeps Tonight

The sun hadn't yet risen when John awoke. Quickly gathering more wood and starting a fire, he cooked up the breakfast scramble. It felt so luxurious to be able to eat a freshly-cooked hot breakfast again. With daylight approaching, this would be a quick meal as John wanted to get back into the woods before he could be spotted. Grabbing a packet of Red Vines and a bottle of water from the broken vending machine, he started running.

Once he got back to his campground, he could pack what he needed to travel and then rest until dusk.

Stopping at various spots on his way back, John looked across the river and tried to plan a route to cross. Getting across the river would be easy but he needed to find a car to get him to Cabella's. In a prior lifetime, John test-drove a Mercedes at a luxury used car dealership somewhere on S. Macadam Avenue. This was a road that hugged the western side of the river from the southern part of downtown Portland, all the way down and through Lake Oswego.

Even in the daylight, it was tough to make out landmarks to trigger his memory. John realized he would have to cross the river and just start walking until he found the dealership. Assuming he found it, would any of the vehicles still have enough battery power to start? That was something John couldn't control so he pushed that thought from his mind. If nothing else, in the time since Liz and the kids passed, John had learned how to adapt to new situations and just handle things on the fly.

The hike back to the campsite was uneventful although John stopped numerous times to see if he might be able to hear anyone on either side of the river. Instead, there was just the river and the birds calling.

Looking forward to avoiding the heat of the day back at the tent, John stopped in his tracks as he came into the small clearing. His tent was shredded and lay on its side. The backpacks were similarly shredded. Whatever had been there had ransacked his stores. Given the condition of the tent and the backpacks, it was clear an animal had been there—a large animal.

John scanned the campsite and saw the hatchet on the ground. Picking it up, he began to walk around the northern part of the island, holding the hatchet in front of him. He checked on the kayaks and noted they were still safely hidden. Just beside them, however, he saw animal prints in the mud. Whatever crossed the river and trashed his campsite had large paws.

It was now clear to him that the island alone could not provide real safety. Quietly, John began to assemble what he would need for that evening. His small backpack was still in good repair, so he loaded it with some water bottles and snacks. The only other items he would need, at least in the short term, were dry socks and shoes. He also put in a couple of small LED flashlights. With that accomplished, John sat with his back to a tree and as close as he could get to the river on the east side of the island. Whether it was a bear or something else, John did not want to be surprised from behind. If something came up behind him now, he would hear the splashing of the water.

The day was warm and it was difficult for him to stay awake. He thought about what he would do when he crossed the river that evening but he also began to reflect on all that had happened over the past year or so. Had it really only been a year since he read the first article about a virus in Ecuador? He knew where his family was but what happened to Hafez? What happened to his friends and business partners? Then he began to wonder about what would happen next. Assuming he was able to find a gun and ammunition, what then? As long as Boulden and the military were still around, he was at risk from them. He was also at risk from whatever wild animals would next attempt to assert primacy upon the planet. If, in fact, mankind's time on the throne was now over, which species was poised to take over?

If he chose to leave Oregon, where could he go? John recognized he had limited survival skills, despite how he'd survived so far, so the thought of living in the mountains was not appealing. It might be nice to live by a warm ocean where he could swim. Southern California was an option but with its huge population, it would be years before the millions of corpses decayed enough to not pose a health risk.

What did the future hold for him? It was clear that John was in mortal danger from both man and animals. How was he to handle those threats? No longer could he rely upon the police and neighbors to provide a measure of civility and security. Now it would just be him, regardless of where he ended up.

A slight cool breeze blew and John was startled to see that he was now in the shadow of the West Hills. It was still much too light to begin the journey, but it was getting close. When it was almost dark enough, he slowly pushed the first kayak out into the river. If he went along the east side of the island, it would be a longer route, but the trees would provide cover from anyone looking for him from Camp Oregon. The sky was clear and the moon was mostly full and in the east.

By the time he crested the southern tip of the island, John decided to take a break and pulled up to the shore. Looking up at the camp, John was surprised to see how different it looked. There were intermittent and small flashes of light and, even from this distance, the sounds were unmistakably of gunfire. The camp itself looked different and it took John several minutes to realize what it was. There were a number of buildings now unlit.

John tried to visualize the camp and which buildings remained from when he was there. Over the past week and as best he could tell, all of them were being used and all were at least partially lit. Now, on the far south side of the camp, there were two buildings that were completely dark. John could see their outline even in the limited moonlight. He couldn't remember what they had been used for but wondered whether this meant Camp Oregon was starting to fall.

The gunfire and the blackout of the buildings certainly suggested there were problems there. While he could have no way of knowing what was going on, he did realize this might be the type of distraction that would allow him to travel down to Tualatin without being discovered.

Pushing off from the shore, John swiftly and quietly paddled toward the western shore. In the limited light, he saw that buildings along the shore were in disarray, whether from fires or the tanks was something he couldn't know yet. As he closed in on the shore, he saw a clump of trees and aimed for them. While still not sure where he was and how close or far he might be from the car dealership, the thought to hide the kayak among the trees seemed wise.

As he pulled into the shore, he stopped and listened. In the distance he could still hear occasional gunfire, as well as the sound of vehicle engines, but there was nothing close. The only noises near to him were the hum of the river, which he almost no longer noticed, as well as crickets and frogs.

Slowly and carefully climbing out of the kayak, John stepped into the water and found it only came up to his knees. He climbed up the riverbank, pulling the kayak behind him. He tossed his small backpack up on the shore and dragged the kayak up. Like he did on the island, John covered it with branches and leaves. Finding a log to sit on, John changed into dry socks and shoes and began walking inland.

Just beyond the trees was a patch of level land, almost a field. Searching his memory, John decided this must be Willamette Park. It was small and ran along the river. It was often used to load and unload boats and kayaks into the river. Now it was just empty and overgrown.

He found one street but was confident that it wasn't S. Macadam Avenue as it was only a two-lane road. He continued and found himself walking through parking lots full of cars and boats. Running a hand alongside the cars, John felt the combination of dirt, pollen and ash that had settled and hardened upon the surfaces of the vehicles.

John was pleasantly surprised to see how well his eyes acclimated to the darkness. Even with only the light from the moon and stars, he could see his way ahead. It was a world of grays and blacks, but he could get by without having to use the flashlight. The next street was much wider and he determined that this must be S. Macadam Avenue. Now the question was which direction he should go. In the distance, John heard a vehicle approaching and ducked behind an abandoned car.

As the noise of the vehicle's engine grew louder, he saw the road start to brighten from the headlights. Without realizing it, John was holding his breath as the noise got louder and the road was illuminated.

A vehicle, clearly a military vehicle of some sort, sped by him. John caught a brief glimpse of the driver in the dashboard light. He looked young but passed much too quickly for John to see anything more.

When it had passed, John ran out into the street to see if its headlights might give him an idea of where he was and which way to go. Unfortunately, it was driving too quickly to be of any assistance in helping him identify exactly where he was.

The decision as to which direction to go was now easy. Rather than walk north and travel toward Camp Oregon, John would walk in the opposite direction. In addition to providing more distance between him and Boulden, John would be able to occasionally use his flashlight, which would be less likely to be seen by anyone with the camp behind him.

Crossing S. Macadam Avenue, John walked toward the first building he saw. His plan was to walk from building to building, knowing that if he heard or saw a vehicle approaching, he could either duck behind a car in a parking lot or run behind the closest building. He also hoped to find a convenience store where he could get some food and drink.

Since he'd landed, he'd drunk three cans of soda and only had two bottles of water remaining. After several blocks, John found his first recognizable landmark. It was a bar called the Buffalo Gap Saloon & Eatery where he had taken Liz years ago, before the children were born. He was now convinced he was going in the right direction, even if he didn't yet know how much further he had to go.

The next building was an office and John noted how most of the first-floor windows were smashed. The building after that had once been a restaurant. There were a few cars and a pickup truck parked in front. This was a good place to take a short break, so John sat down with his back against the front of the building. If he heard any cars, he would have more than enough time to hide.

Reaching into the backpack, John took out a bottle of water, some Twinkies, and a box of cookies. Although he didn't know what time it was, he was comfortable with the thought that dawn was still hours away. If the dealership was within the next couple of blocks, as he believed, he should be there within the next thirty minutes.

The sound didn't really register with him at first. It slowly emerged from the noise of the crickets and the birds. It wasn't the sound of a car engine. It was a clicking or clattering noise. John swiftly crawled over to the closest car and hunched behind it as whatever was causing this odd noise approached.

Even in the limited light, John recognized the shape at fifty feet. It was a large pig trotting down the middle of the empty street. It was completely incongruous as there were no farms nearby and a pig of this size likely wouldn't have been someone's pet. Despite his attempts not to, he envisioned pork chops, ribs, and bacon. A smile came to his lips and John found himself involuntarily salivating.

Reflexively reaching for the hatchet on his belt, John began to think of how he might kill and butcher the pig. He paused and wondered how, even if he could kill it, he would cut it up and cook it. Before he could work out a solution, John heard a low growl and saw a large, dark shape leap out of the shadows right beside him and race toward the pig. It only took seconds for the shape to reach it and take it down. He watched as the shape tussled with the pig and heard a mixture of growling and squealing until both noises stopped abruptly.

John watched all of this and tried to make some sense of the shape hunched over the pig. It appeared to be a large cat—a very large cat. While John could tell that much, he couldn't determine what kind of cat it was, whether a cougar, panther or even a female lion.

John reached for his hatchet but knew he would have no realistic chance should the cat turn on him. He began to wonder where the cat had come from and how long it had been there. Might John have been the initial prey, only to be supplanted by the pig?

He would have shuddered at that thought except for the fact that he was already shaking. John needed to get out of there as quickly as possible. Still hunched over, he started to walk quickly and quietly through the parking lot. The next building was about fifty feet away and John decided to run behind it and create some additional distance from the cat. As he turned away from the road and began running, his foot kicked an empty beer can, sending it clattering.

Instinctively, he turned toward the cat and saw the outline of its head shoot up and look in his direction. John heard a growl, low but loud, arise and he started to run. Behind this building was another road, perpendicular to S. Macadam Avenue and he crossed it and kept running through the next parking lot. Looking at the stores beside him, John realized the road seemed to be curving up and to the west.

Knowing he needed to stay close to the river, John ran across the road and found his way back onto S. Macadam Avenue. He was now at least three blocks from the cat, hopefully, and he just kept running. With no more stores or businesses on this side of the road, he crossed S. Macadam Avenue and found himself right in front of the car dealership. There was a parking lot between a couple of buildings, with the dealership to the south, and John ran through the parking lot looking for a door to the dealership.

Not surprisingly, the double glass doors were smashed so John ran inside. He looked for any desks or other furniture he might find and started piling them in the doorway. It took him fifteen minutes, but the door was now sufficiently blocked that the cat, if it came looking for him, would not be able to get in…at least not through that door.

John sat on the floor and drank his last bottle of water. He was still shaking and completely exhausted. He found the bathroom just in time.

"What the fuck was that thing?" he wondered. It was much larger than a mountain lion and he remembered Dr. Mo telling him about Duke, the polar bear and other animals released from the zoo. John felt overwhelmed. Not only did he have to avoid

Boulden and his merry band of thugs, but he also had to dodge packs of wild dogs and whatever beasts from the zoo were roaming the hills. He wondered not how, but if, he would be able to handle all of this.

In the evolution of man, he, like so many others, had become soft. He was so dependent upon modern technology such as automobiles, electricity, and the Internet, that any semblance of being able to survive in the wilderness was gone. This might be Portland, but it was also now the wilderness. Never again would he experience the joys of fully functional indoor plumbing. He could still drive cars but without any ability to fix an engine or even change the oil in a vehicle, it was only a matter of time before he would be left to just walking.

He didn't know how to grow anything but grass and had limited cooking skills. Would he ever experience a freshly cooked meal again? What would happen if he became ill? He could pick up first aid kits and books but what if he sustained a serious injury?

These were issues and concerns threatening to overwhelm him at any time. All he wanted was to be able, once again, to talk with Liz, Brian and Cassie. All he wanted was to tell them how much he loved them. All he wanted was to be reunited with them. That, however, was still not an option—at least not yet. John stood up, shut down his rogue thoughts, and started looking for a car.

CHAPTER FORTY-TWO

CRYING IN THE NIGHT

There were a couple of things that John needed immediately. First, he had to locate the keys to a car that he could drive out of the dealership. Then he had to hope the car's battery would still be sufficiently charged to actually start. Never having been much of a car guy, he just needed something that would get him down to the suburbs to the south.

Rather than just wandering through the showroom, John went in back and down the stairs to where the vehicles were serviced. There he saw a couple of luxury SUVs, as well as an Audi A5 convertible and an older Saab 9-3 convertible. He ruled out the convertibles immediately as he could picture the big cat leaping into his open car.

Using the hatchet to break open a lockbox located behind the service counter, John grabbed all of the keys and started walking to the SUV closest to the garage door. It took him only moments to locate the right key, but the battery was dead. Three more times this happened and he sat down on a nearby bench and fought the feelings of both frustration and defeat.

He thought a vehicle repair shop like this must have some sort of battery charger and he began to sweep the beam of his flashlight against the walls. Off to the side, he found a couple of them. Wheeling the first one over to the lead SUV, a silver Land Rover, he opened the hood and attached the clamps.

On the charger, he turned one knob to "200 Amp Engine Start." The second knob gave him charging times from 15 to 135 minutes. There was also a setting for "Hold" and John decided to put it on that. He climbed into the Land Rover and turned the key. The engine instantly sprang to life and over the radio he heard the opening guitar chords of Rod Stewart's *Mandolin Wind*.

Sitting with the car running, John listened and momentarily got lost in the words.

> *I recall the night we knelt and prayed,*
> *Noticing your face was thin and pale,*
> *I found it hard to hide my tears,*
> *I felt ashamed I felt I'd let you down,*
> *No mandolin wind couldn't change a thing,*
> *Couldn't change a thing, no, no.*

John didn't even notice the tears running down his face as his eyes closed and his head slumped forward. He might have stayed there forever, but the smell of the exhaust made him cough and he realized that he was actually poisoning himself. John shut the engine off. Climbing out of the car, he detached the battery cables and hoisted the charger into the back of the SUV. He also grabbed a second charger. John had no idea whether or not he would need it but decided it was better to have it than not.

There was a single door to the side of the garage and John peered out. It was dark and he didn't see any movement. Of course, that didn't mean that the cat wasn't out there. Slowly he opened the door a little, just enough to be able to hear whether there were any cars or trucks nearby or any sense any odd movements.

Satisfied it was relatively safe, he closed the door and walked back to the Land Rover. Sitting in the driver's seat, he used the flashlight to illuminate the left side of the instrument panel. He'd once had a car with a dimmer switch for the dashboard lights. He'd played around with it from time to time on longer nighttime drives and didn't know why he hadn't thought of it before.

He found it and, starting the engine up again, he turned down the dashboard lights completely. Checking the fuel gauge, he was pleased to see it was three-quarters full. Stepping back out, he grabbed a hammer from the closest tool bench, and broke out all of the lights in the back of the vehicle. He wasn't going to waste time hunting for the fuses.

John raised the garage door and quickly jumped back into the Land Rover. He started it up and with the headlights off, slowly pulled out into the parking lot.

There was a slight slope up to S.W. Macadam Avenue and John paused just before turning onto the road. The safest route was to drive south staying on S.W. Macadam Avenue as it took him along the river into downtown Lake Oswego, an affluent suburb to the south.

Without hesitation, John turned left and waited as long as possible before turning the headlights on. The brightness actually hurt his eyes. He turned them off but kept the warning lights on. He drove slowly, the limited light coming from the car and the moon allowing him to stay on the road.

While driving, John remembered the many times he'd driven this road in the past. It was a much more scenic drive than taking I-5 and it passed through some absolutely beautiful neighborhoods. He recognized where some of his clients lived, or at least used to live. He wondered whether Boulden's men performed their search and destroy missions in these neighborhoods too. Some of the homes were spectacular and, back in the day, were valued in the millions. John frowned at the thought of their destruction.

With a wry smile, he thought about how much, if not all, of the man-made beauty in the world was going to disappear over the next several years. The works of Matisse, Renoir and Michelangelo would disappear as they fell victim to time and weather. The treasures stored at the Vatican's vast library would eventually disintegrate. The timeless works of art and literature that man had come to so value would disappear over the coming centuries. Eventually, there would be little, if any, evidence of man's existence.

As he rounded a curve in the road, John saw a family of deer leap across. In only a few years, deer and other wildlife would consider this to be their home. While they would fear various predators, they would no longer have to fear man.

Even with the limited light, John recognized buildings as he entered downtown Lake Oswego. His only concern at this point was whether or not there might be roadblocks. Accordingly, he used side roads as he worked his way toward Cabella's. There were a couple of times when the road was blocked by cars either abandoned or crashed. He was always able to either nudge a car out of his way or take a short detour through a neighborhood.

John was almost to Cabella's when he realized the sky was getting light. The sun wasn't up yet but he could definitely see better than before and, more importantly, he could now be seen. He picked up the pace and quickly crossed under I-5 on Boones Ferry Road. Working his way through back streets, John found the gun store and parked the Land Rover in the back of the building. He got out of the SUV and listened. He was trying to see if there was anyone who might have seen him and was following him. All he could hear were the frogs and crickets from the nearby creek. The highway was only a couple of hundred yards away but there was no traffic.

With his backpack on his shoulder, John first looked to see if the back door or loading dock might be unlocked. They weren't, so he walked around the building on the side away from the highway. As he was walking, the sun crested over the trees to the east and John was bathed in sunlight. Even though it was still early in the morning, it was clear that it was going to be another hot day. Taking only a moment to let the sun warm his face, John quickly ran up to the front door. As expected, it was smashed in.

He ducked into the store and saw it was a complete disaster. All the shelves were turned on their sides and clothes and equipment were heaped in piles around the store. Without bothering to waste time on those items, John headed straight to the back, switching on his flashlight as he walked.

The main gun section was located against the wall in the far back corner. A sweep of the flashlight showed all the guns gone. There was nothing on the walls and the display cases were shattered and empty. John made a cursory, and ultimately unsuccessful, inspection of the drawers and the backroom to see if he could find anything.

Sitting down on the floor, his fists clenched, John squeezed his eyes tightly. What he really wanted to do right now was cry. No matter what he did, it never seemed to be enough. This was not his world any longer. He didn't belong here. What the hell was he supposed to do if even the simplest plans failed? If Cabella's was ransacked, didn't that mean that every other gun store was likely empty also? He couldn't very well just go house-to-house looking for a gun.

Suddenly he heard what sounded like a truck in the distance. John jumped up and ran toward the front door to get a better look. The noise was coming from the north and was getting louder. John moved a pile of clothes toward the front door and hid behind it to watch.

It was a small caravan of military and non-military vehicles. John breathed a sigh of relief seeing them traveling south. It was too far for him to see how many people were in the vehicles. Shortly after that, three more cars, all non-military vehicles, also passed by. With the vehicles gone, all was quiet again, so he retreated to the back of the store. He was tired and frustrated and there wasn't anything he could do, at least not until that evening.

Wandering around the store, he found a number of binoculars and picked out a pair with a price tag of $3,500. He couldn't figure out why they were so expensive but decided to use the best. He then crept out of the store and, remaining in the shadows, began working his way to the highway.

There was no noise of vehicle traffic, but he wanted to see if there might be any roadblocks. Creeping up the embankment, he hunkered down beside the railing and peered over it. To the north, he could see where a roadblock had been. Concrete barriers were placed in a configuration requiring drivers to slow down and weave their way through it.

There was a guardhouse to the side, but it was clearly empty. Whoever was to man this roadblock clearly decided that it was time to abandon his or her post. John was encouraged by this.

Returning to Cabella's, John scrounged and found some protein drinks and bottles of water. In the debris were various books on hunting and fishing. He settled down on some clothes and began to read. He started with the fishing manual, as fishing always seemed less violent than hunting. After an hour, John put the book down. Even if he could follow the instructions, the question remained as to whether or not it would be safe to eat any fish he might catch. He'd seen bodies float by on the Willamette River and could only assume the smaller rivers and creeks also had decomposing bodies in them. If he got up into the mountains, the rivers might be fresher but getting up there created a host of other problems.

With fishing put aside, John knew he needed to learn how to hunt. Assuming he could find a gun, it shouldn't be too hard. In the year since civilization collapsed, the deer and elk populations were becoming plentiful. In a pinch, John thought to himself, he could always shoot a cow.

No, he wasn't worried about finding something to kill; the issue was what to do with the animal after he killed it. It seemed wasteful to kill a beautiful animal for just a meal or even two. There was no refrigeration so he wouldn't be able to store any excess meat. In ancient times, he remembered, people salted meats, which just didn't sound like anything he would be interested in.

There was no point in going back to the island yet. If a bear, or whatever else it was, could swim the short span from the shore once, it could, and would, do it again. John remembered there was an REI store just a mile or so away. REI stood for Recreational Equipment, Inc. and was the nation's largest consumer cooperative. It would have skis and bicycles and climbing gear but, sadly, no guns. Nonetheless, John decided to check it out.

It was a very short drive and to his surprise, the store was in reasonably orderly shape. John made mental notes of where items he might need in the future were located. He found more water purifiers and tents. He found clothes for all seasons but most importantly, he found solar powered generators. These were the types of generators Lisa used in the zone. He loaded four of them into the back of the Land Rover.

The vehicles heading south might indicate that Camp Oregon had finally fallen and Boulden wasn't a threat anymore. John started thinking about all the things he might be able to do. Maybe he could find a house, which would provide him with some protection from both the weather and the animals.

In his mind, he pictured the house as an older farm-style with a fireplace and a front porch. It would be next to a creek, which would provide all his water needs for a toilet, bathing and even drinking. The water would need to be treated but he had all sorts of water sterilizers and purifiers.

The generators could be used to power a small refrigerator and stove and even a heater in the winter. Eventually, he would be able to build a pen for some chickens and even have a couple of cows and pigs.

John could visualize this little utopia. It would keep him fed and warm and, most importantly, busy. He would find a laptop and, powered by the generators, he would be able to watch movies. While he didn't like the idea of rummaging through people's homes for guns, he had no qualms about looking for DVDs.

Suddenly he realized he knew where this house was. He wasn't just picking any house; he was picking a specific house. In the next town over, there was an old farmhouse sitting next to Fanno Creek. Just across the street was the Tigard City Library. It would be perfect, as it would provide both books and DVDs. Across the creek was the Tigard Police station. Surely, he convinced himself, they must have guns.

John finished going through REI and loaded up on clothes. He also grabbed a medium sized backpack and a duffel bag and threw them into the SUV. He had a purpose now and was working to control his excitement.

CHAPTER FORTY-THREE

LAWYERS, GUNS AND MONEY

By now, it was dusk and John fought the urge to turn the headlights on and speed down the road. It was only a couple of miles, but he knew it was important to remain cautious. John saw a glimmer of white as he passed the farmhouse and stopped. From the street, he could see that the front door was busted in but, other than that, it looked whole. He continued on the road and crossed Fanno Creek, pulling up to the police station. It was, of course, dark and there were more than twenty police cruisers parked along the side of the building. Assuming their weapons arsenal was intact, there should be enough guns there to last his lifetime.

As much as he wanted to explore the farmhouse right away, he didn't like the idea of being unarmed in the dark. The front door of the station was locked but John took that as a good sign. If it was still locked, the armory was unlikely to have been looted. Looking for a good size rock, John found one and hurled it at the door. The glass cracked but did not shatter. Finally, on his third try, he was able to walk over the glass shards and enter the lobby.

With his flashlight, he looked around. There was a metal door leading to the back, but it was locked. A rock wouldn't be of any help with that.

There was a Plexiglas window leading to a clerk or receptionist area. John couldn't get enough force on his throw of the rock to break the glass. Looking around the lobby, he tried throwing a chair through the Plexiglas, but it just bounced off. He needed something bigger.

John closed his eyes and tried to remember what he knew about this area. There was a municipal building next door and then, down the street, a liquor store and a row of other stores and restaurants. He remembered there was a fishing boat company just down the road and then he realized that the City's Public Works Department was also just down the street.

Returning to the SUV, John drove slowly down the street looking for the Public Works Department signs. On his right he saw a building he recognized as a fire station.

"That might even be better," he muttered to himself and pulled up in front. While the large garage doors were down, John was pleased to find the side door into the station was unlocked. He entered and turned his flashlight on. He was looking for an ax or something the firefighters might have used to open up burning buildings.

Along the side of the building, beside one of the trucks, was a rack with what looked like different types of crowbars. They all seemed to have a fork on one end and various types of claws or pikes at the other. John was surprised at how heavy they were. Each one seemed to weigh at least ten pounds. Without being sure which would work best, John grabbed five of them and put them in the SUV.

Back at the police station, and using a bar with a sharp pike on it, John made short work of the Plexiglas and jumped over the counter. He had never been in the back of a police station before.

The flashlight revealed how it almost seemed like a labyrinth, with very few long straight corridors.

He used the crowbar to open a couple of doors, but they were just offices. Even if there might be a handgun there, he wanted to find the armory, so he kept looking. Further back, he found a metal door set into a cinderblock wall. The wall stood out to him as most of the others in the station were sheetrock.

It would make sense to have a reinforced cement wall to protect the station's weapons. A couple of swings with the crowbar confirmed that he wasn't going to be able to force his way through. With his flashlight pointed at the door, John ran his hand along the edge. There was a slight gap between the door and the doorjamb.

Carefully placing the end of the crowbar into this slot, John tried to pry the door open. It moved but he couldn't gain enough leverage to force it. Encouraged, he raced back to the fire station with the thought there might be something larger he could use. John found a heavier form of crowbar. It was about four feet long and fifteen to twenty pounds.

John threw this heavy-duty crowbar into the SUV and, again, drove back to the police station. He hadn't felt this good in a long, long time. He knew what he wanted to do and how to do it. Climbing over the desk in the lobby of the police station, John dropped the heavy-duty crowbar but didn't worry about the noise.

It took him close to 45 minutes to get the door open. By the time he did, he was drenched in sweat. The room was not particularly large but contained racks of black guns, both standing on the floor and hanging on the wall. Running his hands along the guns, John couldn't help but be impressed with the weapons and with himself.

Most of the guns appeared to be shotguns, given the wide barrel. He picked one up and pumped it once. He didn't dare pull the trigger, remembering what happened with the handgun back on the island. Putting the shotgun back in the rack, he examined the rifles. Many of them were assault rifles of some sort. There were no handguns, John thought, but a shotgun for defense and a rifle for hunting should be sufficient.

He looked all around the room but couldn't find any ammunition.

"What the hell?"

Why wouldn't they keep ammunition in the same room as the weapons? Then he thought about it and realized that it made sense to separate the two. If someone were to find a way to get into the armory, he or she would be harmless without ammunition.

John returned to the hallway and began looking for another door set in a cement-wall that might lead to the ammunition. Sure enough, he quickly found it.

An hour and a half later, he walked out of the police station, drenched and exhausted but with a duffel bag full of shotguns and rifles, together with a couple of handguns he found in the offices. He also had two small backpacks filled with more bullets and shotgun shells than he hoped he would ever need.

It was short drive to the farmhouse. John parked the Land Rover as far away from the road as he could. Loading one of the shotguns, he stepped out of the car and walked around the house. The back door was still intact and only the front door was damaged.

The house was, overall, in good shape although the exterior was starting to show some wear and tear. He would need to replace some of the floorboards on the porch. That could wait.

Walking in, John used the flashlight to inspect the interior. There would be some work to do. It appeared some animals, he assumed raccoons, had ransacked the kitchen. He had no doubt vermin were still living there. They would be fairly easy to address. He would also need to get rid of the refrigerator. He didn't dare open it, knowing that whatever was in there would have rotted over the past year or so. While it would be difficult, he would have to find a hand truck to lift and remove it.

John placed some of the guns and ammunition into a front closet and then walked back to his SUV. While he was excited at the prospect of working on the house, he knew it was too soon. Unless, and until, he could confirm the status of Camp Oregon, he didn't dare set up his own camp. For him, the best-case scenario would be that the camp had just disappeared. The worst-case scenario for him would be that it was still operating. He briefly wondered if he might somehow make peace with Boulden but quickly realized how unlikely that was.

By using back roads and driving slowly, John made his way back to the river to where the kayak was hidden. What he found particularly strange was that there was no traffic noise at all. Before the Curse, there was always a constant drone of engines in the distance. It was like white noise and often not even noticed. Ever since he escaped from the camp, there was no drone but there was always the occasional noise of the remaining vehicles travelling to and from the camp or driving around town. John could pick out noises of individual vehicles. Now, however, there was nothing. No engines meant no vehicles. There was only the steady hum of the river, the crickets, and the frogs. It was unnerving.

Putting a couple of the guns into his backpack, John eased the kayak into the water and slowly paddled back to Ross Island. It was noticeably darker now and it took a while for John to understand why. While Camp Oregon was far up on the hill, the light from the buildings reflected some light all the way down to the river. Now that light was completely gone.

Reaching the southernmost tip of the island, John pulled up to the shore and turned around. It took him a few minutes to find the camp because the entire hillside was dark. When he had left just a few nights ago, there were some buildings gone dark and some gunfire, but the others were still lit. Now there was nothing. Could it really have happened that fast? Could Camp Oregon completely collapse in just a couple of days? John remembered seeing the vehicles driving down I-5 when he was at Cabella's. Had that been part of it? Had people just run away from the camp? If so, where were they going? Was Boulden with them? Was Boulden even still alive?

These were too many questions for John. Rather than risk running into any fleeing soldiers, he decided to return to the buildings along the south side of the island. Hiding the kayak behind a truck, John covered it with a tarp, then quickly walked to the building where he had accidentally discharged the gun. It was just as stuffy as before. He thought he could still detect the lingering scent of the gun he'd fired. It had been a long day and he was tired. It took a little bit of looking but he found a cot likely used by security guards. After having slept on the floor for weeks, John relished lying on the cot. In moments, he was asleep.

He was awakened by the noise of rain on the metal roof. John was used to Portland getting a lot of rain. This was different. This was not a light shower but, rather, a torrential downpour. Looking up at one of the windows, he saw a flash of light and, seconds later, a clap of thunder. It was loud.

John walked to the door and watched as the rain came down in sheets. He could barely see the shore even though it was only 100 yards away.

"Well, God, I guess this is your way of telling me I made the right decision by coming here rather than going to the campsite and sleeping out in the open. I'll take that as a sign of a job well done and will take encouragement from it."

Even though he was speaking softly to himself, his voice sounded strangely loud. Pulling a desk chair out of one of the offices, John sat in the doorway and watched the rain.

"So, what's next? Do I go explore what's left of Camp Oregon to make sure that no one is there?"

It was oddly comforting to be speaking, even if only to himself.

"Nah, that would be stupid. If someone were still there, what would I do anyway? There's really nothing up there that I need. What I really need to do is organize the farmhouse down here."

He started planning what he would do. There was a Home Depot not far from the farmhouse where he could get whatever supplies he might need. He would need to figure out how to hang a new front door and they would have mouse traps.

Once the house was secure, he could begin to retrofit it to be user-friendly. John wondered if he could put rain barrels on the roof of the house and then somehow connect pipes from the barrels to the toilets in order to have flushable toilets.

The Home Depot would also have fencing supplies so he could create a small pasture for cows and pigs. He could also have chickens. With the thought of all of that livestock, John started imagining all the food he could cook. The library would surely have cookbooks and images of fried chicken and pork chops started dancing through his head.

John closed his eyes with a big smile on his face. "Maybe," he thought, "just maybe I can do this." He then fell back asleep.

ॐ

CHAPTER FORTY-FOUR

Celebrate Me Home

The question was how long to stay on the island before starting work on the farmhouse. By staying in the building, he could safely sleep at night. If any bears or other animals swam over to the island, he didn't have to worry. If he saw them during the day, John had his guns so he would at least have some protection.

He'd gone back to the campsite and was able to find a number of undamaged packaged meals, as well as the water purifiers. There was enough food and water, such as it was, for another couple of days so he decided to stay and make sure Camp Oregon really was empty.

Over the following days, he never heard a single car engine. He didn't hear any gunshots, not even from the east side where Tex was. He was so accustomed to the quiet now, any noises other than those of the river, crickets, frogs, and birds were easily noticeable. John began to relax and continued to work on his plans for the farmhouse.

He would likely have to cut down some of the trees in order to open up the land a bit and then fence portions for livestock.

John remembered having to dig postholes for his father when he was still a teenager. He never liked it but knew that he could do it.

By going to one of the local car dealerships, he could get a pickup and start transporting construction supplies and, eventually, livestock and feed. Although he didn't know exactly where, he knew there were farms in the surrounding counties and suspected it wouldn't be too difficult to find cows, pigs and sheep.

John envisioned himself, with work done for the day, using an electric stove to cook a meal and then sitting on the porch as the sun set. He could place cans of beer in the nearby creek, keeping them both cool and close.

One day, he would eventually drive back out to the coast and retrieve his go bag from the Prius. With his laptop and iPhone, he would be able to play music and go through his photographs. From the library, he could read a lifetime's worth of books. Maybe he would even go back to that music store and start playing the guitar again.

Periodically throughout the following days and nights, John would go from end to end, and side to side, on the island to watch and listen. Was Boulden still out there somewhere? With each passing day, he decided it was more and more unlikely. Were Tex and Lisa still alive? From time to time he would see movement on the riverbank but attributed it to animals rather than humans. He saw what looked like smoke one evening but couldn't be sure.

Perhaps he could track down a ham radio and power it up to see if there might be others out there. While it was possible he really was the last man on earth, it was also possible that there were other survivors. There might not be many, but he hoped there were some. He just wasn't that special to be the only person who could survive the Curse.

It was only when he allowed his mind to go still that he wondered about the dark side of his future. Would he always have to be fearful of wild animals? Could he retain whatever remained of his sanity under the weight of crushing loneliness? He did his best to push these thoughts away because they, even more than the thoughts of wild animals, scared him the most.

Maybe he could get a dog…but certainly not a Rottweiler.

❧

After three full days on the island without any suggestion there might be anyone else out there, John decided to leave it once and for all. It was finally time to start implementing his plans for the farmhouse. Despite his confidence, he still waited until dusk to climb into the kayak and start paddling for the shore. If there was someone out there, he might at least be able to see some headlights or even just a flashlight.

There was no point in trying to paddle silently so he just leisurely paddled. The current was swift but no greater than before. By taking his time, he was able to avoid a couple of corpses floating downstream. This reminded him that it would likely be a long time before he dared fish in the Willamette River.

As he paddled, he wondered what downtown Portland must look like. Buildings not destroyed by Boulden would fail from lack of maintenance over the coming years. Rats probably infested them.

"What are the natural enemies of rats?" he wondered aloud.

Certainly, cats would likely be in abundance, as would owls. If the population of cats and birds increased, that would mean that the population of dogs and coyotes would also. There was always the big cat that had scared the crap out of him and killed the pig. He wondered if there were others out there. He wondered if Duke was still out there.

He would expect the deer and elk population to quickly grow and expand into what had been man's domain. Mountain lions would follow them, as would wolves. Bears would also be expanding their territory.

"Jesus," he muttered. "I'm going to be living in the middle of a fucking zoo!"

Pulling up to shore, John pushed the kayak back out in the river. He wouldn't need it anymore and, if he someday decided he did need one, there were plenty of sporting goods stores for him to loot.

The SUV was just where he left it, but it was running low on gas. Gas stations were useless unless he could figure out how to draw fuel from the underground tanks. He stopped at a nearby house and located a garden hose. With the hatchet, he cut a six-foot length and pulled up next to a car. Opening up the gas cap, he fed one end of the hose into the gas tank. With the other end, he began sucking until gasoline flooded into his mouth. Spitting the foul-tasting fluid out of his mouth, John stuck the end of the hose into the gas tank of the SUV.

In order to completely fill it, John had to repeat this procedure two more times. He would have to figure out a better way. Perhaps he would be able to find a pump he could use at a sporting goods store. That, however, was an issue for another day. At least for now, the SUV was fueled up. John popped a couple of pieces of mint gum into his mouth to wash away the taste of gasoline.

Keeping the headlights off, John retraced the drive from the other night. He moved slowly and tried to pay attention to what stores he passed. The locations of the big box stores were easy. What he needed to find were smaller grocery stores which might not have been looted yet. It would also be important to identify where the pharmacies were.

One of the first things he wanted to do the next day was to go to the library and look for first aid books. Driving by REI, John decided to pick up some more supplies. He grabbed a new sleeping bag and some cooking gear. Finally, he filled the SUV with all of the pre-packaged meals he could find. It would be a while before he would be preparing fresh meals and these were better than just a diet of protein bars and cookies.

☙

John found peace over the next several days. He remained too busy to think about anything but the present. From sunup to sundown, he worked on the farmhouse. He located a heavy-duty handcart at Home Depot. He used it to move the refrigerator to the front porch. He backed up a small pickup truck he had located at a neighbor's house, toppled the refrigerator into the truck bed, and drove it to an area behind the local high school. This would become his dump. It was close enough to be convenient but not so close that any animals would follow him back to the farmhouse.

It took him several tries, and several doors, before he was able to install a new front door that would actually latch. It wasn't pretty but it was effective. All he wanted was to be able to sleep at night without fear of intruders and the new door worked for that purpose.

John collected water from the creek and purified it and started to build fences for the future livestock. Using several nets, he had a good supply of soda and beer cooling in the creek. The solar panels were working, and he thought it would be nice to have a small refrigerator to store any meat he might acquire.

It would also be nice to have some music and John thought back to his iPhone in the Prius. Between the iPhone and his laptop, he had a large music library. The public library across the street also had a large, and very eclectic, collection of CDs and DVDs. It would be a lengthy round trip to retrieve these items, so John decided to start the following day early in the morning. This would also give him a chance to visit his family.

He spent the rest of the day clearing brush and starting to dig postholes. He thought he would set up an area for chickens first, which would be the easiest to keep and turn into food. Just thinking about it brought to mind a thick cheese omelet. Once he had the chicken coop set up, he could build pens for pigs and cows.

Before shutting down for the evening, John ate a freeze-dried meal of chicken and noodles but didn't even taste it. He was focused on the next day's journey and building the hen house on his return.

ళ

Up at the crack of dawn John packed the SUV with some food and, of course, his guns. It suddenly occurred to him that he might need something more than this vehicle. Trees might have fallen across roads and there could be cars abandoned and blocking his way. What he really needed was either a heavy-duty Jeep or pickup truck. An electric winch on the front would be helpful but, at a minimum, he wanted something big enough to drag or push any obstructions out of his way.

Landmark Ford was just off I-5 and John found an abundant selection of trucks to choose from. He settled on an F350 even though it didn't have the winch he was hoping for. The biggest selling point was that it used gasoline rather than diesel. While he knew that diesel trucks got better mileage, gasoline was always going to be easier to locate.

John threw a few of the guns in the truck bed and placed the rest in the cab. He put some gas cans in back, after filling them from other vehicles at the dealership. There were some cables and ropes of various lengths, which he placed in the truck bed before heading out.

At this point and with Camp Oregon likely gone, John felt safe enough traveling on the highway during the day. He was actually wondering if he might see someone and, if he did, what he would do. He was curious about what had happened at the camp. More importantly, however, he recognized how lonely he was. A conversation, even with a stranger, would really be welcome.

There were cars abandoned or crashed on the highway, but they were spread out enough for John to weave around them. Just south of downtown, he got on I-405 and then the Sunset Highway driving toward the coast. By staying on these roads, John could skirt downtown Portland.

It was going to be a typical hot summer's day, but it wasn't yet hot enough for the air conditioning. John had all the windows down and was listening to an Eric Church CD he had found back at the farmhouse.

Deciding that he didn't need to fear wandering animals in the daytime, John stayed at a steady 50 mph. Passing through Hillsboro, he saw a large herd of elk in the distance. Someday, he might decide to hunt them and find out what elk tasted like. It would be relatively easy as they moved further and further into what had been cities and towns.

A bigger problem would be what to do with an elk after he killed it. John hoped that the library might have some books on how to cut off the meat. He could store it in coolers for a bit but, without ice, it wouldn't last long. John wondered if he might be able to put the meat into sealed bags and store them in the cool creek, just like he stored his beer. If he got enough solar generators, could he maintain a freezer?

As he approached the Coast Range, a sense of melancholy overcame him. Soon enough he would get onto Highway 101 and knew he would relive the journey back to the cabin with Brian dead in the back seat. How long ago had that been?

The coast was overcast as John got on Highway 101. He decided to drive into Cannon Beach. This little oceanside town was popular with tourists, especially during the summer and John was curious to see what it looked like. It didn't take him long to find out.

Major Boulden's men had been here and much of the town was now just burned shells of buildings. Any houses along the beach not burned were suffering the ravages of coastal weather. Haystack Rock stood as a lonely sentry in the ocean. That natural monument was there well before mankind populated this area and would still be there for millennia afterward. John didn't know if he found that thought comforting or not.

As quickly as possible, he got back on Highway 101 and headed south toward Manzanita. Pulling into town, John noticed how quickly it was deteriorating. He slowed as he drove down Beach Street, trying to find the house he'd barely escaped from. Unconsciously, he began rubbing his thighs, which had been burned so badly that afternoon.

The drive continued toward Nehalem and then up into the hills. Not much had changed but, then again, everything had changed. The truck seemed almost to drive itself as John finally pulled into the driveway of the cabin. Both the cabin and Ray's house were nothing more than charred wood. The military probably destroyed the houses after finding out he had been living there.

His sadness was palpable but not because of the houses. Rather, John was flooded with memories of everything from that first weekend at the cabin until he ran away. Climbing out of the truck, John walked behind what was left of it. The clouds were starting to clear and the sun came out just as he found himself standing in front of the grave.

The edges of the tarps were frayed but with a couple of new tree branches lying on top of them. The broken glass was still there and John took comfort in the fact that his family was undisturbed.

He found the old chair still lying against the foundation. It was filthy but he pulled it out and sat down at the edge of the tarps.

"Well, what a long, strange trip it has been. I think you guys would be proud of me for surviving like I did. I'm sure, wherever you are, you were watching over me and probably protecting me. l wish I could talk with you about it and thank you in person.

"Did I mention I'm the one who apparently infected all of you?

"Did I mention I would be with you now if I wasn't too much of a coward to just kill myself?"

John turned his face toward the sun and let it dry the tears running down his cheeks.

"Goddammit," he whispered quietly. He pulled a handkerchief out of his back pocket, blowing his nose and drying his eyes.

"Oh, yeah, I found a new house to live in. It's got electricity, of sorts, and running water in the form of Fanno Creek. There's not much call for a tax attorney these days so I'm going to try my hand at farming and ranching. First will be the chickens and then who knows?

"How tough can it be to grow wheat? The Tigard Public Library is going to be my best friend for the next couple of years. Maybe I can also get some fresh fruit from the various farms and vineyards."

John stopped talking, knowing he was babbling. Rather than talking, John listened. He listened as the wind moved through the trees. In the distance, he could hear the ocean and wondered who, if anyone, might be out there, on the other side. He might have been there for twenty minutes or for two hours; he had no idea, mostly because he didn't care.

Finally, standing up, John put the chair back against the foundation and then kneeled beside the tarps.

"Liz. Brian. Cat. I hope you are all right wherever you are. If there is a god, I hope he or she or it is taking good care of you. If there is some other level of consciousness, please do me a favor and wait for me. The only thing keeping me going is the hope I'll see all of you again. Don't wander too far away; I'll be there eventually. Wait for me...*please*! I love you all, completely and forever."

John stood back up and brushed the dirt and leaves off his knees. Turning back to the truck, he climbed in and re-traced the route he used in the Prius. He found the accident site quickly and was surprised at how close it was. In his mind, he'd travelled miles before running off the road. In the light of day, however, and without snow, it was barely over a mile.

The Prius was about 30 feet down the embankment. Parking the truck on the side of the road, John secured one end of a rope to the truck's bumper and lowered the other end down. With heavy-duty gloves on, John slowly started to work his way down. The ground was wet and slippery and several times he found himself on his butt holding onto the rope to stop from sliding.

When he got to the vehicle, John reached inside. It took some maneuvering, but he was finally able to grab his go bag. To his surprise, it didn't appear to be damaged. It was in the back seat and had stayed out of the rain.

Running his arm through the straps of the bag, he hoisted it up onto his shoulder and began working his way up the embankment. Finally, back in the truck, John began the drive to his new home. It was time to close the book on his life to date and to begin the rest of his new one. It would be life as a farmer. It would be life as a rancher. It would be life alone but hopefully for not too long.

CHAPTER FORTY-FIVE

Don't Think Twice, It's All Right

J ohn could sense that summer was coming to an end and fall was approaching. The nights were a little cooler and a little longer. Over the prior month, he'd accomplished quite a bit. He'd felled about 20 trees and chopped them for firewood. They wouldn't be sufficiently dry for this winter, but he had also located and stacked several cords of seasoned wood found in the surrounding neighborhoods. He also knew where to find more wood if he needed it.

The front yard was fully fenced. He found a dozen chickens, including one very aggressive and noisy rooster, by exploring local farms in Washington and Yamhill counties. With his flock established, he now had a sustainable source of fresh food. It was too late to plant any crops, but John found fields in the countryside. Both to the south and west, he located orchards ripe with apples and pears. He spent one whole afternoon gorging on grapes at a local vineyard before loading the pickup with cases of wine.

It was more difficult to find cows, as most of them were dead or too sick to be saved. He was able to track down a few that had broken through their fencing and survived by feeding on nearby wheat fields. Using a horse trailer from one of the vineyards, he brought two cows and a bull back to the farmhouse. This gave him hope for milk and steak someday.

John still couldn't bring himself to shoot a deer or an elk but knew he would need to learn someday. The gun store was a huge benefit for this. While it was stripped of guns, the books on hunting were still intact and untouched. He hoped someday to be able to eat fish again, but he would still, from time to time, spot a body floating down Fanno Creek or the nearby Tualatin River. Fishing would have to wait a bit longer. He wondered if it might be safe to go back to the coast and dig up clams.

At night, he would either read books from the library or watch movies on DVD. While the library's DVD collection was modest, there was a lifetime of books for him. In order to safeguard this treasure, he patched broken windows at the library and tried to repair any leaks he found in the roof.

He made a few attempts at writing, thinking his memoirs might be of interest to anyone else who might survive. It was, however, too difficult to write. Invariably, he would break down while writing about Liz and the kids. He just wasn't ready for that yet.

From time to time, he wandered around the area, locating other libraries or stores with useful supplies. One day, John found a short-wave radio set. There was a house only a few miles away with a large antenna alongside of it.

It took more than a week to disassemble the antenna tower and reinstall it at the farmhouse. Using the solar generators, John was able to turn the short-wave radio on and, occasionally, hear someone. Sometimes the voices were in English but most of the time they were in either Spanish or what sounded like Asian languages. Despite his best attempts, he could hear the voices but couldn't figure out how to speak to them.

Despite the frustration with his inability to communicate with other survivors, he took comfort in the fact that at least there *were* other survivors. He was not alone.

Sometimes at night he would hear the howl of wolves and large animals wandering by, close to the farmhouse, but not too close. To scare them away, John would quietly open a window and let loose with a short barrage of gunfire into the air. It was too dark to see what might be out there and he wasn't foolish enough to leave the safety of the house. Nonetheless, the sound of the gunfire seemed to provide a measure of protection to the chickens and cows.

∾

It was an absolutely perfect day. The air was crisp and the leaves on the trees were a pastiche of flaming oranges and yellows. Needing a break, John decided to take a walk. One of his favorite places was in nearby Cook Park. Back in the day, he used to coach Brian and Cassie in soccer there but now the fields were overgrown and wild. The road was impassible to any vehicle other than a four-wheeled truck but today was a day for a walk.

Passing the soccer fields, he continued walking to a bench located just above the Tualatin River. The bench was a memorial to someone's son who'd passed away well before the Curse. On the other side of the river was what used to be the Tualatin Country Club. He could still see a flagpole sticking out of the ground in the middle of a grassy field.

Leaning his shotgun against the side of the bench and placing his handgun on the seat, he sat down. It had been months since he'd seen a body float down this river but today, he spotted three. They were bloated and fortunately the current took them quickly past. John briefly thought about how the sight of the corpses had no effect on him now. He had become at least partially immune to such sights and wondered if that was a healthy thing for him.

The grass had fully returned to its natural state and the pavement on the parking lot was cracked and buckling with various plants popping through the asphalt.

This was John's safe place. While there was really no such thing as actual safety anymore, this was the place where he seemed to find a measure of peace. This was where he could remember the past and contemplate the future without being enveloped by either grief or fear. He ate a large bag of chips and drank several beers. Other than the crunch of the chips, it was quiet and, more importantly, peaceful.

A splashing sound startled him and John turned to see a couple of otters playing in the river. He watched them for over an hour with a smile on his face the whole time. "Maybe I *can* do this," he whispered to the otters.

By mid-afternoon, John gathered up his trash and deposited it into a nearby garbage can. He shook his head realizing that old habits, like not littering, die hard.

The walk back went quickly, as John's bliss seemed to carry him along. The houses he passed were in various states of decay. Some were little more than ashes and others were in the process of being overrun by ivy and blackberry bushes. It wouldn't be long, perhaps only another year or so, before this whole stretch of road would be unrecognizable and possibly impassable.

Walking past the library, John noted how he was going to have to cut back some of the plants in order to keep his treasure trove of books and movies safe. There was no thought of saving these books for posterity but, rather, just for his own personal use and enjoyment.

It was the noise that first caught his attention. It was a crackling sound. He paused to see if he could identify it and then he noticed what looked like a shimmering light reflecting off the windows of the library. Quickly turning around, he raced over to the farmhouse and saw it engulfed in flames.

Reflexively he opened the gate and began looking around for something to use to put out the fire. In his panic, he didn't notice the jeep parked on the far side of the creek, just a hundred yards from the farmhouse. His focus was trying to remember if he had any fire extinguishers or any way to pump the water up from the creek to the fire.

John turned away from the blaze and looked at his pickup truck, wondering if he might have time to race to the hardware store and find something to help. Suddenly, he heard a familiar voice behind him.

"My, oh my, so now we're Farmer John, huh?"

John straightened up, the hair on the back of his neck standing on end. Very, very slowly he turned to face Major Roger Boulden. He was standing on the side of the farmhouse that was not yet aflame. This was nothing like the imposing figure he'd last seen up at the camp. His face was gaunt and, even from a distance, John could see how bloodshot his eyes were. His hair was long and disheveled and the light from the fire seemed to reflect off it, almost making it look as if it was on fire. His left arm was in a sling and what looked like a shotgun was perched in his right arm and pointed at John.

"Yeah…sorry about the fire." His voice dripped with sarcasm. "I wish I could say that I found it like this when I got here but, well, what's the point of lying to you now?"

Noticing the strap over Callahan's shoulder, Boulden said, "Put the shotgun down…slowly."

John took the gun off his shoulder, bent down and laid it on the ground before standing back up.

"C'mon, Callahan, surely you have something to say, don't you? I hope you know that I've been looking for you for months now. I was afraid you might have left the area, but you don't seem like *that* kind of guy. You're not the adventurous type. I pegged you as the kind of guy who would try and stay wherever was most familiar to you. That's why I decided to focus on looking for you around here.

"I've got to give you credit, though. You picked a pretty good spot—a nice little house, the creek right beside you, the library across the street, and, of course, the police station. You've got just about everything you need to get on with your life. Well, at least you did until…" He looked over his shoulder at the burning house and shrugged.

"And you're raising chickens and cows. Damn, I haven't had fresh meat since the camp fell. Oh wait, Callahan, you remember the camp, don't you? You really kind of fucked that up, didn't you?"

John remained still. While it was obvious Boulden wasn't naturally right-handed, he seemed more than capable of handling the shotgun with his right arm. The gun shook a little, but John didn't think he would have much of a chance if he tried to run.

"I don't know what you want me to say," John softly replied.

"What's that Callahan? It's tough to hear you over the noise of the fire."

John could see the smile forming on Boulden's face. He was like a cat playing with a mouse and the hate began to bring John back to life.

"I *asked* what you expect me to say." John's voice was stronger now as he pushed the fear away. Perhaps this was how it was meant to end. If it was, he would not cower to this man.

"That's the thing, Callahan." Boulden seemed to be oblivious to the change in John. "I've been wondering for weeks now what I would say to you and how you might respond. I'd worked out various scenarios in my mind but none of them were particularly satisfying. Of course, the one thing all the scenarios had in common was that you end up dead but that is beside the point.

"The question, when I really think about it, is what I might *want* you to say. I mean, you could apologize for breaking my arm, that might be a start."

John stood there, his eyes locked on Boulden's.

"Yeah, I didn't think so. Of course, you could apologize for effectively killing Dr. Mo. Yeah, that really fucked up morale at the camp. It turns out she was the only one in the medical department who was worth a damn! Who'd a thunk, huh?"

Boulden now began walking toward John.

"Now the big one, I mean the really big one, is that you could apologize for being a carrier of the goddamn Curse and being fucking responsible for killing so many people, even your family. You could apologize for being responsible for the end of any chance we had to survive. Yeah, you could apologize for that, couldn't you?"

Boulden was now about thirty feet from John.

"Why don't you have a hazmat suit on, Major?"

For the first time, John watched a broad smile break out on Boulden's face. As it did, John noticed that he was missing some teeth and others were severely discolored.

"That's one of the other fucked up things about this whole crapshoot. It turns out I'm immune to the fucking virus, at least its most recent mutation. I'm not a carrier like you Callahan but the virus seems not to have much interest in me.

"Hell, maybe Dr. Mo should have been conducting some of those tests on me." He chuckled but it was a dry and humorless sound.

Boulden continued walking slowly with his eyes fixed on John. He didn't see a small rock and stumbled slightly over it with his right foot. He caught himself before falling but his shotgun swung to the left and fired.

John flinched, reflexively taking a step back while simultaneously reaching down to his side and gripping his handgun. Without any hesitation, he pulled it up, pointed it at the center of Boulden's chest, and fired. The sound of the discharge didn't really register with John, but he could see Boulden's body pushed back several times and small circles of red immediately blossomed on his chest.

Lowering the gun, John watched as Boulden collapsed on the ground. While the sun was starting to set, there was still enough light from the burning farmhouse for John to see the body twitch. He couldn't be sure if Boulden was actually moving or if it was that shimmering light from the fire.

Walking slowly over to the body, John saw blood starting to pool out from under the body. Boulden's eyes were still open, with a ghastly smile on his lips. With his right hand, Boulden weakly motioned for John to come closer.

Using his foot, John pushed the shotgun beyond Boulden's reach and then knelt down beside him. Boulden's lips were moving, as if he were trying to talk, but there was only a wet, raspy sound as blood flew out with a cough.

"Do you get it, Callahan? Do you?" Boulden was forcing the words out.

John stared at him. "Get what?"

"You're no fucking different than me. We both would do whatever we could to survive..." He started another cough, this one particularly violent and wracking his body. When he finally settled, Boulden took a deep breath.

"I guess you just did it a little better than me. Ha!"

He started to cough again, and a look of pain crossed over his face. As it stopped, John could see him settle down and his body seemed to try to melt into the ground. It almost looked as if it was deflating. Boulden's eyes took on a dull, glassy look and then he took one last breath.

John sat down on the ground and looked up at the farmhouse. The fire was burning itself out on the right side, but the left side was still going strongly. He watched as the roof collapsed upon itself.

CHAPTER FORTY-SIX

For No One

J ohn sat there until the fire was almost completely out and the sun was fully set. He lay back on the grass and looked up. There were no clouds and the moon was still low in the sky. John lost himself in the millions of stars high above.

"How insignificant am I?" he silently wondered. One being on a small planet circling one medium-sized star in a galaxy containing billions of other stars and countless planets surrounding them.

"What a fucking joke," he muttered as he slowly stood up. Walking over to the chicken coop, he opened the gate. He walked over and opened the door to the cow pen.

"Sorry guys, I really hoped to enjoy you someday but what's the point?"

He could hear the noise of something rustling through the nearby bushes and walked to the pickup truck. Climbing in, he pulled some earplugs out from the center console and turned on his music player. *Shine on You Crazy Diamond* by Pink Floyd was cued up. John closed his eyes and lost himself in the song.

CHASING SHADOWS

Remember when you were young,
You shone like the sun
Now there's a look in your eyes,
Like black holes in the sky.

Opening his eyes, John peered at himself in the rearview mirror. His eyes were red, and he saw he was crying. He wasn't crying for Boulden. In the end, he got what he deserved. No, he realized, he was crying for himself. He knew that Boulden wasn't right. They weren't *anything* alike, but he also understood that he, John Callahan, had really killed someone. It wasn't like the Curse and the spreading of the virus. This was an intentional act by him to shoot and kill another human being.

He understood that he was also crying for a dream he had been chasing to create a life with some measure of normalcy to it; a life that would at least remind him of what things used to be like. The problem, though, was he wasn't a farmer and he never would be; he wasn't safe now and would never be; there was no normal anymore and there would never be.

Regardless of whether he was completely alone or one of a million people or more around the world, there was no going back to what life was like before. Liz was never coming back. Brian and Cassie were never coming back. It would only be a matter of time before the gray skies and winter rains would result in an explosion of depression. Once that happened, John would likely go completely insane without Liz to walk him back from the edge. Even if he didn't, it was possible, if not likely, that one of the animals out there would kill him. No, there was no going back and there was no staying here.

Reaching down to the floor, John picked up some paper and dug a pen out of the glove box. He began writing. It was dark by the time he finished. John pointed a flashlight out the window

355

and could see coyotes sitting beside Boulden. They briefly looked up when they saw the light and John could see blood on their snouts. He turned the light off.

John slept fitfully on the front seat and, upon waking in the early morning light, he stepped out of the truck. It took him about an hour to pack the truck full of as many guns as he could. He took some provisions and water bottles stored in the garage and loaded them into the back of the pickup.

John placed the note in a Ziploc sandwich bag and, using packing tape, secured it to one of the trees in front of the remains of the farmhouse. He climbed back into the pickup and started it up. He eased down the road, heading south. He didn't look back.

EPILOGUE

I, John Thomas Callahan, being of relatively sound mind and body, make this final statement. In my life, I was a lot of things. I was a son and a brother. I was a friend and a tax attorney. Most importantly, I was a husband and a father. Now I am none of those.

I accept responsibility for all the bad things I've done, whether intentional or not. The Curse chose me to allow it to grow and spread. It chose me to infect others and it is far too late for any apologies for that. Anyone who might be entitled to an apology is long gone.

In a misguided effort to fill the emptiness in my heart, I attempted to create a life that I didn't deserve. Somehow, I believed that I could establish a life with order among the chaos. That life, I now understand, would merely be a distorted reflection of the life I once lived—neither complete nor truly satisfying.

Regardless of whether or not I deserved even this mirage of a real life, however, the fact is that nature was never going to allow me to succeed. I am merely a remnant of a species that is no longer welcome in this world. Mankind is no longer the boss and for me to try to live as if it still was, would be pointless. I would spend the rest of my life being Sisyphus and trying to recreate that which is impossible. I don't want that.

With this life over, I've decided to embrace the one thing I always feared in the past. I am going to leap into the unknown. I will travel wherever the road leads me. I am going to explore without any set plan and without any specific destination in mind.

I don't know what I might find out there and my travels may be short or long. Nonetheless, there is nothing left for me here, so I am leaving for parts unknown. There is a part of me that hopes to find community again, perhaps even to find love. I attribute that to my inherent romanticism and not based upon any sense of reality.

The worst-case scenario for me is that I die a painful and lengthy death but, even then, I still hold out hope that I will be reunited with those that I've loved but let down. No, that's not accurate. The true worst-case scenario is that I find no one, lose my grasp on sanity and forget my family. That is truly the only thing I fear at this point.

If you are reading this, I wish you well and hope you find the contentment that eludes me. If, for some reason, we get a second chance at all of this, I hope we do better.

- JTC

ABOUT THE AUTHOR

A lot could be said about the author but, ultimately, the question always comes down to why anything more has to be said. He's written three books so far. Good for him. He's done a bunch of other stuff. Who cares? He's an attorney and lives in Oregon. Wow! Are you impressed yet?

His only *real* accomplishments are his relationships with his family and friends. He's been incredibly fortunate to have a wonderful wife, two great children, an amazing son-in-law, and a granddaughter who is still trying to figure him out. He's got friends who seem to recognize who and what he really is and yet still like him. Go figure!

What else could possibly be said about him that would be more important?

Made in the USA
Columbia, SC
02 August 2022